THE BURYING POINT

A RAY HANLEY CRIME THRILLER

DERIK CAVIGNANO

© 2024 by Derik Cavignano

All rights reserved.

ISBN: 978-1733873321

Library of Congress Control Number: 2024902072

Praise for <u>THE ART OF DYING</u>

14th Annual National Indie Excellence Awards Winner (thriller)

2019 American Fiction Awards Winner (general horror)

2019 Best Book Awards Winner (horror)

14th Annual National Indie Excellence Awards Finalist (horror)

2019 American Fiction Awards Finalist (crime thrillers)

"[A] twisty, gory crime thriller... The satisfying final reveal is a
testament to the author's cleverness."
–Publishers Weekly

"An edge-of-your seat detective thriller that crackles with gore and
wit before delivering a stunning knockout blow. Fans of *The Silence
of the Lambs* should flock to Derik Cavignano's new series debut."
–BestThrillers.com

"Boston gets gory in this enjoyable, horror-tinged crime tale."
–Kirkus Reviews

"The Art of Dying blends drama and horror for a disturbing and
gripping thriller."
–Foreword Clarion Reviews

"A highly suspenseful and delightfully twisted thriller with one of
the creepiest villains in recent memory!"
–Jeff Strand, Bram Stoker Award-winning author

Other Books by Derik Cavignano

THE ART OF DYING
(A Ray Hanley Crime Thriller)

When the bizarre death of a mob foot soldier sparks an escalating war between Boston's Irish and Italian mafia, detective Ray Hanley's relentless search for the truth uncovers evidence of a serial killer obsessed with the art of human suffering.

THE RIGHTEOUS AND THE WICKED

A sci-fi suspense thriller featuring Jacob and Ray Hanley

COLONY OF THE LOST

An ancient evil returns to the site of a lost colony

Acknowledgements

A lot of work goes into making a book like this, and I have many people to thank for the final product. First and foremost, I'd like to thank my wife and kids for putting up with me sneaking off to my office for hours on end to get this book over the finish line. Writing is not my day job, so every hour I spend writing is an hour borrowed from family time.

I'd also like to thank my beta readers for their early insights on the story (Mary Ann Okomski, Bella Cavignano, Jen Campbell, Douglas Ford, and Thomas Michael Thomas). As always, your feedback is instrumental to smoothing out the rougher edges of the story. I'm also indebted to my editor, Elizabeth White, whose expertise helped polish this story into the best version of itself. I also want to thank Officer Ed Campbell of the Danvers Police department for his insights on criminal investigations, police policy and procedure, and some of the local knowledge that's sprinkled throughout this book. I also want to thank the folks at Damonza.com for the fantastic cover design.

And finally, a big thanks to all the readers who've decided to come on this journey. I hope you enjoy the ride.

CHAPTER ONE

Detective Ray Hanley steered his unmarked Ford Explorer through the elaborate gateway of the Forest Hills Cemetery, which resembled a gothic cathedral adorned with stone spires and a trio of arches secured with wrought iron. He parked at the edge of the lot beside a Boston Police car and a state police cruiser.

Climbing out of the SUV, he bowed his head against a steady drizzle and followed an asphalt path that wound through a sprawling expanse of rolling green hills. He trudged through a patchwork of puddles and rounded the bend to where a streamer of yellow police tape undulated in the wind. He ducked beneath the tape and walked toward the trio of officers standing beside an open grave. He nodded to the muscular state trooper who towered over the Boston city detectives and resisted the urge to ask how many cops it took to find a body in a graveyard.

Trooper Ty Garrison, who resembled a mocha-skinned Mr. Clean, removed his campaign hat and ran a hand across his shiny bald head. "First time I've ever seen something like this."

Which said a lot, considering he and Ray had witnessed the grotesque handiwork of a serial killer known as the Artist only a few months earlier.

"Who's got command?" Ray asked.

"Your boys got here first," Garrison said. "It's yours if you want it."

Ray shifted his gaze to detectives Greene and Chang from the 11th Precinct. Like Ray, both men were in their early thirties, although with his youthful face and trendy hairstyle, Chang resembled an Asian pop star more than a city detective.

1

Greene, on the other hand, had a forgettable face and the robotic mannerisms of someone with Aspergers.

Ray turned away from the October wind and drew his sports coat tighter around his broad shoulders. He gestured to the open grave. "What're we looking at?"

Detective Greene stepped aside and aimed a flashlight into the hole, illuminating the disembodied face of a young woman staring up from the depths of the grave. Her eyes were wide and unblinking and streaks of mud were smeared across her cheeks. A damp layer of soil obscured everything except for her head and the curled tips of her fingers, which protruded from the earth like a cluster of worms.

"Christ," Ray said. "Where's the groundskeeper?"

Garrison motioned to a battered yellow backhoe in the distance and waved the man over. The groundskeeper climbed off the digger and approached them with an arthritic gait, his lips pulling into a wince with each labored step. He wore a slate-gray uniform with matching cap and had a frizzy white ponytail that brushed against his angular shoulders.

Ray stared at the groundskeeper for several moments, sizing him up, studying his body language. "What happened here?" he asked. "Did you bury that girl?"

The groundskeeper shifted his gaze to Garrison and the others. "Didn't they tell you?"

Ray glanced at the name embroidered over the old man's breast pocket. "I'd rather hear it from you, Rusty."

"Alright then," Rusty said. "I dug the hole last night, must've been around eight o'clock."

Chang and Greene both scribbled notes on identical department-issued notepads.

"When did you first see the girl?" Ray asked.

"Not until this morning."

"Did you get a good look last night?" Ray asked.

"The backhoe's got a light on it. The grave was empty when I left."

THE BURYING POINT

Ray eyed the sleek granite headstone, its surface glistening with raindrops.

Stanley Morris
Born August 1, 1945
Forever in our hearts

"When is Mr. Morris scheduled for burial?" Ray asked.

"Three o'clock this afternoon."

"Is it unusual to dig the hole so far in advance?" Garrison asked.

"Not when we have a dozen burials scheduled for a single afternoon."

"For the record," Ray said, "are you saying someone came along after you left last night and dumped the body?"

"She wasn't just dumped, Detective. She was buried. And probably two feet below where I'd left off. If not for all this rain, we would've buried Mr. Morris without ever knowing she was there."

Ray imagined a shiny black coffin descending into the grave and entombing the woman forever.

Garrison shook his head. "Almost the perfect damn crime."

"It either took a lot of planning," Ray said, shifting his gaze to Rusty, "or maybe just the right opportunity."

"Was it supposed to rain last night?" Chang asked.

"According to the National Weather Service," Greene said, speaking in his trademark monotone, "rain wasn't in the forecast."

"What time do the gates close in the evenings?" Ray asked.

"Sundown."

"And what time was that?"

"7:12 p.m.," Greene said, glancing at his phone.

"How old would you say that woman is?" Ray asked, eyeing Rusty.

"Gosh, I don't know. Twenty-five?"

"Do you know her?" Ray asked.

"Of course not."

"You're sure?" Garrison said.

"I'm positive."

"Who else was working last night?" Ray asked.

Rusty gestured to the gatehouse. "You can check with Kimberly. She'll show you who clocked in and out and at what times."

"I'll get with her," Chang said, nodding to Ray before hustling toward the gatehouse.

Garrison chuckled. "Ten bucks says he only wanted out of the rain."

"Must've been messing up his hair," Ray said.

"Do you have surveillance cameras on the premises?" Greene asked.

"Just at the front gate."

Ray shifted his gaze to Detective Greene. "Why don't you see if Kimberly can produce the tapes."

"Yes, sir."

As Greene marched toward the gatehouse, Ray caught Rusty sneaking a glimpse at the body. No guilt in his eyes, only sadness. Ray laid a hand on the old man's shoulder. "I assume you've got the equipment to get her out of there?"

Rusty nodded. "I'll get the truck."

***

By the time Rusty returned in a blue pickup, more than a dozen Crime Scene Services technicians were combing the perimeter, laying down bright yellow evidence markers and snapping pictures of the grave site, the surrounding paths, and random scraps of litter.

Rusty climbed out of the truck and limped around to open the flatbed, which held a rectangular casket-lowering device with adjustable chrome rails and several nylon straps designed to cradle a coffin. Garrison grabbed one end of the contraption and waited until Ray had grabbed the other before walking toward the open grave and setting it down in the grass.

Ray stared into the depths of the grave. "What's the best way to get those straps around the body?"

"There's a buckle in the middle," Rusty said. "But someone would need to go down there and fasten them underneath her."

Garrison folded his arms. "Just for the record, there's no way I'd fit."

"I could widen it with the backhoe," Rusty said, thumbs hooked into his beltloops.

Ray brushed rainwater from his eyes and ran a hand through his dark hair. "I don't want to risk disturbing the evidence. Someone's gotta go down there." He glanced over his shoulder and saw Tina Bolton from the medical examiner's office approaching from the parking lot wearing a baggy, blue coverall with long sleeves and hood.

She slipped on a pair of latex gloves and got right down to business. No small talk, no pleasantries. Classic Tina. "Have you determined how you'll extract the body?" she asked.

"We were just discussing that," Garrison said.

"Yeah," Ray said. "You're too chicken to go down there." He gestured to the casket device. "Who's gonna lower me into the grave?"

"What's your plan?" Garrison asked. "You can't just scoop her into your arms."

"Give me a little credit, will you?" He shifted his gaze to Tina. "I'll need the spine boards from your van and a length of rope. Maybe one of your sexy blue coveralls for good measure."

"The van's open," she said. "Knock yourself out."

***

Ray arrived back at the gravesite dressed in blue coveralls and carrying a spine stabilizer board in each hand. He passed one of the boards to Garrison and laid the other one across the support straps of the casket-lowering device.

"Why don't you make Greene or Chang go in?" Garrison asked.

Ray ignored the question. Pulling rank wasn't his style. Besides, he still had plenty to atone for. His last big case had made national news, and for a while, cameras had shadowed his every move. Despite being heralded as a hero cop, taking down the Artist had come at a hefty price, and not a day went by that he wasn't reminded of the cost.

He glanced skyward and cleared his mind, refusing to be dragged back into the Artist's lair, where his victims had hung from the walls like grisly works of living art. By now, the rain had tapered off to an intermittent drizzle, the sun reduced to a pale disk behind a veil of shifting clouds.

"I hope you're not claustrophobic," Garrison said. "Because that is one tightass squeeze."

Ray fished a surgical mask from the pocket of his coveralls and positioned it over his nose and mouth. He glanced into the hole, and for a brief instant, he saw his old partner, Billy Devlin, glare up from the depths of the grave.

Christ, he thought. *Not now.*

"You okay?" Garrison asked.

Ray nodded. "Just be ready with your flashlight." He sank to his knees and shimmied onto the stabilizer board, lying flat over the open grave. The rigid plastic wobbled beneath his weight as it exerted pressure on the straps of the casket-lowering device. "Someone pass me the hand trowel and the rope."

Rusty shuffled toward him and slid the items into his outstretched hand.

"You ready?" Garrison asked.

"Let's get this over with."

Rusty moved to the back of the device and fingered a lever beside the hand crank. "Engaging descent."

Ray felt a sudden sensation of weightlessness as the chrome rails spun counterclockwise, letting out slack in the straps securing the spine board. The surface layer of sodden grass vanished from his peripheral vision, yielding to slick, earthen walls teeming with veiny roots.

Down he went, the straps unfurling, Garrison's light barely penetrating. A shroud of darkness enveloped him as the scent of subterranean decay wafted up from below. "That's far enough," he said, sensing his proximity to the body.

The stabilizer board jerked to a halt, swaying a few inches to the left before glancing off the wall. Ray wedged the blade of the hand trowel beneath his leg and reached into the pocket of his coveralls for a flashlight.

"Everything okay down there?" Garrison's voice sounded muffled and distant.

Ray clicked on the flashlight, and the pasty-white flesh of the dead woman's face materialized just an inch from his own. He recoiled in terror, a silent scream lodging in his throat at the realization he'd narrowly avoided an unholy kiss.

"Christ," he muttered, a wave of revulsion washing over him.

"You okay?" Garrison asked.

"I'm fine," he said, hating the waver that had crept into his voice. "Lift me up six inches." He waited for the height to be adjusted before returning his attention to the dead woman.

Her eyes were wide but vacant, clumps of mud caught in her lashes. A milky pall clouded her irises, dulling what had once been the vibrant blue eyes of an attractive young woman. Her wavy blond hair was matted and damp, and the remnant of a wilted flower was bobby-pinned above her left temple.

A shadow darkened her lips, and it took Ray a moment to realize that flies were swarming into her mouth. He felt his gorge rise and immediately choked it back, focusing instead on the woman's white dress, which was open at the throat and ruffled at the shoulders, the remainder of the fabric submerged in a layer of mud.

He discerned no obvious wounds to her face or throat, which made him wonder if the cause of death was a drug overdose or trauma to the torso. He clamped the flashlight between his teeth, biting it through the mask, and retrieved the hand trowel from beneath his leg. He dug a narrow channel in the mud beneath the woman's shoulders, reaching as far as he could on either side until the channels connected. He repeated the process under her legs and threaded a rope through both channels, tying the loose ends to the holes notched into the side of the stabilizer board.

"Bring me up another six inches."

The chrome rails squeaked as the stabilizer board ascended a half foot into the shaft, the ropes beneath it lifting the body clear out of the mud. Ray feared that going any higher would risk the body folding in half and slipping free of the ropes.

"Hand me that other stabilizer board," Ray said.

Garrison crouched over the grave and lowered it into Ray's outstretched hand. Ray flattened the board against the wall of the grave and angled it beneath the woman's body. He used another length of rope to secure the two boards together.

"Alright," he said, "get us out of here."

The ascent was jerky and erratic, and as they rose toward the morning light, the woman's dress billowed in the breeze. It was the kind of dress that might be worn at a confirmation, all white and floral embossed. Except now it was soiled beyond recognition, and the area over the left breast bore a more sinister stain, the fabric there flapped open to reveal a sunken cavity dripping with mud.

***

When they arrived at the surface, Ray rolled onto the grass and tore off his mask, drawing a breath of fresh air.

Garrison shook his head. "Man, you are out of your goddamned mind."

"A little bit," Ray said.

Garrison reached down and hauled him to his feet. "Some things never change."

Tina had already begun her field examination, crouched over the body with her medical kit opened at her feet.

8

Ray's phone buzzed in the pocket of his coveralls.

Garrison smirked. "You took your phone into a grave?"

Ray shrugged and reached into his pocket. "Forgot it was there." The caller ID displayed the precinct's main number. "Detective Hanley," he said.

Lieutenant Spinonni's voice bellowed in his ear. "I need you back at the precinct."

"I'm in the middle of a crime scene. Just give—"

"I need you here now. Captain's orders." Spinonni hung up.

"What's that about?" Garrison asked.

"I don't know," Ray said, "but it can't be good."

CHAPTER TWO

The 11th Precinct was in Boston's Dorchester neighborhood, which had a reputation as a low income, high crime area that, despite its rich history, was often shunned by tourists in favor of sites with a lower risk of aggravated assault. The precinct occupied a two-story brick building whose south wall was a favorite target of local graffiti artists, including Ray's most reliable informant, RJ, the famed creator of the *Weekly Diss*. RJ's most recent handiwork spoofed the building's distinctive box shape with a message that read:

Allergy warning: May contain assholes.

Ray entered the building and strode past the open grid of desks known as the bullpen, acknowledging a few colleagues with a wave before continuing to Lieutenant Spinonni's office.

The lieutenant sat hunched behind a metal desk, his considerable bulk eclipsing several inches of his workspace. He had a landline wedged against his ear and was berating someone in a colorful tirade of expletives.

Ray folded his arms in the doorway and suppressed a grin. RJ's *Weekly Diss* had once again proved to be spot on.

Spinonni slammed the phone down and glared at Ray. They shared a long history of bad blood, and Ray's recent promotion had only intensified the animosity. "What the hell do you want?"

"You called me back to the precinct."

"The captain wants to see you."

"What for?"

"Don't know, don't care."

"Good talk, Lieutenant." Ray stepped into the hall and continued to the next office, where he found Captain Jake Barnes standing in front of the window with his hands clasped behind his back.

Even at sixty-two, the captain maintained the strict exercise regimen and lean physique from his days as an Air Force colonel, and everything from his police uniform to his crew cut and his salt-and-pepper mustache appeared in neat order.

Ray rapped his knuckles against the doorframe. The captain turned around, but instead of his usual steely gaze, he wore a haunted expression.

"Captain?"

"Get the door, will you?"

Ray pulled the door shut and followed Barnes to his desk.

"I need a favor, Ray. My niece, Cassie... she's missing."

"Christ. Since when?"

"Going on forty-eight hours." The captain's eyes locked on his, sea-green and desperate. "I need you to find her."

"Where was she last seen?"

"My brother's house."

"How old?"

"Nineteen." The captain reached for a photo on his desk and handed it to Ray. "This is her at graduation."

Ray caught a glimpse of her blond hair and felt his skin crawl. He flashed back to the gravesite, his mind retrieving the disturbing image of the dead girl in the muddy dress. He blinked to clear his vision, and when he looked at the photo again, he felt a rush of relief. The eye color was different. The shape of the face too. Christ, that would've been a horrible coincidence.

"She lives in Salem with her parents. My brother and I aren't on speaking terms, haven't been for years. But he agreed to see you."

"Have the Salem Police been notified?"

"That's how I found out. The chief there is an old Air Force buddy."

"You want me to assist with the investigation?"

"I want you to lead it. I've arranged for a temporary transfer. If you're willing, that is. I need someone on the inside. Someone with your tenacity, someone who's not afraid to push boundaries."

Ray clenched his jaw and recalled the last time he saw his partner Billy alive. "That approach doesn't always end well."

"You're the best detective I've got, Ray. I need you to find Cassie... by whatever means necessary. Can you do that?"

Ray drew a deep breath and nodded. "Yeah, Captain, I can do that."

***

Cassie's parents lived in an old Victorian in the heart of Salem's historical district. The three-story home featured slate-gray clapboard siding that yielded to gingerbread shingles on the upper level, where a wrought iron widow's walk stretched between a pair of conical roof turrets that likely offered a million-dollar view of the harbor.

As Ray climbed the stairs to the porch, the muffled discord of an argument filtered through the door. He cocked his head to listen, but the antique oak rendered the words garbled and indistinct. He rang the bell and stepped back from the welcome mat, eyeing a weathered white plaque mounted to the siding.

Built 1711 for Nathaniel Cartwright, Merchant.

A disembodied male voice registered from the interior. "Answer the goddamned door."

A moment later, the door swung inward on a petite blonde in her mid-forties. Her striking blue eyes had the appearance of someone who'd recently been crying. She smiled politely, but it vanished into a frown as quickly as it came, leaving Ray to wonder if he'd really seen it at all.

"Can I help you?" she asked, her breath wafting a hint of gin.

"I'm Detective Ray Hanley with the Boston Police. Are you Elizabeth Barnes?"

The woman held the door open. "We've been expecting you." She motioned into the living room, where a man who resembled a younger but less fit version of the captain sat in a leather recliner wearing designer glasses and a pink Brooks Brothers dress shirt. "My husband, Paul."

"It's about time you showed up," Paul said.

Elizabeth shot her husband a dirty look, then frowned at Ray apologetically. "Please, come in."

Ray wiped his feet on the mat and scanned the living room, which looked like a page from an interior design magazine, complete with high-end furnishings, rustic ceiling beams, and antique flooring polished to a flawless sheen. "You've got a beautiful home," he said as he followed her to a leather sectional accented with nautical-themed throw pillows.

Paul regarded them from the recliner, maintaining a cool distance from his wife. "I don't see how this is going to help. We already went over this with the Salem Police."

"He's trying to find Cassie. That's what you want, isn't it? Or are you too busy to care?"

Paul clenched his jaw and fixed her with an icy stare, the sort of look that suggested she'd pay for the comment later.

"I won't take up too much of your time," Ray said, wondering if the high collar of Elizabeth's blouse hid any bruises.

"My daughter is missing," Paul said, "and you're playing catch-up, so I'm sure you can appreciate my lack of patience."

"I understand how difficult this must be," Ray said. "But I've already read the case notes, and I just want to confirm a few things before asking some new questions." Paul responded with a noncommittal shrug, which Ray figured was the best he would get. "You last saw Cassie on Monday morning when she left for work?"

"That's right," Paul said, making no attempt to disguise the annoyance in his voice.

Ray shifted his gaze to Elizabeth. "Is that when you last saw her as well?" When Elizabeth nodded, he said, "I'm aware that Cassie walked to work that morning, in keeping with her usual routine. A place five blocks from here called Mystical Brew Coffee Cottage."

Elizabeth nodded.

"Do you remember the conversation from that morning? Did she say anything that struck you as unusual?"

"She's a nineteen-year-old girl," Paul said. "She barely speaks to us. If she says anything at all, it's just *yes, no,* or *fine.* I swear social media rots these kids' brains."

Ray jumped in with another question before Paul could go on a tangent. "Have either of you noticed a change in Cassie's mood lately?"

"Not that I noticed," Elizabeth said.

"Did she take her phone with her that morning?"

Elizabeth nodded. "It goes straight to voicemail when I call."

The last ping from Cassie's phone had hit a cell tower a half mile away at 6:45 a.m. on Monday and hadn't registered a blip since. "Was she taking any classes or involved in any clubs or other activities?"

"She wasn't doing much of anything," Paul said. He folded his arms and averted his gaze, as if embarrassed to explain further.

Elizabeth chimed in. "Cassie talked us into letting her do a gap year."

"She talked *you* into it," Paul said. "I always knew it was a bad idea."

"Don't turn this into a fight, Paul. Not now." Elizabeth exhaled slowly, trying to calm herself. "Cassie was a straight-A student, but the idea of committing to college before knowing

14

what she wanted to do with her life terrified her. I found her crying in her room during the application process, sprawled out on her bed and surrounded by papers. It was best for her mental health to take a break."

"None of this would've happened if you'd listened to me," Paul said. "You can keep crying about it if you want to, but you know I'm right."

Elizabeth reached for a box of tissues on the coffee table and dabbed her eyes. After composing herself, she met Ray's gaze. "Cassie planned to travel through Europe with her friend Abby. It would've been a great way to gain perspective and experience a bit of the world, but Abby backed out at the last minute and Cassie couldn't find a replacement. Instead of traveling alone, she took a job at Pickering Wharf serving overpriced coffee to tourists at Mystical Brew."

"And a month later," Paul said, "she started dating some sleazy thirty-year-old. Talk about a waste of potential."

Ray imagined his own daughter all grown up and faced with the same choices. Thankfully, Allie was a long way from deciding on college and was still very much Daddy's little girl. If only she could stay five forever.

"The case notes list Cassie's boyfriend as a public defender named Alex Whitehall."

Paul scoffed. "He represents the dregs of society."

"I don't care who he represents," Elizabeth said. "He shouldn't be dating a nineteen-year-old."

"What can you tell me about their relationship?" Ray asked.

Elizabeth shrugged. "Cassie knows we don't approve of the age difference and doesn't bring him around much. But she swears he's a gentleman."

"Does she spend a lot of nights at his place?"

"Cassie knows the rules," Paul said, "and that's never been allowed."

"Does she have a curfew?"

"Eleven o'clock," Paul said.

"Has she ever run away?"

Elizabeth bristled. "Cassie would never do that to me."

Ray made a mental note of her word choice: *me* instead of *us*. "I didn't mean to offend you."

Elizabeth dabbed her eyes again. "I just want you to bring Cassie home."

"I'll do whatever it takes," Ray said. "That's a promise."

"You can start by searching Alex's house," Paul said. His lips curled into a sneer, giving the impression he was more angry than afraid, as if someone had wrecked his Mercedes instead of kidnapped his daughter.

Ray locked gazes with Paul. "Alex was working at the Salem courthouse when Cassie disappeared."

"I don't give a shit about his alibi," Paul said. "I don't trust him."

"Why not?"

"Because he makes himself out to be some goody-two-shoes public defender, but he's preying on a girl half his age. That makes him a scumbag in my book."

Ray decided not to challenge Paul on his math. According to Captain Barnes, Paul had once studied for the priesthood before switching majors and eventually becoming a hedge fund manager, so he obviously had his own system for rationalizing and rounding.

"What do you think?" Ray asked, turning to Elizabeth.

She was a psychiatrist by trade, and the sole heir to the Cartwright family fortune. Her ancestors were among the first settlers of Salem. According to the captain, the prenup Paul had signed was the curse that kept their marriage together, which was why she self-medicated and he spent most of his time at the office.

"I question his motives for dating Cassie," she said. "It's borderline deviant behavior."

"Don't worry," Ray said. "I'm still gonna rattle his cage, whether he's clean or not. In the meantime, how about showing me Cassie's room."

**

Ray followed Elizabeth up a winding staircase to the third-floor landing, which opened onto a wood-paneled hallway with access to a sitting room, bathroom, and bedroom. Cassie's room accounted for most of the floor. The walls bowed out at either end to accommodate the conical roof turrets, which, as Ray had presumed, offered a stunning view of Pickering Wharf and the sprawling gray Atlantic beyond.

Sunlight streamed through the antique glass windows, illuminating yellow walls and evoking a cheerful ambience that served to counterbalance the toxic family environment. A matching set of white, wood furnishings adorned Cassie's room—a queen-sized bed, clawfoot dresser, chaise lounge, bookshelf, and mirror vanity.

There was a good chance Cassie had run away to escape her overbearing parents, and he hoped her personal effects would provide a glimpse into her state of mind. After a quick scan of the layout, he crossed the room to examine a photo collage tacked to a corkboard between the dresser and vanity. He spotted Cassie immediately, recalling the picture the captain had shown him at the precinct.

Cassie appeared in more than a dozen pictures and seemed happy and well-adjusted; a slender teen with wavy blonde hair and a shy smile, the ghost of a dimple visible on her chin. She was pretty in a subdued way and exuded an innocence the girls around her seemed to lack. Not simply because she wore less makeup and dressed more conservatively—it was something in her eyes. They were a striking shade of amber and possessed an expressive quality that conveyed the awareness of a girl who was wise beyond her years.

The same quality shone through every picture, whether she was on the volleyball court, at the beach, in the classroom, or at a Red Sox game. The same two girls appeared in many of the photos. "Are these her best friends?" Ray asked.

Elizabeth nodded. "They were inseparable in high school. They called themselves the *Three Amigas*." She pointed to a picture of Cassie posing with the girls at a banquet table, a crowd of well-dressed kids dancing in the background. "That's Jessica Ling in the blue dress and Abby Garcia in pink. It was their senior prom."

Judging from the decorative masks and colorful beads, Ray guessed it was a Mardi Gras theme. "Is she still in touch with them?"

"Jessica moved to California to attend Stanford, and Abby is... well, she's been ill."

"What do you mean?"

"She suffered a mental breakdown. Surprising at her age, but thankfully, it happened here in town. She's the one Cassie was supposed to travel to Europe with for gap year. After the trip fell through, she and Cassie both worked at the coffee shop."

"When did she have the breakdown?"

"A couple months ago, around mid-August."

Ray reached into his sports coat for his notepad and jotted down some notes. "Would Abby be able to answer questions about Cassie's disappearance?"

"I doubt it. She was institutionalized, and I don't think Cassie had any contact after that."

Ray made a note and approached the dresser, which displayed a Himalayan salt lamp at one end and a framed photo at the other. A jewelry stand occupied the middle and was adorned with necklaces, earrings, and a variety of moon, star, and crystal pendants. All made of silver. "Does Cassie not like gold?"

"She thinks it's tacky. Probably because I like it."

Ray peered at the photo, which featured Cassie embracing a guy with sandy blond hair and rough stubble across a square jawline, the sun a blazing scarlet disk melting into the lake behind them. "Is this Alex?"

Elizabeth bit her lip and nodded. "That's him."

"When was this taken?"

"Fourth of July weekend. Jessica came home to visit and they drove up to Lake Winnipesaukee. She never told us Alex was going with them."

"All teenagers have secrets," Ray said. "A double life their parents don't know about. You're not alone on that."

"Maybe so, but I've worked hard to keep this family together."

"I'm sure you have."

"We're not perfect," she said, lowering her voice, "and I've probably sided with her father too often. Not because I agreed with him, but because it was easier that way. But now we're paying the price."

"Do you think she might've run away?"

"I don't know what to think, but it's better than the alternative."

"Was your husband ever abusive toward her?"

Elizabeth frowned. "Not physically, but he's hard on her emotionally." She stared out the window at the rolling gray Atlantic. A band of sunlight illuminated her profile, accentuating the fine lines that radiated from the corners of her eyes like the well-worn paths of loneliness and regret. "My husband used to be fun-loving and kind, but now all he does is judge… and we never live up to his standards."

"I'm sure that must be difficult," Ray said, thinking about his own relationship struggles.

She glanced into the empty hallway. "I planned on leaving Paul when Cassie went away to college, but the gap year decision threw a wrench into that." She dabbed her eyes with a tissue. "There were times I wished Cassie would hurry up and leave so I could get on with my life." She buried her face in her hands, shaking her head slowly. "I've been a terrible mother."

Ray laid a hand on her shoulder, and Elizabeth collapsed into his arms, her body hitching with sobs. She buried her face into his chest, hot tears soaking his shirt, her hair smelling faintly of coconut. "I'm sure you did the best you could," he said, patting her back before pulling away. "You can make it up to her as soon as we bring her home."

She drew a deep breath and smiled through her tears. "Thank you, Detective. I needed that."

Ray cocked a thumb at Cassie's vanity, eager to change the subject. "Do you mind if I look through her stuff?"

"Whatever you need."

Cassie's vanity was cluttered with beauty products, including several varieties of makeup, brushes, and lotions. A jar candle was wedged into the back corner behind a bottle of hairspray, the cherry-red wax interior wafting the scent of cinnamon and spice. Its no-frills label advertised a single word: LOVE.

Ray walked over to the bookshelf and scanned the titles, which mainly consisted of dystopian fiction and supernatural romances involving werewolves, vampires, and shapeshifters, the covers all featuring shirtless young men with chiseled abs and brooding expressions. There were also a few books on healing, spirituality, and mysticism. He turned to Elizabeth. "Did Cassie keep a diary?"

"Not that I know of."

"You mind if I look through her drawers?"

"Go ahead."

Ray rifled through her dresser drawers, feeling beneath the clothes but coming up empty. He continued the search elsewhere, but found nothing in her closet, beneath her mattress, or in any other place a young girl might stash her secrets. "Does Cassie have a computer?"

"She has an iPad," Elizabeth said, "but it fits inside her purse and she always takes it with her."

"Have you noticed any personal effects missing from her room? Anything she wouldn't take to work but might throw into her purse if she planned on running away?"

Elizabeth did a slow sweep of the room. "Nothing appears to be missing, although I can't say for sure."

"What about medication? Like an inhaler or birth control pills."

"She wasn't on any."

Ray nodded, feeling that the questioning had run its course. "Can you think of anything else that might help the investigation?"

Elizabeth shook her head.

"I'll get out of your hair now," Ray said. "But do me a favor and take another look for a diary when I'm gone." He handed her a dog-eared business card from his wallet. "In the meantime, I'll be working every angle I can. And I promise you, I won't rest until I find her."

CHAPTER THREE

Ray didn't need thirteen years of police experience to recognize that Detective Elena Martinez wanted nothing to do with him. The animosity was evident from the defiant set of her shoulders, the cocksure tilt of her head, and the way she glared at Chief Sanderson when Ray walked into the chief's office.

Chief Sanderson had pulled Ray aside when he first checked into Salem Police headquarters fifteen minutes earlier. "It's her first case as a new detective," Chief Sanderson had said, "and she's itching to prove herself." He motioned to the bullpen with a caramel-colored hand, his palm etched with a latticework of lines. "She's not gonna like it, but it's good for her development, whether she realizes it or not." The chief's expression was stern, but his eyes were kind. "Why don't you grab yourself a coffee from the break room and meet me and Martinez back here in ten minutes?"

When Ray returned to the chief's office, he stood in the doorway and waited for Martinez to finish venting. Chief Sanderson, to his credit, sat quietly and nodded in all the right places.

Martinez wore a white blouse beneath a navy blazer, her dark hair pulled into a tight ponytail, which cut the air like a scythe as she punctuated her points. Ray guessed her to be twenty-nine or thirty years old.

"What do you mean, 'what do I want'?" she asked. "I want him to stay the hell away from my case."

"I'm afraid you don't have a choice in the matter," Chief Sanderson said.

Martinez shot to her feet in protest and fixed Ray with an icy stare.

Ray put out his hand. "Detective."

Martinez stormed past him without a word.

***

Ray sat behind the wheel of the Explorer and sipped coffee from a Styrofoam cup. "This is terrible," he said, eyeing the layer of grounds clinging to the bottom.

Martinez glared at him from the passenger seat. "I suppose the coffee at your precinct tastes like Juan Valdez harvested the beans and brewed them himself."

"Nah, he quit a while ago, and the coffee's gone to shit ever since."

"Oh great. I'd figured you for a snob, but it turns out you're just a complainer. What's next, are we gonna sit in the parking lot while you bitch about the weather? Or has the bigshot Boston detective already solved the case?"

Ray fired up the engine. "You make a shitty first impression, Martinez. Good thing I like you anyway."

Martinez folded her arms across her chest. "The feeling's not mutual."

"You'll come around," Ray said, reversing out of the parking space.

"What a surprise—another man bragging about how great he is. Why not get it out of the way and tell me how pretty I am."

"Nice try, Martinez, but you're not my type." Ray merged into traffic on Main Street and headed toward Pickering Wharf.

Martinez turned away, but he could see her reflected in the window. She *was* pretty. There was no denying that, and he was under no illusion of how difficult it must be for her to command respect in a precinct full of macho cops.

"For the record, I'm not trying to take anything from you," Ray said. "I only want to find Cassie. And even though the chief put me in charge, I still want your input."

"Then why are we headed to Mystical Brew? Didn't you read my case notes? Or don't you trust me?"

Despite having only a day's jump on the investigation, Martinez's case notes ran twenty pages and showcased a meticulous attention to detail. So far, she'd interviewed Cassie's parents, neighbors, coworkers, and boyfriend and had summarized their alibis, occupations, relationships to Cassie, potential motives, physical appearance, and mannerisms. She'd even risk-ranked their need for follow-up.

"Your case notes aren't the problem," Ray said.

"Then what is?"

"Half of detective work is identifying clues and following the facts, but the other half is abstract. Like when you see one of those paintings that's all blurry up close but turns into a portrait when you move farther back."

"So what's the problem?" Martinez asked.

"I can't see the abstract from someone else's description." Ray turned down East Washington Square and parked a few houses down from Cassie's.

"I thought you said we were going to Mystical Brew."

Ray climbed out of the truck and eyed the stately homes lining the block, their manicured lawns still vibrant green despite the arrival of autumn. Halloween decorations adorned many of the porches—an unholy gathering of spiders, ghouls, and witches looming over a harvest of pumpkins and gourds. But the Halloween spirit was conspicuously absent from Cassie's house, which was situated at the southeastern edge of Washington Square and overlooked the sprawling fields of Salem Common.

"I want to retrace her steps," Ray said, glancing at the park. "See what she would've seen on her commute."

"I already had officers check with every resident from here to Mystical Brew. Nobody saw or heard anything."

Ray began walking south, headed away from the Common. "Page seventeen of your manifesto, if memory serves."

Martinez hurried to catch up.

24

"She could've gotten into a car with someone she knew," Ray said. "Or someone could've dragged her in, kicking and screaming. That early in the morning, most people are just getting up."

"It's a fifteen-minute walk," Martinez said. "She left her house at 6:30 and her phone went off the grid at 6:45, which had to be within a block of work."

"It doesn't mean that's where she disappeared," Ray said. "She might've been pinned down in the back of a car when her phone was turned off."

Martinez buttoned her blazer and scanned the street, her eyes sweeping from left to right and back again. She'd been over this ground once before, but didn't seem to be taking anything for granted. He respected that.

A breeze gusted from the south, rustling through the maples that lined the street, their wavering leaves bleeding orange and gold. It was only the twentieth of October, but the biting wind blowing off the harbor whispered rumors of an early winter.

Ray swept a lock of hair from his eyes, reminded that he was overdue for a haircut. He'd spotted his first grays earlier in the week and spent a few minutes staring at himself in the mirror. The last few months had aged him, sapping the gleam from his liquid-brown eyes. He was usually quick with a joke, but these days nothing much seemed funny.

"What are the odds she ran out on her parents?" Ray asked.

"Probably fifty-fifty."

"Hedging your bets?" Ray asked.

"She hated living with her parents," Martinez said, "but she also could've gone to college to escape them. Her boyfriend dumped her a week ago, so maybe she—"

"Hold up," Ray said. "That's the first I've heard about a breakup."

"Alex told me last night."

"That wasn't in the case notes," Ray said.

25

"Oh, so you did read my notes?"

"Why wouldn't I?"

"I hear that you only follow your own leads."

"Don't believe everything you hear, Martinez. Why wasn't it in the notes?"

"Because it was a late meeting, and my morning got hijacked, as you know."

"Pretty convenient for Alex to say he dumped her," Ray said.

"Her friend Jessica corroborated his story."

"The girl who's going to Stanford?" Ray asked.

"The young woman, yes."

"It's possible Cassie was upset and skipped town," Ray said, "or maybe wandered off and tried to hurt herself."

"Maybe," Martinez said. "But Cassie's a pretty girl, and she walked the same route five days a week. Some pervert could've been watching her for a long time, waiting for the opportunity to snatch her."

"What about her phone records?" Ray asked. "Does the activity support a breakup?"

"She and Alex had a high volume of calls before the breakup. After that, the activity fell off a cliff. She texted and called a couple times, but he never responded."

"She wanted to get back together?" Ray asked.

"That was the gist of it. She felt like the breakup came out of left field, but it was clear from the earlier messages that she was into him way more than he was into her."

"Did you see a spike in calls to Jessica after the breakup?" Ray asked.

"She went from a couple times a month to almost every day for the next week."

"Why isn't any of that in your case notes?"

"Because I haven't gotten to it yet."

"What else hasn't made it into your notes?"

"I'm waiting on a request to access her social media accounts. Her profiles are private, but I got a peek at recent posts from her mom's phone."

"And?"

"Mostly selfies of her and Alex on various dates. A few scattered posts about books, traveling, or animals. Nothing worth following up on. At least not until we get access to her private messages."

Ray ran a hand across his stubbly cheek and gestured to a sign for the commuter bus. "Maybe she hopped on public transit and took a Greyhound out west."

"I told Jessica to call me if Cassie shows up."

Ray nodded. "It's good work, Martinez. You've covered all the bases. I'm impressed."

Martinez shrugged.

"What's the matter?" Ray asked. "Not used to compliments?"

"I don't trust them."

"Why doesn't that surprise me?"

Martinez met his gaze, her dark eyes probing for intent. He hadn't meant it as a slight, but she seemed to interpret it that way. She obviously had a chip on her shoulder, but now wasn't the right time to call her on it.

They continued walking in silence. Ray imagined Cassie plodding along the sidewalk, feeling lonely and dejected, eyes crusty from lack of sleep, probably dreading the long day at the coffee shop and regretting her decision to delay college, only to skip her European tour. He pictured her walking with tunnel vision, unaware of a car slowing at the curb, a man getting out and grabbing her from behind, pressing a hand over her mouth and dragging her off the street.

This time of year, the sun didn't rise until 6:45, which meant most of her walk occurred in the predawn gloom, the sidewalks steeped in shadows. He didn't notice any skid marks in the street or any evidence of a car peeling away in a hurry, but the veil of darkness might've made it unnecessary.

They made a left onto Orange Street and continued past the Custom House, a historic brick building with Corinthian columns and a golden eagle atop a whitewashed cupula. Beyond that, the wooden masts of a replica schooner swayed against the ash-gray sky. The wind off the harbor cut through the street as they approached Pickering Wharf, prying loose the fiery leaves of a nearby maple and scattering them to the wind.

A trolley full of tourists rolled past them before turning left onto Derby Street, headed for the House of the Seven Gables, which the driver announced was built in 1668 and represented one of the oldest surviving wooden mansions in New England. An ad on the back of the trolley promoted their *Ghosts, Witches, and Graveyards* tour, which promised Ray it would inject a *Scream!* into his Halloween.

In eleven days, the streets of Salem would be crawling with trick-or-treaters, and traffic would be snarled for miles in every direction. With any luck, they would find Cassie well before then, because this was the last place on earth he'd want to be stuck on Halloween. He'd fought the crowds here once in his late twenties, and that was more than enough to last a lifetime.

Martinez nudged him in the arm and pointed to a telephone pole, where Cassie's likeness stared back at them, the corners of a missing persons flyer flapping in the breeze.

Have You Seen Me?
Cassie Barnes
Age:19
Height: 5' 7"
Weight: 115 lbs
Missing since October 18
Call the Salem Police Tip Line

Martinez smoothed out the edges of the flyer. "Her family and friends posted these all over town."

Ray recognized the picture as Cassie's senior class photo. In it, she wore an off-the-shoulder white blouse, her wavy blonde hair swept to one side. Her head was turned slightly as she smiled for the camera, her eyes full of promise, oblivious to the dark shadow clouding her future.

Ray felt a pang of sadness for Cassie's parents. They were walking a tightrope of emotions, high-strung and sick with worry, barely keeping it together. For everyone's sake, he hoped Cassie had run away, because if someone had kidnapped her, the odds of her survival were shrinking by the second. The first forty-eight hours of a missing persons investigation were critical. After that, people's memories faded to the point where they began to doubt what they might've seen or heard.

"You think we'll find her?" Martinez asked.

Statistically speaking, Cassie was probably dead, but he wasn't about to say that out loud. "We'll find her," he said, stealing a final glance at the flyer before resuming their walk.

A distant cry of seagulls reached their ears as they continued down Derby Street and approached the harbor. Mystical Brew materialized before them as they turned the corner, a single-story brick building overlooking Pickering Wharf. Its logo featured the shapely silhouette of a witch stirring a cauldron of coffee, the name of the store curled around the image in purple lettering.

A blast of heat buffeted them as Ray followed Martinez inside, the intoxicating aroma of freshly ground coffee awakening his senses. The interior featured exposed brick walls and leather wingchairs arranged in private nooks separated by indoor plants, with crisscrossed strings of vintage lights festooned over the seating area.

A trio of college girls milled about the counter, each dressed in a sweater paired with yoga pants and Ugg boots. They were discussing a biology exam they'd recently taken, one of the girls complaining that their professor hadn't taught them half of the material on the test.

The barista made no attempt to hide her disdain as she made their coffees. She had long raven hair, a silver nose ring, and colorful tattoos snaking down her sinewy arms. She wore shiny black Lycra pants and a V-neck T-shirt cut low enough to expose the lacy edges of her bra.

The case notes identified her as Tracy Lasher. She was twenty-five years old, had bounced around the foster system through her formative years, and spent a month in juvie for shoplifting at sixteen. Two of her coworkers rang up customers to her right—Jason Skylark and Heather Jenkins.

Jason was a twenty-eight-year-old stoner and community college dropout whose parents owned the place and gifted him the title of manager. He had frizzy blond dreadlocks and wore a Rasta hemp sweatshirt with Jamaican flag colors.

Heather was a University of Vermont sociology grad who'd spent two years in Ethiopia digging wells with the Peace Corps before returning home to care for her mom, who was battling breast cancer.

Martinez signaled to Heather as she freed up at the register. "Good morning," Martinez said, flashing her badge. "We wanted to see if you've heard anything from Cassie."

Heather frowned and tucked a dark ringlet of hair behind her ear. "I was hoping you had some news."

"What about you?" Ray said, locking eyes with Jason. "Any word from Cassie?"

"Nah, man, it's been crickets."

"Do you find that odd?" Ray asked.

Jason shrugged. "She was always good about calling when she was running late or needed a day off."

"I'm really worried about her," Heather said.

Martinez nodded. "So are we."

Tracy squeezed past Heather to ring up the college girls, giving Ray the once-over as she worked the register.

"Did Cassie ever mention problems with her boyfriend or any trouble at home?" Ray asked.

"She took the breakup pretty hard," Heather said. "She didn't understand why Alex ended things."

"Do you think she might've harmed herself?" Martinez asked.

"I don't think so, but she did seem a little depressed. She'd thought they might get engaged soon."

"When was the last time you spoke to her?" Ray asked.

"Sunday night," Heather said. "When we were closing up shop."

Ray turned to Jason. "Did she give any indication that she wouldn't be at work the next day?"

Jason shook his head. "She said she'd see us in the morning."

Heather's eyes were glassy with unshed tears. "That's how I remember it too."

According to Martinez's case notes, when Cassie didn't show up to work, Heather called her cell phone and left a voicemail asking if she wanted to talk. She'd assumed Cassie had taken a mental health day to mourn the breakup. It wasn't until eight o'clock that evening that Cassie's mom got worried and called Jason, only to discover that she'd never made it to work that morning.

The door to the coffee shop chimed as a young mom entered with a double stroller. Ray signaled to Tracy before she could wait on her. "Mind if I ask you a couple questions?"

Tracy cocked her thumb at Martinez, who was speaking to Heather in hushed tones further down the counter. "I already talked to your partner. You think because she's a woman she didn't ask the right questions?"

"You don't care much for Cassie, do you?"

"She's not my favorite person."

"Why not?"

"Look, I hope she's okay and all, but she's a prissy little bitch."

"You don't pull any punches, do you?"

Tracy leaned over the counter, a grin tugging at her lips. "You wanted my honest opinion, didn't you? I could've lied and said she was a joy to work with."

"And here I thought honesty was hard to come by these days," Ray said.

"I like to do my part," Tracy said.

"And by that, do you mean stealing from the register?"

Tracy folded her arms across her chest. "What are you talking about?" She sounded defensive, but also amused.

"Those college girls ordered three coffees. You rang up two and pocketed the difference."

"I think you're imagining things, Detective."

"How much do you skim a day? Fifty bucks? More on the weekends?"

"What are you gonna do, narc me out to Jason?"

"You could lose your job."

Tracy smirked. "One thing I've learned—with a body like this, I can get away with almost anything."

"Your parents must be proud."

"My parents are dead." The door chimed with another customer. "Sorry, Detective, but I've got to get back to work."

Ray handed her a business card. "Call me if you hear anything about Cassie."

She tucked the card into her bra, where it disappeared beneath a veil of black lace. "Maybe I will call you… although I doubt you can handle me."

CHAPTER FOUR

Martinez cornered Ray outside the shop. "What was that all about?"

"I caught her stealing from the register."

"It looked like you were flirting."

"I'm married."

"So?"

"Women like Tracy get off on manipulating men," Ray said.

"I think she was right," Martinez said.

"About what?"

"You couldn't handle her."

Ray arched an eyebrow. "Are you making a joke, Martinez?"

A ghost of a smile touched her lips. "I'm just calling it like I see it."

Ray pointed to the building next door. The sign above the window read: *Raven's Wing Books & Magik*. "Have you been in there yet?" he asked.

"It was closed when I left Mystical Brew last night."

"Let's go see what they know."

As soon as they entered, Ray's senses were assailed by a cloying miasma of lavender, sage, and some other pungent incense he couldn't identify. He wrinkled his nose and glanced at Martinez, but she didn't appear bothered by it.

The interior was lit by a series of gothic chandeliers and wall sconces, whose flickering bulbs mimicked the dim glow of candlelight. Curved wooden tables were scattered throughout the floorplan, arranged in a pattern of concentric circles suggestive of a maze. The table nearest to them was stacked

33

with books on mysticism and magic, their titles advertising healing spells, love potions, and success.

Ray picked up a gilded leather volume called *Gardnerian Wicca and the Book of Shadows*. The cover featured an embossed pentagram surrounded by symbols resembling the phases of the moon. "What's this?" he asked, "some kind of satanic bible?"

The shopkeeper appeared beside Ray and laid a stack of books down on a neighboring table. "It has pagan roots," she said, meeting his gaze, "but there's nothing satanic about it." She was in her mid-forties and had dark, pixie hair streaked with accents of pink and green. "Wicca celebrates natural magic derived from the earth and combines ancient folk traditions with certain modern elements."

Ray pointed to the pentagram on the book cover. "Isn't that a symbol of the Devil?"

The shopkeeper, whose nametag said Thalia, shook her head. "It's a common misconception. The points of the star symbolize the five elements—earth, air, fire, water, and spirit. Wiccans don't believe in the devil, nor do we follow a bible."

"Then what's the *Book of Shadows*?" Martinez asked.

"It's a journal of sorts. We use it to record rituals, spells, prayers, dreams, and the like."

"Aren't Wiccans the same thing as witches?" Ray asked.

"Yes," Thalia said, "but the true meaning of that term is quite often misunderstood."

Ray had a dozen more questions, but none were relevant to the case. Martinez fished out her badge, which she wore on a silver chain beneath her blazer. "We're investigating a missing person," she said. "A young woman who works at the coffee shop next door."

"Mystical Brew?" Thalia seemed genuinely surprised.

"Her name is Cassie Barnes," Martinez said. "She's been missing for two days."

Ray opened the photo app on his phone and angled it toward Thalia. Thalia gazed at the picture and touched a hand to her chest, her glossy black fingernails reflecting the candlelight.

"Do you recognize her?" Ray asked.

Thalia frowned. "She looks familiar, but I can't say for sure. I'm not a coffee drinker, so I'm rarely ever over there."

Ray walked over to a nearby table and picked up a jar candle with the word LOVE stenciled across the glass. "She had one of these in her bedroom. Who's your supplier?"

"They're made by a local artist. I'd be surprised if more than a couple shops carry them." She signaled to the young woman working the register. "Fiona, would you come here for a moment?"

Fiona sighed and trudged over to them, her flaming red hair trailing past her shoulders. She had multiple eyebrow piercings and wore a threadbare Slayer concert T-shirt cut into a crop top. She had smoldering green eyes and full lips, which were currently twisted into a frown at being called away from the front desk, where she'd been busy with her phone.

"These officers have a couple of questions."

"About what?" Fiona asked.

Ray showed her the picture of Cassie. "Have you seen this girl? She works at Mystical Brew."

"She's been in here once or twice," Fiona said.

"How recently?" Martinez asked.

"I don't know, a month ago?"

"Do you know her?" Ray asked.

Fiona shrugged. "I get my morning coffee from next door. Sometimes she waits on me, sometimes she doesn't."

"Were you friendly with her?" Martinez asked.

Fiona rolled her eyes. "I don't get in line to make friends."

Thalia smirked. "Fiona isn't known for chitchat. And especially not before coffee."

"Is it fair to say neither of you has any information on Cassie's whereabouts?" Ray asked.

"I'm afraid not," Thalia said. "But I hope you find her. It's terrible to think what might've happened."

Fiona stalked back to the front desk and sat down beside a silver candelabra whose crimson candles oozed rivulets of wax onto the counter like blood. Ray followed her to the register and leaned against the counter beside a sign advertising palm readings for twenty-five bucks.

"You ran off before I could finish my questions."

Fiona stared at him, unable to disguise her annoyance. Her pale skin was lightly freckled, and she was attractive despite her perpetual scowl. She had the air of a loner, a resentful outsider judging from afar.

"How long have you worked here, Fiona?"

For a moment, it seemed she might refuse to answer. "Five years," she said, finally.

"How old are you?"

"Twenty-three."

"What's your impression of Cassie?"

"I don't know."

"You've got no opinion?"

"I hardly know her."

"But you know Tracy, don't you?" The comment made her flinch. "I had a feeling you two might be friends."

"So what? It's not a crime."

"I didn't say it was. And not liking someone doesn't make you a suspect. But whatever you can tell me about Cassie's personality might help us find her. I'll ask you again, what's your impression of Cassie?"

Fiona sneered. "She thinks she's better than everyone else."

"How do you mean?"

"She's a snobby rich girl."

"Has she ever said anything offensive?"

"It's not what she says, it's how she looks at people. Staring down her nose, judging people's hair and outfits."

"You get all that from a look?"

Fiona gestured to herself, indicating her face piercings and goth outfit. "You don't think I can tell when someone thinks I'm a freak?"

"You must be happy she's gone."

"I'm not sad."

"Did you and Tracy team up to make your problem go away?"

"You think dressing like this makes me some kind of monster?" Fiona shook her head. "You're no better than she is."

Ray pointed to a rack of silver jewelry on the counter. "Cassie owns a few pairs of those moon and star earrings, so maybe she didn't look down on you as much as you thought."

Fiona wiped a tear from her eye. "I don't know where she is, okay? I didn't do anything."

Martinez crept up beside Ray and grabbed his arm. "That's enough, Detective. Let's go."

CHAPTER FIVE

"What the hell were you doing in there?" Martinez asked.

"It's called questioning a suspect. Did you miss that day at the academy?"

"She's a kid."

"You didn't hear the whole conversation."

"I heard enough. And just because you triggered an emotional response doesn't mean she kidnapped Cassie."

"You know why I solve a lot of cases? Because I know how to push people's buttons. And yeah, sometimes it comes off as mean, but it gets results. People reveal their true character when they're under pressure."

"You accused that girl of kidnapping Cassie, and without a shred of evidence. I think you're the one who missed a day at the academy."

"What's your problem, Martinez?"

She thrust a finger at him. "People are innocent until proven guilty."

"Look, Cassie's life might be in danger. We can't waste time tiptoeing around people's feelings waiting for a lead to fall into our laps. A case like this has to be worked on instinct."

Martinez was silent for a moment, but the illusion of calm was betrayed by a vein that ticked feverishly near the hollow of her throat. "I'm not okay with you bullying people, and especially not women. If you can't abide by that, I'll transfer off the case."

"I don't care what you do, Martinez. But you don't strike me as the kind of person who backs down from a fight.

You want me to take it down a notch? Fine. But not when it comes to Alex. I promised Cassie's parents I'd rattle his cage."

"I can live with that."

Ray scowled at her. "You don't consider that a double standard?"

"He's a likelier suspect."

"Because he's a man?"

Martinez folded her arms. "You wouldn't understand."

"Try me."

"I don't think so."

"If we're gonna be partners, Martinez, we've gotta trust each other."

"I don't trust easily."

"No shit. What happened to you, anyway?"

"I'm not telling you my life story."

"How about just the CliffsNotes?"

"You know it's rude to pry into people's personal lives, don't you?"

"So I've been told."

"You want a story?" Martinez asked. "I've got one for you. When I was sixteen, I used to take the bus to the mall after class. I didn't have money for clothes or makeup, but I liked wandering through the department stores and picking out things I might buy someday. One time when I was looking at dresses, the mall security guard grabbed me from behind and slammed me against the wall. He told me I was under arrest for attempted shoplifting. He put me in cuffs and paraded me through the store, and I remember seeing a group of rich girls from school pointing at me and giggling. He dragged me into an empty room and questioned me for three hours. It was like a game to him. Some old white guy on a power trip who wanted to shame a Hispanic girl for being poor. That's the kind of shit I've dealt with my whole life. So think about that the next time you interrogate someone."

"Sorry. I had no idea."

"That's not an excuse."

"You're right," Ray said. "It's not. But what ended up happening with the security guard?"

"I reached a point where my anger outweighed my fear, and I kicked him in the balls and stormed out of his office."

Ray couldn't help but grin. "Good for you, Martinez. You've literally been busting balls since you were sixteen. I ought to make you a T-shirt."

"That, I might wear."

They rounded the corner at the Custom House and turned onto Orange Street. "We'll need to run a background check on Thalia and Fiona," Ray said, "just to see if anything pops."

"One step ahead of you," Martinez said. "I put in the request while you were making that little girl cry."

"She's twenty-three," Ray said. "And it's obvious she doesn't like Cassie."

"Are you gonna make Alex cry too?"

"With any luck."

A cold breeze gusted at their backs, skittering leaves across the ground before sweeping them into a whirlwind that blew past them like bats swarming out of a cave. As Ray brushed the hair out of his eyes, he noticed Martinez crouch down at the edge of the street.

"What is it?" he asked.

Martinez fished a pair of latex gloves out of her pocket and wiggled her fingers into them. "An earring. It was under the leaves."

Ray leaned over her shoulder. It was a silver crescent moon with a missing backing, and it was similar to the ones he'd seen on Cassie's dresser.

"It could've been ripped off in a struggle," Martinez said, "by someone dragging her into a car." She picked up the earring with a pair of tweezers and slipped it into a plastic evidence bag she pulled from her blazer pocket.

Ray gazed at the surrounding houses. "You talked to everyone on this street already?"

Martinez retrieved a small leather pad from her pocket and thumbed through the pages. "Everyone except for that one." She pointed to a Cape Cod style home with cedar shingles. "We got no answer when we knocked. But you want to know the good part?"

"What?"

"It's got a doorbell camera."

CHAPTER SIX

Naomi sat on her threadbare sofa, alone and in the dark, a trio of pillar candles burning low on an antique coffee table. The wind from an approaching storm howled in the eaves of her third-floor walkup, the flimsy old windows admitting a draft that incited a wild flickering of flames. With her eyes closed, she could sense it more than see it, the battle between darkness and light played out in a ritualistic dance of shadows.

She drew a deep breath and yielded her mind to the night, allowing it to float untethered into the great void of the universe. A soothing warmth flowed through her, beginning with her head and spreading to her shoulders and torso, enveloping the steep swell of her stomach and working into her legs, feet, and toes.

She could feel her pulse in every inch of her body, the rush of blood coursing through her veins. She cast herself deeper into the void, the feeling intensifying until she could sense the strange vibration of a tiny heart thrumming like alien machinery in her womb.

Sometimes, when she was this deep, this entrenched in the void, she experienced visions—incomprehensible, fantastical visions—and other times she saw premonitions of events yet to come.

A full year before its passing, she'd witnessed herself making love to a priest, riding him cowgirl style in the apse of the church, his dark robes unfurled on the floor around him like a sinister inkblot, his face contorted between agony and ecstasy as a statue of Jesus wept from the cross.

Another premonition struck her now, and she snapped to attention in her living room, the dark warmth of the void replaced by the dim glow of flickering candlelight and the wail of the approaching storm.

They were coming for her. Coming for her baby. Men in dark clothes and ski masks riding through town in a black SUV.

As she got to her feet, the baby responded with a kick to her bladder, releasing a warm trickle of urine down her leg. She cursed her pregnant body and waddled into the bedroom, one hand pressed against her womb, the fleshy nub of her bellybutton poking against her palm. She'd had an innie her entire life, until last week when it popped out like a turkey thermometer.

She sank to her knees before the bed, as if praying, the irony striking her as she groped beneath the box spring and fished out a duffle bag. She laid it on the bed and grabbed an armload of clothes from the dresser, shoving them inside and zipping it shut.

A sense of time usually accompanied her premonitions, but this one felt more imminent than the rest—something measured in hours or minutes, rather than months or days.

Something scraped against her bedroom window like nails on a chalkboard, and she whirled around to see the skeletal branches of an oak whipping in the wind, the gnarled ends rubbing against the panes and cutting streaks in the kaleidoscope of raindrops that clung to the glass.

She slung the bag over her shoulder and wriggled her feet into a pair of loosely tied sneakers at the foot of the bed. A plush blue rabbit with a heart-shaped nose sat on the nearby nightstand. It was the only thing she'd allowed herself to buy for the baby. She snatched it up on her way out of the bedroom and jammed it into her back pocket.

She wanted to take more with her—what little jewelry and keepsakes remained from her broken childhood—but there wasn't enough time. Her purse and keys sat on the foyer table, and she grabbed them on her way out.

The stairwell was dark and treacherous, the thin runner bunched up in several places, creating a tripping hazard made worse by the burnt-out light nobody could reach. The landlord was MIA when it came to things that needed fixing, but he never failed to knock on her door bright and early on the first of the month to collect the rent.

If there was a lesson to be learned there, it was that cokeheads with gambling addictions made lousy landlords. Something to file away for next time because she could never come back here. Which was too bad, because after all these years, she'd finally belonged to something.

But then again, maybe starting over was exactly what she needed, a new life for her and the baby. She could go someplace where nobody knew her, a place where she could reinvent herself, make better choices, become a better person.

Cold needles of rain stung her face as she exited the building and shuffled toward the parking lot. Her car was the rust-colored Camry with the missing panel on the front bumper. A recent dent had knocked the headlight askew, giving it the look of a cross-eyed robot that refused to die.

It figured her car was sandwiched between a Jeep and a pickup owned by those obnoxious dicks from the first floor. She had no choice but to sideways creep to her door, the jacked-up wheel well of her neighbor's Jeep soaking her backside, which these days seemed every bit as pregnant as the frontside.

She opened the door and tossed the duffle bag onto the passenger seat. As she ducked her head and lifted a foot to climb inside, she teetered backward and turned around, expecting to find that her shirt had snagged on the corner of the door. Instead, she saw a black SUV idling in the street, the door closest to her opened to reveal a gaping maw of shadows.

A burly man in a dark hoodie stood behind her, a pair of blue eyes glaring at her through slits in a black ski mask. He held a fistful of her shirt in a meaty paw and was dragging her away from the car.

THE BURYING POINT

For a moment, she thought she might tear loose and escape back to her apartment, but the man adjusted his grip and clamped a hand over her mouth. He snaked his other arm around her throat and squeezed tight, the rock-hard bulge of his biceps constricting her airway.

She screamed as loudly as she could, but the man's calloused hand, which smelled like dirty pennies, muffled the sound. He dragged her toward the SUV with little effort, her thrashing legs failing to slow his progress. The silhouette of her car loomed only a few feet away, an escape capsule that was just beyond reach.

Cold rivulets of rain ran into her eyes, blurring her vision. The last thing she saw before crashing onto the floor of the SUV was a dwindling sliver of light from a nearby streetlamp as the door slammed shut and entombed her in darkness.

CHAPTER SEVEN

Mrs. Landsdale was a seventy-year-old widow with a youthful face and a silver-toned pixie haircut. She'd just returned from visiting her mother's assisted living facility in New Hampshire and was giving Ray and Martinez the unsolicited play-by-play.

"And of course, you know, she got that new hip, but would you believe she was up and walking by the end of the week?"

Ray and Martinez sat opposite her in a cozy living room lit by the glow of a gas fireplace. "That's really something," Martinez said, smiling politely.

They were trying to establish Mrs. Landsdale's whereabouts on the morning Cassie disappeared, but she'd gone off on a tangent and they were struggling to reel her in.

Ray said, "We noticed you have a doorbell camera. If you don't mind, we'd like to see the footage from Monday morning."

"Of course," Mrs. Landsdale said. She reached onto the coffee table for an oversized smartphone in a sparkly blue case.

"Does the camera pick up street traffic?" Martinez asked.

Mrs. Landsdale nodded. "I never could figure out how to change the settings to show just the porch." She accessed the doorbell app and tilted her phone so they could see the display. She scrolled down until it showed Monday's activity, the first alert registering at 4:57 a.m. She tapped it with her fingertip, which loaded a video of a pickup truck zipping past in a halo of headlights. The surrounding shadows made it impossible to determine if the truck was brown or red.

Ray gazed at Martinez. "Cassie left home at 6:30 and was off the grid by 6:45. And we're what, a ten-minute walk from her house?"

"There's a few alerts from 6:39," Mrs. Landsdale said. She tapped the first notification, which showed a grocery store delivery truck lumbering down the street.

Ray pointed to her phone. "Do you have audio on that?"

She shook her head. "The motion alerts only record video."

She pressed the next alert, and Ray's skin crawled as Cassie appeared in the frame wearing ripped jeans and a black wool jacket, her blonde hair tied into a loose ponytail. She held her phone close to her face and trailed one finger across the display, as if scrolling through social media.

The phone's spectral glow illuminated her features, but the graininess of the image made it difficult to read her expression, although her slumped shoulders and shuffling gait conveyed a general sense of sadness. Toward the end of the frame, a battered white Buick sped past her, but her gaze remained glued to the screen.

Mrs. Landsdale looked up from the phone. "Was that her?"

Ray nodded, unable to shake the feeling he'd just seen a ghost.

"Show us the next one," Martinez said, her dark eyes intense.

Mrs. Landsdale tapped the alert, and a red Porsche zoomed down the street at what had to be twice the legal limit. The next clip showed a FedEx truck rumbling past in the other direction.

Ray leaned forward and scanned the notifications, which listed the next one at 6:40. "That could be it," he said.

Mrs. Landsdale's finger trembled as she touched the alert. Although the footage was draped in pre-dawn shadows, it captured the appearance of a white van. Its brake lights glowed bloodred as it steered toward the curb and rolled past the porch, before vanishing from view.

Martinez looked at Ray. "That van was definitely pulling over, and at that speed, it would've stopped right where we found the earring."

Ray sucked in his breath and nodded. "I think we just found our kidnappers."

***

A half hour later, Ray and Martinez stood outside Mrs. Landsdale's house watching the Crime Scene Services team finish their sweep of the area. Aside from Cassie's earring, the scene yielded no obvious evidence, although the crime lab would still need to process the litter collected from inside the perimeter.

"Do you think any of that trash could be left over from Monday?" Martinez asked. "With all this wind, it probably blew here in the last couple hours."

"It doesn't hurt to be thorough," Ray said.

Martinez waved at a patrolman who was ducking under the police tape and exiting the perimeter. "Hey, Frasier, where are you going?"

Officer Frasier halted at the sound of her voice, tension evident in the set of his broad shoulders. He had curly dark hair and the cocksure expression of a brawler. The shoulder patch on his police blues showed the silhouette of a witch riding a broomstick past the moon. "I'm headed to the precinct to finish out my shift."

"I need you to reopen the street to traffic," Martinez said. "And then gather all the surveillance video you can find in this area from Monday morning. We're looking for a white Ford Transit 250 cargo van with no markings."

"You're not my boss, Martinez."

Martinez stepped toward him. "The chief assigned you to provide assistance on this case."

48

"That's right," Frasier said, "but that means I take orders from him, not you." He cocked his thumb at Ray to indicate the chain of command.

Martinez and Frasier stood facing one another like two bullies in the schoolyard, sizing each other up before throwing down.

Ray stared at Frasier until he had the man's attention. "Unless you hear me give a conflicting order," Ray said, "you can assume Martinez is speaking for me."

Frasier smirked. "Don't waste your time giving her special treatment, Detective. She may be a hot piece of ass, but that bitch is a stone-cold lesbo. And between you and me, she only got that promotion because of affirmative action."

Ray clenched his hands into fists. "You better watch yourself, Frasier, or I'll knock your ass out before we're through."

Frasier grinned. "There's that temper I heard about. It's gotten you suspended before, hasn't it? I've got a friend at the Boston Police who tells me all kinds of stories."

"I want that surveillance video," Ray said. "Have it ready by tomorrow morning."

"I'll see what I can do," Frasier said. "Oh, and Martinez, I'd watch my back if I were you. I also hear he got his last partner killed."

***

Martinez stewed in the passenger seat on the ride back from Mrs. Landsdale's house. "I'm perfectly capable of fighting my own battles."

"I never said you weren't. What's the story with that guy, anyway?"

Martinez scoffed. "We came up through the academy together. I beat him once in a hand-to-hand training bout, slammed him face-first onto the mat in front of his buddies."

"I bet that bruised his ego."

"The next time I faced him, he landed a cheap shot during a pause and broke my nose."

"Ouch. Did he get reprimanded?"

"He played dumb, which really isn't a stretch for him. Anyway, flash forward five years. A spot for detective opens up. We both pass the exam, and he assumes the job is his."

"You ask me," Ray said, "they made the right choice."

"Yeah, except he and his buddies at the station act like I didn't earn it."

"Don't let it get under your skin. Guys like that aren't worth your time."

"Easy for you to say."

"You're a good detective, Martinez, and after this case, everyone will know it."

"Thanks," she said. "You're a lot less of a jerk than I'd assumed."

"Don't spread that around. I've got a reputation to uphold."

Martinez studied him for a moment. "It's not true what Frasier said about your last partner, is it?"

Ray clenched his jaw. "Let's just say I've made some mistakes."

CHAPTER EIGHT

Alex Whitehall worked at the Essex County Superior Court, which handled criminal cases for cities and towns throughout the county. His office was located just outside of Salem's historic downtown on Federal Street, where a row of courthouses spanning three centuries loomed over the block.

Ray pulled into a metered spot opposite a massive granite building resembling a Greek temple, which featured six fluted columns and a pediment bearing the epitaph *Registry of Deeds and Probate Court*. It was flanked by a red brick building on the right and a modern concrete and glass courthouse on the left.

"Which one is his?" Ray asked.

"The superior court is in the new building, but his office is in the other one." She pointed to the brick building, which he now saw was connected to a two-story granite block with a pair of columns straddling the entryway, the year 1841 embossed below the roofline.

"Is that where they held the witch trials?"

Martinez pointed across the road. "The original building was over there on Washington Street. It was torn down in 1760."

"You a history buff, Martinez?"

"I worked the trolley tours while getting my criminal justice degree."

"Then I bet you know all of this town's dirty secrets."

They climbed out of the SUV and headed into Alex's building. After clearing security, Martinez led Ray past the law library to the second floor, where the public defender's office was located. Martinez checked in with the receptionist while

51

Ray leaned against the desk and studied the layout, sizing up possible escape routes and areas of attack. It was standard practice for approaching a hostile witness, and although it didn't seem necessary in this situation, he didn't want to leave anything to chance. Not after what'd happened to Billy.

The interior consisted of a maze of cubicles and clusters of filing cabinets surrounded by a copy room, conference room, and a row of offices overlooking Federal Street. It had the feel of a library—people talking in hushed tones, the room so quiet you could hear the electric buzz of the overhead fluorescents.

His brother Jacob worked in an office like this, although he was a CPA rather than a lawyer, but both places had the same atmosphere of slow suffocation, as if the office, itself, was sucking the life out of its employees.

"Mr. Whitehall will see you now," the receptionist said.

Martinez thanked her and led Ray toward the first office on the left. After stepping inside, Ray closed the door behind them.

Alex sat in a leather wingchair, his hands clasped before him on the desk. He wore a shirt and tie, the rough stubble from the Lake Winnipesaukee photo replaced by a clean-shaven look, his sandy blond hair combed neatly to one side instead of tousled.

"Detective Martinez, I didn't expect to see you again so soon. Do you have news on Cassie?"

"We haven't found her," Ray said, "if that's what you mean."

"I'm sorry," Alex said, "but who are you?"

"Detective Hanley, Boston Police. I've been assigned to help with the case."

"That's a little unusual isn't it?"

"Cassie's uncle is a Boston Police captain," Ray said. "He wanted eyes on the investigation."

"Well, the more people on the case the better," Alex said. "Are you close to finding her?"

"We're looking into some leads," Ray said and took a seat beside Martinez opposite the desk.

Alex held Ray's gaze as if awaiting more information. "Your lack of details leads me to believe I'm still a suspect."

Ray studied Alex closely. He was trained to detect when someone was lying, but then again, so was Alex. "What kind of details are you after?"

"I'm not after anything, Detective. I only want Cassie to be safe. We may have broken up, but I still care about her."

"Is that so?"

Alex clenched his jaw. "I assume Detective Martinez has already explained that I was sitting at this desk when Cassie vanished."

"How convenient for you."

"Look, I know what you're trying to do, but I had nothing to do with Cassie's disappearance, which should be perfectly evident from the building's security footage."

"Do you always get to work so early?" Ray asked. "Or only when establishing an alibi?"

"I don't appreciate the insinuation."

"I'm sorry to offend your sensibilities," Ray said. "Would you prefer to have an attorney present? I'd recommend using one from private practice, not one of those second-rate hacks assigned by the state."

"That's real cute, Detective, but if you insist on badgering me, I won't answer any more questions."

"My mistake," Ray said, glancing at Martinez. "I thought everyone liked lawyer jokes."

"What time do you normally get to the office?" Martinez asked, picking up on Ray's cue.

"If I have a morning trial, like I did on Monday, I'm usually in before seven. Otherwise, not until eight."

"Why'd you break off the relationship?" Ray asked.

"We were too different. Cassie's a sweet girl, but I didn't see a future."

"You're thirty," Martinez said, "and she's nineteen; it took you that long to see it?"

"What happened?" Ray asked. "She stop putting out?"

Alex's face reddened. "You don't know what you're talking about."

Martinez adjusted her blazer. "Actually, Jessica told me that Cassie's a virgin. She said you guys only did hand stuff."

"That's none of your business."

Martinez gestured to Alex. "She said you're the one who didn't want to go any further."

Ray lifted an eyebrow. "If you didn't see Cassie as marriage material and you weren't after sex, what exactly was the point of the relationship?"

Alex shifted in his chair. "None of this is relevant to your case."

"You're wrong," Ray said. "The nature of your relationship is very relevant."

"How did you two meet?" Martinez asked.

"She took my order at Mystical Brew, and I guess we both felt a mutual attraction. I honestly thought she was in her mid-twenties when I asked her out. And, yes, I did take it slow with her. I've had a lot of relationships that burned out quick, so when she told me she was a virgin, I decided to give slow a try."

"And how'd that work out?" Ray asked.

"Fine for a while. But eventually the newness of the relationship wore off and I started to see glimpses of her immaturity, which gave me doubts about our future. To be honest, I considered making the relationship more physical at that point to see if it would help, but it sort of felt like—"

"A dick move?" Martinez said.

"I guess you could say that." Alex cleared his throat. "Anyway, I waited around to see if she might grow up a bit or if my feelings would change over time. In the end, neither happened, and I knew it was best for both of us to break it off."

Ray turned to Martinez. "You buying any of this?"

"I don't know," she said. "It seems well rehearsed."

Alex slammed his fist against the desk. "It's the goddamned truth is what it is. And it should be obvious to any detective with half a brain that I had nothing to do with this."

"You're the recent ex-boyfriend," Ray said, "which, statistically speaking, means you did it."

"Did what? Do you have any evidence that Cassie was abducted? How do you know she didn't run away? I mean, she'd just had a breakup, she hates her parents, hates her job… I mean, put it together, will you?"

"What kind of car do you drive?" Ray asked.

"You're wasting your time," Alex said. "Check the security footage, check the phone records, and talk to Judge Reynolds—we were in a meeting together first thing Monday morning."

"We've done all that," Martinez said.

"Then why the hell are you still badgering me?"

"Because a nineteen-year-old girl is missing," Ray said, "and I'm not worried about anyone's feelings except for hers. If you're not the one who did it, then help me figure out who did."

"I don't have the slightest idea," Alex said.

"Do you know anyone who might've wanted to hurt Cassie?" Ray asked. "A friend, coworker, maybe one of your low-life clients?"

"Not that I can think of."

Ray laid his business card on the desk. "You think of anyone, you give us a call."

CHAPTER NINE

Ray trudged up the stairs to his three-bedroom townhouse in Charlestown and tried to bury the day's cases in the back of his mind. He'd promised his wife, Michelle, that he'd be home by six, but coordinating the case's overnight activities took longer than expected, and as always, traffic was a bitch.

He rattled the key in the lock and waited a few seconds, imagining Jason, Allie, and Petey scrambling into the foyer and lining up to jump into his arms. They'd fallen out of the habit these last few months while he recuperated from the gunshot wound he sustained during his showdown with the Artist.

He opened the door and kicked off his shoes. "I'm home," he called, dropping his keys onto the foyer table. He heard the rapid thudding of tiny footsteps and expected to see his three-year-old son, Petey, running in from the living room, but his hyperactive Boston Terrier, Sparky, appeared instead and jumped around his feet with his tongue lolling.

"At least *you* still like me," Ray said, bending down to pet Sparky, who continued to run in spastic circles between his legs. "Come on, Sparky, let's go see the kids." He walked into the living room and found his seven-year-old son, Jason, sitting on the couch wedged between Petey and Allie, their faces illuminated by the glow of an iPad.

"What's the matter, you guys don't say hi anymore?"

"Hi, Daddy," Allie said, not looking up.

Petey lifted a chubby hand and waved.

"What're you guys doing?" Ray asked.

"Watching YouTube," Jason said, making a fleeting attempt at eye contact.

Ray peered over their shoulders. "It's just some kid opening toys."

"He famous," Petey said.

"Famous?"

Jason nodded. "He made twenty-five million dollars last year."

"There's no way that can be right," Ray said.

Allie met his gaze, a blonde corkscrew dangling before her eyes. "How much do you make, Daddy?"

"Not as much as that little brat."

"He's not a brat," Allie said.

"Oh, I know a brat when I see one, and right now I see three."

Jason slid the iPad onto the coffee table and brandished his fists. "That's it, Dad. You wanna go?"

Ray kneeled in front of the couch and struck a defensive pose. "I'm not afraid of you rugrats."

They pounced on him like jungle cats. Jason and Allie latched onto his shoulders, while Petey charged into his stomach and toppled him onto his back. Ray turned onto his side and feigned crawling away, making it a few feet before all three kids jumped onto his back and rode him like a horse.

"Gee-up!" Petey cried, smacking him on the head. "Take us shee Mama." His baby talk had progressed into toddler-speak, but he still tended to mix up his 'S' and 'Sh' sounds.

Ray headed into the hallway toward the master bedroom, but Allie grabbed his tie and tugged it to the right, steering him toward the kitchen. "Good horsey," she said, petting his head while Jason smacked his butt and yelled for him to go faster.

The ceramic tiles in the kitchen were brutal on his knees, but he suffered through it until he'd passed the fridge.

Michelle leaned over the stove, mixing a stir-fry with a wooden spoon, her blonde hair tied back in a high ponytail. She glanced over her shoulder. "Oh, good, you're killing Daddy. That saves me the trouble."

Ray drew a deep breath. "Something smells good."

"It's shirfry," Petey said.

Jason and Allie rolled off his back and padded into the living room, understanding that the ride had ended.

Ray reached up and poked Petey in the ribs. "All right, buddy, you too. This horsey's tired."

"But I like shitting on you, Daddy."

"Don't worry," Michelle said, stifling a grin, "we can all shit on Daddy later."

"Okay, Mama, I hungry though." He pointed a chubby finger at his mouth, then whirled around and chased after Jason and Allie.

Ray peeled himself off the floor and stood up. "Hey, hon, how was your day?"

"Tiring."

He leaned in for a kiss, but she turned so that it landed on her cheek. And instead of reciprocating his hug, her hands dangled limply at the small of his back.

Christ, he thought. *Still?*

Little had changed in the last three months, and he was beginning to wonder if she would ever forgive him for his indiscretion with his old flame, Tina Bolton. Not that it was an excuse, but it'd only happened once, and he'd stopped it before they got past third base. But Michelle had found out, and it shattered the foundation of their marriage. Every day since had been an awkward mix of strained conversation and micro rejections, and he feared things might never return to the way they were before.

"What happened to being home by six?" Michelle asked.

Ray glanced at the clock on the microwave. He was more than an hour late. For those keeping score, it amounted to another mark in the broken promises column. "I'm sorry, but my day got hijacked. I spent most of it in Salem."

"For what?"

"The captain's niece is missing."

"Missing, like kidnapped?"

"It's looking that way."

Michelle pressed a hand against the side of her face, something she always did when she was upset. "My God, that's terrible. How's Captain Barnes?"

"He's taking it pretty hard. I think part of him was holding on to the hope she'd skipped town without telling her parents."

"How old is she?"

"Nineteen."

Michelle shook her head, a multitude of horrifying possibilities swirling in the depths of her eyes. "Are you working it alone?"

"They paired me with a Salem detective."

"Is he any good?"

"She's got potential."

Michelle's lips pursed into a tiny 'O' of surprise. He knew the idea of him riding around with a female cop made her uneasy. He considered telling her that Martinez was gay, but he didn't want to give the impression that her sexuality was the only thing holding him back.

He reached for her hand. "I know you're still upset with me, but I swear it won't ever happen again."

Her eyes glistened with tears. "You betrayed my trust, Ray. And you want to know what's worst of all? It feels like I don't know you anymore."

The words sank in as she drew her hand away, landing like a sucker punch to his gut. She turned around and busied herself at the stove, giving the meal a final, angry stir before removing it from the heat. He could tell from the way her shoulders hitched that she was crying, or at the very least, fighting back tears.

"I promise I'm not gonna let you down. I'll spend the rest of my life making it up to you if that's what it takes."

This time when he held out his arms, she allowed herself to be hugged. "We'll get through this," he whispered, rocking her slowly.

She buried her face against his shoulder, and he could feel her hot tears soaking through his shirt. Her response was muffled, but he heard well enough what she said.

"Only time will tell."

***

Getting three young kids ready for bed was like a high-stakes hostage negotiation with a terrorist cell bent on staying awake at all costs. It was a grueling routine that involved pathological lying, threats, escape attempts, desperate bargaining, and cutthroat plea deals. And tonight was no exception.

Once the kids had their teeth brushed, pajamas on, and bladders emptied, Michelle led the boys to their room while Ray led Allie to hers. Allie climbed into bed and cozied up to their cat, Mr. Snuggles, who lifted his fluffy white head long enough to favor Allie with a slow blink before nuzzling his face between his paws. Sparky lay curled into a ball at the foot of the bed, sound asleep and wheezing softly.

Ray sat on the edge of the bed and brushed a lock of hair from Allie's eyes. "Sweet dreams, Allie-cat." He planted a kiss on her forehead and was about to stand up when he noticed her staring at him, her nose crinkled in the manner she reserved for serious questions.

"Daddy?"

"Yeah, honey."

"Is Momma gonna divorce you?"

Ray sucked air through his teeth. He hadn't expected that. "Of course not. Why do you ask?"

"She seems mad at you."

The kid was observant, he had to give her that. "Did Momma say something to you?"

Allie shrugged.

"Sometimes adults fight, Allie-cat. We get annoyed at each other just like you and your brothers do. But you still love them, right?"

"I guess so."

"Mommy and I love each other very much. There's nothing to worry about."

But a hateful little voice in his mind asked, *Are you sure?*

Allie pursed her lips and seemed to consider it. "If you do get divorced, does that mean I get two Christmases?"

"No, just one boring one."

"But Jenny Erickson gets two."

"Trust me, Allie-cat, you don't want that."

"But it's double the presents!"

He poked her in the belly and stood up. "Goodnight, Allie."

"Will you lay with me, Daddy?"

"Still having bad dreams?"

"I just want to snuggle."

A smile touched his lips. "Scootch over."

He climbed into bed and draped his arm around her. She laid her head against his chest and fell asleep within moments. He watched the steady rhythm of her breathing and hugged her tight, unsettled by the knowledge he wouldn't always be there to protect her, that she would grow older and more independent, venturing further into a cruel and uncaring world. A world where predators skulked in the shadows with dark intentions.

He pictured Cassie's bedroom, a slant of moonlight shining through the bay window illuminating the crisp sheets of her empty bed, everything on her vanity arranged in the exact position as the morning she vanished. He imagined her parents sitting downstairs in the dark, still processing the news about the white van, worry burrowing its way into their brains and festering like an open sore.

Ray waited until he was sure Allie was down for the count before wriggling out of bed and walking into the hallway, where he found Michelle pulling the door to the boys' room shut.

"Don't go in there," she whispered. "Petey's still awake."

Ray cocked a thumb toward Allie's bedroom. "She's out cold."

"I'll just take a peek," she said, tiptoeing past him.

Ray padded down the hall and went downstairs to call Martinez. She picked up on the first ring. "Thanks for covering," he said. "I can get back there in thirty minutes if I have to."

"I got this."

"Do you have eyes on Alex?"

"I'm outside his house right now."

"Is he alone?"

"As far as I can tell. Looks like he's watching TV."

"What's the status of the surveillance footage?"

The angle of Mrs. Landsdale's doorbell camera wasn't wide enough to capture the van's license plate, so they needed to trace it back to other cameras throughout town.

"Frasier's staying late to coordinate the effort."

"The prick from this afternoon?"

"He acts tough," Martinez said, "but I bet he's pissing his pants thinking you might report him to the chief."

"You sure you don't need me?"

"I'll call you if there's any developments."

Ray drew a deep breath. The surveillance review would likely take a couple days, and the list of owned or leased vans of the same make and model within a fifteen-mile radius of downtown would probably take at least until morning.

"Just promise me you won't do anything reckless without calling for backup."

"From the rumors I've heard," Martinez said, "that's the pot calling the kettle black."

CHAPTER TEN

Ray spotted Martinez in the back row of the muster room at Salem Police headquarters, staring at an empty podium and the whiteboard hanging on the wall behind it. The clock above the podium read five minutes to eight and uniformed officers were just beginning to file into the room for roll call.

Ray took a seat next to Martinez and squeezed his broad frame into a stackable plastic chair that seemed better suited to a mall food court. "I figured you as the front of the class type."

Martinez groaned. "Not today." Dark crescents underscored her eyes, and her thick mane of chestnut hair had pulled partway free of her ponytail.

"How late did you stay up watching Alex?"

"Till four in the morning."

"You look like you could use a coffee."

"I feel like I could use ten."

"Let's head over to Mystical Brew after this, see if another visit makes anybody uncomfortable."

"You really do enjoy harassing people, don't you?"

"Best part of the job. You should've seen my old partner in action. Billy had a knack for getting under people's skin and tricking them into revealing things. Trust me, you show up a few times, make some vague insinuations, and all of a sudden you're living rent free in their heads. Next thing you know, they're revisiting the scene of the crime or re-hiding the murder weapon instead of just laying low."

"That's the secret to your success?"

"One of them."

"What are the others?"

"You gotta earn it, Martinez."

She gave him the stink eye. "I wouldn't mess with me right now."

"Last night was a total bust, huh?"

"He watched TV until three in the morning."

"You had eyes on him the whole time?"

"Not exactly, but I could see the screen flickering through a gap in the blinds, and I saw him pass in front of the window at least twice."

"What about Tracy?"

"Officer Jeffries followed her to a bar downtown called Kettle & Cauldron. She and Fiona left with two guys from the band and took them back to their apartment."

"The girls are roommates?"

Martinez massaged her temples and nodded. "The bartender said Tracy has slept with half of the regulars."

"Can't say I'm surprised."

By now, the room was crowded with officers, but the din of conversation dissipated as Chief Sanderson stepped up to the podium. Following roll call, he recapped the overnight incidents, which included a half dozen domestic assaults, three grand thefts, and a suspected arson at an abandoned warehouse.

"We also had another farm-related incident," he said. "Someone carved up a pair of cows over at Heritage Farms. Probably had a hankering for late-night steaks."

The remark drew scattered laughter from the crowd.

Ray eyed Martinez. "How often does that happen?"

"Second time this week."

The chief announced the assignments for the morning shift, including an investigation into the double bovicide, which elicited an audible groan from Officer Jeffries, who was awarded the task.

"I've also got an update on the Barnes case. The crime lab confirmed the earring recovered on Orange Street tested positive for Cassie's fingerprints. We've also received access to her social media records. Detectives Martinez and Hanley, you can stop by my office when we adjourn to pick up the transcripts."

When roll call ended, Martinez flagged down Officer Frasier. "How's it coming with the surveillance footage?"

Frasier glanced at Ray before answering, as if to indicate Ray was the only authority he recognized. "The traffic cameras show the van heading out of town. It's got a bogus paper license plate and no markings or decals on any side." Frasier led them out of the muster room and into the bullpen, where he had the video paused on his computer. "The van took Derby Street to Route 114, which means it's probably headed toward Route 128."

"Are there any shots of the driver?" Ray asked.

"The side windows are tinted," Frasier said, "but this guy was prepared for anything."

"What do you mean?" Martinez asked.

"The camera at Derby and Washington got a good shot through the windshield. I took a screen grab and zoomed it in." Frasier brought up a JPEG file, which revealed the profile of a man wearing a black ski mask. The remainder of the image was grainy, with nothing in the background but a blur of shadows.

"Can't make out his eye color," Martinez said, "but judging from his hands on the steering wheel, he appears white, possibly Latino."

"It's good work," Ray said. "Keep tracing it back. I want to know exactly where that van was headed."

***

The early morning coffee crowd at Mystical Brew resembled a zombified herd of millennials lacking basic social skills shuffling in line while staring at their phones and grumbling about the wait. Martinez snagged a corner table while Ray waded through the herd and ordered a large coffee for himself and a triple shot of espresso for Martinez.

Tracy grinned impishly as she met Ray at the register. "You can't get enough of me, can you, Detective?" She wore another low-cut T-shirt that left little to the imagination. The sleeves of tattoos on her arms featured an intricate pattern of snakes slithering between skulls and hearts.

He handed her a credit card instead of cash. "Keep you from skimming off the top."

"Why don't you tip me the difference?"

"I only tip for good service."

Tracy leaned over the register, her breasts nearly spilling out of her shirt. "Is that good enough for you?"

Ray pursed his lips. "I think you might be in the wrong line of work."

"I'm a woman of many talents."

"I'll bet you are, but right now, I'm only interested in finding Cassie."

Tracy tore off the register receipt and slid it across the counter. "I already told you what I know." She seemed annoyed the conversation had steered away from her.

Ray signed the receipt and added two dollars to the total, not for the peep show or the banter, but because he was a sucker for hourly wage earners.

"I knew you'd tip," Tracy said, a teasing lilt to her voice.

"You got me," Ray said. He walked the coffees over to Martinez, who sat leafing through the social media transcripts.

Martinez reached for the espresso and took a long pull, sighing audibly as she set the cup down on the table. "What'd your girlfriend have to say?" Martinez asked, tilting her head in Tracy's direction.

"I'll tell you what bothers me," Ray said. "She's never offered anything beyond blanket denials. I've never once heard her express any concern about finding Cassie."

Martinez took another sip. "She's a narcissist, and I'm not surprised. She bounced through the foster system from age three until eighteen. If she didn't make everything about herself, she never would've survived. And given her background, it's no wonder she's wary of authority."

"Maybe you're right," Ray said.

Martinez handed him a stack of pages. "Better bone up before Captain Barnes gets here."

The captain was meeting them at the wharf in twenty minutes for an in-person update on the case. Ray stared down at Cassie's social media transcripts, which included Instagram, Twitter, Facebook, and Snap Chat. The messages covered a two-month window and spanned sixty-three pages. Ray and Martinez had started at the earliest date and were reading their way forward.

When 9:15 rolled around, Ray gathered up the pages and followed Martinez outside to the benches overlooking the harbor. Captain Barnes was standing at attention behind the nearest bench, wearing a long trench coat and gazing out at the rolling gray swells. He turned at the sound of their approach, and his haggard appearance caught Ray by surprise.

Good genes and a strict exercise regimen had kept the captain looking youthful for a man his age, but the fine lines radiating from his brow and the corners of his eyes seemed to have branched out and deepened overnight, aging him at least ten years.

"Morning, Captain," Ray said. "How you holding up?"

Barnes frowned. "I'm barely keeping it together." He extended a hand to Martinez. "It's very nice to meet you, Detective. Ray told me about the excellent work you've done so far."

"Thank you," Martinez said, her cheeks reddening. "But I won't be satisfied until we bring Cassie home."

"I like that attitude," Barnes said. "Tell me about the latest developments."

"We've got a couple teams focused on finding the van," Ray said. "One of them is piecing together the van's route through traffic cameras and other surveillance video. The other is compiling a list of owners and lessees of the same make, model, and color in a fifteen-mile radius. We'll bump the lists against anyone with a criminal record and prioritize those suspects."

"The van also had a bogus dealer plate," Martinez said, "so we're looking into any recent arrests or citations where someone used dummy plates."

"Anyone at the coffee shop recognize the van?" Barnes asked. "It could've been one of their regular suppliers, someone who'd taken an eye to Cassie."

"None of the staff recognized it," Ray said. "The manager says they get their supplies from a gourmet coffee company that makes deliveries in a black box truck." He looked at Martinez. "You want to brief him on the rest?"

Martinez seemed eager for the opportunity. "We have another team making the rounds with known sex offenders and anyone with priors for kidnapping or sex trafficking."

"Has anything credible come through the tip line?"

"Not yet," Ray said. "And at this point, her ex-boyfriend's alibi checks out. It seems like they had a normal breakup, nothing that would raise eyebrows about motive."

"You got her social media records?"

"They came through this morning," Martinez said. "But they didn't reveal anything suspicious or incriminating. Your niece seems like a very sweet girl."

Barnes scratched his mustache and nodded, biting his lip to keep it from trembling.

"What's most likely," Ray said, "is this psycho took an interest in her from afar and felt some sick compulsion to possess her. But that also means she might still be alive."

"What makes you say that?" Barnes asked.

"Whoever did this," Ray said, "planned meticulously. He targeted Cassie. He knew her address, her work schedule, her route. He chose a nondescript van with no distinguishing features. He was prepared for the traffic cameras and wore a ski mask, even while driving. My gut tells me this is a long-term play. A capture and hold scenario like with the Ariel Castro kidnappings."

"Long-term feels right to me too," Martinez said. "Whether it's some psycho acting alone or working for a sex trafficking ring."

"Maybe," Barnes said. "Although it's hard to take comfort in either scenario."

Ray hoped he wasn't being too bold in his prediction. It was possible this guy hunted and killed for sport, that Cassie somehow fit his profile of women he'd sentenced to die.

"You've both done a hell of a job," Barnes said, "but I'm concerned about resources. It's time we bring in the state police."

Ray drew a measured breath. "I understand your concern, Captain, and I agree it's the right move if we lose the van, but if we're able to trace it through the cameras, involving the state police will only set us back."

"Sorry, Ray, but Chief Sanderson and I already gave the state police notice. I requested that Trooper Garrison oversee their side of things, given your history. Now, I can hold them off until noon, but that's the best I can do."

Ray nodded slowly, fishing his keys from his pocket. "Come on, Martinez. Let's shake a leg."

CHAPTER ELEVEN

Martinez slammed the passenger door hard enough to rattle the windows. "Now the staties are gonna swoop in and take our case?" She stared at herself in the mirror and breathed an exasperated sigh. "Why didn't you tell me I look like a wreck?" She yanked off her hair tie and strangled her ponytail into submission.

Ray watched her in quiet amusement. She had fire in her belly, and he was glad to see it. It meant she was invested in this case, that she felt a sense of ownership. He wouldn't want it any other way.

Martinez glared at him. "If you're about to make some crack about me being on my period, I swear to God I will knock your teeth out."

"How is it you're still single, Martinez?"

"How is it you're still married?" she shot back.

Ray brayed laughter. "That's it, Martinez, hit me where it hurts." He fired up the engine and shifted into drive.

"That's not the way back to the station."

"We're not going to the station," he said.

"Why not?"

"You said Frasier needed another half hour with the traffic cameras, and they're still working on the lists we requested."

"What do you have in mind?" Martinez asked.

"I want to talk to Abby Garcia."

"The girl who had a mental breakdown?"

"Exactly," Ray said. "She and Cassie were best friends. And they worked together."

"You think Abby's breakdown could be connected to Cassie's disappearance?"

"It's worth checking out."

"Why, so the staties can take that away from us too?"

"We're gonna leverage their resources," Ray said, "not hand over control."

"How're you gonna manage that?"

"Because the captain wants me leading the investigation, and I've known Garrison for years. He won't try to wrestle control."

Martinez punched him in the arm, and her knuckles found the sweet spot between the muscle of his biceps.

"What the hell, Martinez?"

"That's for pissing me off."

"You could've made me swerve into oncoming traffic."

"And you could've told me not to worry about the staties a lot earlier."

"You really want to prove yourself, don't you?" Ray asked.

"I don't want anything to stand in the way of finding Cassie."

"Good, then we're on the same page."

Martinez stared at the road, but her eyes seemed distant.

"You okay, Martinez?"

She drew a deep breath. "This case is personal for me."

Ray turned left onto Essex Street. "You want to talk about it?"

"Maybe some other time."

"Fair enough." He was no stranger to burying things deep.

A few minutes later, they turned onto Lynde Street and arrived at Abby's house, a boxy rowhome with blue siding. A late model Subaru with a Jesus fish bumper sticker was parked in the crushed gravel driveway.

Ray and Martinez climbed out of the Explorer and mounted the stairs to the porch, bits of gravel dislodging from the treads in their shoes and skittering across the floorboards. Martinez rang the bell and hung back until the door swung open on a forty-something Latina woman wearing pink scrubs and a haggard expression, her dark hair streaked with spidery strands of gray.

Ray's first thought was that while Martinez may not have slept all night, this woman looked as though she hadn't slept all year. On top of that, she had an angry purple bruise stamped like a thunderhead across her left cheek.

"Mrs. Garcia? I'm Detective Hanley, and this is Detective Martinez. We spoke on the phone last night. Did we catch you at a bad time?"

Mrs. Garcia touched the gold crucifix dangling at the hollow of her throat. "These days, it's always a bad time." She held open the door and motioned them inside.

Shadows draped the cramped living room, tendrils of darkness stretching into every corner, every crevice. Heavy curtains covered the windows, and a trio of pillar candles on the coffee table produced the room's sole source of light. The kitchen was visible through the hallway, and it appeared equally dark, an unseen candle flickering against oak cabinets.

"Is your electricity out?" Ray asked.

Mrs. Garcia shook her head. "It's the only way I can get Abby to leave her room."

"Migraines?" Martinez said.

"Not exactly, although she does complain about her head when she's lucid." She led them into the living room and gestured to the sofa, her sleeve drawing back to reveal a large flesh-colored bandage. "Would you like to sit?" she asked, before planting herself in a leather recliner.

Ray and Martinez settled themselves onto either end of a microfiber sofa. In the low light, Ray couldn't tell if it was brown or blue. "Do you live here with your husband, Mrs. Garcia?"

"He packed up a few months ago. I haven't heard from him since."

72

"Because of Abby's condition?" Martinez asked.

"He wanted to institutionalize her, but I preferred home care."

"And what is her condition," Ray said, "if you don't mind my asking?"

"The doctors in the psych ward think she has paranoid schizophrenia, but that's because they don't know how else to explain it."

"What happened to her?" Martinez asked.

Mrs. Garcia drew a deep breath. "Well, a few months ago, she started hanging with a different crowd... and then everything changed. She was always a sweet girl, but these kids brought out a rebellious streak. She started talking back, cursing, listening to heavy metal music, staying out all hours of the night. She started dressing all in black—even her lipstick— and her clothes were tight and revealing. I assumed it was just a phase that would run its course. I planned on putting my foot down if it went on much longer. I wanted to enroll her in a private college when the new semester began, somewhere with strict rules like a Catholic university. But I'm an ICU nurse and I have a hectic schedule, and my husband travels a lot for work. So between us, I suppose we let it go on too long."

Mrs. Garcia stared off into space, a tear spilling down her cheek.

"I'm sure you did your best," Martinez said. "All kids go through phases. You couldn't have known how it would turn out."

Mrs. Garcia reached for a box of tissues on the end table and used one to dab her eyes. "I ignored the signs. I could have stopped it from happening."

"What exactly did happen?" Ray asked.

"Abby went out one night and didn't come home. I was working the overnight shift at Salem Hospital, and my husband called me at two in the morning to ask if I'd heard from her. I started to panic and called anyone I could think of who might know where she was, but it was the middle of the night, and the

couple of friends who did pick up knew even less than I did."
She dabbed her eyes again. "The police called me just before
sunrise. They'd found her at the Burying Point."

"The old cemetery?" Martinez asked.

Mrs. Garcia nodded. "She was lying on the ground
beside one of the tombs, laughing up at the sky as if she'd lost
her mind. She didn't respond to the officers, just went on
laughing in the shadow of all those graves."

"Was she hurt?" Ray asked.

"There was no obvious trauma, but the police
transported her to the hospital. The doctors administered a rape
kit and ran a series of blood tests. It came back negative for
rape—thank God—and she had no drugs or alcohol in her
system."

"Her friends just left her there?" Ray asked.

"I don't even know who they were. She was secretive
about the new friend group."

"Was she still hanging out with Cassie at the time?"
Martinez asked.

"Not as much, but they worked together. At the coffee
shop, at least."

"What do you mean?" Ray asked.

"Abby also worked part time at the Salem Witch
Museum. I suspect that's where she met the new group."

Martinez exchanged a glance with Ray. "Did she
exhibit any sign of mental illness before the police found her?"

"No."

"Any family history?" Martinez asked.

"Not that I'm aware of."

"What we're wondering," Ray said, "is if the traumatic
event that caused Abby's condition might somehow be
connected to Cassie's disappearance."

Martinez chimed in. "It's possible Cassie witnessed
something or knew something that somebody wanted to keep
quiet."

It was a stretch, Ray knew, but if you didn't cast the net wide enough or early enough in an investigation, the truth was liable to slip through your fingers.

"Abby didn't talk much about Cassie in the weeks leading up to the morning in the graveyard."

"Would it be alright if we spoke with her?" Ray asked.

Her face paled. "I don't know if that's a good idea."

"It would just be for a minute," Ray said. "And it may help us find Cassie."

"Okay, but don't say I didn't warn you."

***

Abby's room was a full shade darker than the rest of the house, and it took Ray several moments to discern the queen poster bed in the far corner by the blackout curtains. At first, Abby resembled an amorphous collection of shadows on the center of the bed, but when Mrs. Garcia struck a match to light a candle on the dresser, she coalesced into human form.

She lay with her eyes closed and wore a white cotton nightgown with long sleeves and three black buttons extending down the neckline. A tousled mane of dark hair spilled over her shoulders and obscured all but a narrow swatch of the pillowcase. The air inside the room felt thick and stagnant, redolent with the animal stench of a zoo enclosure.

Ray wrinkled his nose and cleared his throat, wondering how in the hell a teenage girl could smell so bad. He glanced over his shoulder at Mrs. Garcia, who stood near the door with her face drawn in concern.

He directed his gaze toward the bed and, for the first time, noticed the restraints that secured Abby's arms to the frame, the white nylon straps camouflaged against the linen comforter. He nudged Martinez in the shoulder and gestured to the restraints, but she nodded as if she'd already seen them.

Abby's nostrils flared as Ray and Martinez approached the bed, her body thrashing under the sheets as if tormented by a nightmare from which she couldn't awaken. A floorboard creaked underfoot, and Abby's eyes snapped open, her lips curled into a snarl.

Ray held up his badge. "Abby? We'd like to ask you a few questions."

Her eyes were mostly pupil, and they blazed with a furious energy, like a cornered beast ready to strike. A growl emanated from her chest—deep, resonant, and ominous, like the grinding of rocks. She sat up to the full extent allowed by the restraints and regarded them with a leering grin.

The air closest to the bed felt different, as if an artic blast had flooded the room with a swarm of charged particles. It prickled Ray's skin with gooseflesh and coaxed every hair on his arms and neck to stand on end.

Abby uttered a throaty chuckle—a gravelly sound, more animal than human.

Mrs. Garcia made the sign of the cross and reached for the crucifix dangling from her necklace.

"What the hell's going on?" Ray asked.

"Something took hold of Abby in that graveyard. Something evil."

Ray turned back to the bed and found himself caught in the crosshairs of Abby's hateful gaze. There had to be another explanation—multiple personality disorder, insanity, or just plain faking it. Martinez seemed rattled, but she held her ground.

"What happened, Abby?" Ray asked. "Did someone do this to you?"

Abby's eyes rolled back to the whites, a crooked grin creasing her lips. "E tenebris, bestia resurget."

The bedroom door slammed shut with a reverberating bang, creating a gust of wind that extinguished the candle and plunged the room into darkness.

Abby repeated the nonsense phrase.

E tenebris, bestia resurget
E tenebris, bestia resurget

THE BURYING POINT

E tenebris, bestia resurget

As Ray reached for the flashlight clipped to his belt, he heard a creak of bedsprings, followed by the shuffle of feet. He sensed movement to his right and swept his arm out to feel for Martinez, but all he encountered was dead air.

Martinez screamed as he clicked on the light, the beam lancing through the dark. He angled it at the bed and saw Abby's arms wrapped around Martinez's shoulders, the nylon restraints torn in half and fluttering at the bedside.

He marveled at the force necessary to tear those restraints. It shouldn't have been possible. Not even for a grown man in peak physical condition. Abby was drawing Martinez toward the bed, her hands now on the detective's cheeks, as if she meant to kiss her.

***

Martinez stared into the depths of Abby's eyes, mesmerized by the appearance of golden spirals of light, which seemed to ebb and flow like the birth, growth, and death of galaxies, as if the wheels of time were winding down like a broken clock until the seconds ran backward. A dark rent opened in the cosmic vista, revealing a gaping black maw that threatened to swallow her into the belly of oblivion.

In a distant world, Martinez felt herself mimicking Abby's movements, her lips parting to receive the dark seed of creation. But the exchange was disrupted by a rough pair of hands yanking her backward, and her jaw snapped shut with an audible click.

A flood of images flickered before her eyes like the clattering of an old movie reel's labored revolution, a movement like—

The hub, the spoke, the wheel of infinity.

Martinez watched Abby's hands slip away as Ray drew her back. His flashlight struck the ground and reflected off the ceiling. The air before Abby's face suddenly contorted like melted plastic, her features blurring and stretching until it

77

revealed a face behind her face—an abomination with galaxies for eyes and a blooming flower of fangs spiraling down into infinity.

A wooden crucifix spun against the wall, etching unholy spirographs into the paint. A jet of vomit streamed out of Abby's mouth and splattered against Martinez's cheek—hot, sticky, and teeming with wriggling black insects.

Martinez stumbled backward and screamed, clawing at her hair and stomping on the insects squirming over her feet. Ray steadied her with an arm across her back, and she leaned against him for strength.

"Let's get you cleaned up," he said.

She realized from his tone that he hadn't seen the insects, hadn't seen what lived behind Abby's face. She touched her cheek and examined the bile glistening on her fingertips.

"She threw up on me." Martinez gazed down at the sick on her blazer and shoes, but no longer saw any insects.

Because they were never there.

The crucifix wobbled against the wall and slipped off the nail, clattering against the hardwood below. The spirographs it had traced into the paint bore the unsettling likeness of a horned beast.

"Do you see that?" Martinez asked, pointing to the image.

Ray clenched his jaw and nodded.

In the last few moments, Mrs. Garcia had crept up and jabbed a needle into Abby's arm. "It's a sedative," she said, noticing them looking. She smiled apologetically at Martinez. "You can clean up in the washroom."

***

Martinez stripped off her blazer and dropped it into the tub, dunking it beneath the running water. Gooey bits of pinkish white vomit slogged off the fabric and swirled into the drain— just your garden variety teenage puke, not a nightmarish swarm of insects summoned from the bowels of hell.

She squirted a stream of shampoo onto the blazer and rubbed the sides against each other until it was lathered up, then rinsed it under the faucet and wrung it dry before hanging it over the shower curtain. Next, she washed her face and hair in the sink—lathered, rinsed, and repeated. She gazed at herself in the mirror, her chestnut eyes still bloodshot from lack of sleep, a spattering of tiny freckles showing against her olive complexion.

She'd splashed water onto her blouse, and now the lacy blue edges of her bra were visible through the cheap fabric. At five-foot-five and 120 pounds, Martinez figured she qualified as petite, but she was cursed with her mom's big boobs, and the last thing she needed right now was another detective ogling her like a disgusting perv. To his credit, Ray seemed better than most guys, but he was still a man.

When she emerged from the bathroom, Ray was talking to Mrs. Garcia in the kitchen. He barely looked up when she entered the room.

"Has she ever said that before?" he asked. "Bestia resurge?"

Mrs. Garcia nodded. "E tenebris, bestia resurget. It's Latin."

"For what?"

Mrs. Garcia whispered, as if afraid of who—or what—might hear. "It means out of the darkness, the beast shall rise."

"Christ," Ray said.

Mrs. Garcia made the sign of the cross, although for her blasphemy or his, she couldn't say.

"Did she take Latin in school?" Ray asked.

"Two years. She thought it would help with law school." She shook her head and frowned. "It's a shame how things don't work out the way you planned."

"Did your daughter keep a diary?" Ray asked. "It could help us in our search for Cassie."

"Not exactly, but there is something I'd like you to see." She went into Abby's room and returned a minute later with a distressed leather journal. It was bordered on all sides with symbols resembling Celtic runes. The title of the work was embossed in gold: *The Book of Shadows.*

Martinez reached for the book and turned it over in her hands. They'd seen something very similar at Raven's Wing Books and Magik Shoppe.

"I don't want it in my house anymore."

Martinez flipped through the pages and felt the hairs bristling on the nape of her neck. She wanted to get the hell out of here, and fast. She handed the book to Ray. "We'd better go."

He studied her for a moment, his liquid-brown eyes concerned, yet probing. Probably wondering why the hell she had freaked out so badly in there. To his credit, his eyes hadn't wandered to her chest, at least not yet.

Mrs. Garcia walked them to the door. "I couldn't bear to read more than a few pages of that... that garbage, but if you come across anything that explains what happened or who's responsible, will you please let me know?"

"Of course," Martinez said.

"I'm sorry for what you're going through," Ray said. "I hope for your sake Abby gets back to normal."

"Thank you. Father Maroney from St. Margaret's stops by three times a week for a blessing and that seems to help."

"Has he performed an exorcism?" Martinez asked, her mind still reeling from the face behind Abby's face.

"Not yet. He's still trying to convince the bishop it's warranted. But I hope he gets permission soon, because I've seen some horrible things in there... and I don't know how much more I can take."

CHAPTER TWELVE

Ray and Martinez sat in the Explorer, *The Book of Shadows* resting on the console between them like a cursed relic. Ray met Martinez's gaze. "I pictured that visit going a lot differently," he said.

Some of the color had returned to Martinez's cheeks, but she still looked shell-shocked. "What the hell happened in there?" she asked.

Ray started the engine. "I'm still trying to wrap my head around it."

"She broke the restraints," Martinez said.

"They probably got worn down from chafing against the bedframe. No way she's strong enough to do that otherwise."

"But how do you explain the door slamming or that thing with the crucifix?"

Ray shifted into reverse and backed out of the driveway, gravel popping beneath the tires. "If there was a window open behind the blinds, it could've suctioned the door shut. Happens in my house all the time."

"Come on, Ray, didn't you see the marks the crucifix left on the wall? What did that look like to you?"

"I know what it looked like, Martinez. But coincidence or not, we can't let it distract us from finding Cassie."

Martinez seemed as if she wanted to say more, but she clamped her mouth shut and turned toward the passenger window, her ponytail swishing defiantly.

Ray recalled how Abby's hands had cupped Martinez's cheeks, the restraints dangling from her wrists, both of their lips parting as if to kiss. The whole sequence felt surreal. When he'd

81

tried pulling Martinez away from the bed, it'd felt as if he were swimming against a rip current, and he got the sense whatever was happening wasn't meant to be interrupted. He was dying to know what Martinez was thinking right then—what she was seeing—but it was a rabbit hole he couldn't afford to go down.

They rode to the station in silence and headed straight to Officer Frasier's desk. It was ten thirty, which meant they still had ninety minutes to head off state police involvement.

"How's it going with the van footage?" Ray asked.

"Not good," Frasier said. "We lost the trail."

Ray swore. "Show us what you mean."

They huddled behind his workstation, staring at a monitor displaying a satellite map of the city. Frasier pointed to a spot on the map. "We last sighted the van here, just over the border on Route 114 in Peabody. It made a right turn onto Margin Street, heading into Danvers."

Ray studied the map. He'd expected the van to continue west on 114 and pick up I-95. "Have you gotten access to the traffic footage in Danvers?"

"That's the problem," Frasier said. "Danvers doesn't have traffic cameras."

"You're kidding," Ray said. "What kind of city doesn't have cameras?"

Frasier shrugged. "It's a local decision; privacy concerns and all."

"We'll have to ask businesses along the road for their security tapes," Martinez said.

It was a good suggestion, but now that the van had crossed town lines, they definitely needed state police. Ray scanned the map again and pointed to a mushroom-shaped body of water at the north end of Danvers. "How secluded is that reservoir?" he asked.

"Secluded enough," Martinez said.

Ray sucked in his breath. "Let's go talk to the chief."

"About what?" Martinez asked.

"I think we ought to search that reservoir, but we're gonna need help."

***

Ray parked the Explorer along the eastern edge of the Putnamville Reservoir, pulling onto the shoulder of Locust Street and rolling up to Trooper Garrison's state police cruiser. The street was lined with trees that had been stripped bare of their leaves by the October wind. He and Martinez exited the SUV and pushed their way through a dense tangle of underbrush. Thorns snagged their pants legs as they scaled to the crest of a wooded embankment that rose twenty feet above the road.

Garrison stood at the edge of the reservoir, one boot planted on the concrete wall that bordered the water. He looked like a giant silhouetted against the blue sky, the cold autumn sunlight reflecting off the surface of the water and making Ray squint.

"See anything?" Ray asked.

Garrison shook his head. "Not from here."

Ray cocked a thumb at Martinez. "This is Detective Martinez, my partner on the case."

Garrison shook her hand. "My condolences."

"Is that supposed to be a dig at me?" Ray asked.

"Obviously." He grinned at Martinez. "How many department rules has Ray broken so far?"

"None that I'm aware of."

"Give it time," Garrison said.

"I hear you two go way back," Martinez said.

"Yeah, we've got history. Mostly me saving Ray's sorry ass." He looked at Ray. "Remember what we found the last time we stood near the water like this?"

"We fished out Danny the Mule."

Danny was the Artist's first victim—or the first they'd found, anyway—and the investigation had sparked a mob war that led to the bloodiest summer in Boston's recent history.

"Where are the dogs?" Martinez asked.

"Should be here any minute," Garrison said. "Along with a chopper equipped with the latest search and rescue technology."

"We might be wasting our time," Martinez said. "We have no evidence Cassie is actually here."

"It's been three days," Garrison said. "The odds of finding her alive have plummeted, and we've got to start the search somewhere."

"What if you don't find anything?" Martinez asked.

"We'll try some other secluded spots in the vicinity."

"I'd rather focus on finding the creep who took her," Martinez said. "This feels too much like giving up."

Ray couldn't say he blamed her. "We've got a long list of individuals and businesses that own white Ford Transit vans, so there's plenty of leads to chase. We can start with the guys who've got a criminal record and divide the rest up between the Salem cops and Garrison's team."

"How big of a list is it?" Garrison asked.

"A hundred seventeen in a fifteen-mile radius of Cassie's house. And that doesn't count the ninety-seven sex offenders we have to interview."

Garrison grimaced. "We'll take whatever you can't handle. In the meantime, I've got a unit contacting local businesses along Margin Street to review security footage, but until we get a hit on that van, we're flying blind."

"We'll take all the help we can get," Ray said. "Let's agree to check in every couple of hours."

"Works for me," Garrison said.

Martinez seemed anxious to get started on the list and had already taken a step toward the street. Ray lingered for a moment. "Hey, I meant to ask… whatever happened with that girl we dug up at the Forest Hills Cemetery?"

"You didn't hear?" Garrison said. "Someone cut that girl's heart clean out of her chest, possibly while she was still alive."

CHAPTER THIRTEEN

"There he is."

Martinez pointed to a white male in his mid-twenties with curly, dark hair lumbering across the parking lot of the Broad Street apartment complex carrying a five-gallon bucket of paint supplies. He'd grown out his beard and packed on a few pounds since his last mugshot, but Ray was certain it was him.

He nodded to Martinez and they climbed out of the Explorer, approaching the man from either side as he opened the rear door of a white cargo van bearing the logo *Van-Go Commercial and Residential Painters*.

"Eddie Fischer?" Martinez said.

The man whirled around, his eyes wild with panic. He dropped his shoulder and barreled into Martinez, sending her sprawling onto the pavement before darting off like a spooked animal.

Ray charged after him, weaving between a pair of pickup trucks and racing to the end of the lot, where a wrought iron fence marked the boundary of Broad Street Cemetery and a ring of skeletal oaks presided over the barren grounds like a circle of mourners.

As Eddie made a running leap to scale the fence, Ray hooked an arm around his waist and yanked him backward, sending them both tumbling onto the pavement. Eddie popped up like a jack-in-the-box and hoofed it toward the van. Martinez stepped into Eddie's path and used his own momentum to judo toss him against the van, leaving a man-sized dent in the side panel.

Eddie sat on the ground, his back against the wheel well, and stared up at Martinez in confusion.

Martinez drew her gun. "Salem police! Don't move."

Eddie's shoulders slumped. "Why didn't you say that in the first place? I thought you were someone else."

Ray walked over to Martinez. "You didn't give us a chance, but now you've made me curious."

Eddie shrugged. "I owe people money. The kind who break your legs when you miss a payment."

"I hear those credit unions can be a real bitch," Ray said.

"Do you know why we're here?" Martinez asked.

"Is one of my taillights out?"

"This isn't a joke," Ray said. He held out his phone, which showed a grinning photo of Cassie. "Did you kidnap this girl?"

"I don't know what you're talking about."

"You ever see her before?" Martinez asked.

Eddie shook his head. "I've been keeping my head down, man, I swear. I started my own business. I don't want no trouble."

"How'd you afford the van?" Ray asked. "They're not cheap."

"I borrowed money from a loan shark, and as you might've guessed, I'm a tad behind on the payments."

"You're not dealing drugs anymore?" Ray asked.

"I'm clean, I swear. Take a look in my van if you don't believe me."

"Gladly," Martinez said and climbed into the back of the van.

"You did a few years for rape, didn't you?" Ray asked.

Eddie clenched his jaw. "It was consensual."

"Not when the girl's fifteen," Martinez said, pausing her search of the utility shelves.

"I had only just turned eighteen," Eddie said, "and she was my girlfriend. Her dickhead dad pressed charges and ruined my life."

"You ever been to Mystical Brew Coffee Cottage?" Ray asked. When Eddie hesitated, Ray said, "And don't lie to me."

"Yeah, I've been there."

"When?"

"A couple months ago. But I swear I didn't take that girl."

"I don't believe you," Ray said. Which wasn't exactly true, but he wanted to see how Eddie held up under pressure.

"I'm not lying, I swear. I bet the whole town's been to that place at least once."

"You're doing a lot of swearing, Eddie," Ray said.

"Please, you gotta believe me. I'm trying to get my life together. My business is just getting off the ground. If business keeps up, I'll have my debts paid off in a few months." Eddie's shoulders hitched like he was about to cry.

Ray sucked in his breath. Christ, he was starting to feel sorry for the kid.

Martinez hopped out of the van. "He's clean."

"Where were you on Monday at 6:45 a.m.?" Ray asked.

"Uh, getting ready for work. I was hired to paint a bunch of these empty units. Wait, how did you know where to find me?"

"Because we've been watching you," Ray said.

"Why?"

"Because you fit the profile and own the right kind of van."

"What time did you leave for work on Monday?" Martinez asked.

"Uh, my normal time. I guess around seven thirty."

"Can anyone vouch for that?" Ray asked.

"There's a couple of electricians working in the building. They see me here every morning."

Ray ran his hand over the *Van-go Painters* logo on the side of the van. It looked like a custom vehicle wrap rather than a magnetic decal. He tried peeling a corner up with his thumbnail, but it held fast.

"How long have you had this wrap?" Ray asked.

"About four months."

"What'd it cost you?"

"Almost two grand."

"You ever take it off?"

"I don't know how. And anyway, why would I? It'd be like throwing two grand in the toilet."

"Tell you what," Ray said. "You show us a receipt for that wrap, and we'll get out of your hair."

Eddie appeared relieved. "I've got it in the glove box."

***

Ray eyed Martinez as she fastened her seat belt. "You think Eddie's telling the truth?" he asked.

"It seems like he is."

"Based on what?"

She ticked off the reasons on her fingers. "The receipt for the vehicle wrap confirmed it was put on months ago. He maintained eye contact during questioning. He answered directly, wasn't evasive, and those electricians corroborated his arrival time on Monday."

"They didn't sound too sure of themselves," Ray said. "It was a weak corroboration at best."

"Maybe, but he seemed like he was telling the truth. And besides, you've got to heat those vehicle wraps with a propane torch to get them off. They get ruined in the process. I don't think he'd throw away two grand, especially when he's in debt to a loan shark."

"How do you know so much about wraps?"

"I spent a few summers working at my cousin's auto body shop. Now, would you please stop testing me?"

"It's your first case. I'd be doing you a disservice if I didn't give you a few pointers."

"I don't need your mansplaining."

"Christ, Martinez, you're a pain in my ass. Go ahead and suggest the next move already."

A ghost of a smile touched her lips. "We make sure the company Eddie used doesn't have a record of selling him a replacement wrap."

"What else?"

"We revise our list to focus on plain white vans or ones using magnetic decals."

"Exactly," Ray said. "And then we cross reference that with suspects having prior convictions. Let's ask the team to work on a revised list. Until then, we can continue with the next targets."

"Now you're getting it," Martinez said.

"Getting what?" Ray asked, knowing that he was setting himself up.

"Being a mentor. You sucked in the beginning, but you're starting to show promise."

Ray gave her the side-eye. "You're a piece of work, Martinez."

She gestured to the upcoming intersection. "Take this next left."

After Ray made the turn, Martinez said, "I heard Garrison talking about that girl you dug out of the grave. Were they able to ID her?"

"They're still working on it. Why, you looking to boss your way onto another case?"

"No, it's just violence against women is a trigger for me."

"Is that why you became a cop?"

"It's one of the reasons. It's also why Cassie's case feels so personal."

"Something happened to you when you were younger, didn't it?"

Her nod was barely perceptible, and Ray could tell by her tortured expression she was reliving whatever demons haunted her past.

"You can tell me if you want. I've been doing mandated therapy since my partner got killed. Trust me, it helps to get it out."

"Have you made any progress?"

"I no longer want to punch my therapist in the face."

"That sounds like real growth," Martinez said, "but I don't think I'm ready to share."

"You want to know why I became a cop?" Ray asked. "My dad got mugged while we were waiting for the subway in downtown Boston. He tried to be a hero but wound up bleeding to death in my arms. The punk who killed him got away."

"I'm sorry," Martinez said.

"It was a long time ago."

"My dad died when I was thirteen," Martinez said. "He was killed in a hit-and-run on Route 114. And my mom, she couldn't cope. She started drinking, and when that failed to numb the pain, she turned to prescription drugs. A year or so later, she started dating her dealer, this tatted up biker gang lowlife named Stu. He moved in after a few months and weaseled his name onto her bank account. Normally, it wouldn't have been much, but it had the proceeds from my dad's life insurance and his pension benefits from the electrician's union.

"Anyway, Stu was a horrible excuse for a human being, and he turned my mother into a mousy, fearful woman I no longer recognized. And once he'd bullied her into submission, he turned his attention to me. I was fifteen when he first raped me. After that, it became a nightly occurrence. He'd stumble home from the corner bar around one in the morning, crawl into my bed, and slap me awake. He was especially fond of choking me until I passed out."

"Christ," Ray said. "Did your mother know?"

"She refused to believe it, said I was looking for attention. It didn't help that she was pretty much doped up 24/7. Anyway, I worked up the courage to run away when I was sixteen, and I never looked back."

"I'm sorry you went through that."

Martinez shrugged. "Whatever doesn't kill you only makes you stronger, right?"

"So they say."

***

By the end of the shift, Ray and Martinez had interviewed a dozen people and developed a list of questions for the other investigators to leverage. Back at the station, Martinez typed a summary of their findings into the department's case management software, including any suspicious behavior, motives, alibis, or items requiring follow-up.

Meanwhile, Ray called Garrison to check in on the reservoir search. "You find anything?"

"We came up empty," Garrison said. "Not even the dogs picked up a trace."

"What about the water? Did you have divers?"

"We had a whole team. They found an old console TV in there—believe it or not—but no sign of Cassie. After the reservoir, we searched a few of the parks along I-95 in Danvers, but that didn't turn anything up either."

Ray shoulders sagged in relief. "We need more footage of that van."

"My team got a hit about a half mile from the last sighting," Garrison said. "Same road, same direction."

"That's it?"

"It's all we have for now. Most of the businesses in that area don't have any cameras. It's looking like it'll be a long and tedious process."

"We don't have that kind of time," Ray said.

"You're assuming she's still alive."

"Until we know otherwise," Ray said, "every damn second counts. Are you with me?"

"Yeah, I'm with you. I'm just not optimistic."

"It's the captain's niece we're talking about."

Garrison sighed. "Let me see what I can do to secure more resources for the surveillance footage."

"Good."

"Anything interesting come out of the interviews today?"

"No smoking guns," Ray said. Which didn't mean anything now, but if an alibi crumbled under closer examination, it could be a turning point. It would be a grind for sure, involving countless hours of old-fashioned police work to eliminate hundreds of potential suspects, but at this point it was all they had.

"I've got a night crew dedicated to the case," Garrison said. "Anything breaks, they know to call me, and I'll get in touch with you straightaway."

Ray thanked him and hung up. He walked over to Martinez, who sat slouched at the computer, her face bathed in liquid crystal luminescence. She looked exhausted.

"How's it coming?"

"I finished logging our stuff, but I want to read the other teams' reports before wrapping up."

"I'll save you the trouble," Ray said. "Nobody identified any significant leads on the kidnapper, but we did get the background checks on Thalia and Fiona."

"And?"

"No priors for either. Thalia is listed as the owner of Raven's Wing Books & Magik. She apparently runs a coven out of the place. You want to explain to me what that means?"

"It's a meeting place for Wiccans to practice their religion."

"You mean witchcraft?"

"Yes, but in the context that Thalia explained to us. Pagan beliefs, white magic—that sort of stuff."

"It's a real religion?" Ray asked. "Not just a way to drum up business or claim a tax exemption?"

"It's got a network of believers, just like any other religion."

"If you say so." He glanced at the clock on the bullpen wall, which read 6:55. If he left now, he could still catch Petey before bedtime. "How about we call it a day?"

Martinez rubbed her eyes and nodded. "I've got a feeling I'm gonna sleep like the dead."

CHAPTER FOURTEEN

Martinez pushed open the door to her three-story walkup and eyed the narrow wooden stairway that twisted a rickety path up to her apartment. Being a gym rat, she normally didn't mind the climb, but right now she found herself wishing more than anything for an elevator.

After trudging up thirty-two steps, she unlocked the door to her apartment and shuffled inside, feeling along the wall and flicking up the light switch. A narrow interior hallway stretched left to the bedroom and bathroom and right to the living room and kitchen. She stalked into the bedroom and unshouldered her messenger bag, laying it at the foot of the antique vanity that doubled as her desk.

She caught a glimpse of her reflection in the mirror. God, she looked like hell. Hair unkempt, eyes puffy. She peeled off her blazer and slung it over the chair, then stripped off her clothes and padded into the bathroom for a shower.

As the hot needles of water pelted her shoulders, she imagined it washing away the day's stresses, from the bizarre encounter in Abby's bedroom to the hours of interrogating suspects afterward. Despite rinsing off the vomit in Abby's bathroom and changing into a spare set of clothes at the station, she'd felt soiled and violated all day.

The lingering revulsion dredged up a memory from her mid-teens, and she found herself transported back to her childhood bedroom, where she lay crying soundlessly in the dark, resisting the urge to wipe away the semen leaking down her thighs for fear of waking the slumbering beast beside her.

She worked a squirt of shampoo into her hair and shuddered at the memory. She'd never intended to tell Ray about her childhood trauma. She was the kind of person who built walls instead of windows, who sectioned off her life and limited people's access to only the parts they needed to see. Work was work, past was past, and personal was personal. No one at the gym knew her beyond her workout regimen, no one at the station knew her beyond her case experience, and very few in her personal life knew her beyond the present.

And yet, she'd shared her most closely guarded secret with a man she'd known for only two days. A man she'd resented at first, pegged as arrogant, macho, and condescending. But Ray was different from the other men she knew. He had an easy way about him. Gregarious, yes, a touch of ego, sure, but beneath that was an openness that seemed genuine, a vibe that suggested a caring and trustworthy soul.

But what if she was wrong? What if she'd misjudged him? What if he betrayed her?

She leaned into the hot stream of water and bowed her head, watching soapy rivulets roll down her body and swirl into the drain. It was too damn late now, wasn't it? One more regret to add to the pile.

She cranked off the water and snatched the towel she'd draped over the shower door. She patted herself dry, then wrapped the towel around her hair and padded into the bedroom. A framed photo of her ex sat atop a Queen Anne style dresser she'd picked up at a yard sale. It featured Stephanie standing at a scenic overlook in the White Mountains, a sprawling vista of forest and lake in the backdrop, her shoulder-length blonde hair ruffled by the wind.

She thought for sure Stephanie would come around, shrug off their last fight, and accept her apology, but yesterday's text dashed any hopes of that. After ghosting her for a week, Stephanie sent her only two words: *It's over*.

Martinez wiped her eyes and laid the picture face down on the dresser. Somehow, in the space of a week, Stephanie had transformed from the kindest woman she'd ever met to a stone-cold bitch. Funny how people changed once they considered you an outsider.

She retrieved a pair of flannel pajamas from the top drawer and slipped them on. This is what she got for putting herself out there, for trying to have a life as well as a career.

Life isn't fair, Elena. We must all do our best with the hand we're dealt.

It was something her papi had told her on more than one occasion, usually after she'd stormed into her bedroom to throw herself a pity party. One time, after she'd had a fight with her best friend, Papi had presented her with a white box wrapped with a sapphire ribbon. She gazed up at him from the bed, her tears forgotten.

What is it?

Open it. A smile creased his lips, his kind eyes magnified by thick glasses, without which he had to squint to see anything.

She tugged at the bow until the velvety ribbon fell away and fluttered onto the bed. The box measured the length of a magazine but was half the width. It was heavy for its size, almost leaden. She opened the lid and parted the tissue paper to reveal a handheld mirror shaped like an old-fashioned fan, the inset glass surrounded by pale pink porcelain embossed with ornamental roses.

I want you to remember, Elena. Whenever you gaze into that mirror, you'll see a girl who is strong, beautiful, and capable of anything.

She beamed at Papi, grateful for his kindness, his understanding, his uncanny ability to cheer her up. She turned toward the vanity now, where the mirror lay beside a can of hairspray and a perfume diffuser. Aside from a few outfits stuffed into her backpack, the mirror was the only thing she took from her mother's apartment on the day she walked out for good.

She padded over to the vanity and picked it up, feeling the reassuring weight in her hand. When she angled it toward her face, it showed tears welling in her eyes.

I miss you, Papi.

She wondered, as she often did, what would've happened if Papi hadn't been killed in that crash, if that confused old lady had picked another day for her hair appointment or had taken a cab instead of getting behind the wheel. Maybe Martinez would've been a doctor instead of a cop and would've treated abuse instead of suffering from it. Maybe her mom would've been comfortably retired instead of a strung-out junkie.

But all the maybes in the world couldn't change the hard reality of her past, and so she dealt with it the way she always did—by cloaking herself in steel and allowing the world to break against her armor.

Latest victim: Stephanie Frederickson.

She towel-dried her hair and stalked into the kitchen, scowling at the notion of changing herself to make a relationship work. She refused to surrender her spirit to fit someone else's ideal; let a weaker woman make that trade.

She yanked open the freezer and pulled out a boxed dinner—sesame chicken with edamame and rice. It wasn't exactly a feast fit for a queen, but she'd long ago resigned herself to the role of a pauper, and so she had no reason to complain.

After dinner, she retreated into her room and flopped onto the bed, but sleep eluded her. Her mind kept circling back to the bizarre encounter in Abby's room, and the face she'd glimpsed behind the face—the abomination with a blooming flower of fangs. It had to be her imagination, some twisted delusion born out of a lack of sleep. Yet it had seemed frighteningly real.

She recalled Abby's cold hands on her cheeks, the girl's hypnotic gaze luring her closer, until she was staring into spiraling pools of golden light.

It wanted to use her... occupy her.

She realized her mind had swapped pronouns and she was no longer referring to Abby as *her* but *it*. And maybe she was delusional, maybe she'd wake up in the morning and think herself crazy for even considering it, but was the thing inside Abby seeking another host?

It might explain the jet of vomit, the hot bile teeming with strange black insects. She felt certain the Abby-thing was aiming for her mouth, that it meant to transfer its consciousness into her.

She could never tell Ray. He would think she was batshit crazy, just another woman who couldn't handle the stress of the job. And maybe it was true. Maybe she'd suffered a full-scale mental breakdown and was destined for the looney bin.

She peeled herself out of bed and picked up the mirror from the vanity. She stared at her haggard reflection, her hair wild and dried into loose corkscrews. She drew a deep breath and recited the mantra Papi had taught her.

"I'm strong, beautiful, and capable of anything."

She repeated it until she felt some semblance of herself returning. She eyed the messenger bag at the foot of the vanity, the faux leather bulging where the *Book of Shadows* pressed against it, like a diseased rat in the belly of a snake. Abby's mother wanted it out of her house, and after everything that'd happened, Martinez doubted it was a good idea to bring it into her own. But here she was, drawing it out of the bag and shuffling back to bed with it.

She'd lost her cool for a moment, doubted her sanity, and now she needed to prove she could handle it, that it was only fatigue and stress and nothing more.

The black, leatherbound volume featured an embossed pentagram surrounded by golden runes resembling Celtic knots. A thin blue stone was set into the center of the pentagram like a watching eye, its whorled imperfections lending it the appearance of a watery planet viewed from space.

Martinez settled onto the bed, drawing the covers around her legs, and propped the book against her inclined knees. She flicked open the brass swing clasp securing the pages, and the book flopped open in her lap. It began with a brief introduction on the history of Wicca before yielding to a section of lined journal pages on a thick stock of fibrous paper.

Martinez read about Wicca's pagan roots and the resurgence of modern paganism in the 1950s, which the book credited to Gerald Gardner, who spent his early years living on a plantation in the far reaches of the British empire in Sri Lanka and Borneo, where he was influenced by the beliefs of the natives, ceremonial magic, and the occultist writings of Aleister Crowley.

Gardner returned to England later in life and established a coven. His writings and religious traditions spread over the subsequent decades and gained acceptance as *Gardnerian Wicca*. Gardner embraced the early Wiccan tradition of worshipping a Horned God and a Mother Goddess, which had roots tracing back to the Stone Age. While some Wiccans viewed the deities as largely symbolic, others believed in their literal existence or in the existence of other pre-Christian gods.

More universal, however, was the Wiccan belief that magic exists in the natural world in the form of energy, which can be manipulated to produce a desired result. The addition of offerings and talismans like crystals and herbs aided in the channeling of energy to create the power necessary to cast a successful spell.

The introduction went on to describe the significance of the seasons, the lunar cycles, solar festivals, and the eight pagan sabbats. It described basic spell techniques, circles of protection, the difference between crafting and casting, and how to center, raise, and ground energy. It warned against the use of black magic and cited the law of threefold return, which was an old pagan adage that harmful magic will return to you threefold.

THE BURYING POINT

The section concluded with a summary of common spells for love, luck, money and health, and a final blessing that read:

> *May the energy of the Universe*
> *Calm your mind,*
> *Mend your heart,*
> *And fill your spirit*
> *With the divine wisdom*
> *Of the God and Goddess,*
> *Blessed Be!*

Martinez turned to the first of the journal pages and found a hand-drawn pentagram with a word written at each of the star's five points: *Spirit, Air, Fire, Water, Earth.* Beneath this was another pentagram drawn inside a circle, along with explanatory notes.

Pentacle = a protection sigil

<u>NOT</u> a symbol of the Devil! Wiccans do <u>NOT</u> worship the Devil!

There were several more notes on the page, and Martinez imagined Abby attending her first meeting with a coven of Wiccans and coming home to record what she had learned.

"Magic is the science and art of causing change to occur in conformity with will." –Aleister Crowley

Magic is a <u>law of nature</u> that is not well understood.

Triple Goddess = A trinity of the Maiden Goddess, Mother Goddess, and Crone Goddess… representing virginity, fertility, and wisdom.

The Horned God = animals, the hunt, the natural world, and man. Also, death and the afterlife?

"If it harm none, do what ye will."

Martinez turned to the next page.

My first spell!

Things for the altar (use TV tray)
-Incense
-Plate with sliced apples, honey, and rose petals
-Goblet of red wine
-Athame (dagger)… letter opener okay?
-Bell
-Two candles (one in front of object representing Goddess and one in front of object representing Horned God)
-Bowl of salt
-Rose quartz crystals
-Drawing of a pentacle

Instructions
-Cast spell during the waxing moon
-Clear mind / meditate
-Draw circle of protection on the floor with chalk
-Call on the elements and gods for power
-Raise energy
-Recite the following words like a chant (and hope it works!)

To find true love, I conjure thee,
To make my heart brim with ecstasy.
An enchantment cast to the universe wide,
Ensnares a man… and makes a bride.

Martinez rubbed her eyes and frowned, the threat of sleep at last catching up to her. She closed the *Book of Shadows* and set it down on the nightstand. The blue stone inscribed into the pentagram stared at the ceiling like a watchful eye.

Abby and Cassie, she thought. Two girls lost to the world in vastly different ways. Could there be a connection? Or was her tired mind grasping for the slightest hint of a lead?

She reached for the bedside lamp and clicked it off, plunging the room into an obsidian darkness. Her leaden eyes slipped shut and she felt herself drawn into a suffocating vortex of sleep, where a terrifying gauntlet of nightmares awaited her, and the thing that was no longer Abby grinned in the shadows, its razor-sharp fangs like a blooming flower of madness spiraling down into infinity.

CHAPTER FIFTEEN

Four days had passed since Cassie disappeared on the road to Mystical Brew. Four days since a man in a ski mask dragged her into a white van and sped away to do God knew what to her.

Ray gripped the steering wheel and guided the Explorer over the Tobin Bridge, the sun rising over the steely peaks of the city behind him and bathing the road ahead in golden-orange light. He'd worked this type of case a dozen times in his career, and it rarely ended well. If Cassie wasn't dead, she was likely suffering in ways that defied the imagination, and he needed to do everything in his power to bring her home.

When Ray arrived at Salem Police headquarters, he checked in with Chief Sanderson, who informed him the overnight shift had yielded no significant updates, no additional sightings of the van, no material suspects of any kind.

"There's gotta be something," Ray said. "That van didn't just disappear." He was standing in the doorway to Sanderson's office, his arms folded across his chest.

"I wish I had better news." Sanderson's eyes were dark and mournful.

"I owe the captain an update at noon," Ray said. "I can't tell him there's been no progress."

"I'm afraid you don't have a choice."

Ray rubbed a hand across his stubbly cheek. "Who worked the sex offender list last night?"

"Officer Jeffries."

"I think we ought to release the footage of the van to the public," Ray said. "Turn up the heat and see what shakes out."

"I'm not sure we're ready to show our hand just yet," Sanderson said.

"We don't have time to play cat and mouse."

Sanderson's expression soured. "It'll flood the tip line with thousands of well-intentioned but useless reports from the public."

"The state police have the resources to handle it," Ray said. "Isn't that why we got them involved in the first place?"

"You don't follow orders very well do you, Detective?"

"In my defense, it seemed like more of a suggestion."

Sanderson grinned wryly. "Pass it on to Captain Barnes. Let him make the call."

"Fair enough," Ray said. He turned around and almost walked straight into Martinez. "Christ, Martinez—eavesdrop much?"

"Why didn't you wait for me?"

"You weren't in yet, and I wanted to get an early start."

Her accusing look softened. "Fine. Let's catch Officer Jeffries before he punches out."

They found Jeffries in the break room, eating a jelly doughnut. Officer Frasier was needling Jeffries as he poured himself a coffee. "One more of those, Tubby, and your blood's gonna turn to jelly."

Jeffries ignored the comment and smeared a napkin across his lips, somehow managing to avoid a glistening speck of jam at the corner of his mouth. He was indeed a big guy, but not fat exactly, and had a boyish, gap-toothed face that reminded Ray of a cross between Howdy Doody and an offensive lineman.

Martinez nodded at Jeffries. "Chief said you worked the sex offender list last night. Any leads?"

"Not really. They all denied knowing Cassie, and of course everyone had an alibi. One guy was out of town when Cassie was taken. Another guy was at work. A couple others swore they were still asleep and said their parents could vouch for them." Jeffries rolled his eyes. "You wouldn't believe how many of these guys still live in their parents' basements."

"Did you leave enough details in the case files for us to follow up on alibis?" Martinez asked.

Jeffries nodded. "It's all in there."

"Anyone in particular we should start with?" Ray asked.

Jeffries answered without hesitation. "Shane Davis. Dude gave me the creeps."

"What makes you say that?" Ray asked.

"Just... I don't know. The way that he looked at me during questioning, like he was amused by it all. Like Cassie being missing was somehow funny or that she deserved it."

"What's his rap sheet?" Ray asked.

"Lewd and lascivious. Seems he likes flashing teenage girls in the park."

"Anything else?" Ray asked.

"He was also picked up for public masturbation, petty theft, and loitering."

"No violent crimes?" Martinez asked.

"Nothing on record."

"Where's he work?" Ray asked.

"He's an exterminator."

Martinez nodded as if she'd suspected it all along. "Those guys are always creepy."

Jeffries wiped a hand across his cheek and stifled a yawn. He'd put in a double and seemed ready to crash. "At least it was better than investigating dead cows."

"What was the deal with that, anyway?" Ray asked.

"Someone snuck onto the farm in the dead of night and butchered a couple of cows. Second time it's happened this month."

"Probably some city kids looking for a sick thrill," Martinez said.

"What'd they do to them?" Ray asked.

"Slit their throats."

"I've heard of cow tipping," Ray said, "but that brings it to a whole new level."

"That's not the worst of it," Jeffries said.

"What do you mean?" Ray asked.

"They also cut out their hearts."

Ray stared blankly at Jeffries, not sure he'd heard correctly. "Cut out their hearts?"

"That's what the vet said. Neat, too, like some ninja butcher."

"Any suspects?" Martinez asked.

"It happened at night. Nobody saw anything."

Ray thought about the girl they'd found in the open grave. She was wearing a white dress, her hair adorned with flowers, her heart missing. He and Garrison had both assumed it was a revenge killing, a scorned lover's symbolic payback for being dumped. Just a coincidence, or something more?

He tapped Martinez on the shoulder. "Come on."

"Where are we going?"

"To see an old friend."

***

Frank Eastman squinted at Ray from across the table, the weathered lines on his ruddy brow creased in his trademark expression of agitated curiosity. He brought a coffee mug to his lips and sipped loudly, his sharp gray eyes shifting between Ray and Garrison before settling on Martinez.

"What'd these two knuckleheads drag you into??"

Martinez cocked her thumb at Ray. "Said he'd tell me when we got here."

"Christ almighty." Frank's voice was deep and gravelly, the result of smoking a pack a day for better than fifty years. "He say anything else?"

"He said you were his very first partner. A real ballbuster. And a cranky old sonofabitch."

Frank lit a cigarette. "He forgot tough as nails."

Ray swatted at the plume of smoke. "Come on, Frank, I thought you'd quit."

"That was before I was in remission." He inhaled deeply and blew smoke at the ceiling. "My place, my rules. What's this about, anyway? I got a case to work."

Since retiring from the force ten years ago, Frank had started his own private investigation and security installation business.

"We've got a couple of cases that show signs of occult activity," Ray said. "I know you were an expert back in the '80s."

Frank nodded slowly, his eyes suddenly distant, as if reliving the past. "The Satanic Panic. What a shit show." He scowled across the table. "I bet the three of you weren't even born yet."

Martinez furrowed her brow. "What does that mean, the Satanic Panic?"

Frank met her gaze. "Hyped up allegations of ritualistic child abuse perpetrated by devil worshippers."

"Sounds like a load of bullshit," Garrison said.

"It started with a couple of books," Frank said. "Then the evangelicals added fuel the fire. Next thing you know, panicked parents across the country were leveling accusations against preschool teachers. Some of the parents ended up hiring quack child psychiatrists who dabbled in repressed memory hypnosis."

"What the hell is that?" Ray asked.

Frank folded his arms. "They hypnotized kids in an effort to recover memories, but ended up planting suggestions that led to false recollection."

"I thought that wasn't admissible in court," Garrison said.

"Not anymore, but back then, it spread across the country like the witch trials."

"So it *was* bullshit," Garrison said.

Frank gave a noncommittal shrug. "The media circus diverted attention from the real thing. Some of it was copycat stuff inspired by the hype, but there was an authentic element mixed in, some dark shit that took place in the shadows."

"Like what?" Ray asked.

"It ran the gamut, everything from murder and mutilation to kidnapping and theft. What are you seeing on your cases?"

Ray told him about the girl they'd found in Forest Hills Cemetery, the odd way she was dressed, and how someone had cut her heart out. He explained what Officer Jeffries had witnessed on the farm in Salem, how someone had mutilated the cows and removed their hearts with neat precision.

Frank listened closely, nodding in the right places. He stubbed out his cigarette and frowned. "The heart's an important organ in satanic rituals. It's used in black masses. They believe it adds power to the ceremony, increases the odds of success."

"What do they get out of the ceremony?" Ray asked.

"Whatever they ask for." Frank held his gaze as he sipped his coffee. "Did the girl show any other signs of trauma? Anything to indicate she was restrained or dressed like that against her will?"

"There was some bruising, I think," Garrison said. "But no obvious sign of trauma other than to her chest. We'll know more after the autopsy on Monday."

"If this was the work of a satanic cult," Frank said, "she might've thought she was participating in a ritual as a symbol of innocence. That might explain the white dress and flowers in her hair."

"Would someone in a cult ever willingly sacrifice themselves?" Martinez asked.

"Doubtful," Frank said. "Satanists are notoriously selfish. They celebrate anything that gives them pleasure, even if it means someone else's pain."

"What are the odds this was the work of a satanic cult versus some guy getting revenge on an ex-girlfriend?" Ray asked.

"I interviewed a lot of ex-cult members in the '80s. Your case has a few similarities to what I've heard."

"Like what?" Ray asked.

"I talked to this one guy who fled southern California. The cult leaders there wanted him dead for spilling secrets to the police. He said the cult used to rob graves for body parts. They even sacrificed a couple of drifters during a black mass. He said they disposed of the bodies in a cemetery, burying them a foot below the surface of a freshly dug grave... like your girl."

Ray exchanged a glance with Martinez. "What about the cows—you ever see anything like that?"

"Sometimes they harvest the organs for their rituals. It barely gets any attention from police. These cows, were they blood let?"

"What, like drained of their blood?" Martinez asked. When Frank nodded, she said, "Their throats were slit. Let me ask Jeffries if the ground was saturated with blood." She pulled out her phone and texted Jeffries.

"What other signs should we be looking for?" Garrison asked.

"Sometimes it depends on the denomination. If you're talking about Santeria, they leave behind signs like corn kernels, voodoo dolls, or coins in multiples of seven. They also like to behead their victims."

"What the hell is Santeria?" Ray asked.

"It's a mix of a tribal religion and the worshipping of Christian saints," Frank said.

"My grandmother told me about that once," Martinez said. "She was born in Cuba, and the practice was brought there by West African slaves."

"What about satanists?" Garrison asked, his brow wrinkling as if he found the word distasteful.

"They relish in making a mockery of Christianity," Frank said. "The black mass is a perversion of a Catholic mass. The high priest recites the liturgy backward and uses unholy symbols like inverted crosses, goat heads, and black candles. In extreme cases, the candlewax is made from human fat, the Eucharist is made from human flesh, and the wine is the blood of a sacrificed baby, preferably unbaptized. Sometimes, the mass is performed skyclad, which means naked, and the ritual resembles an orgy."

"Come on," Ray said. "You can't be serious."

"I wish I wasn't. I've seen some shit I'd rather forget."

"Like what?" Garrison asked.

Frank sighed, as if reluctant to summon the ghost of old memories. "I had a case where a young couple vanished. At first, we thought they were runaways, but we eventually got a tip they were targeted by a satanic cult. We tracked them to an abandoned church in the woods of New Hampshire. We must've spooked them during a black mass because they left behind a bunch of paraphernalia—candles, pentagrams, a chalice full of blood. We even found a heart buzzing with flies on the altar. It turned out to be human."

Ray grimaced. "Did you make any arrests?"

Frank shook his head, regret etched into the lines of his face. "They scattered. We never found another trace."

"Damn," Garrison said. "That is some freaky shit."

"How do we catch these guys?" Ray asked.

"You can start with a manual I wrote back in the day on occult crime scene investigation," Frank said. "The department doesn't use it anymore, but I've got an old copy kicking around."

A series of images flashed through Ray's mind—the slaughtered cows, the dead girl in the graveyard, the crucifix in Abby's bedroom scratching out the rudimentary lines of a horned beast. "We'll take whatever you got."

***

They stood outside the weathered Victorian that doubled as Frank's home and the headquarters of Eastman Security and Alarms. The cold October wind buffeted the wooden sign hanging from the front porch, threatening to strip away the remaining curls of paint.

Garrison leaned against his state police cruiser, arms folded across his giant's chest. "We got a positive ID on the girl from the cemetery. Her name's Brittany Cooper. Want to guess where she's from?"

Ray felt his arms crawl with gooseflesh. "Salem?"

"Close," Garrison said. "Danvers." The next town over. "She was a student at Boston College. Her parents didn't even realize she was missing. They contacted us after seeing her picture on the news."

Martinez frowned. "Do you think there could be a connection to Cassie? They're about the same age, and from that picture you showed me, they even look similar."

"I hope not," Ray said. "I'd hate to think Cassie suffered the same fate." He eyed Garrison. "When'd you find this out?"

"Her parents came to the morgue last night to ID the body."

"Are there any suspects?" Ray asked.

Garrison shook his head. "All I know right now is that she lived on campus and didn't go home often. I'm meeting with some of her classmates later this morning to get more details."

"If there is a connection," Ray said, "we could be one step closer to finding Cassie."

A voice inside his head added, *Dead or alive.*

CHAPTER SIXTEEN

Shane Davis's green Toyota pickup appeared a mile shy of rolling into the nearest junkyard and disintegrating. The rusted flatbed contained a jumbled heap of poles, nets, and traps, and the roof displayed a magnetic placard in the manner of a pizza delivery sign. But instead of a steaming hot pizza, Shane's logo featured a dead cockroach with cartoon X's for eyes and the words *BUG OFF!* looming over the corpse.

Ray and Martinez sat in the Explorer and observed Shane from across the street. He stood on the porch of a nearby duplex, chatting up an attractive woman in her early thirties. The woman was half turned toward the door, one hand clutching the knob, as if desperate to escape the conversation.

They climbed out of the SUV and hailed him from across the street. "Shane?" Ray said. "We need a word."

The woman slipped inside as Shane turned around, a flicker of relief registering on her face.

"What's this about?" Shane asked, descending the stairs with obvious hesitation.

Martinez flashed her badge. "Salem Police. We have a few questions."

"I already talked to the cops."

"Maybe you didn't pass the test," Ray said.

Shane approached the truck carrying a battered metal canister with a spray hose attachment. A shock of red hair framed his alabaster face like a mane, his feral gray eyes spaced so far apart it was unnerving. He set the canister down on the flatbed. "You can't harass me like this."

"Spare us the victim routine," Ray said.

"I told you guys, I was home when that girl was taken."

111

Ray glanced at Martinez. "You buy that?"

"I have my doubts."

"I'm telling you, I was home sleeping."

"Can anyone vouch for you," Ray said, "besides your mom?"

"I don't go into work until eight. I was home when it happened."

"She's the sort of girl you like to spank it to in the park, isn't she?" Ray asked. "You see a girl like that, and something happens up here?" He tapped the side of his head. "You can't control yourself, am I right?"

Shane shook his head. "You don't know what you're talking about."

"We've seen your rap sheet," Martinez said. "And I think my partner is right. You wanted to take the next step, you wanted Cassie all to yourself."

"I don't know anything about that girl."

Ray folded his arms. "Her house is on your list of clients. And we know you like chatting up the pretty girls."

"Even though it makes them uncomfortable," Martinez added.

"You can think whatever you want, but it doesn't change the fact that I didn't do it."

"When was the last time you serviced her house?" Ray asked.

Shane averted his eyes. "I don't even know where that girl lives."

"I find that hard to believe," Ray said. "You know where all the pretty girls live, don't you, Shane?"

"What about her?" Martinez asked, showing him a picture of Brittany Cooper on her phone. "Have you seen her before?"

Shane shook his head. "Doesn't look familiar."

"Do you mind if we look inside your truck?" Martinez asked.

"Not without a warrant."

"You hiding something?" Ray asked.

"I know my rights."

"Sounds like you've been through this before," Ray said, "which doesn't say much for your character."

Shane gave him the finger and pushed past them to the truck. A moment later, the engine roared to life and a stinking cloud of exhaust belched into the air.

Martinez swatted at the fumes and coughed into her hand, watching as Shane peeled wheels down the street. "I don't think he likes you much."

"Any guesses what he was hiding?" Ray asked.

"Drugs probably. Seems like a stoner to me."

"Let's get someone to follow him, see where he goes."

As Martinez called in the request on her radio, Ray wondered about the odds of Shane being their man. He didn't have any obvious connections to a white van, and the last time he'd visited Cassie's house was a month earlier to trap squirrels in the attic.

Martinez returned the radio to her belt. "What do you think?"

"It was hard to get a read on him," Ray said.

"A neighbor saw him leaving the house around 7:45."

"He could've left before six," Ray said, "and then came back."

"True," Martinez said. "But what about that other guy? Eddie, the painter? He could've scrubbed down the van, gotten a new wrap. Maybe he has a buddy who works at the garage and did it for him off the books."

"I don't know," Ray said. "I got the sense Eddie was telling the truth, but maybe he's just a good liar. We ought to keep an eye on him too."

Martinez's phone buzzed with a text alert. She squinted at the screen. "It's Jeffries."

"What's he saying?"

"He says there was hardly any blood around the cows." She slid the phone into her pocket. "It could be a coincidence."

Ray shook his head. "I don't believe in coincidence."

***

Ray braced himself for the pungent aroma of incense as they walked into Raven's Wing. "Goddamn place makes my eyes water," he muttered.

"I think it smells nice." Martinez gestured to the back of the store. "Why don't you let me handle Fiona this time?"

"Be my guest. Just don't let her play you."

Martinez shot him a withering gaze, and he had to bite his lip to suppress a grin.

"Did I say something funny?"

"Don't take this the wrong way, Martinez, but you're the only woman whose thoughts I can read."

"Oh really? What am I thinking right now?"

"Something very close to *fuck you*."

"That was an easy one. How about now?"

"Still *fuck you*."

"Hmm... you're finally getting me."

Ray followed her to the back of the store, where they found Fiona unpacking a box of crystal pendants at a counter cluttered with racks of cheap jewelry. After separating the contents of the box, Fiona threaded a silver chain through a pink quartz pendant and hung it on an empty rack. She was halfway through the next one when she noticed them coming. Ray couldn't decide if the look that crossed her face was surprise, annoyance, or fear.

"You again?"

"We've got a couple of follow-up questions," Martinez said.

Fiona let out her breath in a huff. "I told you everything I know about that girl." She twirled a lock of flaming red hair around one finger and regarded them with her smoldering green eyes.

"This isn't about Cassie," Martinez said.

Fiona gestured to the pile of pendants. "Can you make it quick? I've got, like, this whole box to do." Her Metallica T-shirt had rips in all the right places, and Ray noticed Martinez's gaze lingered for an extra beat before she asked her next question.

"Cassie had a friend she worked with at Mystical Brew, a girl named Abby Garcia. Do you know her?"

"A little. Is she missing too?"

"No," Martinez said. "But she had a nervous breakdown."

"Is that, like, a crime now?"

Martinez ignored the comment. "Her mom said she'd been hanging with a new crowd. It's possible one of them knows what happened to Cassie, but we don't know who they are."

"Why don't you ask Abby?"

"She's not able to communicate right now," Martinez said.

Fiona blinked at them. Ray thought she might ask a question, but she held her tongue.

"Did Abby ever attend one of Thalia's meetings for the coven?" he asked.

Fiona gestured to the front of the store. "You'll have to ask Thalia."

Martinez pulled out her phone and accessed a picture of Brittany Cooper. "Have you ever seen this girl?"

Fiona shook her head, her face unreadable. "I don't know her." She reached into the pile of pendants. "I'm sorry, but I really have to get back to work."

Martinez stared at her for a moment, but it was clear Fiona was done talking. Ray nudged Martinez in the shoulder and led the way past a display of healing spells and natural remedies. He spotted Thalia ringing up a preppy couple at the front of the store. They seemed comically out of their element, as if they'd taken a wrong turn on the way to a charity auction in the Hamptons.

Ray eyed a flyer taped beneath the cash register.

Interested in Wicca?

115

Join us Saturday, October 23 @ 8PM
Ceremonial Magick
Ask for Details

Thalia met Ray's gaze as the preppy couple whispered to each other and snickered on their way out the door. "You're back," she said, brushing aside a colorful lock of her pixie hair.

"You don't look happy to see us," Ray said.

"People make a lot of judgements about my way of life. Especially those who know nothing about it."

"I'm not judging," Ray said. "I'm only interested in Cassie."

"I'd like to help you, Detective, but I've already told you what I know."

"Cassie used to work with a girl named Abby Garcia," Ray said. "Did she ever go to any of your meetings?" He nodded to Martinez, who brought up Abby's senior photo on her phone.

Thalia frowned. "I do remember her. She came to a few meetings about six months ago."

"Why only a few?" Ray asked.

"Sometimes, people are curious. They want to see what it's all about. Other times, they're searching for something spiritually and want to see if Wicca feels right for them."

"And what was Abby's deal?" Ray asked.

"It wasn't a good fit."

"Why not?" Martinez said.

"She was looking for something…" Thalia hesitated. "*Darker.*"

"What do you mean by that?" Ray asked.

"Wiccans practice white magick. We don't wish harm on anyone. We connect to the spiritual realm and leverage those forces for good. We ask for things like healing, protection, understanding, and love. But calling upon the spirits to do harm…" She shook her head reproachfully. "You never know what might answer."

"Is that what Abby did?" Martinez asked.

"She wanted revenge on a cheating ex-boyfriend. I tried to steer her toward healing, but she refused to embrace it."

"So what'd you do?" Martinez asked.

"I asked her to leave the coven."

***

A few minutes later, Ray and Martinez once again found themselves at Mystical Brew.

Heather Jenkins handed Ray a coffee over the counter. "Are you any closer to finding Cassie?" she asked, her brow wrinkled in concern.

"Not really," Ray said. Which wasn't exactly true, but he wasn't in the habit of oversharing; he'd been burned one too many times before.

None of the employees had recognized Brittany Cooper when Martinez flashed her photo a few minutes earlier, and neither had Thalia when they asked her before departing. Granted, it was a long shot given that Brittany was from Danvers and was living away at college, but you never knew when you might get lucky.

Jason—the stoner manager—tugged at one of his ratty blond dreadlocks and stared into space. "That totally bums me out, man."

It took Ray a moment to realize Jason's remark was a delayed response to the exchange with Heather.

Tracy directed an eyeroll at Jason as she rang up a customer. Despite the bitchy attitude, she was the most efficient of the three employees. She winked at Ray after her customer shuffled toward the door. "Are you packing heat under that sports coat?" she asked.

"You'll have to use your imagination."

Tracy pursed her lips and nodded, pretending—or maybe not pretending—to undress Ray with her eyes.

Martinez sipped her coffee and scowled at Ray before turning back to Heather. "When was the last time you saw Abby Garcia?"

"Sometime in early August."

117

"Before her mental breakdown?" Martinez asked.

Heather nodded. "We used to hang out all the time, but I didn't see her much that whole summer."

"Why not?" Martinez asked.

"She went through a bad breakup and was depressed for a while."

"What caused the breakup?" Ray asked.

"I'm not sure, but I know they were fighting about money. Her boyfriend was developing some kind of relationship app and had suckered Abby into lending him money from her travel fund—you know, the gap year she and Cassie never went on? Anyway, the app never got off the ground, and Abby was out a few thousand dollars."

"Is that why she got the job at the Witch Museum?" Ray asked.

Heather nodded. "She wasn't getting enough hours here."

"Abby's mom mentioned she fell in with a bad crowd at the museum," Ray said. "Do you know anything about that?"

A shadow crossed Heather's face. "Abby started getting into goth. Like, really into it. I guess it was an outlet for her depression. But some of the people she started hanging out with..." Heather trailed off.

"What about them?" Martinez asked.

Heather crossed her arms, hugging her elbows. "They were super creepy. I didn't like it when they came in here."

"What was creepy about them?" Martinez asked.

Heather thought about it for a moment. "Have you ever looked into someone's eyes and just known they were evil? It was like that."

Ray and Martinez exchanged a glance. In their line of work, it happened all the time.

"How often did they come in here?" Ray asked.

"Twice that I know of. Both times, it was two guys and two girls."

"What did they look like?" Martinez asked.

"Early twenties, I guess. Dressed in all black. Leather pants, black lipstick, spiky silver dog collars. Lots of tattoos."

"You remember any of the tattoos?" Ray asked. "Anything in particular that stood out?"

Heather's brow crinkled as she scanned her memory bank. "One of the girls had a tattoo of a bat protruding from her cleavage, its wings spread like it was taking flight. I didn't get a good look at the others. Once I realized they were here for Abby, I hid out in the back room. It was just a bad vibe, you know?"

"Did they have any interaction with Cassie?" Martinez asked.

"Not that I know of. But Cassie and I didn't have the same schedule. They could've come around when I wasn't working."

"You stopped hanging out with Abby once these new friends came into the picture?" Ray asked.

Heather nodded. "All she wanted to talk about was dark magic and the spirit world. I felt like she was trying to recruit me into a cult."

Ray and Martinez exchanged another glance. Maybe this rabbit hole ran a whole lot deeper than they'd imagined.

CHAPTER SEVENTEEN

Monument Liquors derived its name from its proximity to the Bunker Hill Monument and was conveniently located just three blocks from Ray's townhome. It carried all the essentials for an impromptu date night, including Michelle's favorite brand of Sauvignon Blanc, a bouquet of long-stem roses, and an assortment of chocolate-covered strawberries.

Ray balanced the items in his arms and approached the counter where the heavyset Latino proprietor, Sam, greeted him with a warm smile. "How are you doing, my friend? Hot date tonight?"

"If I'm lucky." He and Michelle hadn't been intimate since she learned of his indiscretion with Tina three months ago, so he figured it was a longshot at best. "How you been, Sam?"

"Living the dream," Sam said, gesturing to the interior of the store, where a dozen or so customers were rummaging through the shelves for their libation of choice.

Ray laid the items on the counter and reached into his pocket for his wallet, but Sam shook his head. "Your money's no good here, my friend."

"Come on, you don't owe me anything."

"You saved my life."

"It's my job," Ray said. "That's why you pay taxes." He peeled fifty bucks out of his wallet and slipped it into Sam's breast pocket. "Buy yourself something pretty," he said, and winked.

***

"I'm home!" Ray kicked off his shoes and tiptoed around a sprawling minefield of LEGO. "Where is everyone?"

Michelle's voice emanated from the bedroom. "The kids are upstairs playing Hot Wheels."

As she said it, he could hear the unmistakable sound of cars zipping around a battery-powered track. Ray headed toward the master bedroom with the goods from the liquor store. "I brought you something."

Michelle reacted to the flowers and wine with bewildered amusement. "What's all this?"

Ray handed her the flowers, his brow wrinkling at the sight of her hair and makeup already being done. "I'm taking you out to a nice dinner. I lined up Sheila Morrison to babysit."

Michelle frowned. "I'm sorry, Ray. Megan and I are going out for a girls' night. I told you that last week. Don't you remember? Lucy said she'd watch the kids if you weren't home yet."

Ray groaned. "I forget."

She tilted the flowers toward her nose and breathed in. "It's a nice surprise, but maybe next time we can plan ahead?"

Ray felt his shoulders sag. "Sure. You look gorgeous, by the way."

"Thanks," she said, allowing Ray to kiss her on the cheek. "Why don't you keep the babysitter and go out with Jacob?"

Ray sighed and nodded. "I guess I could do that."

***

Jason and Allie swarmed Ray as he entered the bedroom, leaping up from beside the whirring orange racetrack and rushing toward him. Ray squatted down and hugged them, feeling Allie's wild blonde mane tickle his face.

He caught a glimpse of Petey watching them from afar, glaring at him like one of the wildlings from *Lord of the Flies*. As Ray released the older kids, Petey let out a guttural growl and charged him. Ray allowed himself to be knocked backward onto the floor, wrestling with Petey until the chubby animal sat triumphantly on his chest like a lion upon a wildebeest.

"That's it, you little gremlin!" Ray seized Petey by the shoulders and rolled him onto the floor until they'd reversed positions. The wrangling hiked up Petey's Lightning McQueen T-shirt and exposed the smooth white mound of his belly.

Ray planted his lips against Petey's stomach and blew a raspberry. Petey flailed around like a fish out of water, laughing and crying hysterically. After a few seconds, Ray lifted his head to give Petey a breather, but Petey locked eyes with him and shrieked, "Again! Again!"

Before Ray could acquiesce, Jason and Allie pounced on their little brother, taking turns as they blew the sloppiest raspberries Ray had ever seen. Petey kicked his legs and squealed until an unexpected fart reverberated in his diaper, which sent Allie and Jason scrabbling away to the far corners of the room.

Petey sat up and eyed them sheepishly. "I think I poop."

Allie held her nose and ran out of the room. "Gross!"

Jason lifted his shirt over his face and followed his little sister into the hallway.

Ray grinned at Petey. "It happens to the best of us, buddy. Let me get that pull-up off you."

"No," Petey said. "Mama do!"

Michelle appeared in the doorway a moment later wearing black jeans, high heels, and a tight red sweater. "I'm off the clock, kiddo." She tossed a fresh pull-up to Ray and kissed Petey on the forehead. "Thanks for waiting until Daddy got home."

"Welcome, Mama."

"Such good manners," Michelle said, pinching his cheek.

"Yeah," Ray said, "he's a real prince."

"Did you decide to keep the sitter?" Michelle asked.

"I'll text Jacob after I take care of this, uh, situation. Where are you going, anyway? Maybe we'll meet you out for a double date."

"It's girls' night, Ray."

"Oh, right," he said, trying not to sound disappointed. "I'll see you later."

He felt a twinge of jealousy as she walked away, knowing she'd be a magnet for every sleazy guy she met at the bar. That kind of thing never worried him before but, now that he'd given Michelle a reason to get revenge, how far would she be willing to go?

Allie came back into the room and tugged at his pantleg. "Do you want to see my Halloween costume, Daddy?"

"Of course. What are you gonna be?"

"A kitty cat!" She clapped her hands excitedly, gazing up at him with her bright-blue eyes. Michelle's eyes.

"I bet you'll be the cutest kitty on the block."

"Can I put it on?"

"Sure, why not?"

Jason trotted into the room. "Mom said we couldn't wear our costumes until it got closer to Halloween."

"It's fine," Ray said. "Just be careful not to rip them. What are you dressing as?"

Jason puffed out his chest. "Batman!"

"Nice! What about you, Petey?"

"I bee."

"What?"

"I *bee*." Petey planted his hands on his hips and stared at Ray as if he was the dumbest dad in the world. Then he started running around the room making buzzing noises, holding his finger out from his nose like a stinger.

"Bzzzzzzzzzzzzzzzzzzzzzzzzzzzzz! Bzzzzzzzzzzzzzzzz! Bzzzzzzzzz!"

He poked Ray in the stomach with his stinging finger, stabbing him repeatedly like an insect version of Helter Skelter. "I *killer* bee."

Ray turned to Jason. "You'd better sleep with one eye open, because your brother might grow up to be a serial killer."

"I not kill sheereal."

That sent Jason into a giggling fit. He flopped onto the lower bunk and rolled around, clutching his stomach.

It was moments like this that made Ray wish he could freeze time and prevent his kids from ever growing up, keep them in a protective bubble forever. To think that his mistake with Tina had nearly robbed him of these moments made his stomach lurch. And he had no one to blame but himself.

Allie called out from across the hall. "Petey, do you want your costume?"

"I coming!" he said, darting for the door.

"Not so fast," Ray said. He grabbed Petey by the shoulders and guided him onto the floor. "Let's get you into that pull-up."

***

Ray sat at a back booth in his favorite neighborhood bar and waited for his brother to arrive. Despite being a straight-laced CPA, Jacob was notoriously late to everything, which Ray attributed to his workaholic tendencies and inability to quit anything halfway through. It seemed he was always finishing an email or wrapping up a memo or putting the final touches on a proposal, which meant delaying his departure from the office until everything was completely buttoned up.

Ray sipped a Heineken and watched the TV above the bar, which was airing the American League championship series. The Red Sox had lost a heartbreaker to the Yankees in the divisional series a few days earlier, and he was rooting for the Bronx Bombers to suffer a throttling at the hands of the Astros.

Ray caught sight of Jacob entering Quinn's during the commercial break. He was dressed in a navy-blue suit, designer glasses, and a paisley tie knotted tighter than a hangman's noose. He seemed out of his element among the boisterous crowd of blue-collar workers enjoying a round of hard-earned drinks. Ray watched with a bemused grin as his brother struggled to politely navigate a crowd that was as reluctant to part as it was unaccustomed to politeness.

When he finally reached Ray's table, Jacob slipped into the chair and shook his head in exasperation. "Felt like I was running the gauntlet back there."

"It's about time you showed up."

"Sorry, my meeting ran—"

Ray cut him off with a wave of his hand. "I'm already bored with that story."

"Thanks for the brutal honesty."

"That's nothing. If I'd said you walked in here like a monkey with a stick up its ass, that would've been brutal."

"Then I appreciate your restraint."

"Now loosen your tie and order a drink. It's Friday night, for Christ's sake."

Jacob raised a hand to flag down a barmaid, but instead managed to look like a schoolboy asking permission to use the bathroom.

"Hey, Kathy!" Ray yelled to the rail-thin brunette. "Get my brother a drink, will you?"

"You got it." Kathy winked at Ray as she weaved between the tables carrying a teetering tray of empties.

"You gotta be more assertive," Ray said. "Stop being such a doormat."

"Good idea," Jacob said. "How about I start by breaking that beer bottle over your head?"

Ray brayed laughter and clapped Jacob on the shoulder. "That's the spirit."

Jacob sat back and loosened his tie. "Think we'll have more fun than the girls tonight?"

"We damn well better."

"How are things with Michelle?"

Ray shrugged. "Not great. She's on guard all the time. I feel like I'm constantly being judged. And she barely lets me near her."

"I told you it would take time to earn back her trust." Jacob held out a hand to accept the beer from the barmaid.

"I get that," Ray said. "But it's been the same since I moved back in. I mean, why take me back in the first place if she's not gonna try?"

"She'll come around. But you need to be patient."

"I am being patient."

"The timeline isn't yours to control. If you want her back, you'll have to shut your mouth and wait."

Ray grumbled. "I liked you better as a doormat."

Jacob lifted his beer and offered a toast. "To brighter days."

Ray nodded and raised his drink. "To brighter days," he said and clinked glasses. They both took a long sip. "What's been going on with you?" Ray asked. "You and Megan still trying for a baby?"

"Yeah," Jacob said, a hint of dejection in his voice.

"What's it been, four months?"

Jacob took another sip of beer. "Six. And I'm starting to get worried."

"Come on, Jacob. You can't let that get into your head. Six months isn't a long time. Try to enjoy yourself. Spice things up, make it interesting."

"How long did it take for you and Michelle?"

"Probably about three months with Jason and Allie."

"What about Petey?"

"We didn't plan it with him, just let nature take its course. Trust me, it'll happen for you guys soon."

But Jacob didn't look convinced.

"You don't have to believe me," Ray said. "Just promise me you won't put too much pressure on yourself. I know how you get."

"Maybe you're right."

"Course I'm right. You remember how nervous you used to get before your high school swim meets? What do you think will happen if all your little swimmers throw up in the pool?"

Jacob lowered his beer. "That happened *one* time."

Ray met his gaze, and they busted out laughing, struggling to regain their composure before losing it all over again.

"Thanks," Jacob said finally. "I needed that."

"Me too," Ray said. "Me too."

CHAPTER EIGHTEEN

Martinez drove to the Salem Witch Museum at the end of her shift and parked in a metered spot near the Common. Originally built as a Unitarian church, the museum was a brownstone-and-brick Gothic Revival structure with two octagonal towers rising up from the foundation and framing an arched doorway and an impressive medieval window laced with ornamental wrought iron.

Martinez went inside and purchased a ticket from a lanky teen who gave the impression he'd been wrongly convicted and sentenced to a lifetime of boredom. "Do you know Abby Garcia?" she asked, handing the kid her credit card. "She used to work here."

The kid shook his head. "I just started here." He ran her card through the machine and handed her the receipt. "The tour starts in fifteen minutes."

Martinez retreated to the other side of the room and leaned against the wall, watching as the anteroom filled with groups of tourists bundled in puffy jackets and hats. She'd visited the museum years ago for a high school field trip but didn't recall much of the experience, except that it managed to be educational and creepy.

At the top of the hour, the kid from the ticket booth herded them into a dark room where a circle of red light displayed the names of the witch trial victims. Afterward, a glowing figure of the Devil materialized to gloat about how the Puritans cowered in his presence.

Martinez scanned the crowd for other museum employees but couldn't see past the shadows. The exhibit progressed into an immersive retelling of Salem's witchcraft hysteria, which was acted out by mannequins on lighted stages. It was accompanied by creepy sound effects—the shrill cries of the afflicted girls, the creaking of a hangman's noose, the tortured moaning of a man pressed beneath the weight of stones.

The next phase of the tour led them into a room that displayed a timeline of witchcraft throughout the ages, including an entire section dedicated to notorious examples of European witch hunts. The lighting was better in here, and Martinez spotted a raven-haired woman in her twenties observing the crowd from the back of the room, her lips curled into a scowl. She wore a nametag on her black dress and had multiple piercings protruding from her eyebrows, nose, and lips—all silver to match the pentagrams dangling from her ears.

Her frown deepened as Martinez started toward her, reluctantly switching to a neutral expression as she shifted into customer service mode.

"Can I help you?" the woman asked.

The high neckline of her dress didn't quite extend to her throat, and Martinez noticed the dark apex of a triangle tattooed on the pale ridge of her collarbone—one on either side, like the tips of a bat's wings. Martinez glanced at the girl's nametag.

"Hello, Danielle. I'm Detective Elena Martinez with the Salem Police. I'd like to ask you a few questions."

Danielle shifted her feet nervously. "What's this about?"

"I want you to tell me what happened to Abby Garcia."

Danielle shook her head. "I don't know. I, um, I hardly knew her."

"We have witnesses who've seen you together on multiple occasions."

Danielle's eyes flitted about the room. "I can't talk here."

"I also need you to tell me about Cassie Barnes."

Danielle shook her head. "I don't know that name."

"Then let's start with Abby."

"I'm sorry, I just... I can't talk right now."

"Then how about I bring you in for questioning?" Martinez opened her blazer to reveal the silver gleam of handcuffs.

"No, wait! I'm working a haunted house on Sunday night. It's at the old warehouse on Church Street. Meet me there at eight o'clock, and I'll tell you everything I know."

***

Martinez unshouldered her gym bag and dropped it onto the floor of the hallway. Despite the blustering cold of the autumn night, she was sweating beneath her coat. A warm trickle of perspiration rolled down her spine as she peeled the coat off and hung it in the hall closet. She wore black leggings and a doubled up pink sports bra that accentuated her toned midriff. The double layer was constricting as hell—like a straightjacket for her boobs—but if she wanted to run the treadmill without putting on a show for a bunch of jacked-up perverts, it was the price she had to pay.

She ambled into the kitchen and rummaged in the fridge for something to whip up for dinner, settling on leftover chicken and bowtie pasta from a few nights ago. She dumped the food onto a plate and popped it into the microwave.

She switched on the radio to brighten her mood, but the universe twisted the knife by playing her and Steph's song, the kitchen suddenly filling with James Arthur's voice crooning, "Just say you won't let go."

Martinez lunged for the stereo and stabbed the power button, cutting off Arthur before he could repeat the line. "Huh-uh," she said. "You shut your damn, dirty mouth."

After dinner, she cleaned up, showered, and changed, but thoughts of Steph pursued her at every turn. She climbed into bed and eyed Abby's *Book of Shadows*. It made for an effective distraction the last time she'd read it, although she'd paid the price with nightmares.

Or maybe the nightmares had stemmed from what she'd seen in Abby's bedroom, or what she'd *thought* she'd seen. Because now that she'd gained a little distance from that day, a little perspective, she knew it couldn't be real. It was almost certainly a delusion, a hallucination brought on by stress and lack of sleep.

She snatched the book off the bedside table before her conscious mind had a chance to tell her it was a bad idea and flipped it open to where she'd left off. The next several pages contained more notes about rituals, potions, and spells—everything from luck and love to health and money. After that, Abby had written a series of diary entries.

April 19
None of this is working. I'm not getting better. Am I doing it wrong?

April 21
Maybe I don't have the patience for this. The healing spells are worthless. And Max is never coming back. He's got a new girlfriend—some prissy bitch named Amanda. I am such a waste. No one will ever love me. I feel like dying.

May 10
I was wrong before. I'm not the problem, it's Max. I see that now. He's the sickness and the disease. A lying, cheating, thieving ASSHOLE! And I don't feel guilty for saying that anymore. I've neglected myself for too long. It's MY time now. I hope he dies and ROTS in HELL. And chokes on the worms that'll feast on his insides!

Underneath this, Abby had sketched a young man writhing on the ground, his clothes in tatters. He clutched at his face as worms wriggled in his eye sockets.

That's what you deserve, Max!

Fuck healing. Fuck white magic. Fuck Glenda the Good Witch.

And FUCK all you <u>witches</u>, <u>bitches</u>, and <u>snitches</u>!

I WANT REVENGE!!!!

CHAPTER NINETEEN

Garrison felt a pang of nostalgia as he steered his cruiser through the tree-lined entrance to Boston College, passing an array of gothic stone buildings with ornate spires and belltowers that loomed over a latticework of landscaped quads that were lush green in the warmer months, but had faded to a washed-out beige with the onset of fall.

He hadn't been on campus since completing the second semester of his freshman year, when his mama was diagnosed with breast cancer and was forced to quit the two jobs that were funding his tuition. He'd applied for a financial hardship, and the school had done its best to accommodate him. But his mama's medical bills and subsequent funeral expenses drained their savings, and he hadn't heard from his dad since he walked out of their lives five years earlier, leaving Garrison and his kid sisters without even a simple goodbye.

He'd come so close to breaking out of the old neighborhood, but the ghetto had a way of dragging people back into its clutches, like an alley cat toying with its prey. And while some folks greeted him with sympathy, there were plenty who thought it served him right for trying to prove he was better than them.

After dropping out of school, he settled back into their rundown apartment in the Roxbury projects and found a full-time job in construction. Two years later, he enrolled in night classes at UMass Boston, but by then, he'd given up on his dream of being a doctor—dealing with his mama's illness had exposed him to the ugly side of corporate healthcare and had left a bad taste in his mouth. He ended up pursuing a degree in criminal justice, but wondered now if the invisible strings of the ghetto had subconsciously manipulated him into setting limits on his own potential.

As he stared out his windshield at a group of well-dressed students walking to class in designer jackets and scarves, he couldn't help but wonder how different his life would've been if he'd never dropped out. Maybe he'd be living a quiet life in the suburbs married with a couple of kids instead of barely making ends meet in a dangerous and unpredictable job.

Still, he loved the work and had few regrets. But now that he was back on campus in the shadow of the cathedral-like buildings, the reality of it sucked the wind out of his lungs, like an unwanted visit from the ghost of Christmas past.

Never mind that, his mama's voice said. *Life only moves in one direction, and if you keep looking back, it'll run your ass over.*

Mama was never short on colorful advice, and in the years after his father split, she spooned it out in dollops, doing everything in her power to keep the family together.

Garrison drew a deep breath and climbed out of the cruiser, making his way across the parking lot to Maloney Hall, where the campus police had their offices. A female officer checked him in at the front desk, her graying hair tied in a stubby ponytail, her eyes the color of washed-out denim.

"I'm Trooper Garrison," he said. "I called earlier about questioning Brittany Cooper's roommate."

"I'll just need some ID."

Garrison reached into his pocket and fished out his credentials. The officer checked it against the computer to ensure it matched what he'd given over the phone. "You'll be meeting with Jennifer Colby," she said. "We conducted an initial interview last night before we knew the state police were involved." She handed Garrison a one-page report. "She's waiting for you in that conference room."

Garrison took a minute to read the report, then reached into his back pocket for his notepad and strode over to the conference room.

***

Jennifer Colby sat hunched over her phone, texting at a speed that would shame the world's best court stenographer. She had auburn hair, a milky-white complexion, and a smattering of freckles across the bridge of her nose. Her hazel eyes were swollen and bloodshot, which Garrison attributed to a recent bout of crying.

He knocked softly on the inside of the door. "Jennifer? I'm Trooper Garrison with the State Police."

She laid her phone down and straightened in her chair.

"I understand you were roommates with Brittany Cooper."

She nodded wordlessly.

"I'm sorry for your loss. Were you and Brittany close?"

She wiped a tear from the corner of her eye. "Brittany was one of the nicest people I've ever known. She was smart and beautiful, the type of person whose laugh was so infectious you couldn't help but join in, even if you were in a bad mood." Jennifer shook her head and drew a shuddering breath. "I can't believe she's gone."

"Tell me about the day you last saw her."

"It was Tuesday afternoon. I'd just come back from history class, and she was getting ready to go out."

Garrison jotted it down on his notepad, recalling how they'd found Brittany early Wednesday morning after the overnight rain washed away the bottom layer of dirt from someone else's freshly dug grave.

"Did she say anything about where she was going?"

"She went out with her friend Holly."

"How well do you know Holly?"

"I don't, really. All I know is that Brittany met her on the quad a few weeks ago, at the end of September."

"Did you ever meet her?"

135

"No, that was the weird thing. Brittany was secretive about her, almost like she had to keep her apart from her other friends."

"Why would she do that?"

"Because I think they were more than just friends."

"Can you elaborate on that?" Garrison asked.

"I followed her once, maybe a week after she met Holly. I got on the Green Line a couple of cars behind her. She got off near BU, and I watched from across the street as Holly greeted her with a big hug and a kiss. A *long* kiss."

"Brittany was gay?"

"She never talked about it, but when I look back on it now, it makes sense."

"How so?"

"I've seen her flirt with guys at parties, but never witnessed a hookup. She's never mentioned any crushes from high school. And she's always been a little touchy-feely with the girls in our group."

A tear escaped Jennifer's defenses and rolled down her cheek. There was a box of tissues on the table, and Garrison slid it toward her. She pulled a tissue from the box and wiped her eyes.

"I'm sorry," Garrison said. "I know this is hard."

"It's just… things changed between us after I saw her kissing Holly."

"You confronted her about it?"

Jennifer nodded. "I guess I felt betrayed that she never told me. Like, all those nights we cozied up on the couch watching movies… was she hoping something would happen? I know I shouldn't care, but it just bothered me. And now I can't help but wonder if that makes me a bad friend or maybe, like, a secret homophobe." She dabbed her eyes with the tissue.

"How were things between you and Brittany after that?"

"A little strained. Eventually, she told me the story of how she came out of the closet her junior year of high school, and it didn't go well. She said her family was a bunch of stuck-up Puritans who practically made her wear a scarlet *L*. Anyway, her mom convinced her to hide her sexuality in college, especially since BC is a Catholic university."

Garrison frowned. It made what happened to her even more tragic. "You really never met Holly?"

"No, I only saw her from across the street that one time."

"What did she look like?"

"Um, she was white with dark hair. Gave off kind of an '80s metal vibe."

"Any tattoos?"

"I don't know. She was wearing a denim jacket and leather pants, but she definitely seemed like the type who'd at least have a tramp stamp."

Garrison glanced at the report he'd gotten from the front desk. "You told campus police Holly's last name was Radnor." When Jennifer nodded, he said, "There's no record of anyone by that name attending BC. Now or ever."

Jennifer seemed legitimately shocked.

"It's possible Brittany lied to you about it," Garrison said. "Or maybe Holly lied to her." Which raised the possibility Brittany might've been targeted.

"I don't know why Brittany would lie about that," Jennifer said. "I mean, if she met a new friend, why would it matter where?"

It was a good point, but he felt the need to pivot. "What was Brittany wearing the last time you saw her?"

"A white linen sundress. Real pretty, with lace trim."

"What was the weather like that day?"

"Cloudy. Kind of cool, which is why I thought the outfit was strange. But she insisted on wearing it, said she was gonna take a jacket, but never did."

"Did she say where she was going?"

"She mentioned some kind of, like, hippy festival where you dance under the moon and thank Mother Earth for a bountiful harvest."

"Do you have any idea where it was held?"

Jennifer frowned. "I wish I'd asked more questions, or insisted on going with her. Instead, I just let her walk out the door. And now she's gone forever." She lowered her head and sobbed into her hands.

Garrison jotted a final note in his pad, paraphrasing what Jennifer had said. Brittany hadn't headed for a hippy festival… it was a goddamn pagan ritual.

CHAPTER TWENTY

The trailhead for Salem Woods began in a parking lot past the high school and municipal golf course. At this late hour, there were only a few cars on the lot, and the one working streetlight cast a jaundiced glow that failed to penetrate beyond a dozen feet.

Ray parked next to a Toyota Prius with a pentagram decal on the rear window and a bumper sticker with a picture of a broom that read, *Yes... I Can Drive A Stick.* He climbed out of the Explorer and spotted a dark figure lurking in the shadows near the trail. He zipped up his jacket against the raw October chill and approached the figure, his eyes beginning to adjust to the darkness.

"You're late," Martinez said. Her hair was tied up in a ponytail and she wore a puffy jacket paired with black leggings.

"Traffic was a bitch," Ray said. "You know where they're meeting?"

"Abby's *Book of Shadows* had details on the covenstead."

"The *covenstead*?" Ray asked.

"It's a gathering place for witches. The more who come, the greater the power."

Ray glanced at his watch and saw that it was 8:05, which meant the meeting was just getting started. He gestured to the trailhead. "After you."

The woods swallowed them as they hiked along a trail choked with underbrush. A towering wall of trees pressed in on either side, their skeletal branches stripped of leaves, twisted black limbs silhouetted against a violet sky. A yellow moon rose above the canopy, three-quarters full and obscured by a shifting veil of clouds.

"You afraid of the dark, Martinez?"

She scowled at him, but in the pale light of the moon, he could see a hint of fear dancing in her eyes. And he wondered, not for the first time, what exactly had she seen at Abby's bedside?

They walked slowly, leaves crunching underfoot, a steady wind blowing through the canopy rattling the limbs like a graveyard of bones. Somewhere, an owl hooted, and Martinez caught him flinching.

"What's the matter, Ray? Do you want to hold my hand?"

"Very funny."

They continued up a low rise and curved left before crossing a wooden bridge over a stream, its black water rippling with moonlight. They walked in silence, ascending a steep hill and passing a broad cliff face with scraggily ferns growing from its crevices.

Martinez nudged him on the arm. "There should be a footpath up here that branches off the main trail." She brushed past him and led the way, drawing a finger to her lips to keep him quiet. She started down a narrow path where the underbrush had been trampled.

Ray followed her through a dense tangle of vegetation that had turned brown with the season. It obscured their view of the trail for a hundred yards before emerging into a grove of birch. There was a clearing beyond the grove about half the size of a football field.

An oblong boulder rose like an ancient monolith from the center of the clearing. A fire burned in a circle of rocks near the boulder, and a dozen women dressed in dark robes danced around the monolith, their voices rising and falling in a rhythmic cadence.

Ray crouched behind a cluster of birch and stared at the scene. It was almost mesmerizing to watch. Martinez squeezed in beside him, sharing the scant cover provided by the spindly, white trunks. He wondered if their dark clothing was visible from the circle or if the shadows were sufficient to conceal them.

Martinez was so close he could feel the heat of her breath against his neck. "You smell that?" she whispered. "They're burning sage."

He nodded slowly, his gaze transfixed on the women cavorting around the fire, around the monolith. "Is that Thalia?" He pointed to a robed figure near the fire. The orange flames illuminated her pixie hair as she placed an object on an altar adorned with white candles.

Martinez leaned over his shoulder for a better view and nodded.

"What do you think they're doing?" he asked.

"They're giving devotion to the god and goddess. That's a protection circle. The cone of power moves through the center."

"Protection from what?"

"They're tapping into the spiritual realm and using its power to bend energy to their will. They have to be careful not to attract the wrong attention... or anger the wrong gods."

Ray looked at Martinez, the pagan firelight dancing in the depths of her eyes. "You believe in this stuff?"

"No, I...." She let out her breath. "I don't know what I believe anymore."

"Maybe you should quit reading Abby's *Book of Shadows*."

When Martinez made no response, Ray cocked his head and listened to the chanting, trying to make sense of the words that drifted on the wind.

Spirits of fire, come to us,
As we dance the magic circle 'round.
We are the circle within the circle,
Both the spider and the web.

We come from the Goddess,
And from her we take our form.
We give thanks to the woodland spirits,
And pay homage to the hoof and horn.
The spirit of the wind guides us,
Through the years and past our fears.
And to the Earth we shall return.

The chanting ended on that last line, as if the ritual had drawn to a close. The women stopped dancing and broke away from the circle, some chatting, some giggling. One-by-one, they walked over to Thalia and hugged her, exchanging the words, "Blessed be."

Ray rose from his crouched position and stepped away from the shadows.

Martinez regarded him with alarm. "Where are you going?" she asked, her voice a harsh whisper.

"I want to see what's on that altar." He strode into the clearing, making no effort to mask the sound of his approach.

Thalia whirled toward him, a startled whimper escaping her lips. She stood paralyzed, rooted to the ground, torn between fight and flight. Another woman—a redhead—pulled a gun and pointed it in his direction.

Ray held up his hands and moved into the firelight. "Police. Put down your weapon."

Thalia placed a hand over her heart. "Detective Hanley? You scared us half to death. What are you doing lurking around in the dark?"

"Put the gun down," he repeated, eyeing the redhead. She was young, maybe early twenties, and it took a moment for him to recognize her—the clerk from Raven's Wing.

"It's all right, Fiona," Thalia said. "Put it away."

"You have a permit for concealed carry?" Ray asked.

Fiona reached into her purse and brought it out, angling it so he could see. He nodded in approval, and she slipped the .22 and the permit back into her purse.

"May I ask why you're spying on us?" Thalia asked. She was trying to play it cool, but she was obviously rattled.

Tracy Lasher from Mystical Brew emerged into the light, her raven-black hair spilling over her shoulders. A coy grin tugged at her lips. "I bet he was curious what a witch wears underneath her robe."

"Mind if I have a look at that altar?" Ray walked toward it without waiting for an answer, keeping one eye on Fiona. "Martinez, make sure she stays away from her purse, will you?"

Thalia folded her arms. She was dressed in a purple robe, in contrast with the others, who wore black. "You won't find any sacrifices, Detective. Like I told you, our religion is a peaceful one. Our magic works through our minds and our feelings, and this is a sacred space you're violating."

He gazed down at the altar, which turned out to be a TV tray draped in white cloth. It held a variety of objects: candles, sage, incense, flowers, corn, salt, water, chalice, bell, wand, dagger, and pentagram. He leaned toward the chalice and sniffed the dark liquid inside—red wine. "What's the dagger for?"

"It's an athame, a ceremonial blade. And before you jump to conclusions, it's used to direct energy and draw boundaries. It's not used to cut anything."

Martinez came up beside him. "What about the other objects?" Her tone was curious rather than accusatory.

"Everything has a purpose," Thalia said. "None of it evil, I can assure you."

"Is this the sort of ritual Abby participated in?" Ray asked. When Thalia nodded, he said, "And you're certain Cassie never came?"

"I believe I answered that question already. And while I'd like to help you, I'd appreciate if you didn't trample on my right to religious expression. You realize that Wicca is protected under the first amendment? If you keep harassing us, I will file a complaint."

"We're not looking to harass anyone," Martinez said. She tugged Ray's arm. "Let's go."

***

Martinez didn't say another word until they'd hiked down to the parking lot. "What were you thinking?" she asked. "You almost got shot. And you scared the living shit out of a bunch of innocent women."

"I wouldn't call Tracy innocent."

"Is this a joke to you?"

"Come on, Martinez. We had to make sure they didn't ditch any evidence in the woods."

"Next time, give me a heads-up before you storm into something that could turn into a hostile situation."

"You're right," Ray said. "I'm sorry."

Martinez blinked at him. "Did you just say I'm right?"

"What, you don't think I know how to apologize? Come on, let me buy you a beer."

CHAPTER TWENTY-ONE

The Pink Sailor wouldn't have been Ray's first choice for a bar—or even the twentieth—but he'd allowed Martinez to pick the venue, and she was currently sipping a beer and relishing in his discomfort.

"I thought you might want to expand your horizons," she said.

Ray drank a Heineken and eyed the stage at the back of the bar. "I used to pull the same shit on my old partner."

"How's it feel to be on the receiving end?"

The bar erupted in raucous applause as a drag queen contestant sashayed off the stage wearing nothing but a pink wig and a neon-green mermaid tail.

Martinez giggled—something he'd never imagined her doing. "You should see your face."

"I don't have a problem with this," Ray said.

"Then why are you cringing?"

"Because no mermaid should have that much back hair."

"Valid point."

"What's the deal, you come here so you don't get hit on?"

"I like the energy. And I can let my guard down. No creepers to ruin my time."

"Why don't you tell them you're lesbian?"

"Because I'm not."

Ray arched an eyebrow. "So… bisexual?"

"Pansexual."

"What the hell does that even mean?"

"It means attracted to a person, not a gender."

"How's that different from being bi?"

"We love the heart, not the parts."

Ray chuckled. "Billy would've lost his mind over this conversation."

"Your old partner?"

Ray nodded. "Garrison and I were always busting his balls. He was a lovable curmudgeon, you know?"

"Was he a good detective?"

"Before he lost interest in the job, he was the best damned detective around."

Martinez raised her beer. "To Billy, then."

They clinked glasses. Ray finished his Heineken and set the bottle on the bar. "What's your take on Thalia's little gathering tonight?"

"No smoking guns," Martinez said, "except for the one you almost got shot with."

"It doesn't rule them out."

"Thalia's isn't the only coven in the city."

"You think Abby's friends from the Witch Museum are part of a coven?" Ray asked.

"Thalia thought Abby had moved onto something darker. So maybe not a coven, but a—"

"Satanic cult?"

"That's the sense I get from her *Book of Shadows*."

"You've read it?"

"I'm halfway through."

"Anything useful?"

Martinez shrugged. "It starts off fairly tame but takes a dark turn about twenty pages in."

"How so?"

"You can almost see the transformation, the change in her voice, the loss of innocence. The writing grows dark and brooding, like a flowering rot. Pages filled with strange symbols and morbid poetry, riddles wrapped in blood and death." Martinez stared past him, her eyes assuming a haunted look.

"What happened in Abby's bedroom?" Ray asked. "You saw something, didn't you?"

Martinez signaled to a shirtless bartender for another beer. "I don't know."

"Come on, Martinez. No judgement."

Martinez pressed her lips into a tight purple line, and Ray figured she'd said all she intended to on the matter. But then her shoulders slumped and she leaned forward, her hot breath tickling his ear.

"I saw a face," she whispered. "Lurking behind Abby's. It was like something out of a nightmare. Dark, monstrous. Bristling with fangs." She drew back and folded her arms, daring Ray to challenge her. "You think I'm crazy, don't you?"

"I saw how you reacted at her bedside. And you know what they say: you can't believe in God without the Devil."

Martinez shrugged off his comment. "I'd barely slept the night before. It could've been a hallucination."

"Who are you trying to convince, Martinez? Me, or you?"

"I don't want to distract us from finding Cassie."

"Abby's new friends came into Mystical Brew," Ray said, "so if they're somehow responsible for her condition, maybe it's not a distraction."

"We'll find out tomorrow night."

Martinez was referring to the meeting she'd arranged at the haunted house with Abby's former coworker, Danielle—the woman with the bat tattoo on her chest. They wanted to hear what she had to say before approaching anyone else from the Witch Museum.

"You think we'll get anything out of her?" Ray asked.

"She seemed spooked. There's definitely something she didn't want her coworkers to overhear."

"But she told you she doesn't know Cassie," Ray said, "so unless she can identify someone who does, it might be another dead end." He reached onto the bar and passed Martinez a fresh beer. "What we need is to find the van. If we can do that, we can get Cassie and her kidnapper all in one shot."

Martinez stared into her drink. "Is it normal to have so many suspects?"

"There's nothing normal about this case."

Martinez ticked off the suspects on her fingers. "There's the boyfriend, Alex. Tracy from Mystical Brew, plus Thalia and Fiona from Raven's Wing. Then there's the exterminator, Shane, not to mention Abby's friends and whoever the hell cut Brittany Cooper's heart out."

"We could also be dealing with a random crime of opportunity," Ray said. "Some pervert in a van who spotted her walking alone."

Martinez frowned. "She's been missing for five days now. Do you think we'll find her? Alive, I mean?"

Ray finished his beer and set the empty on the bar. "I sure as hell hope so."

CHAPTER TWENTY-TWO

The tunnel was long and narrow, steeped in shadows, the way ahead lit by flickering torchlight. Naomi's captors marched her down the passageway like a lamb to the slaughter. The two men behind her held torches and wore black ski masks, their combined bulk eclipsing the width of the tunnel. Whenever Naomi glanced backward, they grinned at her like hyenas before a kill.

She found it difficult to keep pace. Her back ached, and she was exhausted, her fingers and toes swollen like sausages. She stared at the broad back of her third captor—the one leading this unholy procession. She might be able to knock him down and push past him, but there was no way she could outrun them in her condition. She couldn't fight one man, let alone three.

She cupped the swell of her belly, gritting her teeth at another painful kick from her unborn son. She knew it was a boy from an earlier vision—a vision in which she'd witnessed a crying babe extracted from her womb, his bloodied limbs kicking in protest as the high priestess lifted him into the torchlight and leered at him through the slits of her goat's mask.

She'd been a fool to think she could skip town, a fool to believe she could outrun her destiny. Somehow, the Temple of Six had divined her plans, and now here she was, ready to pop, and the torchlight was already aflicker.

A stitch burned in her side, and she slowed to catch her breath. One of the men behind her swatted the back of her skull, and she cried out in pain. She could already feel a knot swelling in the place where the man's big ring had struck her.

He was known to the congregation as Luther, and the ring symbolized his status as a lieutenant of the Six, a protector of the Temple. He wore it on his left hand—a grinning Baphomet with rubies for eyes.

"Where are you taking me?" Naomi asked, injecting a hard edge into her voice, trying not to show weakness. "What do you want?"

"You betrayed your oath," Luther said. "The child belongs to the Temple."

"You don't understand," Naomi said. "I was only going away for the weekend. I was planning to come back, I swear."

Luther swatted her again, this time so hard she stumbled into the wall and fell to her knees. The other men spat in her face as they hauled her to her feet.

She studied their eyes but couldn't identify them. Some of the congregants never showed their faces—before, during, or after a ritual—always worshipping behind a goat's mask. If they were wearing their ceremonial robes, she might be able to identify their rank from the symbols on their sleeves.

One of the men slapped her ass. "How about we show her a good time? Put another baby in this bitch?"

"She carries a sacred offering," Luther said. "We mustn't defile it."

"What about after she delivers?"

Spider. His name's Spider.

"Once she's served her purpose," Luther said, "her corpse is yours to entertain."

Spider leered at Naomi. "Hear that? You and I are gonna make some real magic."

Naomi punched Spider in the throat. He fell against the wall of the passageway and slid to the floor, gasping for breath. "Try it," she said, "and I'll haunt you for eternity."

Luther grabbed Naomi's arms and yanked them behind her back. He glared down at Spider, shaking his head in reproach.

The other man kicked Spider in the thigh. "Come on, you pussy, get up."

Luther pushed her forward, and she picked up the pace, her footfalls grating against the floor of the tunnel. None of them had noticed the bulge in her back pocket, the thin fabric of her jeans concealing the plush blue rabbit with the heart-shaped nose she'd grabbed on the way out of her house—the only thing she'd ever purchased for her unborn son.

It's probably what had gotten her caught in the first place. Someone from the Temple must've been assigned to watch her and make sure she didn't become attached to her offering.

In the beginning, she was resolute in her commitment to the Temple. She had succeeded in her mission, and all that remained was to offer up the spawn of the priest. Her own flesh and blood would help to fulfill the prophecy and unleash an unimaginable power.

But something changed the first time she felt the baby kicking inside her and realized she was connected to another life. She'd done some terrible things in her teenage years, and all the violence and hatred began to weigh on her, things she could never take back.

But with the baby—with Daniel—it would be like starting over again. She would be reborn a new woman, a mother, and she would leave the broken shell of a girl behind.

She kept the change of heart to herself, didn't utter a word to anyone. And then one day, she found herself staring through the window of a toy store. There, on a shelf, was a plush blue rabbit with a heart-shaped nose. And in that moment, she wanted more than anything for Daniel to have it.

It was her only slip, but they must've seen it. And now she would pay the price.

As they rounded the corner, she caught her first glimpse of a dingy cell with rusted metal bars. Luther shoved her inside and slammed the door shut with an echoing finality.

She wrapped her hands around the bars and pulled, but the door refused to budge. "Please let me out of here. I'll do anything."

Luther sneered at her through the bars. "You made your promise, Naomi, and now your fate is sealed. One way or another, it ends for you on Halloween night."

CHAPTER TWENTY-THREE

The first thing Ray saw when he trudged out of his bedroom on Sunday morning was all three kids sitting on the living room couch watching cartoons and eating cereal from a giant mixing bowl, which rested atop of Petey's naked lap.

"Did you pour the entire box in there?" Ray asked.

"We were hungry," Jason said.

Petey plunged his chubby hand into the bowl and ate *Special K* from the hollow of his fist. Allie reached over his shoulder and mined the pile for dried strawberries.

"You guys really like that stuff?"

"Ish yummy," Petey said, his eyes glued to the TV.

"Where's you diaper?"

Petey pointed to the corner of the room, where last night's diaper sat on the floor, expanded to almost comical proportions. "It full."

"And no one thought to get you a fresh one?"

"He wanted to dry off first," Allie said.

"With his butt on the couch?"

Petey wiggled the lower half of his body, grinding his cheeks into the cushions. "It feel *gooood*!"

That sent Jason and Allie into a full-on giggle fit, and Ray couldn't help but join in. "What is wrong with you?"

Allie rubbed the curly blond tangles of Petey's hair. "He's a baby animal."

"Yeah, he's something alright."

Allie scrunched her nose at him. "Why are you all dressed up, Daddy?"

"I've gotta work."

"But it's Sunday."

153

"It's a special case."

Jason peeled his eyes off the TV. "But we're supposed to go to the corn maze today."

"I know," Ray said, "but you'll have fun without me." The harvest festival was one of his favorite events with the kids—hayrides, corn maze, hot apple cider, costume contest.

"But who's gonna hide in the maze and scare us?" Allie asked.

"I'm sure Grandma will."

Allie was indignant. "Grandma doesn't know how to be the corn monster!"

Michelle leaped out from behind the bookshelf, taking them all by surprise. "I'm the corn monster!" she growled.

The kids screamed, and Petey flipped over the bowl of cereal and jumped off the couch. Jason started to laugh. "You got us good, Mom."

Petey glanced down at himself and giggled. "I naked."

"I see that," Michelle said. "Daddy's doing a fantastic job at parenting."

"Daddy hasn't had his coffee yet," Ray said.

"And neither has Mommy," Michelle replied.

"How do you already have a pull-up in your hand?" Ray asked.

"Because I think ahead." Michelle crouched down and helped Petey into an Elmo pull-up, then grabbed the discarded diaper from last night and followed Ray into the kitchen. "Forget something?" she asked, holding the bloated thing near his face.

"I didn't pee in that."

The look on her face suggested that she was no longer accepting jokes, so he quickly added, "I'll clean up the cereal as soon as I have coffee."

"Oh, so you do have brain activity before your first cup?"

"It's very limited," Ray said. "Probably wouldn't show up on a scan."

Michelle tossed the diaper in the trash and washed her hands at the sink, her hair hanging down in wild blonde corkscrews. She looked adorable in her fleece pajama bottoms and a faded blue T-shirt with no bra. He had to fight the urge to wrap his arms around her and squeeze her tight.

"You really have to go to work?" Michelle asked.

"We've got a few leads that need chasing, and we don't have the same quality backup that we do here in the city."

"You can't work the afternoon shift and go in after the festival?"

Ray shook his head. "The chief's gonna be there and Captain Barnes is supposed to drop by."

"So you're stranding me with all three kids and your mother at the harvest festival."

"I'll make it up to you."

She laid a hand on his chest and met his gaze. "Just find Cassie and then promise you'll take a few days off."

***

When Ray arrived at Salem Police headquarters, he spotted Cassie's ex-boyfriend, Alex, walking out of Chief Sanderson's office. Ray signaled to Martinez, who was sipping a coffee nearby, and they intercepted Alex near the exit.

"What happened?" Ray asked, stepping into Alex's path. "You decide to confess?"

Alex was dressed in khakis and wore a sweater over his collared shirt, as if auditioning for a spot in the J.Crew catalog. "You've been harassing my client."

"You'll have to be more specific," Martinez said. "He harasses a lot of people."

"Thalia Blackthorne."

"We've had a few conversations," Ray said.

"My client believes you violated her First Amendment rights."

"I thought you were a public defender," Ray said. "You know, one of those lawyers who was picked last for the debate team."

"That's very funny, Detective. But I turned down a lot of firms so I could serve the greater good. I also do pro-bono work for marginalized groups."

"Well, aren't you a Boy Scout," Ray said. "Where are you headed, anyway? Is there a nerd convention in town?"

"I'm going to church. Maybe you've heard of it."

"Praying for your soul?" Martinez asked.

God love her, she was catching on.

"Praying for Cassie's safe return," Alex said. "Which I'm sure will bear more fruit than a team of investigators barking up the wrong tree."

Chief Sanderson yelled at them from down the hall. "Hanley. Martinez. My office. *Now.*"

"I'll leave you to your ass reaming," Alex said, smirking as he headed for the door.

***

Ray strode into Chief Sanderson's office with Martinez trailing a few steps behind. Captain Barnes was already there, seated opposite the desk and looking like he'd aged five years in as many days. He nodded in Ray's direction and then glanced at Sanderson, ever the stickler for chain of command.

Sanderson motioned for them to sit and then proceeded to stare at Ray for a long moment, as if sizing him up.

"If you're trying to intimidate me," Ray said, "you'll have to do better than that."

To his credit, Sanderson didn't blink. "I want you to stay away from Thalia Blackthorne and her employees. If either of you finds new evidence that warrants additional questioning, you come see me first. Understood?"

Martinez nodded, but Ray wasn't ready to give in. "I don't know what Alex told you," he said, "but all we've been doing is weeding out suspects."

Sanderson straightened in his chair. "There's a line you can't cross, Detective, as I'm sure you know."

"We never crossed it," Ray said.

Sanderson leaned forward. "But you flirted with it, didn't you?"

"People betray themselves when you fire them up. Like I told Martinez, we don't have time to tiptoe around people's feelings."

Sanderson let out an exasperated sigh and turned to Captain Barnes. "Is he always like this?"

Barnes nodded. "Frustrating as hell, but he's got damned good instincts."

"Don't talk to Thalia again without clearing it with me first," Sanderson said.

"I hear you," Ray said. Which wasn't exactly agreement, but he doubted the chief would push it any further.

"As much as I hate to admit it," Martinez said, "Alex may be right. I don't think Thalia's involved."

"Alex is full of shit," Ray said. "Going to church? Come on."

Chief Sanderson scowled. "A superior court justice has vouched for Alex's character, and it should go without saying that it's in the best interest of this department to stay in the good graces of Justice Reynolds.

There was a sharp knock at the door. Ray turned to see Garrison leaning his hulking frame into the office.

"Sorry to interrupt," Garrison said, "but you guys ought to take a look at this."

Captain Barnes stood up, a shadow of hope crossing his face. "What is it?"

"Traffic surveillance footage. Our analysts detected a gap in the recordings."

"A gap?" Ray said. "Where?"

"Right after the Water Street bridge in Danvers."

"Wait a second," Ray said. "I thought Danvers doesn't have traffic cameras."

"They don't have red light cameras, but there's still surveillance on a few stretches of roadway."

"Did somebody hack the system?" Sanderson asked.

"Who would have that kind of reach?" Martinez said.

"The firewalls in that system aren't worth shit," Garrison said. "The guys in IT told me a fifteen-year-old in his basement could've hacked it."

"Are you sure the van went over the bridge?" Barnes asked.

"We picked it up on a gas station camera heading right for it, and the trail goes cold after that."

"In both directions?" Martinez asked.

Garrison nodded.

"What's in the vicinity of that camera?" Ray asked. "Any place the van might've taken her?"

Sanderson stood up. "We need intel on any warehouses or storage units nearby. Wooded areas too."

Garrison reached into his back pocket and pulled out a rolled-up stack of papers. He laid down three different aerial maps on the chief's desk and tapped his finger against a long rectangular building near the river. "This warehouse is home to a dozen different industrial companies, from shipping and storage to construction, welding, and propane."

"What's over here?" Barnes asked, pointing to the other side of the river.

"That's a boatyard and marina. The one next to it is retail space with a liquor store and a Dunkin' Donuts."

Sanderson turned to Martinez. "Find out if any of those businesses use the same model of Ford Transit van."

"I've got a team standing ready," Garrison said. "We're prepared to hit the warehouses and boatyard, question anyone who's around."

"What about searching the premises?" Barnes asked.

"We'll search any place that lets us, and we'll get a warrant for the ones who don't."

"What about the footage?" Ray asked. "Can the IT guys restore it?"

"They're working on it. I'm hoping for an update this afternoon."

"Mind if we ride along with you?" Barnes asked.

Garrison rolled up the maps and slipped them back into his pocket. As a state trooper, he was the only one who had jurisdiction in Danvers. "As long as you guys stay in your lane," he said, "you're welcome to observe."

CHAPTER TWENTY-FOUR

Chief Sanderson ruled against the field trip to Danvers, insisting they should avoid the appearance of interfering in a state police investigation. When Ray reminded him Cassie's case was a Salem Police matter and the staties were merely assisting, Sanderson suggested Ray get the hell out of his office.

"I think you might be wearing out your welcome," Martinez said, glancing up from the business records displayed on her computer.

"Are you kidding? The chief loves me, he just doesn't know how to express it."

Martinez snorted, then abruptly covered her mouth. "It's a miracle you're still married."

"More like I'm dangling by a thread."

Martinez chuckled. "Aren't relationships the worst?"

Ray motioned to the computer. "You find anything useful in there?"

"A few of the warehouse employees have criminal records. And one of the companies leases Ford Transits from a local dealer, but none fitting our model year."

"What are the convictions?"

"Possession of narcotics with intent to distribute, domestic battery, breaking and entering, and driving under the influence."

"Any of those guys live in Salem?" Ray asked.

"The guy with the DUI."

"Probably not worth our time, assuming Garrison hasn't already gotten to him."

"Have you checked in with Garrison?" Martinez asked.

"I was only able to grab him for thirty seconds, but he said they interviewed dozens of people and managed to search about sixty percent of the premises."

"What about the other forty percent?"

"He's setting up a surveillance detail until the warrants come through. Should have them by tomorrow."

"Are they logging everything into our case management system?" Martinez asked.

"Supposed to be." Ray felt the tremor of someone's approach and turned to find Officer Jeffries standing behind them.

"I guess we're missing all the excitement," Jeffries said, a frown creasing his boyish face.

"Garrison's gonna be up to his eyeballs in paperwork," Ray said. "At least we'll skip that part."

"I like filing the reports," Martinez said. "There's something satisfying about sifting through the details, organizing the confusion, and identifying breadcrumbs to the killer."

"I've seen your paperwork," Ray said. "It's like you're auditioning to be teacher's pet."

Martinez punched him in the shoulder. "I'm not anyone's pet."

"You ever thought about the FBI?" Ray asked. "You'd make a good agent."

She eyed him skeptically.

"I'm serious. As long as you don't mind being surrounded by assholes."

"It just so happens I've had a lot of experience with that lately."

"Uh, hey," Jeffries said. "You asked me to report back on Alex?"

"What'd you find?" Martinez asked.

"He went to the episcopal church near the courthouse."

"He stayed the whole time?" Ray asked.

"He left about an hour after mass let out. I peeked inside and saw him helping to clean up."

Ray grunted and rolled his eyes.

"I know you want to hate this guy," Martinez said, "but we should probably focus somewhere else."

"What about Shane Davis?" Ray asked. "Weren't you tailing him too?"

Jeffries nodded. "He spends a lot of time frequenting dive bars and strip clubs. Always alone. The only other places I saw him go were work and his mom's basement. His boss says he's not the best employee—too chatty with the customers—but he's more reliable than most."

Jeffries dug into his pocket and struggled to extract his hand. "I also wanted to show you this." He held up a plastic evidence bag containing a bulky silver ring in the shape of a grinning goat's skull with pointed horns and rubies for eyes.

"Where'd you get that?" Martinez asked.

"Remember that farmer whose cows were mutilated? He found it in his field yesterday, half buried in mud."

"Did you take it to Evidence?" Ray asked.

"I wanted to show you guys first."

"Hold it still," Martinez said. "I want to get a picture."

Ray leaned in for a closer look after she snapped the photo, hoping to see an inscription, but it was blank inside. Nothing but smooth silver, devoid of any markings.

"Do you think we can get prints off that?" Martinez asked.

"Not likely," Jeffries said. "The farmer wiped it clean after he found it. Said he didn't realize it might be evidence at the time. I'll submit it anyway and see what they can do."

"Keep us posted," Martinez said. "And make sure you log it into the case file."

"I will."

As Jeffries trudged away down the hall, Martinez leaned back in her chair and sighed. "It feels like we've got a dozen threads, but they're all worthless if we can't connect them."

"I bet that's some kind of cult membership ring," Ray said. "You see anyone in Thalia's coven wearing something like it?"

"I don't think so, but it was dark."

"Let's stop by Mystical Brew, see if anyone there remembers Abby's friends with a ring like that."

Martinez furrowed her brow. "You're not planning to ask Thalia are you?"

"We'll start with Tracy for now."

"The chief said we couldn't question anyone in the coven."

"No, he said to stay away from Thalia and her employees."

"I'm sure he also meant the coven."

"We're questioning the workers at Mystical Brew about their customer history. It's different."

"I don't know…"

Ray stood up. "Grab your coat, Martinez, and don't forget rule number twenty-three of being a detective—not everything is black and white."

***

The line for Mystical Brew stretched out the door, and it fell upon Ray and Martinez to coax a crowd of reluctant college students to look up from their phones long enough to realize that not only did other people exist, but also that forming a line involves moving forward and using all available space. The crowd's reaction to this new knowledge ranged from slack-jawed surprise to dramatic eyerolls.

"The future of America," Ray said, as he and Martinez shuffled in from the cold. "God help us all."

Behind the counter, Tracy and Heather were busting their asses making specialty drinks that required mixing, frothing, and infusion, while Jason plodded along at a leisurely pace, glassy-eyed and unquestionably stoned. When the crowd thinned, Martinez showed Mystical Brew employees a picture of the grinning goat's skull ring. "Have you ever seen this? Maybe on one of Abby's friends from the Witch Museum?"

"I don't think so," Heather said. "But sometimes it's so busy in here that I barely register people's faces."

"True that, man," Jason said. "It's like the world's a blur sometimes, you know?"

"If you worked any slower," Tracy said, "you wouldn't have a pulse."

"Good burn," Jason said, his dreadlocks swaying as he nodded and laughed.

"What about you?" Ray asked, turning to Tracy.

"I've never seen it, but it looks like something I'd wear."

Ray observed Tracy's tight leather pants, chrome-studded belt, and barely there Metallica crop top. "It does go with your outfit."

Tracy met his gaze over the counter. "You should see what's *under* my clothes. That would really blow your pants off." She winked at Martinez. "And maybe yours too."

"We'll have to take your word for it," Ray said. "What about the coven? You ever see anyone wearing a ring like that?"

"I thought you were supposed to stay away from the coven," Tracy said, a teasing lilt to her voice.

"Where'd you hear that?" Ray asked.

"A little raven told me."

CHAPTER TWENTY-FIVE

"I don't trust her," Martinez said, climbing into the Explorer. "It doesn't mean she's lying about the ring, but she strikes me as a narcissist who'll say anything to boost her own ego."

"I can't argue that."

"Are you attracted to her?" Martinez asked.

Ray arched an eyebrow. "Are you?"

"Like I told you, I love the heart. And hers is as black as night's plutonium shore."

"Is that a Poe reference?"

"Tis the truth," Martinez said, "and nothing more."

Ray reversed out of the parking lot and merged into traffic. "I've got a hunch Abby's friend from the Witch Museum might recognize that ring."

"If she doesn't," Martinez said, "we can always take it to the public."

"Maybe as a last resort. We don't want to tip our hand any sooner than we have to."

It was nearing six o'clock when they arrived at the stately old Victorian where Cassie grew up. As they climbed out of the SUV, Ray exchanged a glance with Martinez and wondered if she found this part of the job to be as difficult as he did. He could go toe-to-toe with an armed assailant with zero hesitation, but when it came to navigating the raw emotion of a grieving family, his confidence was shaky at best. These situations required a delicate balance of empathy and reassurance, while walking a fine line between bringing the family up to speed and not compromising the more sensitive elements of the investigation.

Ray shrugged off the unease as best he could and mounted the stairs to the porch. As Martinez rang the bell, he eyed the historical register plaque that dated the house to 1711. There was something about the old house and the wealthy family that nagged him, but before he could give it more thought, the door swung open.

Elizabeth Barnes stood in the foyer wearing yoga pants and a white cable knit sweater, her blonde hair tied into a loose ponytail. "Come on in, detectives."

After an exchange of greetings, Elizabeth brushed past them to close the door, and Ray caught a whiff of gin on her breath.

"You have news about Cassie?" Elizabeth asked.

"We have a general update on the investigation," Ray said, "but nothing specific about Cassie."

"Is your husband home?" Martinez asked.

Elizabeth gave an exaggerated shrug. "I told him you'd be here at six, and yet he still felt the need to go to the office this afternoon. On a *Sunday,* no less." She snorted in derision and motioned for them to follow her into her opulent living room.

Once they were seated, she reached for a highball glass on the coffee table and drank slowly and deliberately, as if trying to pass a field sobriety test. "Cassie's dead, isn't she? Is that what you're here to tell me?"

"No," Martinez said, leaning forward. "And none of the evidence suggests that."

"But the statistics do, don't they?"

"Every case is different," Ray said. "And we've uncovered a number of leads that are being investigated as we speak."

"Like what?"

"All I can say right now is that we've found an area of interest based on the traffic footage of the van."

"How close are you to finding her?"

"It's difficult to say," Ray said.

"But we're getting close," Martinez added.

"Who do you think took my girl?"

"Our best theory right now," Ray said, "is that Cassie might've been the target of cult activity."

Elizabeth drained the last of her glass and set it down hard, her eyes narrowing to slits. "We should've burned all the witches when we had the chance. Now, they flock to this town like it's some kind of mecca." She shook her head. "Do you know I can trace my ancestry in this town to before the witch trials? Cassie and I are direct descendants of John Proctor. Do you know who he was?"

Martinez nodded. "He was one of the judges who presided over the trials."

"That's right," Elizabeth said. "And he executed more witches than all the others combined."

"He's also the only one who never repented," Martinez said.

"That's true," Elizabeth said. "He went to his grave convinced the people he condemned were real witches who earned their trips to hell."

Ray sucked in his breath, his mind suddenly making the connection that had eluded him on the porch. "Does the name Brittany Cooper mean anything to you?" he asked.

Elizabeth tensed up, a frown creasing her lips. "Do you mind if I get another drink?"

"Not at all," Ray said. He turned to Martinez after Elizabeth headed into the kitchen. "How do you know all that history about the witch trials?"

"I told you, I used to be a trolley driver for one of those Salem history tours. You know, for a detective, you don't listen well."

"I've been reading Frank's handbook on occult crime," Ray said. "The one he wrote during the Satanic Panic. These cults, they're big on symbolism. They attach significance to historic events, important dates, and bloodlines."

He could tell by the look in Martinez's eyes that she'd made the connection too. "Cassie wasn't a random target,"

Martinez said. "She wasn't profiled for her age or her looks. It was her family."

"Exactly," Ray said. "Her ancestry makes her the perfect victim of a Salem-based cult... or maybe a coven of witches looking for revenge."

"Halloween is right around the corner," Martinez said. "It's a high holiday for the occult. They call it *Samhain*."

Ray had read about Samhain in Frank's handbook. It was supposed to be when the dead return to walk the earth, when the veil between this world and the spirit world is at its thinnest. A night when occult groups call upon demons and make sacrifices to gain their favor.

"Do you think they could be keeping Cassie alive?" Martinez asked, her voice low. "To use as a sacrifice?"

Before Ray could answer, Elizabeth staggered into the living room with her highball glass filled to the brim, her unsteady gait sending splashes of gin onto the gleaming hardwood floor.

When she reached the sofa, she set the glass down on the coffee table and dropped back into her seat, then looked at them as if she'd forgotten something. "Can I offer either of you a drink?"

Ray and Martinez shook their heads.

Elizabeth reached for her glass and took a long sip. "You were asking about Brittany."

"That's right," Martinez said. "Do you know her family?"

Elizabeth nodded gravely. "Years ago, her mother and I volunteered at the Salem Historical Society. Her family's roots go back as far as mine."

"Is she from Salem too?" Ray asked.

"As far as I know, she's always lived in Danvers."

Martinez turned to Ray. "Part of Danvers used to be called Salem Village. It's where the hysteria surrounding the witch trials began."

Elizabeth's hand shook as she drew the glass to her lips. "I've heard the news reports about Brittany, the awful things that happened to her. She and Cassie are about the same age. Both have long, blonde hair. I can't help but think that whoever did this might be the same person, that whatever they did to Brittany, they may also have—" Elizabeth broke off and covered her face, a heart-wrenching sob escaping her lips.

Martinez laid a hand on Elizabeth's shoulder and let her cry it out for a minute. "We don't know anything for sure, but we're working with the state police to determine if there's any connection."

The front door opened suddenly, and Paul Barnes stomped into the living room. "What did I say about starting without me?"

Elizabeth glanced up, her eyes bloodshot and swollen with tears. "You're a half hour late, Paul. Do you think these detectives have time to sit around waiting for you to make an entrance?"

Paul eyed the half-empty highball glass. "How many gin and tonics have you had?"

Elizabeth picked up the glass and took a drawn-out sip. "A lady never counts."

Paul's cheeks turned scarlet, and his eyes gleamed like marbles behind his rimless glasses. "Don't disrespect me in my own home, Elizabeth. I won't tolerate it." He turned to Ray and Martinez. "I apologize, detectives, but would you mind repeating your update?"

"You didn't miss much," Ray said, and proceeded to catch him up.

"What about Alex?" Paul asked, once Ray had finished. "You said you were going to rattle his cage. Did you search his house?"

"We've looked into him," Ray said. "And trust me, I did rattle his cage. But there's no evidence to suggest he took her, which means we don't have probable cause for a warrant."

"Not to mention," Martinez said, "he gave me a walkthrough of his house on the first day of the investigation. We went through every room, including the basement. It's obviously not as thorough as a search warrant, but if Cassie were there, I would've seen her."

Paul's shoulders slumped as he sat down on the sofa as far away from Elizabeth as possible. He peeled off his glasses and rubbed his eyes. "I've been trying to busy myself, distract my mind from the constant worry. But I just..." He shook his head. "She's our baby girl."

Elizabeth muttered something under her breath, but Paul didn't seem to notice.

Ray leaned toward them. "Has anyone ever threatened your family because of your ancestor's role in the witch trials?"

Elizabeth shrugged. "Not that I recall."

"No, nothing like that," Paul said. "What else can you tell us about the investigation?"

Ray stood up, and Martinez followed. "I'm sorry," Ray said, "but that's all we have for now."

CHAPTER TWENTY-SIX

According to Martinez, the five-story building on the eastern corner of Church Street was once a confectionary that pumped out the kind of hard candies old ladies struggled to pawn off on their grandkids when Ray was growing up. The brick exterior was so worn that it appeared sandblasted, the traditional reddish hues covered in white splotches from mineral salts leaching out of the material over the better part of a century.

There was a line outside the building with more than a dozen people queued up behind a barrier of velvet ropes. Two hulking bouncers manned the entrance, each wearing a pissed-off expression that could roughly be translated as, *I'd rather be kicking your ass.*

The bouncers granted access at five-minute intervals, and each time the heavy metal doors parted, Ray caught the sound of disembodied screams, maniacal laughter, or the screeching violins from *Psycho*.

"This place needs to get over itself," Ray said as they shuffled to the front of the line.

Martinez pointed to a sign near the door that advertised a $30 ticket price, a 16+ entry requirement, and boldface warnings for pregnant women, people with heart conditions, and anyone prone to vertigo or epilepsy.

"We can only let in twenty people at a time," the bouncer said in answer to Ray's comment. He was tall and muscular, his skin as smooth and dark as the night around them. Big hands, no rings. "The isolation adds to the experience."

"How many floors are used for the haunted house?" Martinez asked.

"It's the whole building. All five levels. And definitely not for the faint of heart." He accepted their money with a grin and waved them toward the door. "You'll be scared. I guarantee it."

"For thirty bucks," Ray said, "I'd better have a heart attack."

The second bouncer pulled the double doors open slowly, triggering the theatrical sound of creaking hinges to pipe through hidden speakers.

Martinez drew a deep breath. "I hate haunted houses."

"Then you came to the wrong place, lady." The bouncer pointed into the yawning cavern of darkness. "Follow the glowing arrows through the exhibits all the way up to the top floor, then take the back stairs down to the exit. Until then... *have a pleasant nightmare*," he said, doing a second-rate imitation of the Crypt Keeper.

Ray chuckled at the cheesy routine and stepped inside with Martinez. A second later, the doors swung shut and the hidden speakers broadcasted the sound of heavy chains barricading them in. It was pitch-black inside, the only source of light coming from the glow-in-the-dark arrows lining the floor. Ray could barely see Martinez standing next to him.

A menacing voice suddenly reverberated through the room.

"THERE'S NO ESCAPE FROM THE MANOR OF THE DAMNED. ALL WHO ENTER SHALL PERISH IN THE LABYRINTH OF MADNESS. FIVE LEVELS OF SPINE-TINGLING TERROR AWAIT YOU. AN ENDLESS NIGHTMARE THAT WILL SHATTER YOUR MIND, DEVOUR YOUR SOUL, AND FEED WHAT REMAINS TO THE CREATURES THAT LURK IN THE DARK.

The voice dissolved into the maniacal laughter Ray had heard earlier from the street. "You ready?" he asked.

"I can't believe we have to go through this just to interview a suspect."

"Where are we meeting her?"

"Fifth floor. She said to look for the headless bride."

"Should be hard to miss."

Another voice broadcasted through the speakers, the tone less ominous this time. "For your own safety, please remain on the path of lighted arrows. Thank you and enjoy your visit."

As they approached the first arrow, Ray heard moaning somewhere to his right, followed by a rustling in the darkness like the shuffling of feet. The moaning grew louder, as did the shuffling, all around them now. And still, they couldn't see a damn thing.

He walked beside Martinez, their hips brushing together as they bumbled through the darkness. A hollow click registered from above and suddenly a rotting corpse dropped from the ceiling, suspended from a rope and dangling not three feet from their shocked faces.

Martinez grabbed Ray's shoulder and screamed.

"It's a dummy," Ray said. "Just a dummy." But there was panic in his voice.

Then the dummy's eyes snapped opened and its jaw unhinged. Its arms shot forward, reaching for them as it gnashed its teeth.

"Sonofabitch," Ray muttered. "That scared the sh—"

Martinez screamed again, and Ray whirled around as strobe lights suddenly filled the room. Something seized his ankle, and he glanced down to find a zombie-like creature covered in festering sores slithering on its belly and grinning up at him.

"Brainzzzz," it moaned. "Eat your brainzzzz!"

He jerked his foot away and saw that it had gotten Martinez too. Not a dummy this time, but an actor wearing some pretty damn convincing monster makeup.

Martinez grabbed his hand and squeezed it, half-screaming, half-laughing. "Ray, look!"

There were zombies all around them now, the strobing lights creating a dizzying 3D effect that seemed to multiply their numbers.

"Brainzzzz! Eat you brainzzzz!"

Disembodied screams rang out all around them, followed by the wet chewing sounds of zombies feasting on human flesh.

"Remind me not to bring my kids here," Ray said.

They followed the arrows around a bend and into a narrow corridor lit by artificial torches. There were shelves cut into the faux stone walls ahead that resembled storage compartments. As they drew nearer, he saw bones strewn across the shelves and then he understood.

"Catacombs."

Martinez groaned. "Wonderful."

"Just be ready. We know what to expect now."

Martinez cocked her head to the side and shushed him. "Do you hear that? It's like a high-pitched chittering."

Before Ray could respond, he detected a blur of movement overhead. "What the—"

A colony of bats streaked toward them, their mechanical wings flapping as they zipped along an invisible wire. Some flew low enough to catch in their hair or strike the backs of their heads with soft, rubbery thuds. As they swatted away the bats, a trap door opened beneath their feet and they plunged into a chute, which slid them into a subterranean catacomb where the dead began to rise.

Zombies in various stages of decay emerged from the catacombs and lumbered toward them. "Brainzz…. Eat your brainzzzzzzz."

Ray and Martinez hurried to the other end of the narrow chamber and arrived at a stone stairwell. This time, the glowing arrows pointed up. Ray groaned. "We have five floors of this? Do me a favor, Martinez. Next time a suspect wants to meet, you pick the location."

Martinez gave him a look that said, *No shit,* before grabbing hold of the wrought iron handrail. They ascended the stairs to the second-floor landing, where they encountered a large metal sign posted to the wall.

THE BURYING POINT

Salem Institute for the Criminally Insane.

"Seriously?" Martinez said. "People actually pay for this stuff?"

The rest of the tour was a blur—a dizzying gauntlet of knife-wielding lunatics, killer clowns, and hostile spirits, all of them competing to be the scariest in the building. Halfway through the fifth floor, they nearly collided with a headless bride in a blood-soaked wedding dress. She lumbered toward them with her arms outstretched, glowing a spectral white under the blacklights and speaking to them in an ominous voice.

"Take my hand, o lost soul, and feel the kiss of darkness, for even true love turns to rot, and death feasts upon the spoils."

Martinez waved a hand at the corpse bride. "Danielle? It's Detective Martinez."

Danielle flinched at the mention of her name, then motioned for them to follow her into the shadows. A scream rang out from the floor below, and Ray and Martinez exchanged a glance before pursuing her into the darkness. Danielle drew to a halt a few feet from the back stairway, where the glow of an exit sign illuminated her silhouette.

Up close, they could see the ruin of the bride's neck was actually a mask, the eyeholes camouflaged in glossy smears of blood.

"Why here?" Martinez asked. "Why not talk to me at the museum?"

"It's not safe."

"Why not?" Ray asked.

"Because they're watching me."

Martinez leaned in. "Who?"

"The Temple. They've gone too far."

"What are they?" Martinez asked. "A cult?"

It was hard to tell through the costume, but she appeared to nod. "Abby was my friend."

"What did they do to her?" Martinez asked.

"She wanted to tell, but they found out."

"What did they do?" Martinez asked again.

"They performed a ritual."

"What kind of ritual?" Ray asked.

"A possession. Something to drive her mad… or kill her. Something that couldn't be traced back to the Temple."

"What about Cassie Barnes?" Ray asked. "Or Brittany Cooper? Did the Temple—"

There was a click as the power went out and the building plunged into darkness, triggering a series of disembodied screams that echoed across all five floors.

Ray felt a rush of air at his back, a tremor of footsteps vibrating the old floorboards. The strobe lights suddenly activated, and the next few seconds played out like the stuttering frames of a silent film with gaps in the footage.

He saw the corpse bride leaning away from them… in the next frame, she had spun halfway around, the wedding dress rippling with momentum… next, he saw the treads of her sneakers improbably facing the ceiling… then the top of her costume suspended in the air, her hair flying as if she were airborne.

Martinez cried out, piecing it together before his brain could fully grasp the situation. "Danielle!"

Martinez ran down the steps after her, but in the final, strobing frame, Ray saw Danielle crumpled against a concrete wall far below, frozen in a kind of half-somersault, her head bent at a ghastly angle.

Ray ran into the center of the room and yelled, "Police! Turn on the lights, it's an emergency!"

The lights sputtered on a moment later, so bright they hurt his eyes. He ran to the stairwell and saw Martinez crouched down next to Danielle. There was blood on the third step from the top, some more splattered on the walls a few steps below, and a whole pool of it where she lay on the next landing.

Martinez had peeled her off the wall and laid her flat so she could administer chest compressions, but Danielle's head lolled at an unnatural slant.

"Martinez?"

She glanced up at him, shaking her head. "I can't get a pulse."

"Keep trying. I'll call for an ambulance."

He reached into his pocket for his cell phone and dialed 9-1-1. When he finished speaking with the dispatcher, he glanced around the room at the dozen or so actors dressed in ghoulish costumes and a trio of teenaged boys who appeared to be customers. He reached into his sports coat and showed them his badge. "Did anyone see what happened?"

Head shakes all around.

Ray pointed to a guy wearing a bodysuit with painted-on bones, which under the blacklights made for a pretty convincing skeleton. "Do you have any way to contact the bouncers outside?"

"There's a radio in the back room."

"Go get it and bring it to me." His eyes swept over the crowd. "Nobody leaves until we've taken your statement."

There was a good deal of mumbling and complaining as the skeleton fetched the two-way radio.

Ray called out to Martinez. "How's it going down there?"

"Still no pulse."

"Shit."

The skeleton—who turned out to be a shaggy-haired kid who couldn't be more than twenty—returned a minute later with the handheld radio.

Ray nodded in thanks and depressed the talk button. "This is Detective Hanley with the Salem Police. We have a situation on the fifth floor that requires an ambulance. Nobody leaves the building until we've cleared them. Do you copy?"

"10-4," the bouncer said. "The ambulance is just pulling up."

"Send them up the back steps."

"You got it."

Ray handed the radio back to the skeleton kid, who had taken a couple paces toward the stairs and was craning his neck for a look. "What happened?" the kid asked. "Who got hurt?"

"That's close enough," Ray said, indicating an invisible line about five feet from the stairway. "Do me a favor and make sure nobody crosses that line."

"Uh, sure."

Ray used his phone to snap pictures of the fifth-floor landing from various angles, including one facing out to the factory floor. He walked down the stairs toward Martinez, snapping pictures of the blood spatters and the latex mask that had slipped off Danielle's head as she'd fallen. It now dangled over one of the steps like a freakish snakeskin.

Martinez was still administering chest compressions, and he took pictures of that too, trying to record as much as he could before the EMTs trampled through what might be a crime scene.

"Did you see anything?" Ray asked.

Martinez looked at him, her hands still pumping against Danielle's chest. "I felt someone pass by, but it happened so fast. Then the strobe lights kicked on and everything was so disorienting."

"We were four feet from that landing," Ray said. "No way she just tripped."

"Unless something spooked her," Martinez said, "and she decided to run."

Ray groaned. "She was about to tell us if there was a connection to Cassie. And now she's dead."

Martinez continued performing chest compressions, seeming not to notice the way Danielle's head was lolling to the side. "Maybe there's a chance..."

"Her neck's broken, Martinez. She's not coming back."

The echoing of footfalls emanated from the stairway below as the EMTs ascended with a stretcher and medical bags.

Martinez stood up to let them through and gave them a quick rundown on the situation. The lead EMT was a middle-aged woman with severe features and a long, dark braid that reached halfway down her back. She pulled on a pair of blue latex gloves as her associates went to work with a defibrillator.

"We'll take it from here, ma'am."

CHAPTER TWENTY-SEVEN

By the time the EMTs carried out Danielle's body, reinforcements from the Salem Police department had arrived. Ray established command of the scene and assigned the officers a variety of tasks, including guarding the exits, interviewing witnesses, and collecting Danielle's clothing from the hospital to be logged as evidence.

The witnesses included twelve customers and seventeen employees, which worked out to roughly three interviews per officer. Ray supplied the officers with a standard series of questions, including:

1. Did you see what happened?
2. Where were you when the lights came on?
3. Did you see anyone leave the building?
4. Did you see or hear anything suspicious?
5. Do you know the victim? If so, what's your relationship?
6. Do you recognize these pictures of Cassie Barnes and Brittany Cooper? If so, describe how you know them and the nature of your relationship.
7. Do you recognize the Baphomet ring in this picture? If so, where have you seen it before?
8. Have you ever heard of a group called the Temple?

The answers they received were pretty much "no, no, and more no." Even more discouraging, none of the witnesses exhibited suspicious behavior or provided evasive answers, which either meant they were accomplished liars or they'd seen about as much in the dark as Ray and Martinez had.

Ray folded his arms and watched the state police Crime Scene Services team log evidence from the fifth floor. They collected bits of trash and strands of hair, snapped pictures of sneaker prints, and swabbed the blood from the stairs. It was almost certainly an exercise in futility, but he couldn't take any chances.

Martinez leaned against the wall near a steel door, which was marked with a spray-painted symbol depicting a goat's head set against a six-pointed star. They had just walked up and down five flights of stairs at each of the emergency exits searching for clues that might've been left behind by a fleeing assailant. They came up with nothing.

Ray wiped his brow with a napkin from Mystical Brew, then balled it up and shoved it into his pocket, marveling at the fact Martinez hadn't broken a sweat.

"Somebody had to see something," Ray said.

"That kid in the skeleton costume was only a few feet away when the lights came on."

"His outfit glows under the blacklight," Ray said. "If he pushed Danielle, we would've seen him."

"Maybe whoever did it was wearing all black," Martinez said.

"That could explain it," Ray said, "except that nobody we interviewed was dressed in all black."

"If someone pushed her, where would they have escaped to?"

As they glanced around the room, Ray spotted Officer Jeffries ducking beneath the police tape. "Hey, Jeffries," Ray said. "What'd you find?"

Jeffries cleared his throat and shuffled toward them. "I've got the guy who runs this place. He's waiting for you downstairs."

Ray patted his shoulder. "Good work."

As they headed downstairs, Martinez turned to Jeffries. "Was the crime lab able to recover any prints off the Baphomet ring?"

"It was wiped clean," Jeffries said. "Just like we thought."

When they reached the first floor, they found Officer Frasier chatting with the haunted house's manager, who reminded Ray of a midlevel bookmaker due to his slicked back hair, fake tan, and a burgundy leather jacket that might've been swiped from the set of Starsky and Hutch.

"Is this your operation?" Ray asked.

"My bread and butter, baby." He held out a hand. "Steve Rancic."

Ray and Martinez introduced themselves. "You got an office down here?" Ray asked.

"Right this way."

Rancic led them across the old factory floor, the walls painted a matte black to enhance the spookiness factor when the lights were out. A dark knob protruded from the rear wall, and as they got closer, Ray realized it was a door. Inside, there was a cramped office with a small desk, two chairs, and a sound board that Ray figured controlled the lights and effects.

"What's the radio for?" Ray asked, pointing at the walkie-talkie sitting on the desk.

"I've got spotters who signal me when to trigger the effects. It's a hell of a lot cheaper than motion sensors."

"Do you have any cameras?" Martinez asked.

"Just one of those internet cameras watching the bouncers collect money. It's the only way I know these shits aren't stealing from me."

"Any others?" Ray asked.

"Nah, that's the only one. Got it hooked up to my computer here." He motioned to the laptop sitting open on his desk.

"How long has Danielle worked for you?"

"She the dead girl?"

Martinez bristled. "Yes, Mr. Rancic. The dead girl. Your employee."

"You got a picture?"

Martinez showed her a photo of Danielle lying in the stairwell. As Rancic studied the picture, Ray noticed his lip twitch, either in revulsion or maybe suppressing a smirk.

"I recognize her," Rancic said. "She's worked here a couple of seasons. What happened? Did she fall down the stairs?"

"We think she was pushed," Ray said.

"Did anyone see it happen?" Rancic asked.

"We can't share those details right now," Ray said.

"So you two detectives just happened to be in my haunted house the moment a murder happens?"

"Who said we were here when it happened?" Martinez asked.

"The bouncers told me."

"Do you know why someone would want to hurt Danielle?" Ray asked. "Has she had any problems with any of the employees?"

"Not that I know of, but I'm not exactly what you'd call an attentive boss."

"What's that supposed to mean?" Martinez asked.

"I rent this place a few months out of the year, pay minimum wage to a bunch of teenagers who run around scaring the shit out of people in the dark. They get a costume, watch a one-hour training video, and that's it."

"Do you have a list of all your employees over the last two years?" Ray asked.

Rancic chuckled. "I don't do everything by the book, if you know what I mean."

"Why don't you explain it to us," Martinez said.

"You guys don't have any ties to the IRS, do you?"

"We're after a murderer," Ray said. "We're not interested in your tax records."

"Well that's good, because I don't keep any. This is what you'd call an under-the-table kind of business. I don't have employee files or none of that shit. Everything I do is cash only, and I pay whoever's here when the lights come on at the end of the night."

"What if someone's late?" Martinez asked.

"You show up late, you don't get in. And if you don't get in, you don't get paid. It's a simple business model."

"How many people you got working here at a time?" Ray asked.

"About twenty."

"We interviewed seventeen tonight," Ray said. "How many showed up?"

"Like I said, I don't keep track. If they're here, they get paid. And if I start to notice we're getting light, I find replacements."

"You only have the two exits?" Martinez asked.

"That's right."

The bouncers told them earlier that none of the workers had left near the time of the incident, so in theory everyone was accounted for. Except the bouncers could be lying. Or maybe the killer found a good hiding spot and laid low until everyone was released.

Martinez showed Rancic her phone. "Have you ever seen these girls or heard the names Cassie Barnes or Brittany Cooper?"

Rancic shook his head. "Can't say that I have. Couple of lookers though."

"What about this ring?" Martinez asked. "Have you ever seen anyone wearing something like this?"

"Doesn't look familiar."

"What about the Temple?" Ray asked. "Anyone ever talk about a temple around here?"

"The only temple I know of is that Jewish place down the street."

Ray folded his arms. This conversation was going nowhere. "You got anything else, Martinez?"

She shook her head.

Rancic leered at her. "How about you give me your number in case I think of something more?"

Martinez handed him a business card.

"After Halloween, I turn this place into a winter wonderland, but then I'm off to Cabo. You should come with me. I bet you're a knockout in a bikini." Rancic held his hands in front of his chest, estimating how Martinez would fill out a bathing suit.

Before Ray could register what was happening, Martinez grabbed Rancic's arm and twisted it behind his back. She seized his thumb with her other hand and yanked it so far in the wrong direction that Ray expected the bone to snap.

Rancic dropped to his knees and let out a high-pitched shriek. "Ow! Ow! Stop!"

Martinez relinquished her grip and stormed out of the office.

Ray smirked at Rancic. "I'd put her down as a *no* for Cabo."

CHAPTER TWENTY-EIGHT

"You really think she was pushed?" Garrison asked. He was seated across from Ray and Martinez at Kettle & Cauldron, a bar and grille near the Salem waterfront.

It was the kind of place that served mediocre food but had a decent drink selection and live music every night. The interior consisted of floor-to-ceiling wood paneling that was painted all black, the lingering odor of spilled beer seeming to permeate every surface.

Ray set his burger down and wiped his mouth on a cheap paper napkin. "Someone ran past us, and a split second later, Danielle tumbled into the stairwell."

"And you didn't see anything?" Garrison asked.

"It was pitch dark," Martinez said. "At least until the strobe lights made everything look like a psychedelic hallucination."

"Something hit her hard enough to knock her mask off," Ray said. "I don't see that happening just by tripping."

"Did you interview her family?" Garrison asked.

"She doesn't have any," Martinez said. "Her mom overdosed on heroin when she was sixteen and there's no father listed on the birth certificate."

"Any roommates?" Garrison asked.

"Boyfriend," Ray said. "Which explains why we're eating in this shithole."

"He works here?" Garrison asked.

Ray motioned to the bar, where a tattooed meathead with a buzz cut was mixing drinks. "His name's Evan Brody."

Garrison sipped his Diet Coke. "Does he know his girlfriend's dead?"

Martinez nodded. "Officer Jeffries tracked him down last night and got him to ID the body."

"How'd he take the news?" Garrison asked.

"Jeffries said he seemed pretty shocked," Martinez said.

Ray balled up his napkin and tossed it onto his half-eaten burger. "I'm gonna talk to him."

He got up and strode over to the bar, where Evan was sopping up a spill with a dirty rag. He had a muscular build and a sleeve of tattoos spiraling up both arms, his too-small black T-shirt likely hiding more ink.

"Evan Brody?" Ray asked.

"Let me guess," Brody said. "Another cop."

"Detective Hanley."

"Is this about Danielle?"

"I want to ask you a few questions."

"I already talked to the cops last night."

"Officer Jeffries said you were here when Danielle was killed."

"Is he the fat cop?"

"Let's go with big-boned, but yeah. And anyway, I'm sorry for your loss."

"She was a good kid."

"How long did you live with her?" Ray asked.

"About a year."

"How'd you get along?"

"Pretty good."

"No fighting?"

"Nah, we were tight."

"Then why would your neighbors tell me you were always fighting?"

"Because my neighbors are shitheads who don't know how to mind their own business. Me and Danielle watch a lot of horror movies, got a whole system on surround sound. That's probably what they've been hearing."

"Sounds like an honest mistake," Ray said. "But I'm surprised you're at work today. I mean, your girlfriend just died."

"You think the owner of this place gives a rat's ass? I already got two strikes. I miss one more day, and I can kiss this job goodbye."

"Not easy finding work with a criminal record, is it? What was it, aggravated assault?"

"It was self-defense."

"You just happened to be carrying a lead pipe when someone took a swing at you?"

Brody clenched his jaw. "Why are you here? You get a rise out of harassing people in mourning?"

"Did you hire someone to push Danielle down the stairs?"

"What? Hell, no. She was my girl. And that fat cop said it was an accident."

"I think she may have been pushed."

"What makes you say that?"

"Did Danielle ever mention being afraid of anyone? Maybe somebody she worked with at the Witch Museum?"

"If she was, she never mentioned it."

"I understand you also work at the Witch Museum," Ray said.

"Just a couple days a week."

"Did you work there on Friday with Danielle?"

"Yeah, why?"

"My partner saw her there. She said Danielle was acting real skittish. Any idea why?"

Brody folded his arms. "No idea."

"What about the Temple?" Ray asked.

"What temple?"

"Danielle said people from the Temple were watching her."

"I don't know anything about that."

188

"I get the sense it's a cult," Ray said. "Something pagan, maybe even satanic. Something that uses symbols just like the one on your forearm." Ray pointed to Brody's tattoo. "That's a Baphomet, isn't it? A goat's head symbolizing the Devil?"

Brody chuckled. "You know how many people in this town have a tattoo just like it?"

"You ever see anyone wearing a Baphomet ring? A grinning one with rubies for eyes?"

"Doesn't ring a bell."

"What about the names Cassie Barnes and Brittany Cooper? Do they mean anything to you?" Ray showed him their pictures on his phone.

"Never heard of them."

"What about Abby Garcia?"

"Nope."

"Are you sure? She used to work with you and Danielle at the Witch Museum." Ray showed him another picture.

"Okay, yeah. I remember her. She had some kind of mental breakdown, didn't she?"

"How do you think that happened?"

Brody shrugged. "Some bitches be crazy."

A middle-aged guy in a Kettle & Cauldron polo shirt whistled for their attention. "Hey, Evan, you got paying customers waiting for their drinks over there."

"Alright, I'm on it," Brody said, then turned back to Ray. "I guess we're done here."

Ray rapped his knuckles against the bar. "I wouldn't bet on it."

                              ***

As Ray turned to leave, he discovered Garrison lurking a few feet behind him. "I don't remember asking for back up."

"Just making sure I didn't need to save your sorry ass."

They exited the restaurant and joined Martinez outside, where the wind blowing off the harbor cut like shards of ice.

"For the record," Ray said, "I can handle myself just fine."

Garrison winked at Martinez. "You know how many times I've rescued this fool from the brink of death?"

"Don't listen to him," Ray said. "His ego's bigger than his biceps."

Garrison held up a hand and wiggled his fingers. "Five times. *At least.*"

"You really keeping count?"

"It's not a small number," Garrison said.

"Some guys play it safe," Ray said. "Others play it to win."

Garrison shook his head. "I don't even know what to say to that, man."

Martinez cocked her thumb at the bar. "What'd you get out of him?"

"The usual denials. We ought to watch him for a while."

"Did you interview anyone else from the Witch Museum?" Garrison asked.

They had finally moved away from the bar and were in the process of climbing into the Explorer.

"We did the rounds this morning," Martinez said. "The manager is a sweet older lady in her mid-sixties, and besides Brody and Danielle, all of the other employees are either grandmotherly types or high-school kids who work part-time."

"Did any of them admit to working at the haunted house?" Garrison asked.

"No," Martinez said. "And the haunted house staff didn't recognize them either."

Ray turned to Garrison, who looked like a kidnapped giant in the back seat. "Any new developments with the warehouse search?"

"We're still sifting through all the details, but it's starting to feel like a dead end."

"There's got to be a reason someone deleted five minutes of video from that location," Martinez said.

"Maybe the guy switched cars or made an exchange in the parking lot," Ray said. "Or maybe it was a turnaround point."

"We reviewed the footage in both directions," Garrison said. "The van never came back over the bridge."

"Can't your IT guys restore the missing tape?" Martinez asked.

"Whoever hacked the system also restricted the admin rights needed to restore the video. They're working on getting it back, but I can't get anyone to commit to an ETA."

"So, we've got a pervert in a van who's also a computer expert," Ray said. "Not exactly a stretch, except we can't be sure that's the motive."

"Let me guess," Garrison said. "You've got a hunch."

"More like we're starting to see the connections," Ray said.

"Okay, let's hear it."

"Cassie and Brittany both come from families who can trace their roots to the witch trials," Ray said. "And Brittany grew up near the spot where the accusations began."

"Brittany grew up in Danvers," Garrison said, "not Salem."

Martinez said, "The part of Danvers where Brittany grew up was originally called Salem Village. There's a historical marker at the end of her block for the Salem Village parsonage."

Garrison folded his arms. "What's a parsonage?"

"It's a minister's residence built by the town," Martinez said. "And the minister who lived there in 1692 was Reverend Samuel Parris."

"And?" Garrison asked.

"He had a slave named Tituba who told his niece and daughter tales of witchcraft from her time in Barbados. The girls later accused Tituba of being a witch, and since she lacked any social standing as a slave, she was arrested. The authorities eventually beat a confession out of her, along with the names of other suspected witches in town."

Garrison scoffed. "Same shit, different century. You're saying Brittany's ancestors lived next door to all that?"

"It's not just the location that ties Brittany to the witch trials," Martinez said. "It's her bloodline."

"What are you talking about?" Garrison asked.

"She's a direct descendant of Reverend Parris," Martinez said.

Garrison blinked at her. "You're shitting me."

"It's not just Brittany," Ray said. "Cassie's ancestor was a judge in the witch trials, and he was unrepentant to his dying day."

"Both of their ancestors were notorious witch haters," Martinez said. "In a city that's become a modern-day mecca for witches."

"And you think that's why they were targeted?" Garrison said.

Ray nodded. "Something big is going down, and we're just six days from Halloween. The Temple is planning something. It's why they killed Danielle, why they did something to Abby that drove her insane. At first, it seemed like we were chasing shadows, but now I think it's all connected."

"But what's their endgame?" Garrison asked. "Some symbolic act of revenge?"

Ray thought about what he'd read in Frank's occult crime manual. "The Temple doesn't want them for the symbolism. It wants them for their blood."

CHAPTER TWENTY-NINE

Garrison mulled over Ray's comment. "What you're saying sounds crazy, but I'll be damned if it doesn't fit." He brought them up to speed on his interview with Brittany's roommate, including her secret romance and the trouble they were having locating her girlfriend, Holly.

"What about Brittany's phone records?" Martinez asked. "They've gotta contain something that would help find the girlfriend."

"Holly's number is from a burner phone," Garrison said. "And the only texts she sent were short on details. Most of their communication was through actual talking, which I didn't think teenagers knew how to do anymore."

"Can you triangulate the cell tower pings and find out where Holly lives or works?" Ray asked.

"Holly was extremely careful. She only turned the phone on once a day, and always on campus. The very first ping recorded for that number happened on the outskirts of campus, which makes me think she targeted Brittany from the beginning."

"What's Brittany's family dynamic?" Martinez asked.

"No siblings," Garrison said. "Her parents are holy rollers. They didn't approve of Brittany's sexuality and insisted it was just a phase. Other than that, they seemed like loving parents and were about as distraught as you'd imagine."

"What about Brittany's phone?" Ray asked. "Can we use it to locate where this ritual was held?"

"She turned it off before she left campus, and as far as we can tell, the only location both phones pinged at the same time were either on campus or in public places nearby."

"Whoever these guys are," Ray said, "they're smart and organized, which makes them dangerous."

"And before you ask," Garrison said, "I can't find any information about a pagan harvest festival on the night Brittany was murdered."

"I doubt they would've advertised it," Martinez said.

"For all we know," Ray said, "the whole purpose of the ceremony could've been to remove Brittany's heart."

"But for what?" Garrison asked.

"To use in another ritual," Martinez said. "As an offering to the Six."

"What the hell are you talking about?" Ray asked.

"It's something I read this morning in Abby's *Book of Shadows*."

CHAPTER THIRTY

From page 66 of Abby Garcia's Book of Shadows.

I felt it this time... the power, the energy. Flowing through me like I was some kind of god. Danielle was right. This shit is real. And we can ask for whatever we want—no groveling, no dropping to our knees, no begging like weak fucking Christians.

There's strength in the darkness, an untapped well that's ours for the taking. The Temple of Six holds the keys to anything we could possibly want.

Last night, I asked the Six to punish Max, to make that asshole pay for his betrayal. And this morning, I found out he'd crashed his car and rolled it into a ditch. They had to pry him out of the wreckage with the jaws of life.

He shattered his knees, his pelvis, and even fractured his skull, all because he's too arrogant to wear a seat belt. And now he may never walk again.

I figured the least I could do was send him flowers, so I delivered a single black rose to his hospital room, along with a note that said, "I guess *you're* the broken one now."

The old Abby would've felt sorry for him, would've rushed over to the hospital and fawned over his sorry ass, feeling guilty for ever wishing him harm.

But the old Abby is dead. She was weak and pathetic. A submissive, whiny, people-pleasing bitch. The new Abby is fierce and fearless. She makes no apologies for going after what she wants.

From page 71 of Abby Garcia's Book of Shadows.

DERIK CAVIGNANO

We gather at dusk to whisper their names,
And summon the Six from out of the flames,
A legion of darkness to rival the Prince,
We harness their power and bathe in their strength.

From page 77 of Abby Garcia's Book of Shadows.

Darkness blooms like a flower,
In the woods, at the witching hour,
When silken petals of obsidian hue
Unfurl and spread to subdue
The fading vestiges of the day,
Which die gasping in dismay,
Choked by shadows creeping lithe,
While night beckons…
And grinning demons rise.

From page 81 of Abby Garcia's Book of Shadows.

To the point and past the nurse,
Where sunlight yields to life's long curse,
And through the halls of torchlit walls,
Where conjured thoughts of decay and rot,
Harken back to the rites of yore,
With darkness, blood, and dripping gore,
Where dancing flames paint the night,
As the Temple prepares for sacrifice,
With the offer of a virgin heart,
The gates that hold the Six shall part.

CHAPTER THIRTY-ONE

"Well?" Ray asked, "what do you think?"

Frank stubbed out his cigarette and scowled at them from across the conference room table, a tendril of smoke curling up between them like the essence of a genie. "Christ almighty," Frank said. "You really stepped in it this time."

"Have you ever heard of them?" Martinez asked. "The Temple of Six?"

Frank shook his head and frowned, the slight twist of his lips deepening the creases lining his face, which radiated from the corners of his mouth like cracks in a windshield. "It's the ones you never heard of that you've gotta worry about."

Garrison looked at Martinez. "What do you think these guys are planning?"

Before heading to Frank's house, they'd stopped off at Martinez's apartment to grab the *Book of Shadows*. Martinez laid it on the table before them and flipped open the leatherbound volume to a page she'd earmarked.

"Read these poems," she said.

They all leaned over the book and scanned the text, the stale reek of Frank's ashtray wafting up from the table and making Ray wrinkle his nose in disgust.

Garrison leaned back in his chair and shuddered. "That shit gives me the creeps."

Ray turned to Martinez. "You've had more time to study this than we have. Let's hear your theory."

Martinez brushed a lock of hair from her eyes. "Like you said earlier, I think they're planning something on Halloween. And removing Brittany's heart was part of their preparations. They'll use it as an offering to the Six." She pointed to one of Abby's poems. "If I'm interpreting this right, the Temple worships six demons who they believe have a combined power greater than the Devil himself." She shifted her gaze to Frank. "Last time we met, you said the heart adds power to a ritual and increases the odds of its success. Given Brittany's bloodline, the Temple probably believes her heart holds even greater power, especially if they perform the ritual in Salem."

Frank nodded. "The greater the sacrifice, the greater the reward. Which is where Cassie comes in."

"Do you think she's alive?" Garrison asked. "Or would they have harvested her organs too?"

"A live sacrifice is the ultimate offering," Frank said. "But it may have come down to opportunity."

Ray furrowed his brow. "You're saying something went sideways with Brittany, that they would've preferred to keep her alive?"

"Call it an educated guess," Frank said.

"But what's in it for the Temple?" Garrison asked. "What do they get in return?"

Martinez pointed to the *Book of Shadows*. "There's a passage in here about wealth and immortality."

"So the Temple gets an eternity of riches in exchange for murdering a couple of innocent girls?" Ray asked.

"Not exactly," Martinez said. "The girls are only the key."

"The key to what?" Ray asked.

Martinez leaned forward. "To opening the gates of hell and releasing the Six into our world."

"Come on," Garrison said. "That's crazy. None of this is real."

"No," Ray said, "but the Temple *thinks* it's real, which puts them at a disadvantage because they've gotta follow certain protocols."

"It may help to know these demons," Frank said. "If we can decipher their nature, maybe we can figure out what the

Temple needs for the ceremony. And if that involves stealing certain objects, it could lead us right to them."

"What are their names?" Ray asked. "The six demons?"

Martinez opened her mouth to answer, but Frank cut her off. "Best not to say it out loud. There's power in names and speaking them is almost as bad as praying to them."

"Come on," Garrison said. "You don't really believe that."

Frank fixed him with a steely gaze. "I've seen enough to know we shouldn't take any chances." He lifted a gnarled finger and leveled it at them. "You should all remember that."

Martinez reached for the *Book of Shadows* and rifled through the pages. "Here," she said, stepping back to let them read.

The Legion of Six
- *Malsedar*
- *Tortomal*
- *Sangudon*
- *Septival*
- *Exilenus*
- *Dolotrell*

Frank squinted at the names. "I don't recognize any of them."

"I searched a few demonology websites," Martinez said, but I couldn't find a match even though the sites had hundreds of names."

"I might know a guy who can help," Frank said.

"Who?" Ray asked.

"Someone I got acquainted with back in the heyday of the Satanic Panic. Last I talked to him, he was working at the Hub City Bookshop down in Spartanburg, South Carolina. He's got a side gig where he deals in rare texts and specializes in the occult. If anyone recognizes the names of those demons, it'd be him."

Ray leaned back in his chair. "We need to find out where the Temple plans to hold their ritual." He motioned to Martinez. "Let me see that poem again—the one that mentions a sacrifice."

Martinez flipped back a few pages and pointed to the text.

> *To the point and past the nurse,*
> *Where sunlight yields to life's long curse,*
> *And through the halls of torchlit walls,*
> *Where conjured thoughts of decay and rot,*
> *Harken back to the rites of yore,*
> *With darkness, blood, and dripping gore,*
> *Where dancing flames paint the night,*
> *And the Temple prepares for sacrifice,*
> *With the offer of a virgin heart,*
> *The gates that hold the Six shall part.*

Garrison ran a hand across his cheek, his fingers tracing the shadow of a goatee. "Do you think she could be talking about an abandoned hospital?"

"There's that old insane asylum in Danvers," Ray said. "The one that's supposed to be haunted."

"They turned that into condos," Martinez said. "It used to have a system of tunnels running underneath it, which became a magnet for paranormal investigators. I heard that one or two of the tunnels may still be there, but they're sealed off."

"We should definitely check that out," Garrison said.

Ray reached for the *Book of Shadows* and flipped forward a few pages. Abby's entries ended after page eighty-four, leaving a series of blank pages up to page one hundred. After that, a final gilded page marked the end of the book. Ray was about to snap the book shut, then hesitated.

"What is it?" Martinez asked.

THE BURYING POINT

Ray rifled back to the last entry. "There's a page missing. It's torn so neatly, I almost didn't notice." He lifted the book and angled it into the light. "Hey, Frank, you got a pencil?"

Frank pointed to the far corner of the room, where a dot matrix printer sat on a TV tray. Beside it was a rusted coffee can crammed full of pens and pencils. "Help yourself."

When neither of them moved, Garrison stood up with a groan. "You gotta be kidding me." He retrieved a number two pencil from the can and tossed it to Ray, who caught it one-handed.

"What do I owe you now?" Ray asked. "Five lives plus a pencil?"

Garrison eased his giant's frame back into the conference room chair. "Just show us what you found."

Ray turned the pencil sideways and rubbed the tip across the page, creating an etching from the impressions left by Abby's pen. Many of the words were unintelligible, but what they could make out was a disjointed entry from August 28th.

> *...I don't know... this... anymore... gone...*
> *...too far... innocent... will die. Need...*
> *...get out... warn... police.*

Ray turned the book so that everyone could see.

"August 28," Martinez said. "That's two days before the cops found Abby in the graveyard with her mind scrambled." She pointed to the bottom of the page. "There's something else there."

Ray etched over the spot with his pencil, revealing a circular symbol with six pointed stars and the inscribed head of a Baphomet.

Martinez stared at the page, her eyes growing wide. "I recognize that symbol."

"From where?" Ray asked.

"It's painted on a door... at the haunted house."

CHAPTER THIRTY-TWO

When Ray and Martinez rolled up to the boxy blue rowhome on Lynde Street, they spotted Mrs. Garcia sitting on the stoop in pale green scrubs, staring out at the road and hugging her knees against the cold. They climbed out of the Explorer and approached the house, the crushed gravel driveway crunching underfoot.

"Everything okay?" Martinez asked.

Mrs. Garcia stood up and swept a graying lock of hair behind her ear. "Detectives? I didn't expect to see you again."

"We wanted to ask you a few questions," Ray said.

"About what?"

"We think what happened to Abby was deliberate," Martinez said. "And whoever did it may be involved in Cassie's disappearance."

"Just don't repeat that to anyone," Ray said. "It could compromise the investigation."

As Mrs. Garcia made a lip-zipping gesture, a sudden roar emanated from within the house.

"What the hell was that?" Ray asked.

"Father Maroney's in there with Abby. He finally got the bishop's permission for an exorcism."

"Do you mind if we go inside?" Martinez asked.

But Ray had already stormed inside the living room. He'd forgotten how dark Mrs. Garcia kept the place. She claimed it had a soothing effect on Abby, that it kept her demons at bay, but as Ray fumbled blindly past the sofa, he wondered if the opposite was true.

The scent of burning sage permeated the air, masking the underlying stench of a caged animal. The door to Abby's room yawned open. She was thrashing on the queen poster bed, her wrists secured by nylon restraints.

Father Maroney loomed over her, his black robe draped with a purple stole. He was younger than Ray expected—early forties, with a slight build and rakish brown hair. He clutched a leatherbound Bible in one hand, and a bulbous silver wand in the other, a tool Ray recognized as a holy water sprinkler.

"By the power of Christ, I command you—release this child!"

Abby kicked off the bedsheets and bent her legs, the motion drawing up her nightgown and exposing a dark thatch of pubic hair.

Father Maroney drew closer to the bed, making the sign of the cross with the holy water sprinkler. He chanted a prayer in Latin, then followed it with one in English.

"All things in heaven and earth shall bend the knee in the name of Christ our Lord."

Abby uttered a throaty chuckle, and the voice that followed was raspy and laced with malice. "You've eaten from the forbidden fruit, priest. God has cast you from his garden."

Father Maroney sheathed the wand of holy water in his rope belt and gripped the Bible with both hands, showing Abby the golden cross embossed on its cover. He chanted another prayer in Latin, his voice rising.

> CRUX SACRA SIT MIHI LUX,
> NUNQUAM DRACO SIT MIHI DUX.
> VADE RETRO SATANA!
> NUNQUAM SUADE MIHI VANA!
> SUNT MALA QUAE LIBAS.
> IPSE VENENA BIBAS!

Abby spread her legs and raised her pelvis, swaying her hips and moaning, offering the priest a view of her labia, which glistened in the candlelight.

Father Maroney brandished the Bible, wielding it like a shield. "May the holy cross be my light. Let not the dragon be my guide."

"Your god has deserted you," Abby said.

"Be gone, Satan!"

"It's not Satan you should fear but the coming of the Six."

"May the Lord God lay hold of the beast and cast it into the abyss."

Abby let out a guttural laugh. "Get on your knees, tainted priest, and suckle from the flower of ecstasy.

"Do not tempt me with thy vanities, demon!"

Abby lashed out with her foot and kicked the Bible out of his hands. It sailed through the air, pages rustling, before striking the floor with a reverberating smack. Before Father Maroney could step back to pick it up, Abby's legs snaked around his body and pinned his arms against his sides.

Father Maroney let out a startled grunt, and Ray lunged forward, grabbing a fistful of his robe. But Abby's reflexes were cat-quick, and she drew the priest toward her like a praying mantis snatching its prey. Except instead of dragging Father Maroney into her jaws, Abby wrapped him in a leglock and buried his face in her crotch.

Father Maroney flailed his legs, his feet kicking against the hardwood as Abby's thighs squeezed his head in a vice.

Abby's laughter echoed throughout the room. "Take this body and eat it," she said, mocking the Eucharistic Prayer.

Martinez appeared beside Ray and wrapped her arms around Father Maroney, trying in vain to free him.

"Recant your faith, priest, and drink the blood of the new and everlasting covenant!"

Ray and Martinez pulled together, but Abby held the priest in an iron grip. *Christ*, Ray thought. *How the hell is she this strong?*

Father Maroney's legs stopped flailing, his feet barely scraping against the hardwood.

"He's suffocating!" Martinez said.

Ray relinquished his grip and rushed toward the headboard, intent on putting Abby in a sleeper hold.

"Be careful, Ray! Don't look her in the eyes."

He wanted to tell Martinez that she was being crazy, that there was a perfectly logical explanation for what was happening. That he could stare into Abby's eyes all day long and see nothing but an advanced case of psychosis.

Except everything about the situation felt wrong. The air around Abby seemed dense, and the closer he got to her, the more difficult it was to breathe, the hair on his arms bristling as if electrified.

Ray wasn't the religious type, but he had an open mind and trusted his instincts. He understood you couldn't possibly know everything, that some things existed beyond the plane of human comprehension. And when he looked at Abby writhing on the bed, her eyes rolled back to the whites, it was almost as if he could sense the energy trapped within her, something dark and terrible trying to claw its way out.

Her head swiveled as he stepped past her, tracking his movement, and he suddenly felt faint, as if he'd stood up too fast on a hot day. He swayed on his heels, the bedroom reeling around him, disappearing altogether as if he was stumbling through the fog of a dream.

He half-felt, half-sensed dark things zipping around his peripheral vision, like giant bats buzzing around his head. An ominous voice called out to him, and he wasn't sure if he was hearing it with his ears or with his mind.

Raaayyyy.
You're a sinner, Raaayyy.

Suddenly he saw an image of Tina kneeling before him, his boxers pulled down around his ankles, the wet heat of her mouth closing around him.

Join us, Raaayyy.
It's where you belong.

Abby grinned at him, and he knew he must be going insane, because somehow her mouth had transformed into a geometric spiral of fangs, like a jagged staircase descending into the black void of infinity.

"Ray!"

It was Martinez's voice, and it snapped him out of it. He lunged for the bed and swept his arm around Abby's neck. Her flesh felt hot and feverish, oiled with sweat. He engaged the sleeper hold, the crook of his elbow wrapped around her throat as he pushed against her head with his other arm.

At first, she went rigid, and he thought she might throw him like a rodeo clown. But after a few seconds, her body relaxed and her legs went limp, sending Martinez and the priest stumbling backward into the bedroom wall.

Ray jumped away from the bed, a wave of revulsion sweeping over him at the lingering sensation of her touch.

Martinez helped Father Maroney to his feet, his face smeared with a garish scimitar of menstrual blood. She escorted him to the living room, but he kept on going, fleeing out the front door without a backward glance.

Abby moaned from the bed, slowly regaining consciousness. When her eyes opened, her gaze settled on Ray, and she regarded him with unadulterated hatred.

He returned her gaze and approached the footboard. "Where's Cassie?" he asked. "Where's the Temple holding the ritual?"

Abby sat bolt upright, roaring her now familiar refrain.

E tenebris, bestia resurget!
E tenebris, bestia resurget!
E tenebris, bestia resurget!

***

Ray pulled Abby's bedroom door shut and spotted Mrs. Garcia in the kitchen talking to Martinez.

"I don't know what to do. Abby seems to be getting worse every day."

"Has the bishop been to see her?" Martinez asked.

Mrs. Garcia shook her head. "Father Maroney says the bishop isn't experienced with exorcisms. He barely gave Father permission to perform this one."

"From what I saw," Ray said, "I'm not convinced Father Maroney knows what he's doing."

"He told me he trained at the Vatican in some special program."

Ray gazed at the front door, which Father Maroney had left wide open in the wake of his retreat. "You sure he passed the course?"

Mrs. Garcia drew a deep breath, her shoulders sagging. "I don't know where else to turn. Abby's hardly lucid anymore, and when she is, she's crippled by migraines and stomach cramps."

"Maybe you should try another priest," Martinez said. "Father Maroney might be in over his head."

Or tainted, Ray thought, recalling Abby's words.

"I suppose I may have no choice. I just… I can't believe this is happening." She wiped her eyes with the heel of her hand. "I should've forbidden Abby from seeing her new friends. I should've thrown her occult paraphernalia into the trash. I thought it was just a phase, but now look what's happened."

"I'm sorry," Martinez said. "But it might comfort you to know that Abby tried doing the right thing in the end."

"What do you mean?"

"She wrote something in the *Book of Shadows*," Ray said. A page was torn out, but we could decipher the impression of a few words."

"What did it say?"

"That things had gone too far," Martinez said. "And that she planned to contact the police."

"We need to see what else was on that page," Ray said. "Do you have any idea where it might be?"

"Abby ripped the page out during one of her episodes."

"Where is it now?" Ray asked.

"It's gone."

"What do you mean gone?" Martinez asked.

She lowered her eyes and frowned. "She ate it."

CHAPTER THIRTY-THREE

"What time is it?" Garrison asked. He was seated across from Ray and Martinez in one of Mystical Brew's leather wingchairs.

"Seven forty-five," Ray said, frowning at a recent text alert from Michelle.

When are you coming home?

Sorry, he texted. *Gonna be another late one.*

"We should head over to the haunted house at eight," Martinez said. "Get there right when it opens."

Again? Michelle responded.

Sorry, Ray texted. *But we're getting close.*

Okay, but the kids really miss you.

I miss you guys too, he responded, noting she'd left herself out of the equation. *I'll take time off when this is over. I promise.*

Garrison pointed to Ray's phone. "What's the matter? You in the doghouse again?"

"My home away from home," Ray said.

The sound of shattering glass diverted their attention to the counter, where Jason stood holding an empty serving tray next to his Bob Marley T-shirt. He stared down at the floor and shook his head, his confused expression suggesting he was as high as a kite. "Ah, man," he said, "that's a lot of glass."

It was a slow night at the coffee shop, and Jason had let the staff go home a half hour earlier. Before they left, Ray asked if they'd ever heard of the Temple of Six, but none of them had. Martinez had gotten a similar response when making the rounds at Raven's Wing.

Ray swallowed his last sip of cappuccino and stared at the ring of foam clinging to the inside of the mug. The circular pattern reminded him of the spiral of fangs he'd glimpsed when Abby grinned at him. Martinez had mentioned seeing something similar on their first visit—another face lurking behind Abby's. It sounded nuts, but what were the odds they'd shared a hallucination.

He wasn't ready to accept that Abby was possessed by a demon, but he'd seen enough that he couldn't rule it out either.

"You two have been awfully quiet since we got here," Garrison said. "What happened at Abby's?"

Ray and Martinez exchanged a glance.

"You saw it, didn't you?" Martinez asked. "The face?"

"I don't know what I saw, Martinez."

Garrison knit his brows. "What are you talking about? Some freaky ass paranormal shit?"

"Just to give you an idea," Ray said, "the priest ran out of the house and never looked back."

"Come on." Garrison turned to Martinez. "Is he for real?"

"It's the truth."

"What do you think Abby meant when she said Father Maroney was tainted?" Ray asked.

"I don't know," Martinez said, "but maybe that's why the exorcism didn't work."

"Assuming you believe in that stuff," Ray said.

"I believe it," Garrison said. "When I was five, we moved into the top floor of a multifamily in Dorchester, and that place was haunted as hell."

"What happened?" Martinez asked.

"The place was old," Garrison said. "A mansion from the 1800s that fell into ruin and got chopped up into apartments. It was the kind of place that just felt *wrong*, you know? Even at five, I felt it. And it wasn't anything I could put my finger on. There were no visions, no voices—at least, not then—but I wouldn't set foot in my parents' bedroom. Not even for all the candy in the world.

"We lived there for a few weeks before we noticed that something was playing with my toys while we slept. We'd wake up and find all my letter magnets from the fridge scattered across the floor and the hands of my Fisher Price clock moved from where I'd set them. You remember those teaching clocks with the yellow hands that you had to move yourself? It was one of those.

"At first, my mom thought I was sneaking out of my room at night and making a mess. But after she confronted me and realized I was telling the truth, she looked like she'd seen a ghost. After that, she started arranging the fridge magnets in alphabetic order before bed, so she'd be able to see if anything was disturbed.

"She didn't tell me until years later, but one night she woke up to someone calling her name in the bedroom, even though my dad and I were fast asleep. When she climbed out of bed and went into the kitchen, her name was spelled out in the refrigerator magnets. And not just *Bea*—the name everyone called her, the only name I knew her by—but *Beatrice*, scrawled across the fridge at the height of a child a few years older than me."

"That's pretty creepy," Martinez said. "What'd she do?"

"She called the church and had the apartment blessed. And that was the end of it. But ever since then, I've hated haunted houses. Fake or not, that shit gives me the heebie-jeebies."

***

They stood outside of the velvet ropes to the haunted house and waited while the bouncer flirted with a couple of teens dressed like slutty renditions of Wednesday Addams. After typing one of the girls' number into his phone, the bouncer waved the pair through.

"Wear that outfit when you drop by my apartment," he said. "And bring your friend along; I'll show her a good time too."

The girls giggled and waved before vanishing through the battered steel door of the haunted house.

When the bouncer turned back to collect their tickets, he flashed Ray and Garrison a cocksure grin, as if he was the biggest stud in town.

Martinez glared at him. "Give me your phone."

The bouncer stared at her in confusion, his expression morphing from alpha male to omega dumbass in the space of a second. "Do you want my number too?"

Martinez reached behind the bouncer and plucked the phone out of his back pocket. Then she seized his pinky finger and yanked it backward until he dropped to his knees with a yowl.

Ray elbowed Garrison in the ribs. "I love it when she does this."

"Ow! Hey! What the hell?"

Martinez stared down at the bouncer and spoke to him in a calm voice. "How old are you?"

"Twenty—ow—five."

"And what about those girls?"

"I don't know."

Martinez twisted his finger back even farther.

"Ow, stop! You're gonna break it!"

"How old were those girls?" she repeated.

"I don't—ow—sixteen!"

"That's more like it," Martinez said. "When I let go, you're gonna delete that girl's number from your phone, aren't you?"

"Yuh... yes."

When Martinez relinquished her grip, the bouncer staggered to his feet and hugged his hand to his chest. As she passed him the phone, Ray could sense anger radiating off the bouncer like heat. Guys like him weren't used to being humiliated. He seemed like he wanted not just to punch her, but to bash her face in.

"Delete the number," Martinez said, showing her badge.

The bouncer scowled but did as she asked. Afterward, he shoved the phone into his pocket and puffed out his chest.

"We need access to the haunted house," Martinez said.

The bouncer folded his arms. "I don't see any tickets."

"We're on police business," Martinez said. "And I don't think I need to remind you that a woman died here yesterday."

The door to the haunted house swung open before the bouncer could answer. The manager, Steve Rancic, stepped out, wearing maroon slacks and a leather jacket over a polyester shirt, the top two buttons obscured by a wild thatch of chest hair. He looked like the manager of a 1970s disco, and Ray honestly had no idea if his outfit was meant to be a costume.

"What's going on here?" Rancic asked.

The bouncer pointed at Martinez. "This bitch assaulted me."

Rancic chuckled. "You gotta be careful with this one. She's a feisty little minx."

"We need another look around," Ray said.

"Do you have a warrant?" Rancic asked.

"Why?" Ray asked. "You got something to hide?"

"I'm running a business. I can't afford any disruptions."

"We're not gonna bother anyone," Garrison said. "Just gonna poke around a little."

"You're welcome to come in, but without a warrant, you're no different than any other paying customer."

"How much?" Garrison asked.

"Thirty dollars."

"Seriously?" Garrison said.

Rancic shrugged. "My condo in Cabo doesn't pay for itself." He leered at Martinez. "Did you change your mind about my invitation?"

Martinez folded her arms. "Do you want to keep all your teeth?"

"You got any cash?" Ray asked, looking at Garrison. "All I've got is a card."

"Me too," Martinez said.

Garrison grumbled as he withdrew ninety dollars from his wallet.

Rancic accepted the money with a shit-eating grin and waved them through the velvet ropes. "Right this way."

CHAPTER THIRTY-FOUR

When the heavy steel doors of the haunted house swung shut behind them, a familiar recording warned there'd be no escape from the manor of the damned. It was pitch-black, and Ray's eyes hadn't yet adjusted to the darkness. He could sense Martinez and Garrison huddled beside him as the building suddenly came alive with the sound of moaning zombies. When the glowing arrows appeared on the floor, Garrison shuffled forward and walked right into the first trap.

The rotting corpse dropped from the ceiling and dangled from its noose, landing so close to Garrison that one of its skeletal limbs knocked the campaign hat right off his head. Ray would've enjoyed the moment more if Garrison hadn't stomped on his foot when he jumped back and screamed, but it was still pretty damn amusing.

Martinez doubled over in hysterics as Garrison scooped up his hat and scowled at them. "You knew that was coming, didn't you?"

"You want us to hold your hand?" Ray asked.

"Where's the damn door?" Garrison asked. "The one with the symbol?"

Ray opened his mouth to answer, but the zombies responded for him.

Brainzzzz. Eat your brainzzzz!

"It's on the fifth floor," Martinez said.

Garrison shook his head. "No way I'm trekking through five floors of this shit."

A zombie crawled past on its belly and seized hold of Garrison's ankle. "Brainzzzz."

Garrison yelped in surprise and kicked the costumed teen in the shoulder.

"Ow, watch it!" the kid said, rolling over and crawling away.

"You don't ever grab a man's leg like that," Garrison said.

"We can take the back stairwell," Martinez said, "bypass the exhibits."

"Dammit," Garrison said. "Why didn't you say that in the first place?"

"And spoil the fun?" Ray said. "Where'd you learn to scream anyway, the Girl Scouts?"

Martinez snorted. "I've never heard a Girl Scout make a sound like that."

Garrison waved a finger at them. "I'm not digging this new dynamic."

Martinez led them away from the moaning zombie herd and directed them to the back of the building. The stairwell came into focus just as the strobe lights activated, eliciting disembodied screams from across the floor.

"This place is a nightmare," Garrison said.

"Try dropping through the floor and landing in the catacombs," Ray said. "I guarantee you'd shit your pants."

Garrison shook his head in disbelief. "Worst ninety bucks I ever spent."

The stairwell was intended to be the exit for those who'd made it to the top of the haunted house. A sign posted beside it read, *No Reentry,* and a section of velvet ropes directed people to a gray steel door that would deposit them into the alley behind the building.

As they started their ascent, Ray flashed back to Danielle tumbling down the same stairwell, her hair billowing over her shoulders as the mask of the corpse bride flew off and landed on the steps like a deflated balloon. He recalled the sickening thud of her head smacking the concrete, followed by

216

a series of rolling thumps as her body tumbled down to the next landing, her neck cocked at a ghastly angle.

His gut told him that she was pushed, but proving it wouldn't be easy. Their only chance was to track down the cult and pit the members against each other with a promise of leniency.

They passed a few customers on the stairwell descending toward the exit, laughing and gasping and saying things like: *"Holy shit, that was crazy;" "Bro, I almost had a heart attack;" "Mikey legit pissed his pants."*

As their voices trailed away, Ray nudged Garrison in the arm and said, "You're the Mikey of our group."

Garrison gave him the finger as they reached the fifth-floor landing, where the strobe lights were in full effect. A guy in a clown mask was screaming like a lunatic and lunging at customers with a bloody butcher knife.

"Come on," Martinez said. "I think the door's over here."

They followed her to the right and traced the length of the wall, stopping about a third of the way in where a black steel door was set into the brick. Someone had painted a white symbol in the middle of the door—a Baphomet drawn over a six-pointed star, all of it inscribed within a circle.

Martinez tried the knob. "It's locked."

"Let me see." Ray jiggled the knob. "A credit card should do the trick."

Martinez grabbed his arm as he reached for his wallet. "We can't do that. Not without a warrant."

"Rancic gave us permission to poke around," Ray said.

Martinez shook her head. "Poke around doesn't mean breaking into locked areas. Anything we find will be inadmissible in court."

"You're right," Ray said. "But if we ask Rancic for permission, he'll probably say no. And it could take days to get a warrant. I'd rather find Cassie alive and wind up tainting the evidence than play it by the book and be too late to save her."

Martinez looked at Garrison for a second opinion.

"It's a moral dilemma," Garrison said. "But I agree with Ray. The benefits outweigh the risks."

Ray pulled out a credit card and jimmied the lock. "Sometimes you gotta work outside the lines, Martinez. Just be careful you don't stray too far because it can be a slippery slope." He pushed against the door, which opened with a drawn-out creak.

Garrison glanced over his shoulder. "Coast is clear."

Ray closed the door after they'd stepped inside, locking it with a button on the interior knob. Garrison retrieved a flashlight from his utility belt and clicked it on, illuminating a narrow stone stairwell winding down into darkness.

A layer of dirt coated the stairs, and as they made their descent, they kicked up loose particles, which floated like pixie dust in the bright arc of Garrison's beam. Their footfalls echoed as they wound deeper into the heart of the building, and Ray wondered why they hadn't arrived at another landing. By his estimation, they'd traversed at least twenty-five steps.

"Where are the light fixtures?" Martinez asked.

Ray glanced up at the ceiling and realized it wasn't simply a matter of the lights being off. It was a complete lack of hardware—not a single bulb, wire, or junction box as far as the eye could see.

Garrison lifted a hand and signaled for them to stop. He pointed his flashlight at the stairs ahead of them. "No one's been down here," he said. "No footprints anywhere."

"That symbol has to mean something," Martinez said.

"Let's keep going," Ray said. "And see where this leads."

They resumed their descent, and Ray counted forty more steps before they reached the bottom. There was nothing down there except for a heavy steel door marked with an *Emergency Exit* sign, the muffled sound of city traffic emanating from beyond.

Garrison laid a hand on the door's horizontal push bar. "I guess we're out of luck."

"Wait!" Martinez said.

Ray and Garrison turned to look at her.

"What is it?" Ray asked.

"Don't you feel it?"

"Feel what?" Garrison asked.

"Wind," Martinez said. "It's coming from behind us."

"She's right," Ray said, his pulse quickening.

Martinez approached the rear wall opposite the emergency exit, moving methodically along the gray stones and feeling for the source of the draft. The wall narrowed where it met the overhanging stairs, and Martinez crouched down and squeezed herself into the tight cavity, flattening her palms against the air like a mime trapped in a box. She waved at Garrison. "Give me a light."

Garrison shone the flashlight where she indicated, revealing a softball-sized stone that appeared loose. Martinez gripped the stone in both hands and wiggled it, drawing it out of the wall. She placed it on the ground between her feet and peered through the hole.

"What do you see?" Ray asked.

Martinez inserted her arm into the hole and reached down, triggering an audible click that resulted in a section of the wall shifting slightly, revealing the dark outline of a hidden door. Martinez pulled it all the way open, the muscles of her neck straining with the effort.

"Holy shit," Garrison muttered. "It's a tunnel."

Martinez ducked inside without waiting for them. Ray reached into his sports coat and unbuttoned the strap on his holster. He nodded to Garrison, who slipped inside without a word. Ray picked up the stone and slid it back into place before pulling the door shut, leaving it open just a crack in case they needed to make a hasty exit.

***

The tunnel sloped down more than a dozen feet, the walls and ceiling lined with weathered bricks, the floor earthen and hardpacked. Martinez knew from her days as a tour guide that the variations in the bricks' size and color meant they were handmade and dated back to the mid-1800s.

A torch hung on the wall beside her, its wooden handle threaded through an iron ringlet. The top was blackened and bulbous—some kind of fabric covered in pitch. She brought her nose to it and detected the faint aroma of a burned-out campfire.

"Was it used recently?" Ray asked.

"Hard to tell," she said. "Definitely not in the last couple of days."

Ray leaned in and took a whiff. "It's not fresh, but who knows?"

Martinez felt a twinge of annoyance at Ray's double-checking, but then again, she'd failed to identify the missing page in Abby's *Book of Shadows*. And while she could accept the fact she had more to learn, the glaring oversight made her blood boil. She was better than that, dammit.

But you found the tunnel, Mija.

Even in death, Papi's voice was kind and reassuring. And although it helped a little, it also reminded her of her mother, who was probably out roaming the streets, selling her body for heroin. It would kill Papi to know the woman he adored had fallen so far, that his death had driven her to a lifetime of addiction and all the manner of hell that went with it.

The flashlight momentarily blinded her as Garrison swept the beam across the walls. "There's some scuff marks on the ground," Garrison said. "Maybe we'll find footprints farther ahead."

They resumed walking, traveling the length of a football field before Martinez felt a cool wind gusting from above. Garrison must've felt it too, because he shone the flashlight on the ceiling, where a brick was missing on both sides.

"Looks like ventilation shafts," Garrison said. "I can't tell for sure in the dark, but I bet they reach to the surface."

"This place reminds me of Abby's poem," Martinez said. "Look at this." She pulled her phone out of her pocket and showed them a snapshot from the *Book of Shadows*.

> To the point and past the nurse,
> Where sunlight yields to life's long curse,
> And through the halls of torchlit walls,
> Where conjured thoughts of decay and rot,
> Harken back to the rites of yore,
> With darkness, blood, and dripping gore,
> Where dancing flames paint the night,
> As the Temple prepares for sacrifice,
> With the offer of a virgin heart,
> The gates that hold the Six shall part.

"You can check torchlit walls off your Bingo card," Ray said, "but I don't know about the other parts."

"Is there a hospital around here?" Garrison asked. "Could we be beneath one?"

"I don't think so," Martinez said.

Ray ran his hand over the wall. "These bricks look old. I bet this tunnel's been around a long time."

"Yeah, but for what purpose?" Garrison said.

"It's an old smuggling tunnel," Martinez said.

"A smuggling tunnel?" Ray asked. "From when?"

"They were built in the 1800s by wealthy merchants and politicians."

"Why?" Garrison asked. "That's too early for Prohibition, isn't it?"

"It wasn't alcohol," Martinez said. "At least not then. They did it to avoid paying taxes on the spice trade. Ships would land at the harbor, and before the goods got weighed at the Customs House, half the product would disappear into hidden tunnels."

"Wait a second," Ray said. "Aren't we more than a mile from the harbor right now?"

"The tunnels ran between the wharf and different homes and businesses across town. There was even an underground train station to haul cargo."

"Is there a map of these tunnels?" Ray asked.

Martinez shook her head. "They're mostly on private property, and the ones on public land that haven't collapsed are used by the utility companies. My old boss said there's probably a whole network out there nobody knows about."

"Why have I never heard of that?" Garrison asked.

"You're not the only one," Ray said. He motioned to the darkness ahead, which was damn near absolute. "Let's see where this takes us."

They set out once again through the tunnel, following the hardpacked trail as it curved right and joined up with another passageway branching off to the left. There wasn't any debate on the road not taken, since the path on the left was strewn with fallen bricks and mortar, not to mention a few rotted beams and piles of earth that sealed off any possibility of safe passage.

"I guess we go right," Garrison said, leading them past the debris field.

A few minutes later, Martinez drew to a halt. Ray and Garrison stopped to look at her.

"Do you hear that?" she asked. "Voices… coming from over there."

Ray turned to Garrison. "Kill the light, will you?"

Garrison clicked off the flashlight. They stood huddled together on the path, blinded by darkness, completely motionless. They all heard it now—a female voice mingled with a bunch of men, the words muffled and unintelligible.

Martinez's eyes were beginning to adjust to the darkness, and she could discern a few narrow slants of light projected onto the wall of the tunnel, as if filtering through cracks in the mortar.

"There's something on the other side," she whispered.

They crept further into the tunnel, hugging the right side, which split into a passageway that sloped upward into a narrow gap between walls. Ray crouched down and peered through one of the cracks in the masonry. As Martinez and Garrison squatted beside him, Ray muttered, "Holy shit."

Martinez was about to ask him what was wrong, but then she saw it for herself. They were staring down into the nave of a church, where more than a dozen congregants had gathered to worship. But this was no ordinary mass.

The robed man officiating the mass stood in the apse beneath an upside down cross. Tar-black candles burned on the altar, protruding from holes bored into a trio of human skulls. He wore an elaborate goat's mask and read from a leatherbound volume, his words sounding brutal, alien, and blasphemous, like no language she'd ever heard before—a Catholic mass read backward.

The congregants wore a less elaborate variety of goat's mask, but unlike the high priest, they wore nothing else, their naked bodies lithe and glistening, bathed in the golden glow of candlelight.

A woman in a black robe materialized from behind the high priest, wearing a goat's mask that was even more elaborate than his. She sauntered over to the center of the transept holding a golden chalice and carrying herself with an air of nobility. The congregants gathered around her, bending in supplication at her feet.

The high priest laid the book on the altar and led the congregation in a guttural chant, the responsorial sounding like the frenzied bark of hyenas fighting over a kill. Then all at once, the voices fell silent, and the priestess shrugged her shoulders, causing the robe to slide down to the floor and revealing a perfectly contoured body, her bare breasts exposed to the nave.

She raised the chalice over her head and uttered something halfway between a prayer and a growl before tipping the chalice forward and spilling the contents onto herself. The bright-red surge of what looked like blood coated her breasts in a glistening sheen as dark rivulets trickled down to her abdomen and legs.

The congregants mewled like feral cats and pressed forward, jockeying for position as they removed their masks and licked blood off her body, starting at her feet and working higher until they lapped it from between her legs and suckled it from her breasts. The priestess moaned in pleasure, her hips swaying in a rhythmic circle until her pelvis shuddered uncontrollably, a scream rising in her throat as she reached the pinnacle of climax.

She sank slowly to her knees and laid down on her back, spreading her legs as the congregation mounted her, one after the other, their faces a mask of shadows in the flickering light.

"What the hell is going on?" Garrison whispered.

"It's sex magick," Ray said. "Frank's manual says it's supposed to harness the power of orgasm to increase the strength of their spells."

Martinez drew a finger to her lips. "Shh, they'll hear us." She pulled out her phone and accessed the video app, angling the lens against one of the larger peepholes. The congregants' faces were obscured by shadows, but maybe they could enhance the video enough to make a positive ID.

"There's gotta be a way in there," Ray whispered.

Martinez knew what he was thinking—they could bust the cult for trespassing and then leverage the charges for information on Cassie, squeeze them until the lower guys cracked.

Garrison stood up and brushed past Martinez. "I bet there's a door somewhere." He aimed the flashlight at the ground and shielded the beam with his hand, trying to prevent the glow from being detected through the peepholes.

Martinez followed the beam's trajectory as it illuminated the narrow gap between walls and washed over an impassable barrier of stone.

Garrison and Ray tiptoed past Martinez, their feet scuffing against bits of loose mortar that someone had chiseled away to create the peepholes. She was about to shush them again, but they quieted as soon as they returned to level ground, the soft thud of their footfalls tracing the path parallel to hers.

After a long silence, she whispered into the dark. "Did you find anything?"

Ray's voice drifted back to her. "There's a locked door at the end of the tunnel."

"Can you open it?"

"We're working on it," Garrison said.

Martinez slipped the phone back into her blazer pocket and leaned forward to peer through the wall.

Ray and Garrison argued in harsh whispers as they struggled with the door. One of them pushed too hard and rattled the frame, sending a ripple of concern through the throng of gyrating congregants, who glanced up and froze like a bizzarro pack of prairie dogs.

"They heard you!" Martinez said, watching as the congregants scrambled into the pews and grabbed their robes, some pausing to put them on, others running into the sacristy, the small room to the right of the apse.

The high priestess rose to her feet and slipped on her robe, hurrying to join the high priest, who shoved the candles, skulls, and chalice into a black duffle bag.

There was a loud crash as the door flew open, and Martinez saw Ray and Garrison charge out into the nave, yelling, "Stop, police!"

Most of the congregants had already fled into the sacristy, but a couple of burly men remained behind—masked, robed, and armed with bo staffs. They held their ground as Ray and Garrison approached, wielding their bows in a lethal cross shoulder spin that suggested they were skilled in mixed martial arts.

Ray reached for his gun, only to have the weapon swatted away in a flash. Garrison drew his too, but suffered a similar fate, one end of the bo disarming him, the other striking him in the shoulder and making him yelp in surprise. Ray dropped to the ground to avoid a strike. He rolled across the tiled floor and reached for the Taser at his belt, the arm of his sports coat straying into the outer ring of blood from the ritual.

Garrison spun to the left, narrowly avoiding a jab to the face. He backpedaled to a nearby pew and hurled a Bible at the assailant's face. It hit the guy's mask, knocking it askew, and in the split second before he could adjust it, Martinez caught a glimpse of Evan Brody.

The crackle of Ray's Taser shifted her attention from Brody to the other assailant, who had a wired lead attached to his stomach, snagged dead center in his robe. The man dropped to his knees and jittered with a surge of electricity.

Garrison crouched low and charged Brody, but Brody sidestepped and followed through with a savage blow to the back that dropped Garrison like a sack of grain. A moment later, Brody swung the bow in a hacking motion that severed the Taser's wire. He reached into his jeans pocket and tossed something onto the ground between them.

"Take cover!" Ray yelled.

He and Garrison flung themselves in opposite directions as a cylindrical object clattered to the floor within a dozen feet of them. It detonated with a concussive bang and a flash of light that left Ray and Garrison writhing on the floor of the nave, covering their faces as a plume of smoke billowed into the air and obscured the congregants' retreat.

Martinez abandoned the peephole and rushed through the tunnel into the church. She dropped to one knee between Ray and Garrison. "Are you guys okay?"

Ray rolled over and groaned. "They hit us with a stun grenade."

Martinez pointed through the dissipating smoke to the sacristy. "They went through that door," she said. "There must be another tunnel."

Ray groped for the nearest pew and hauled himself to his feet. Garrison was in worse condition, and Martinez had to use all her strength to help the big man up.

Ray attempted to charge ahead, but his equilibrium was off, and he wound up stumbling into the pews like a drunk.

Martinez rushed forward and hurried through the door to the sacristy. The room was small, maybe ten-by-ten, with barely enough space for a desk, a bookshelf, and a couch. But the congregants were nowhere to be seen, and there were no obvious doors or hiding places.

The interior consisted of worn gray carpeting and drab walls devoid of any cracks that might suggest a secret door. She planted her hands on her hips. Where the hell had they gone?

And then she saw it—a tuft of rug curled against the wall beneath a rack of garments. Not glued down and slightly out of place. "Guys!" she yelled. "I found it!"

She slid her fingers beneath a corner of the rug and peeled it back, revealing a layer of dusty planks with a trap door cut into the center. She was reaching for the door's rusted iron handle when Ray and Garrison staggered in.

"Wait up," Ray said. "We're coming with you."

"But you're in no cond—"

An explosion ripped through the underground tunnel and rattled the floor like an earthquake. The shockwave blew the trapdoor clean off the hinges and struck Martinez on the side of the head.

She fell backward onto the desk and gawked at the ceiling, only vaguely aware of blood running down her cheek. She could hear Ray and Garrison calling her name, but their voices grew distant as darkness crept into her field of vision and spread like an ink stain, until her entire world had faded to black.

CHAPTER THIRTY-FIVE

A second explosion sent Ray staggering toward the wall. He extended his arms to cushion the blow but ended up colliding with Garrison and falling onto the desk beside Martinez.

Martinez groaned, her eyes fluttering open. She glanced around the room, confusion clouding her face. "How long have I been out?"

"Not long," Ray said. "Maybe ten seconds."

"What happened?" Martinez asked.

"They rigged the place to blow," Garrison said. "They probably had a couple of strategically placed charges in case they ever got caught."

Ray knew from Frank's manual that performing a black mass inside a Catholic church would've been the ultimate score, since the power attained from the ritual depended on making a mockery of a Catholic mass. And by sneaking in and out through the tunnels, the cult members had the full run of the place, which would leave them plenty of time to clean up the evidence.

A flickering glow emanated from the nave, and Ray suddenly realized that any latent prints or other DNA evidence left behind by the congregation were about to go up in flames. He slammed his fist against the desk and swore. "Come on," he said, "we'd better get out of here."

Martinez eased herself off the desk, wincing as she fingered the bloody welt on her forehead.

"You need a hospital," Ray said. "You might have a concussion."

Garrison lifted her into his arms. "Let's boogie."

Ray followed them out of the sacristy and into the nave, where an explosion had ripped a hole into the floor and reduced the surrounding pews to splinters. The seats that hadn't been destroyed were all ablaze, the ceiling above them turning black, the paint blistering.

Ray figured they had a minute, maybe less, before the fire consumed the ceiling and spread to the walls, sucking oxygen from the air and superheating the church to the point where survival would be impossible.

Garrison ran with Martinez cradled in his arms, her head buried against his chest. He crossed the apse and maneuvered around a trail of burning hymnals, making a beeline to the opposite end of the church where the flames were less intense.

Ray followed closely behind, one hand cupped over his mouth to protect against the billowing clouds of smoke. They hugged the aisle along the leftmost wall and were halfway to the rear exit when a flaming beam dropped from the ceiling and crashed into the center of the nave.

"Come on," Ray said, "keep going."

When they reached the exit, Ray risked a glance over his shoulder. The whole interior was engulfed in flames, a roaring inferno stretching from floor to ceiling.

Garrison threw the doors open wide and they stormed out into the night, gasping and wheezing. They retreated to a spot across the street and sat down on a cold granite curb, watching the flames spread across the roof to consume the spire.

A warble of sirens rose in the distance, but the old church collapsed long before the first truck arrived, reduced to a twisted pile of burning wreckage, like a signal fire from the depths of hell.

CHAPTER THIRTY-SIX

When Ray pulled up to the entrance of Salem Hospital, he found Martinez leaning against a light post with a bandage on her forehead and an ID bracelet on her wrist. Her hair was pulled back into her usual ponytail, but a dark purple crescent underscored her left eye, as if she went three rounds against the champ to secure her release.

After last night's CT scan registered a mild concussion, the doctor insisted Martinez remain overnight for observation. But Martinez, being her stubborn self, initially refused, and when an orderly accidentally blocked her exit, Ray had to intervene before things got ugly.

Ray waved to her as he shifted into park and rolled down the window. "How was your night, Martinez? You make any more friends?"

Martinez showed him both middle fingers before climbing into the Explorer. "Just get me some coffee."

"I thought you weren't supposed to have caffeine after a concussion."

"It was a mild concussion, so I'll get a mild roast."

"Makes sense." Ray turned right onto Highland Ave, heading toward Mystical Brew.

Martinez opened the glove box and rooted through it. "Do you have any sunglasses? This light is killing me."

Ray reached up to his visor and passed her his aviator glasses. "Shouldn't you be taking the day off?"

"I'm fine." She slipped the glasses on and settled back into the seat. But her posture was stiff, as if too much movement was hurting her head.

"You sure you're okay?"

Martinez massaged her forehead and groaned. "I think I need to reexamine my life."

"It could've happened to any of us. You were in the wrong place at the wrong time. Don't let that discourage you."

"That's not what I mean."

"Then what do you mean?"

"When I got discharged from the hospital, you were the only person I could think to call." She drew a shuddering breath and turned away from him. "I don't have any family or any close friends. How pitiful is that?"

"Give yourself a break, will you?" Ray said. "You had a rough childhood. You had to put up walls to protect yourself. And you did that better than anyone. I mean, Christ, you're one of the toughest people I know. And a hell of a good detective."

"That means a lot," she said. "Probably more than it should."

"I'm no shrink," Ray said, "but maybe it's time you took down some of those walls and let a few people in. You don't need a fortress to protect yourself anymore."

A ghost of a smile formed on Martinez's lips. "Maybe you're right."

When they got to Mystical Brew, Ray ordered two coffees from Tracy and delivered them to Martinez, who was sitting at a back booth with the sunglasses still on.

"What do you remember about last night?" Ray asked.

"Do you mean before or after those guys kicked your asses in the church?"

Ray grunted. "The last thing I expected was to get attacked with a bo staff. Who the hell uses a bo staff?"

"It's a common weapon in taekwondo. If I'd brought mine, those guys would've gone down for the count."

"I believe it."

"It tells us something about the Temple though," Martinez said.

"Go on."

"Some of their members are trained in martial arts. Demolition too."

"You think they're ex-military?" Ray asked.

Martinez was silent for a moment. "Oh my God," she said, finally. "Brody."

"What?"

"Danielle's boyfriend—Evan Brody. I saw him in the church. Garrison hit him with a Bible, and it knocked his mask askew."

"You're just remembering that now?"

Martinez pointed to the bandage on her forehead. "Concussion."

Ray stood up. "We'd better take these coffees to go."

***

Brody was a no-show for his job at Kettle & Cauldron. His manager said he'd called out sick, but he wasn't home when Ray and Martinez visited his apartment. When they got back to headquarters, they gathered in the briefing room with Chief Sanderson, Captain Barnes, and Garrison.

Martinez brought them up to speed. "Brody is an ex-Marine and a second-degree black belt. He served eight years and was honorably discharged."

"You're sure it was him?" Sanderson asked. "How long was his mask loose?"

"Only for a second," Martinez said. "But we'd just interviewed him earlier in the day, so his face was fresh in my mind."

"I doubt that's strong enough to support a warrant." Sanderson looked at Ray and Garrison. "Did either of you recognize Brody?"

"We were under attack," Ray said. "If his mask slipped off, I didn't see it."

"Me neither," Garrison said.

"Did you see any tattoos?" Captain Barnes asked.

Ray shook his head. "They were wearing full-length robes."

Garrison gazed across the conference table at Martinez. "What about that video you took through the peephole? Was the crime lab able to enhance it?"

"No. The quality was too bad."

Sanderson drew a deep breath. "I'll go out on a limb and request the search warrant for Brody, but don't be surprised if it gets rejected. In the meantime, we'll put out an APB."

"I think we should hold off on the APB," Ray said. "If the media picks up on it, we risk sending Brody into hiding."

"Isn't he already in hiding?" Sanderson asked.

"I've got a hunch it's only precautionary," Ray said.

"What gives you that idea?"

"Brody doesn't know Martinez ID'd him," Ray said. "They weren't even in the same room together. And Garrison and I had no idea who he was. I think he's just being cautious, waiting to see if his name hits the papers in connection with the church fire. If it doesn't, I bet he emerges from hiding."

"But we went to Kettle & Cauldron to ask about him," Martinez said. "He might take that as a sign we recognized him."

"Not necessarily," Ray said. "I told him at our last visit I wasn't done with him yet."

Sanderson motioned to Captain Barnes. "What do you think?"

"If Cassie's still alive," Barnes said, "then every second counts."

"If she's alive," Ray said, "she'll stay that way until Halloween. But if Brody's face gets plastered on the news, we might never see him again, then we'll lose the link to Cassie."

Barnes fingered his mustache. "Why don't we stick with the search warrant for now and keep the rest quiet."

Sanderson nodded. "I'll put in the request to Judge Reynolds. Are there any other updates before we adjourn?"

"I've got one on the church," Garrison said. "The state's arson experts are working with Salem Fire to sift through the rubble, but the preliminary reports say that everything's charred beyond recognition."

"What about the tunnel?" Martinez asked.

"It's completely caved in, and the structural engineers advised us against digging it out."

That meant the only evidence salvaged from the church was the blood used in the ritual. Ray had gotten some of it on his sleeve when he dropped to the ground to avoid Brody's attack. DNA analysis was expected back from the crime lab within the next twenty-four hours.

In the meantime, Ray couldn't help but wonder if the destruction of the tunnel reached all the way back to the haunted house. He got up from the conference table. "There's something else I want to check out."

CHAPTER THIRTY-SEVEN

Steve Rancic's claims of being a savvy businessman had always smelled like bullshit to Ray, and now that he saw the dilapidated apartment building Rancic called home, he knew he was right to trust his instincts. The five-story brick walkup had a trash-littered stoop and a row of broken windows that had been repaired with cardboard and duct tape.

A gang of tough-looking teens loitered on the stairs wearing baggy clothes and baseball hats cocked to the side. Distrustful eyes followed Ray and Martinez as they approached, their boisterous trash-talking cutting off abruptly.

A teen sporting a red Adidas hat looked at Martinez and raised his hands defensively. "We didn't do nothing, Officer Martinez."

"We're not here for your crew, Manny. And it's *Detective* Martinez now."

"Ooh," another teen said. "The lady is moving up."

Martinez gestured for them to clear a path to the door, and they obeyed without question.

Ray suppressed a grin and followed Martinez past the teens and into the building. As they headed up a creaky wooden staircase to Rancic's third-floor unit, Ray said, "You have history with them?"

Martinez smirked. "The last thing these gangbangers want is to get beat up by a girl in front of their homies... *again*."

"You are a true badass, Martinez."

She looked at him and shrugged, as if to say, *what'd you expect?*

When they arrived at apartment 317, Ray rapped his knuckles against the door. "Rancic, open up."

Footfalls emanated from within as someone crept toward the door to gaze out the peephole, their stealth betrayed by creaky floorboards.

"We hear you," Martinez said. "Open the door."

A chain jingled, followed by the metallic snap of deadbolts disengaging. The door swung open to reveal Rancic wearing nothing but a pair of silky black boxer briefs. He was lean but muscular, his chest covered in a thick thatch of reddish-brown hair.

"You interrupted my workout," Rancic said. He gestured to his torso and leered at Martinez. "You want to reconsider Cabo?"

Ray pointed to Rancic's chest. "I doubt she's into shag carpeting."

Rancic's eyes narrowed as he noticed the bandage on Martinez's forehead and the nasty shiner below it. "What happened to you?"

Martinez folded her arms. "None of your damn business."

"I'd hate to see the other guy," Rancic said, elbowing Ray like he was in on the joke. "Am I right?"

"What do you know about the tunnel below the haunted house?" Ray asked. He kept the question deliberately vague to see how Rancic would react.

"The trap door?" Rancic said. "It drops into the catacombs and—"

"We're not talking about the attraction," Martinez said. "We want to know about the tunnel to the church."

Rancic wrinkled his brow and glanced at Ray. "What's she talking about?"

"There's a hidden tunnel that can only be accessed through a stairwell that goes directly from the fifth floor to the ground floor."

"I don't know any stairwell like that."

Ray studied Rancic's face. He seemed legitimately perplexed, but then again, the guy was a professional huckster.

236

"There's a symbol on the door," Martinez said. "A circle with a six-pointed star and a Baphomet in the center."

"I know the door, but I don't have a key to it."

"Bullshit," Ray said.

Rancic held up a hand. "No, I'll prove it to you." He pointed to the foyer table, where a ring of keys sat atop the distressed wooden surface. "That's the only set of keys I have. They open a half dozen different doors, but not the one you're talking about. We can go down there right now and try them out."

Ray swept his gaze over the tiny apartment. Nothing seemed out of the ordinary. No weapons, no occult paraphernalia, no news clippings plastered to the walls. Just your garden-variety shithole. "You mind if we take a quick look around?" Ray asked.

"I'd rather you didn't, but I got nothing to hide."

Rancic motioned for them to follow and proceeded to give them the two-dollar tour, giving them a peek into the bedroom, the bathroom, and the closets. And he was right—there was nothing incriminating, nothing illegal. Just a whole lot of vintage porn on VHS.

"Just say the word," Rancic said, "and I'll let you borrow some." He winked at Martinez. "I've got guy-on-girl, girl-on-girl, guy-on-girl-on-guy."

Martinez held her thumb and forefinger an inch apart. "I am this close to hurting you again."

"Sorry," Rancic said. "I didn't figure you for a prude."

"Who drew the symbol on the door?" Ray asked. "The one you don't have a key to?"

"I hire a bunch of artsy goth kids and let them go nuts with the spooky shit. All I do is buy the paint and supplies. It's like free fucking design, which is why I can afford that place in Cabo."

"You're a regular Warren Buffett," Ray said.

"I know you're busting my chops," Rancic said, "but Buffett lives on the cheap, just like I do."

"What about the Temple of Six?" Martinez asked.

"Never heard of it."

***

Although it would've been satisfying to catch Rancic red-handed, the visit wasn't a total loss. They followed Rancic to the haunted house, where he demonstrated that none of his keys fit the lock to the door with the Baphomet symbol. Ray got Rancic's permission to jimmy the lock with his credit card, and all three of them took the stairs down to ground level.

Several of the stones comprising the hidden door had been blown into the stairwell, and when Ray shone his flashlight into what remained of the door, he could see nothing but rubble, as if the whole tunnel had collapsed in the explosion.

"It doesn't prove anything," Ray said after Rancic drove away from the haunted house in a dented red Subaru. "He might keep the key to that door separate from the others."

Martinez buckled her seat belt and slipped Ray's sunglasses onto her face. "It's possible the landlord never gave him a key."

It was true that Rancic didn't own the building. Their research showed it was owned by a real estate investment trust that was, itself, owned by a hedge fund. The haunted house was just one of a hundred properties in the trust's portfolio.

Earlier that morning, they'd spoken to the property manager who oversaw the buildings in the fund, but she wasn't aware of a key to that door either.

Ray exhaled sharply and eyed Martinez in the passenger seat. "You may be right about the key, but I'm not ready to cut Rancic loose just yet."

CHAPTER THIRTY-EIGHT

Father Maroney poured himself another shot of Jack Daniel's and held it up to the light, staring into the depths of the rich amber liquid until his eyes blurred with double vision. Had it been fifteen years already? Fifteen years since his apprenticeship with Father Abruzzi at the Church of the Holy Staircase in Rome?

He was a young man back then, practically a boy, fresh out of the seminary, full of optimism and idealism, inspired by the work of Father Candido Amantini and his protégé, Father Gabrielle Amorth, whose urgent call to bolster the ministry of exorcism had rallied him to the cause.

Few people understood the gravity of the situation, the degree to which the Devil meddles in the affairs of the living. His legion lurks in the shadows—watching, waiting. Seeking to prey upon the weak and the vulnerable, desiring to corrupt the body and subvert the soul. The Devil is as cunning as he is manipulative, the most powerful of all the angels. But his pride led him to mount a rebellion against God, and when the insurrection failed, he and his followers—angels no more—were cast down from heaven to lick their wounds on Earth.

In the two years Father Maroney had trained in Rome, he'd attended hundreds of exorcisms. He'd seen firsthand the work of the Devil, the wickedness wrought upon the world of man. He'd casted demons out of men, women, and children, and he'd liberated homes of diabolical infestations. Some of the exorcisms had taken multiple visits over the course of days or even weeks. But in the end, he'd subdued the demons in the name of Christ and cast them into the fiery pits of hell.

All of them, that was, except for the demon residing within Abby Garcia.

He drank another shot of whiskey and relished the trail of liquid fire that slid down his throat and blossomed within his stomach, enveloping him in a tingling warmth like the reassuring weight of a security blanket.

In all his years performing exorcisms, he'd never encountered a demon as formidable as Abby's. When he laid hands upon her and performed the rites, the demon refused to speak its name, its nature, or how and when it entered the body. It showed no fear at the invocation of Christ. It did not scream, did not wail. It resisted him every step of the way with brute force, cruel tricks, and mockery.

That reminded him of the most recent humiliation—the near suffocation as Abby drew his face into the swampy heat between her thighs. He'd gagged on the fetid stench of her unwashed body and felt the maddening tickle of pubic hair against his forehead as a disembodied laughter echoed in his ears.

Had he imagined what came next? The horrible feeling of something sinuous and snakelike emerging from her genitalia and pressing against his lips, trying to force its way inside his mouth.

Tainted priest.

The demon's words returned to him in a mocking lilt.

Father Maroney poured himself another shot and drank it with a trembling hand. He returned it to the table with a heavy fist, which jolted the bottle, almost toppling it.

Despite all his piety, all his training, he'd been played a fool. He knew better than to underestimate the cunningness of Satan, and yet he'd fallen victim to the beast's carefully laid trap. It'd only taken one misstep in the form of a pretty young woman who spoke to him after mass. He'd dismissed her wanton gaze as eagerness to learn the gospel. And when she asked to return later that evening for a private Bible study, he knew he should have refused.

But one mistake led to another, and soon he'd violated his vow of celibacy and defiled both himself and the church. Not once, but many times. And when their affair came to an end, the woman revealed her demonic intentions. A black mass would be held in his church, and he was welcome to attend.

He'd lost his temper and threatened to call the police, but the woman merely smiled. "All those times you fucked me," she said. "In the pews, on the floor, against the altar... it's all on video. Do you want to be defrocked, Father Maroney? Or worse, excommunicated from the Church?"

He should have resisted, but his pride got in the way. And so he turned a blind eye to their blasphemy. And in return, he kept his status as a respected member of the clergy, one of the rising stars in the diocese.

But in truth, he was no better than the Devil himself.

CHAPTER THIRTY-NINE

"You gotta be shitting me," Ray said.

"Do I look like I'm in the mood to shit anybody?" Martinez asked. She pointed to her computer monitor, which was open to the website for St. Gregory's Parish. "It says it right there."

Ray leaned over her shoulder and stared at the boldface name underneath the heading *Our Pastor*.

"Father David Maroney," he said. "What are the odds?" He handed Martinez her coat. "Let's go."

Father Maroney lived around the corner from the church in a modest home that had the Spartan look of a parsonage. When the Father answered his door, he regarded Ray and Martinez with bleary eyes. He reeked of booze, and when he motioned them inside, he staggered to the kitchen table like a drunken sailor.

"Can I offer you a drink?" Father Maroney asked, motioning to a half-empty bottle of Jack Daniel's. His voice had the deliberate cadence of a drunk feigning sobriety.

"We're on duty," Ray said, joining him at the table. "I assume you heard about the church?"

Father Maroney folded his hands. "One of the parishioners notified me. I haven't worked up the courage to go there myself, but I… I hear it's a total loss."

"I'm afraid so," Martinez said.

"Do you have any idea what caused the fire?" Father Maroney asked. "I heard rumors of a gas line explosion, but the church isn't hooked up for gas."

"Does the Temple of Six mean anything to you?" Ray asked.

Father Maroney hiccupped. "No."

"We think a cult did this," Martinez said. "One that practices black masses. We suspect it's not the first time they've used your church."

Father Maroney frowned, and the fine lines that radiated from his eyes and accentuated his brow creased deeply, for a moment making him appear like a much older man.

"Have you ever seen evidence of cult activity in your church?" Martinez asked.

Father Maroney nodded slowly.

"Like what?" Ray asked.

"Small things here and there. The lights left on. Things moved around. Black candle drippings on the altar."

"Why didn't you go to the police?" Martinez asked.

"I was afraid of—" He hiccupped again. "Of what the parishioners would think."

"So you did nothing?" Ray said.

"I changed the locks, made sure all the windows were secure. It's been quite a while since I've seen anything suspicious."

"The other day in Abby's bedroom," Ray said. "What did Abby mean when she said you were tainted?"

Father Maroney flinched as if Ray had slapped him. "We are all sinners, Detective. All of us are tainted in the eyes of the Lord… in one way or another."

"Do you really think Abby is possessed?" Martinez asked.

Father Maroney nodded. "Hers is a particularly troubling case."

"Can you bring in reinforcements?" Ray asked. "Send for the bishop?"

Father Maroney chortled. "The bishop wouldn't know a demon if it pissed in his tea."

"He doesn't believe?" Martinez asked.

"He's too much of a skeptic to be an effective exorcist. He'd rather not have anything to do with that sort of… *unpleasantness*, as he calls it. So he delegates the work to me."

"Are you sure it's a demon," Ray asked, "and not some kind of psychosis?"

"She exhibits all the signs," Father Maroney said.

"And what are those?" Ray asked.

"Displays of superhuman strength, speaking in tongues, and knowing what's hidden, to name a few."

Ray had a flashback to Abby's bedside and the intrusive voice that had spoken up in his mind and called him a sinner. It showed him an image of Tina going down on him right before he'd pushed her away, and not from his own vantage point, but from someone who'd been watching.

"We heard Abby's doctors diagnosed her as paranoid schizophrenic," Martinez said.

Father Maroney scoffed. "Most doctors aren't trained to recognize the difference between afflictions of the mind and those of the spirit." He raised a finger and pointed at them, one eye squinted shut as if to prevent double vision. "Under Canon Law, a priest cannot perform an exorcism until he determines with moral cert… certitude that the victim is truly possessed by demonic forces and not merely suffering from physical ailments or psychological issues."

"How do you decide that?" Ray asked.

"By consulting with doctors whom I'm acquainted, doctors who have experience in these matters. You've seen her condition for yourselves. What do you think?"

"I'm open to the possibility," Martinez said.

Ray thought about the dizziness he'd experienced in Abby's bedroom, the dark things that had zipped around his peripheral vision, and the strange way Abby's mouth had transformed into a geometric spiral of fangs. It took him a moment to realize Father Maroney and Martinez were both staring at him, waiting for an answer.

"Well?" Father Maroney asked.

"Let's just say I'm on the fence." But a part of him knew better, the part of his brain that existed beyond reason, where survival relied upon primitive instinct and primal fear.

"This cult," Ray said. "The Temple of Six. It's very important that we find them. We think they murdered at least one girl and kidnapped another to sacrifice on Halloween. Can you think of anything else that might help our search? Anything you might've found in the church or any direct encounters you've had with these people?"

Father Maroney shook his head, but his eyes appeared haunted. "This town... it's a hotbed of evil. You should start your search with the witches, pagans, and satanists who sell their wares in every corner shop. People think it's harmless, a bit of spooky fun, but these trinkets and chants and seances, they all serve the Devil. They'll tell you it's white magick, but I assure you, all magick is black. And you must never invite the darkness inside.

"I've seen the many faces of the beast, and with every new shop that opens, every new witch who casts a spell, every pew that remains empty, every church that shutters its doors or burns to the ground, the beast grows stronger. The forces of darkness are gathering, detectives... so you'd better be careful."

Father Maroney reached for the bottle of Jack and poured himself another shot, then raised his glass in a toast. "May God have mercy on our souls."

CHAPTER FORTY

After coordinating the overnight assignments at the shift change, Ray waved to Martinez as she climbed into her Corolla and drove off the lot. He was about to head home himself when he caught a glimpse of a woman signaling to him from across the street.

She was strikingly beautiful, the kind of woman who could stop a man in his tracks. She wore a black cocktail dress made of a shimmery fabric that glittered under the streetlights. It showed off her toned legs and accentuated every curve of her body. She held a tire iron in one hand and a cell phone in the other, although it took Ray a moment to process those last couple of details.

"I'm sorry to bother you," she said, "but I have a flat. Would you mind giving me a hand?"

"Uh, sure. No problem."

He followed her to the side of the road where a yellow Jeep Wrangler was parked with a deflated rear tire. She bent over in front of him and pointed to the jack, which she'd positioned under the frame near the wheel well. He averted his eyes as her dress inched up, not wanting to come across as a creepy pervert.

"I heard you can crack the frame if you put it in the wrong spot," she said.

"You've got the right spot. You just need to use that rod as a lever to crank it."

"Like this?" She grinned over her shoulder as the back of the Jeep began to lift.

"You got it."

"Are you a cop?" she asked.

"Boston Police detective."

"What are you doing in Salem?"

"Long story. Aren't you cold in that dress?"

Her lips curled into a devilish grin. "That's funny, most men think I'm hot in this dress."

"I can see their point," Ray said.

She went to work removing the lug nuts. "I appreciate that you're not trying to take over. I've always wanted to do this myself."

"Yeah, I got that impression."

"Most guys would insist on helping, thinking that it'd increase the odds of getting into my pants."

"You're not wearing pants," Ray said.

The woman laughed and pointed a manicured finger at him. "Oh, you're sneaky. You act like a feminist, but you're just here for the show."

Ray held up his hands. "I'm just kidding. I'm honestly trying not to look."

The woman's grin returned. "If we're being honest, I don't mind if you look. But I will accept a hand swapping out the tire."

Ray pulled off the tire and replaced it with the spare.

"What's your name?" the woman asked as she tightened the lug nuts. "I'm Amanda."

"Ray."

"This may sound forward, Ray, but do you want to get together sometime?"

Ray frowned, suddenly feeling uncomfortable. "I'm married."

Her devilish grin made another appearance. "We could keep it casual, no strings attached."

"I don't think so."

She eyed him skeptically. "I saw the way you were looking at me. Are you really turning me down?"

"I'm married," he repeated.

Amanda pursed her lips, forming a damn near irresistible pout. "It'll be our little secret."

"I can't, I'm sorry."

Amanda folded her arms. "Can I ask why?"

"Because I love my wife. And I hurt her once. I won't ever make that mistake again."

"Not even if she was guaranteed to never find out?"

"Not even then."

"How about I give you my phone number in case you change your mind?"

Ray shook his head and turned away. "Have a nice night, Amanda."

***

Ray was halfway home when Jacob called him in a panic.

"Thank God you picked up," Jacob said.

"What's going on?"

"I just overheard something that you should know."

"What?" Ray asked.

"Are you sitting down?"

"I'm driving. Spit it out."

He could hear Jacob drawing a deep breath. "Michelle hired a private investigator to honey trap you."

Ray slapped the steering wheel. "You're kidding me."

"I'm sorry you had to find out this way."

"Christ, Jacob. I could've used that information fifteen minutes ago."

"Oh shit."

"How long were you sitting on that?" Ray asked.

"I called as soon as I heard. What happened? What did you do?"

"What do you think?" Ray asked, relishing the opportunity to torture his little brother.

Jacob groaned. "I have a friend who's an excellent divorce lawyer."

"You think we can get a two-for-one discount?" Ray asked.

"What do you mean?"

"Well, after I had sex with that woman, I gave her your number and said that you'd probably be interested."

"What? Why would you say that? Oh my God. Megan's gonna kill me!"

Ray erupted in laughter. "Relax, little brother. I passed the test."

"You didn't do anything?"

"That's right."

"And you didn't give her my name?"

"Well, that I did."

"Oh my God."

"Seriously, Jacob, you're too easy. It's not even fun."

"Wait, so you turned her down?"

"Of course I did."

"Thank God! Was she pretty?"

"Yeah," Ray said. "She was pretty."

"So… are you gonna confront Michelle? Because if you do, you didn't hear it from me."

"Don't worry, I won't rat you out."

"Are you mad?"

"Honestly," Ray said, "I'm glad she did it. How else would she ever know for sure?"

"You're not gonna say anything? Just pretend like it never happened?"

"It's probably for the best."

***

"Daddy, come see what we built!"

Allie grabbed Ray by the hand and led him into the living room, where Jason and Petey stood in front of a tower of wooden blocks that reached up to Jason's chin. Ray's mom had dropped off three baskets of blocks last weekend after rediscovering them in a forgotten corner of her attic. Seeing them had transported Ray back more than twenty years to when he and Jacob used to spend hours tinkering with different designs in order to build the tallest structure possible.

"Will you help us get it to the ceiling?" Jason asked.

"Yeah," Petey said, dancing in a circle. "To the sheeling!"

Ray eyed the stock of raw materials. "All right, but we'll need to start from scratch. Everyone grab a block from the basket."

Allie scrunched her nose. "But don't we need to knock it down first?"

"Oh, we're gonna knock it down," Ray said, wielding a block and taking aim.

The kids erupted in cheers and snatched up their own blocks as Michelle walked into the room. "What are you guys doing?" she asked.

Jason grinned. "Demolition."

Michelle shook her head. "Is it a coincidence that you were all playing so quietly before your father got home?"

"That's because they were doing it wrong," Ray said.

Michelle arched an eyebrow and gave him a playful shove. "All right then," she said, staring down at the kids. "Demolition it is."

The words had barely rolled from her lips before the kids threw their blocks and the tower collapsed in a tumultuous implosion of wooden rectangles raining onto the floor.

Allie plugged her ears against the commotion, and Sparky, who'd been nosing a bone in the corner of the room, began barking like a maniac.

Petey clapped his hands in delight. "I love breaking shings!"

***

They never did manage to reach the ceiling, but the kids seemed satisfied with a tower that stood as tall as Ray. Or at least they were until Sparky chased a tennis ball right through it and showered everyone with an avalanche of wood. After dinner, Michelle surprised them with a bushel of pumpkins and three sets of kid-friendly carving tools. The kids insisted on carving the pumpkins themselves and refused to accept any constructive criticism, which led to a serious degradation in the quality of the final product.

Luckily, the kids didn't see it that way and marched up to bed happily. Once they were settled down for the night, Ray and Michelle arranged the jack-o'-lanterns on the front porch and stepped back to soak in the view.

"I can see the headline now," Ray said. *"Pumpkin Family Butchered In Their Own Home. Suspect Still At Large."*

Michelle snickered. "Did you see Petey's? It looks like someone bashed its face in with a baseball bat."

Ray nodded gravely. "It's truly horrifying."

Michelle burst out laughing, and when Ray joined in, she slapped his arm and shushed him, but that only made them laugh harder. When they finally regained their composure, they walked arm-in-arm into the house.

"Let's have a glass of wine," Michelle said, leading him into the kitchen.

"What's the occasion?"

Michelle smiled at him. "A rare night of domestic bliss."

"Just like old times," Ray said.

Michelle poured them both a glass and tucked a lock of hair behind her ear. "Here's to old times."

Ray lifted his glass. "And to all the new times yet to come."

CHAPTER FORTY-ONE

The Danvers Lunatic Asylum had a notorious reputation as a psychiatric hospital that opened in the late 19th century and grew into a sprawling complex of gothic-style buildings that housed more than a thousand mental patients who were subjected to a variety of questionable treatments, including electroshock therapy, prefrontal lobotomies, and straitjacket confinement.

The red brick buildings were connected by a labyrinth of underground tunnels that provided shelter for doctors and nurses shuttling between wards during the cold New England winters. Designed with self-sufficiency in mind, the campus generated its own power from an onsite plant that ran on steam and pumped electricity through the tunnels.

Although most of the complex was torn down and converted into apartments in the early 2000s, the administrative buildings were preserved for their architectural features, which included gothic spires and gabled roofs. The remaining wards were replaced with updated modern replicas, and the tunnels beneath were sealed off during construction.

Martinez had heard rumors some of the tunnels were still accessible under the residences, but she had it on good authority it was nothing more than urban legend. The abandoned power plant was another story, however. It sat on a remote wooded section of the complex, boarded up and covered in graffiti, its brick smokestack still reaching into the sky like a cancerous finger.

A single tunnel snaked out of the plant and made a gradual U-turn in the direction of the administrative buildings. Martinez could see the faint evidence of its existence, as if the ground around it had eroded just enough to discern its outline. She clicked on her flashlight and followed the shadow of the tunnel a few hundred yards into the woods, where an exposed cross section terminated like a drainage pipe, the gaping black maw of the opening muzzled by a chain link grate.

A friend of hers from the Danvers Police had found a body at this location a year earlier, and while the city kept sealing off the tunnel, people kept finding new ways to access it.

It was pitch-dark at this end of the complex, but the moon was nearly full, its eerie light turning the swaying canopy of trees into a host of skeletal shadows that lurched over the ground like phantoms escaped from the asylum's cemetery.

Frost-hardened leaves crunched beneath her feet as she approached the opening. The beam of her flashlight washed over the grate, illuminating a section where someone had cut the galvanized steel links away from the pole.

Something moved in the woods nearby, the stealthy sound of a snapping twig commanding Martinez's attention. She whirled toward the sound, staring out into the night, but it failed to repeat itself.

Probably just an animal. A skunk, or maybe a raccoon.

After a long moment of deafening silence, she crouched down and peeled the fencing back with both hands, clenching the flashlight between her teeth as she squeezed her body through the gap. One of the severed links snagged her blouse and tore the fabric halfway up her back, exposing her bare skin to the frigid caress of autumn.

Shit!

The grate snapped into place behind her, making a sudden metallic clank like the slamming of a prison door. She bit her lip against a scream and cursed under her breath instead. She had nothing to prop the grate open with, which meant she'd lose precious seconds should she require a quick escape.

She drew a deep breath to steady her nerves and aimed her light into the tunnel, illuminating a blackness so absolute that it appeared solid. The tunnel measured fifteen feet across, but her light failed to penetrate more than a couple feet in either direction.

So far, the tunnel seemed as empty as it was abandoned, with an overturned gurney and a rusted old wheelchair the only relics to suggest this once served as a medical facility. A moldering rot permeated the air, a wet fungal odor mingled with the stench of decay. Somewhere up ahead, the muted echo of water dripping from the ceiling registered at such even intervals that it seemed to be marking the passage of time.

Martinez swept the flashlight in increasingly wider arcs, revealing horizontal pipes running the length of the wall, the flaking paint suggesting the tunnel was once gleaming white from top to bottom. But the antiseptic cleanliness had since faded beneath a scrim of moss, the spaces in between spotted with fuzzy dark clusters she guessed was some kind of toxic mold.

Thankfully, she'd come prepared with a surgical mask, which she paused to slide into position on her face. As she stared ahead into the darkness, Abby's poem whispered through her mind.

> *To the point and past the nurse,*
> *Where sunlight yields to life's long curse,*
> *And through the halls of torchlit walls,*
> *Where conjured thoughts of decay and rot,*
> *Harken back to the rites of yore,*
> *With darkness, blood, and dripping gore,*
> *Where dancing flames paint the night,*
> *As the Temple prepares for sacrifice,*
> *With the offer of a virgin heart,*
> *The gates that hold the Six shall part.*

She was convinced it contained a hidden message, something she could solve in time to rescue Cassie from ritualistic sacrifice. She'd passed the old nurse's barracks on her way to the power plant, so she could check off that element of the poem. But what about the point? Could that be some kind of geographical feature?

It didn't quite fit in with this place, but maybe she was missing something. She could give another checkmark to the halls of decay and rot, and maybe the torchlight was poetic license. But what did Abby mean by sunlight yielding to life's long curse? Was it a reference to being institutionalized?

The rest of the poem depended on the ritual itself, which wouldn't happen until Halloween, but this place seemed like the perfect setting for a sacrifice. But as she tiptoed forward in the dark, she didn't see any signs of occult paraphernalia. No upside-down crosses, no skulls, no Baphomets, no black candles. Not even a trace of occult graffiti or any abandoned altars.

Then again, she was only halfway through the tunnel, and so far, she hadn't encountered anything that resembled a hidden door or passageway. She was about to write the trip off as a total bust when she heard a rustling up ahead where the tunnel curved to the left.

She clicked off her light and flattened her body against the wall, wondering if whoever was whispering had noticed the glow of her flashlight. She hadn't yet rounded the bend, which meant the light might not have penetrated around the corner. She cocked her head to listen but couldn't decipher the words over the maddening echo of dripping water.

She held her breath and inched forward, the fingers of her right hand curled around the grip of her gun. She transferred her weight from her back foot to the front, moving soundlessly. The whispering voices continued, more urgent now. Two men, maybe more. She could pick out every few words, her eyes detecting a ghostly green light emanating from their direction.

"...picking... pulses... can't... orb..."

"...there... see... thermal..."

Martinez's foot caught the cratered edge of a pothole. She twisted her ankle and fell in a heap, the sudden whiplash sending a jolt of pain radiating through her head and making the wound behind her bandage throb in time with her pulse.

"The fuck, bro? What the hell is that?"

"Dude, don't—"

A hulking form emerged into Martinez's field of vision, backlit by his companion's flashlight. He wore a clunky pair of headphones and held something rectangular in his hands, like an old satellite phone. His jaw dropped open when he registered Martinez's Glock aimed at his heart.

"Holy fuck, it's got a gun!"

"Salem Police!" Martinez yelled. "Drop it!"

The man raised his hands over his head, but didn't let go of the instrument. "It's an EMF detector."

The other guy stepped out from behind his friend, holding a device with a long antenna. He was half the size of his companion and had shaggy hair and a scruffy beard. "Please, we just—"

"Who the hell are you?" Martinez asked, no longer certain these guys belonged to the Temple.

"We're ghost hunters," the big man said. "We've got our own YouTube channel."

The skinny guy shook his head. "You scared the shit out of us, bro. This place is like crawling with paranormal activity. Fucking dials are all lit up."

Martinez clicked on her flashlight and directed the beam at their equipment. She let out her breath in a long, shuddering sigh, trying to slow her racing heart. "How far back does that tunnel go?"

"About fifty feet before it dead-ends at that wall."

Martinez followed the path of the man's flashlight and saw nothing but brick. She pushed past them, wincing as her ankle bore her full weight for the first time since twisting it. She couldn't discern any entry or exit points. No trap doors, no visible seams of any kind.

"Who are you looking for?" the burly guy asked.

"I can't believe you came here alone," the skinny guy said.

"Have you ever heard of the Temple of Six?" Martinez asked.

They shook their heads in unison. "Nah, man, but that sounds spooky as shit."

Martinez sighed. "All right, let's go. No more trespassing."

"We were about to wrap anyway," the burly guy said. "Come on, Ben, let's get out of this lady's way."

Ben pulled a business card from his pocket and handed it to her. "Check out our YouTube channel. We're the BS Ghost Ravagers."

Martinez raised an eyebrow. "BS?"

"Yeah, Ben and Steve. Subscribe to our channel, and don't forget to smash that *Like* button."

"How about you get out of here before I smash your equipment?"

"Somebody's got a temper," Ben muttered as he approached the exit.

Martinez rubbed her forehead, her fingers brushing the edge of the bandage. Now that the adrenaline had drained from her system, she suddenly felt exhausted. "Where's your car?" she asked, realizing she hadn't spotted another vehicle on her way in.

"We live in the complex," Steve said.

After they peeled back the fencing and exited into the brisk autumn air, Martinez watched the men amble along a paved pathway toward the front of the complex. When they disappeared around the bend, Martinez turned and walked toward her car. As she got within a dozen feet of it, another twig snapped in the woods.

Martinez drew her gun and aimed into the shadows, where the branches of a spruce rustled with the furtive movement of something trying to stay concealed. "Don't move!" she barked. "Salem police. Come out slowly and put your hands where I can see them."

A hush fell over the woods, the night becoming so quiet Martinez could hear her own pulse thumping at her temples. And then came another rustle, softer this time. Stealthy. Like someone shifting their weight, considering their options.

"Any sudden movements," she said, "and I *will* shoot. This is your last warning."

A sigh drifted through the trees. "All right. You got me. I'm coming out."

That voice, Martinez thought. *It sounds like—*

She held her ground as a brawny pair of hands emerged from the branches, palms turned outward to show that he was unarmed. His body came next, creeping out of the shadows until the moonlight fell upon his face.

Frasier!

He was dressed in his police blues and grinned smugly at her.

"What the hell are you doing in the bushes?" Martinez asked.

"When I saw you leaving the precinct, I could tell you were going after a lead."

"So you followed me?"

"Are you gonna put that gun down?"

Martinez lowered her weapon. "Why did you follow me?"

"I wanted in on the action."

"You're supposed to be staking out Evan Brody's apartment."

"I should've gotten that detective job, Martinez. We both know I'm more qualified. But ever since the chief showed up, the whole department has gone woke. The only thing missing from my resume is dark skin and a pussy."

Martinez clenched her jaw and resisted the urge to pistol whip the sonofabitch. "Why were you hiding in the trees, Frasier?"

"I heard a noise and went to check it out."

"Don't give me that bullshit. You want me to notify the chief you deserted your post? Or are you gonna man up and tell me what this is about?"

Frasier folded his arms. "Fine. I wanted in on the action, wanted the glory of taking down the bad guys… especially since you went without backup. And don't think I won't tell the chief that either."

"That doesn't explain why you were lurking in the trees."

"I followed you into the tunnel, but when you stumbled into those ghost hunters, I realized the whole thing was a waste. So, I hightailed it out of there."

Martinez nodded. "You didn't want to get caught leaving your post with nothing to show for it."

"You gonna rat me out, Martinez?"

Damn right she should rat him out. Although giving him a pass might help bury the hatchet. "Just get back to your post, Frasier, and don't ever pull a stunt like that again."

CHAPTER FORTY-TWO

There weren't many things that made Ray uncomfortable, but being alone with Tina was near the top of the list. She sat across from him at her desk, her wavy brown hair spilling over her shoulders, her hazel eyes regarding him in a way that was both familiar and analytic, as if she were simultaneously reading his thoughts and staring into his soul.

"I'm surprised you came," Tina said. "It feels like you've been avoiding me."

"Just trying to keep it professional."

"If that were true, you wouldn't have changed your behavior after what happened between us."

"Come on, Tina. These last few months have been hard enough as it is."

"And yet I'm the one who's all alone."

"Let's not do this, okay?"

"You know, once upon a time, we planned to make a life together."

"That's ancient history. You've gotta let that go."

"I have let it go."

"Doesn't sound like it."

Ray glanced over his shoulder at the sound of Garrison's approach.

"Am I interrupting something?" Garrison asked.

"No," Tina said, "you're right on time."

Ray gave Garrison the stink eye. "Is he?"

"Don't blame me," Garrison said. "I spent ten minutes looking for a spot."

"Why do you insist on doing everything by the book?" Ray asked. "Just double park out front for Christ's sake."

"It's a bad look for the department," Garrison said. "And if you want to climb the ranks, they pay attention to that stuff."

"I've climbed as far as I want to go," Ray said.

Tina and Garrison exchanged a glance, and he knew they didn't understand. None of the Type A personalities ever did.

Tina cleared her throat and opened her laptop. "Are you ready for the preliminary autopsy results on Brittany Cooper?"

Ray wanted to say that he was ready five minutes ago, but Garrison answered first. "Sure, let's hear it."

"As you know, someone extracted Brittany's heart while she was still alive, but did so in a way to preserve the organ." She motioned to her computer and angled the screen so they could see a picture of Brittany on the exam table.

Her body had been rinsed of graveyard dirt, and she looked pallid and waxen on the stainless-steel surface, her long blonde hair matted against her head. There was a gaping hole in her chest cavity the size of a cantaloupe, and through the gap they could see the gleaming white curvature of her ribcage, and a spongy grayish-pink organ Ray guessed to be her lungs.

Tina tapped her finger against the screen. "The first blow struck here, puncturing her chest at the sternum. Judging by the pattern of cuts across the bone and cartilage, I can say with a high degree of confidence the murder weapon is a fixed blade hunting knife with a serrated edge nearest to the hilt."

"How big of a knife was it?" Garrison asked.

"Five to six inches."

"How do you know she was alive?" Ray asked.

"Because of the blood stains on the sleeves of her dress."

"How does that prove anything?"

"It was a long-sleeved dress," Tina said. "And there was blood underneath her arms—not pooled there, but spattered. As if she was on her back fighting off an attacker when the first strike severed her aorta."

"Christ," Ray said.

"It gets worse."

Garrison narrowed his eyes. "How could it possibly get worse?"

"Some of the arterial gushing also landed on her face, and while she lay there thrashing and screaming, she ingested a modest quantity of blood. I found the evidence in the contents of her stomach. It couldn't have gotten there if she was dead."

"My God," Garrison muttered.

"Help me understand how the scene unfolded," Ray said. "Someone pushes her to the ground and stabs her. She starts to fight back, but bleeds to death as her arteries are severed?"

"In a nutshell," Tina said. "Except this wasn't a one-man job."

"What do you mean?" Garrison asked.

"Judging from the bruising, I think the killer knelt on her legs while he cut her. But somebody else pinned her arms. At some point, Brittany was able to free her arms, which led to the blood spatters we observed."

"It might've been her girlfriend, Holly, who held her arms," Garrison said. "Brittany might not have been able to break free if it was a man."

"Wait a minute," Ray said. "If she managed to get her arms out, she probably clawed at her attacker."

"You're right," Tina said. "We found skin cells under Brittany's nails."

"You're kidding," Ray said, feeling a surge of adrenaline. The Temple had finally made a mistake. They dumped Brittany in the grave and assumed she'd never be found. "How long will it take to run a DNA match?" he asked.

"We have to send it to a special lab. It'll take at least a week."

"We don't have a week," Ray said. "Halloween is in four days. You need to put a rush on it."

"I'll see what I can do."

262

"What else do you have?" Garrison asked.

"There's two other things you should be aware of," Tina said. "The first is that the killers drained Brittany's blood before disposing of her body."

"What's the second thing?" Ray asked.

Tina advanced to the next picture on her laptop, which displayed a nasty gouge carved into Brittany's back. It was in the shape of an upside-down lowercase 't' with a half circle rising up from where the lines crossed.

"What is that?" Garrison asked.

Ray clenched his jaw, recognizing the symbol from Frank's occult manual. "That's the inverted cross of satanic justice."

CHAPTER FORTY-THREE

The muster room at Salem Police headquarters had been converted into a war room, complete with maps and photos plastered against every wall. Each corner of the room had been dedicated to a different victim, with lines of colored string tied from one pushpin to the other to signify known connections.

Ray watched Garrison add a few of Brittany's autopsy photos to the wall between Cassie and Danielle before writing 'DNA evidence pending' on a rolling whiteboard. After Garrison shared the update from their debrief with Tina, Martinez asked about the symbol etched into Brittany's back.

"It's called the inverted cross of Satanic justice," Ray said. "They carve it into the body as an act of vengeance against a traitor or an enemy."

Garrison pointed to the genealogy section of the whiteboard. "Brittany's ancestor was a prosecutor in the witch trials, so we think the symbol relates to her family's role in the hysteria. And one of Cassie's relatives served as a judge. It's why we think these cases might be connected. Bloodlines are important to these cults."

Chief Sanderson leaned back in his chair and steepled his fingers. "I appreciate the similarities, but we've got to be careful not to jump to conclusions. Remember, Danielle didn't even recognize Cassie's name when you questioned her. We don't want to fall into the trap of disregarding new evidence if it doesn't fit the broader theory."

"Understood," Garrison said. "It's only part of the puzzle, and we don't have the whole picture yet."

Ray noticed Captain Barnes sitting quietly beside Sanderson, his eyes distant, as if he'd lost faith in their ability to find Cassie alive.

"Were there any sightings of Evan Brody last night?" Ray asked.

Chief Sanderson gestured to Officer Frasier, who shrugged and said, "We had units watching Brody's apartment, Kettle & Cauldron, and his gym. He was a no-show on all fronts."

"What about the warrant to search his apartment?" Ray asked.

"It was denied," Sanderson said.

"Denied?" Ray asked. "What the hell for?"

"I told you not to be surprised. Judge Reynolds didn't feel as though we had enough evidence."

"You gotta be kidding me," Ray said.

"I've worked with Judge Reynolds for many years, Detective, and I trust in the judge's decisions."

Ray was about to share his own opinion of the judge, but Martinez chimed in before he could bury himself.

"What about Rancic?" she asked.

"He stayed home and watched dirty movies all night," Jeffries said. "I wish I could unsee what I saw through those binoculars. That guy is into some nasty stuff."

"I told you he was a dirtbag," Martinez said.

"That was never up for debate," Ray said. "But I think we ought to expand our surveillance to Danielle and Brody's coworkers. I guarantee some of them are members of the Temple."

"It's a reasonable request," Sanderson said, "but we're already running at capacity."

"I can put resources on it," Garrison said.

Sanderson nodded. "Thank you, Trooper Garrison." He glanced around the room. "Are there any other updates?"

"I've got a couple more things," Garrison said. "The crime lab tested the blood on Ray's jacket—the sample he picked up from the ritual in the church. Turns out it's not human."

"Let me guess," Martinez said. "It's cow's blood."

"The lady wins a prize," Garrison said.

"I bet it's from that farm I investigated," Jeffries said.

Ray leaned forward. "It would be a mistake to think this cult is any less dangerous because of it. Come Halloween, it'll be human blood in their ritual." He noticed Captain Barnes stiffen in his chair, and although he felt sorry for the guy, it needed to be said.

Chief Sanderson eyed Garrison over the conference table. "You said there were a couple things. What else do you have?"

"Our IT guys managed to recover a few seconds of the hacked traffic camera footage."

Captain Barnes snapped to attention. "What does it show?"

"I only had a quick peek, but I didn't see any new revelations."

"I'd like to see it," Barnes said.

"We can pull it up on my laptop," Sanderson said, "if someone doesn't mind fetching it."

Martinez raised her hand. "I'll get it."

When she returned with the laptop, Sanderson plugged it into the projector and passed it to Garrison, who used it to log into his state police account. A few moments later, the wall-mounted screen at the front of the room showed a white Ford Transit cargo van with no markings rolling across the Water Street bridge in Danvers. The camera was mounted high on a pole, so the angle of the shot was downward facing, showing the van from above.

Garrison paused the video as the van passed the camera. "This is where the recovered footage begins." He pressed a button and resumed the video, which showed the van continuing for three seconds before the footage ended.

"That's all there is?" Barnes asked, his shoulders sagging.

"I told you it wasn't much. They're still working to see if they can recover more."

"Let me see that again," Ray said. "Zoom in and slow it down."

Garrison backed it up and hit play, adjusting the speed and magnification. As the van crawled across the screen, Ray noticed a blurry gray line enter the frame from above and strike the back left corner of the roof.

"Right there!" Ray said. "You see that?"

When nobody answered, Garrison rewound the tape and played it again.

"It's bird shit," Ray said.

Officer Frasier chuckled. "What's the big deal?"

"The big deal is that it takes us from a plain white van to something with an identifying mark."

Barnes leaned forward. "What are you getting at?"

"We know the warehouses right after the bridge weren't the final destination," Ray said, "because Garrison's men searched the area with a fine-toothed comb. But what if they pulled into the lot to swap cars or maybe even turn around?"

Garrison shook his head. "My team scoured that footage. The van never goes back over the bridge."

"Your team was searching for a plain white van," Ray said. "But what if the purpose of the pitstop was to disguise it? They could've molded a vehicle wrap around it or slapped on some magnetic decals. Would your team have scrutinized a van heading back that wasn't plain white?"

Garrison blinked at him. "Maybe not."

"If the Temple abducted Cassie," Martinez said, "they'd hide her in Salem. Maybe driving over the bridge and wearing a ski mask through the traffic cameras was their way of throwing us off the trail."

Captain Barnes pointed at Garrison. "I want all your resources reviewing that tape. I don't care what logos are on the side of the van. If it's the same make and model, and it's got bird shit on the roof, I want to know about it."

CHAPTER FORTY-FOUR

"Are you sure this is a good idea?" Martinez asked.

"Probably not," Ray said.

Martinez drew to a halt halfway up the courthouse steps. "Then why are we doing it?"

"Because I want answers."

"I don't think the chief's gonna like it."

"Then stay here and let me handle it," Ray said. "No reason for us both to stick our necks out."

"We're partners, aren't we?"

Ray grinned. "Took you long enough to admit it."

She rolled her eyes, and they ascended the remaining steps together. When they reached the courthouse entrance, Martinez said, "At least tell me that you have a plan."

Ray held the door open and followed Martinez inside. "It's more of a poke than a plan."

"What's that mean?" Martinez asked.

"We find the bear, we poke it, and we see what happens."

Martinez slapped a hand against her forehead. "That's on me for asking."

After clearing security, they walked upstairs to the second-floor reception desk. Martinez paused to check in, but Ray kept on going as if he had every right to be there.

The receptionist—a matronly woman wearing an orange knit sweater—stared at him with unease. "Can I help you, sir? You're, um, not allowed inside without an appointment."

"That's okay," Ray said, flashing her a grin. "I know my way around."

"Sir…"

Her voice trailed off as he rounded the corner and entered a maze of low-walled cubicles, a row of well-coiffed heads visible above the workstations, giving the impression the building was infested with lawyers. Which made him wonder, could you fumigate for that?

Alex's office was across from the cubes, a bank of filing cabinets strategically placed in the middle of the floorplan so the junior attorneys couldn't see into his office from their seats.

Alex stood up behind his desk at the sight of Ray. "Detective, what are you doing here?" He sounded surprised, but not panicked. "If this is about Cassie, I don't have anything else to tell you."

Ray leaned against the doorjamb. "I want a word with your boss."

"Judge Reynolds?"

"Where's his office?"

"Why do you—"

The receptionist stormed around the corner, frazzled and winded. "I'm sorry, Mr. Whitehall, I tried stopping him."

Alex waved her off. "It's alright, Susan. I'll handle it."

Martinez arrived a moment later looking uncomfortable, her gaze shifting between Ray and Alex.

"You can't just barge in here and expect an audience with the judge," Alex said.

"Your boss denied a search warrant in Cassie's case," Ray said, "and I want to know why. And so should you, seeing as the suspect isn't the guy standing right in front of me."

Alex considered this for a moment, the tension in his jaw easing. "Follow me." He led them down the hall to a corner office with Judge Reynolds' name posted on the door in gold letters.

Alex knocked and went inside ahead of them, his body blocking their view of the desk. "Excuse me, Judge Reynolds? There's a couple of detectives here with questions on a warrant."

Ray couldn't hear the judge's reply, but Alex motioned them inside. Maybe it was sexist, but Ray had imagined the judge to be a wrinkly old man with a shock of white hair. Instead, the person behind the mahogany desk was an attractive woman in her early forties with long, dark hair, full lips, and emerald-green eyes. If Ray had seen her on the street, he would've sworn she was a model.

Judge Reynolds regarded them for a long moment, and Ray got the sense she knew exactly what he'd been thinking. "Whom do I have the pleasure of speaking with?" she asked, a ghost of a grin creasing her lips.

"Good morning, Your Honor," Ray said. "I'm Detective Hanley and this is Detective Martinez. We were hoping you might reconsider the warrant on Evan Brody."

"And why should I do that, Detective?"

"Because searching Evan Brody's apartment is critical to finding Cassie, or at least proving he had a hand in blowing up the church."

"I'm sorry, but the evidence I've seen doesn't support that conclusion."

"But we saw him," Martinez said. "He assaulted my partner in the church."

Judge Reynolds appeared skeptical. "According to the report I reviewed, he was wearing a mask."

"He was," Martinez said, "but it got knocked loose."

"For how long?"

"Only a second, but—"

"Did *you* recognize him?" Reynolds asked, turning to Ray.

He shook his head. All of this was in the report, but she clearly wasn't buying it. "I was in the middle of defending myself. I guess I missed it."

"You admit you never saw his face."

"That's right," Ray said. "But the guy had the exact same build as Brody. And I trust my partner. If she says she recognized him, then I believe her."

"We'd just interviewed him a few hours earlier," Martinez said, "so his face was fresh in my mind."

Judge Reynolds folded her hands on the desk. "And describe for me again where you were standing when you identified him."

"I was in the next room, looking through a hole in the wall."

"You mean like a peephole?"

"Uh, yeah," Martinez said.

"I assume you had to squint?"

"Yes."

"Just to clarify," Reynolds said, "the suspect's ID was confirmed by an officer standing in another room while squinting through a peephole, and all she saw was a tiny fraction of the man's face for a split second?"

"We're not asking for an arrest warrant," Ray said. "We've seen enough to know this guy is probably guilty. If we search his house and find out that we're wrong, then no harm, no foul."

"I disagree," Judge Reynolds said, leaning over her desk. "What you're suggesting violates the Fourth Amendment, which protects American citizens against unreasonable search and seizure. I have no doubt you're good detectives—and you may even be right about Mr. Brody—but unless you can provide more compelling evidence, I see no reason to amend my decision. And until that time, I don't want to see your faces in my office again. Is that clear, detectives?"

CHAPTER FORTY-FIVE

"Do you think she'll tell the chief?"

"Don't sweat it, Martinez. That's why we pay our union dues. Besides, she agreed to talk to us."

"She had some good arguments though, didn't she?"

Ray grunted. "She could've given us the benefit of the doubt." He shifted into drive and pulled onto Federal Street, leaving the row of courthouses in the rearview mirror. "You want to stop at Mystical Brew for coffee?"

Martinez fingered the wound on her forehead where a line of dark stitches showed beneath the translucent bandage.

"Come on," Ray said. "I'll tell the chief it was my idea. You won't get in trouble."

"It's not that. I'm still thinking about Abby's poem. There's something we're missing."

"You're lucky you didn't get yourself killed at that mental hospital. Next time you want to go rogue, do me a favor and call me first."

"Are you seriously lecturing me after all the stories I heard about you?"

"All the more reason not to repeat my mistakes."

"Is it true what Frasier said the other day?"

"What, that I got my last partner killed?"

"I can't imagine that was really your fault."

"You weren't there."

"I understand if you don't want to talk about it."

Ray checked the rearview mirror and switched lanes. "We've gotta trust each other with our lives, Martinez. You have a right to know."

He drew a deep breath, then explained how everything went south after he tracked down the Artist. "If I'd just waited for Billy to show up before going inside, things would've turned out different. Instead, Billy walked right into a trap, and I couldn't do anything except watch him die. My shrink tells me I'm not the one who pulled the trigger, but I for damn sure put him in that bullet's path."

"You couldn't have known that would happen."

"No, but I should've anticipated the risk. I was too caught up in the endgame, and Billy paid with his life. So now I go to his son's soccer games whenever I can, take the kid for ice cream afterward, and try to keep Billy's memory alive. His ex-wife's not gonna talk him up, you know? So I'm all he's got."

Martinez laid a hand on his shoulder. "You're a good friend."

"I don't know, Martinez. I'd say the jury's still out on that."

A few moments later, Ray's phone rang. He accepted the call, and Garrison's voice boomed through the speakers.

"We found it, Ray. You were right. They slapped some decals on the van and drove it back over the bridge."

Ray tightened his grip on the steering wheel. "Where'd it go?"

"We don't have an exact location, but based on where the footage disappears, we've triangulated an area near Derby and White Streets. It's adjacent to a warehouse complex on the waterfront. I'm headed there now with a couple of units."

Ray pressed down on the gas. "We're on our way."

When they arrived at the site, they found a trio of state police cruisers blocking the entrance to the complex, blue lights flashing. Ray parked on the matted grass beside the cruisers and climbed out of the Explorer, falling into step beside Martinez.

He counted six warehouses spread across several acres of gravel-strewn land that jutted into the harbor, most of which were constructed in a hybrid of concrete and corrugated steel.

He spotted signs for at least a dozen different businesses, including propane, granite, sheet metal, welding, and boat engine repair. Trucks and vans belonging to the businesses were parked in front of the buildings, and Ray could see Garrison and the other troopers inspecting the vehicles, jotting down license plate numbers and taking note of the makes and models.

Gravel crunched underfoot as Ray and Martinez strode into the complex. A frigid wind gusted off the harbor, working its icy fingers between the buttons of Ray's sports jacket. Martinez hugged one arm across the front of her blazer and pointed to a security camera, which was mounted to one of the buildings and angled toward the main drive.

Ray signaled to Garrison, and the big man trotted over holding his hat down in the wind. "What kind of decals are we looking for?" Ray asked.

"Magnetic ones that say Joe's Plumbing."

Ray chuckled. "That's original."

"A bunch of criminal geniuses," Garrison said.

"Was there a logo?" Martinez asked.

"It had black lettering and a silver pipe wrench with drops of water falling from it."

"Was there a phone number?" Martinez asked.

"Yeah, but it's out of service. Never been assigned to anyone. But get this, they had decals on the roof too. That's why we overlooked it at first."

"What'd it say?" Ray asked.

"No Flow, Call Joe."

"Well, at least that part's original," Ray said.

A warble of sirens rose in the distance, and they turned to see a column of Salem Police cars racing toward the complex from Derby Street."

Ray winced. "Do me a favor, Martinez. Get on the radio and tell those guys to turn off their—"

CHAPTER FORTY-SIX

The explosion sent them all flying. The concussive force of the blast pitched them face-first into the gravel as the nearest warehouse erupted into a cataclysmic fireball that rose hundreds of feet into the sky.

For a split second, the bitter cold was replaced by a searing heat that singed the hairs on the back of Ray's neck. He tucked his head between his arms and curled into a fetal position as the world around him went eerily silent.

Garrison hauled him to his feet, yelling something that Ray couldn't hear. Martinez appeared at his side and pointed to the row of squad cars, a thin line of blood trickling down her cheek. He followed their lead and wriggled underneath a state police cruiser as an avalanche of flaming debris rained onto the windshield and slammed against the roof.

It was over a few seconds later, and they crawled out from under the cruisers, clothes torn and covered in dust. They were scraped and bloodied but otherwise okay. Most of Garrison's men were further into the complex when it happened, safely sheltered between buildings. But one of them had been approaching Garrison when the warehouse blew, and he had a piece of shrapnel buried deep in his shoulder, the entire left sleeve of his uniform soaked a glistening crimson.

The trooper staggered toward them like a soldier fleeing a warzone, his eyes rolling back as a prelude to faint. Ray rushed forward and caught the trooper in his arms. "Give me a hand," Ray said, his own words sounding faint and muffled, as if he were underwater.

Garrison grabbed the man's legs, and they carried him to a Salem Police cruiser that was just arriving with Officer

Frasier behind the wheel. Martinez opened the rear door, and Ray and Garrison loaded the trooper into the back seat as gently as they could. Martinez climbed in after him and sat on the floor to keep him secure.

"No time for an ambulance," Ray said, addressing Officer Frasier.

Frasier nodded without a word and peeled out of the parking lot, tires spewing gravel. After the squad car disappeared around the corner, Ray and Garrison turned to face the warehouse, which had been transformed into a burning heap of rubble, its steel walls warped and blackened beneath hungry yellow flames. Several large sections of roof were strewn across the gravel lot, tendrils of smoke curling up from its jagged metal edges.

Garrison ran a hand over his head, his hat nowhere in sight. "No way in hell that was an accident."

"They saw us coming," Ray said. "They had it rigged to blow just like the church."

"But how are they always one step ahead of us?" Garrison asked.

Ray pointed to the burning building. "There was a camera on that warehouse, and we didn't exactly come in under the radar."

Garrison swore. "I hope you're prepared for a long-ass night."

***

The next two days passed in an exhaustive whirlwind of investigative work. Between Garrison's team and the Salem Police, they interviewed thirty-one workers from the warehouse complex and performed dozens of background checks, trying to determine if any of the workers had a passing connection to the white van or any relationship that could be linked to Cassie, Danielle, Brittany, Abby, or Evan Brody. The sheer volume of the work stalled the entire investigation, and Ray worried they were losing precious time.

In the meanwhile, he learned that the land beneath the warehouse complex originally belonged to the Customs House and was used to weigh and store goods that were subject to import taxes. By the 1920s, the original buildings were razed and the land was sold to a private investor, who transformed it into an industrial complex.

The warehouse that exploded was a tool manufacturing business until the 1970s, when it was purchased by the city of Salem to stockpile salt and sand for use on the roads in wintertime. In 2001, it was sold to a cement company that went belly up three years later.

When the bank foreclosed on the mortgage and attempted to resell the property, an environmental study concluded that it was full of asbestos. The estimates to remove the asbestos were so costly the bank realized they'd never be able to get the building off their hands. And so it had sat vacant ever since.

The Salem Fire Department concluded the destruction of the warehouse was caused by a gas line explosion, but the devastation was so severe there was no way to determine if it was an accident or if it had been rigged to blow. The EPA assured them the asbestos probably vaporized in the flames, but Ray wasn't entirely convinced.

This morning, he parked a hundred yards from the site and leaned against the Explorer, watching a bulldozer clear the debris. Martinez handed him and Garrison coffees. Over the last forty-eight hours, they'd been taking turns making runs to Mystical Brew.

Garrison cocked a thumb at Ray. "Not that anyone's counting, but that's the sixth time I've saved your ass."

"What, because you helped me stand up after the explosion? I think that's stretching it."

Garrison looked at Martinez for confirmation.

"Don't drag me into this." She pointed to the debris field. "As soon as that's clear, we should take a look. It's right around where those old smuggling tunnels are rumored to be."

Their working theory was that the Temple leveraged the warehouse as an entry point to the tunnels, which provided access to some kind of underground lair where they'd imprisoned Cassie until it was time for the ritual. Although the security camera on the nearest building didn't have sufficient range to reach the front of the destroyed warehouse, it did have footage of the kidnap van disappearing around back. Unfortunately, with the distance and the window tinting, it was impossible to identify the driver.

According to the bank's foreclosed asset manager, the camera Martinez had spotted on the destroyed warehouse wasn't installed by the bank, and they didn't have access to the security footage.

"We sometimes have problems with squatters," the manager had said. "Especially on properties like that where we aren't able to dispose of them on a timely basis."

Ray sipped his coffee and watched the bulldozer scoop debris into an idling dump truck. "How close are we to finding the vendor who made the Joe's Plumbing decals?"

"No luck with any of the local dealers," Garrison said, "but there's literally thousands of businesses who sell those over the internet."

"What about the DNA from under Brittany's nails?" Martinez asked.

"The search came back negative on the criminal databases. But we're trying the genealogy sites next."

"It's two days till Halloween," Ray said. "We're running out of time."

"I'll check in with the station and see if anything's come through the tip line," Martinez said.

Chief Sanderson had hosted a press conference following the warehouse explosion and had linked it to both the church fire and Cassie's disappearance. He concluded his remarks with an appeal to the public for help in catching those responsible and had identified Evan Brody as a person of interest wanted for questioning. He'd also shown pictures of the van with the Joe's Plumbing decals and had asked for help locating it.

"While you do that," Garrison said, "I'm gonna take a run to the hospital to visit Trooper Devin."

"How's he doing?" Martinez asked.

"The shrapnel sliced clean through his muscle. His arm might never be the same again." Garrison lowered his head, his eyes glassy with unshed tears.

Ray draped his arm around Garrison's shoulder. "We're gonna get these sonsofbitches. I promise."

CHAPTER FORTY-SEVEN

How many days, Naomi wondered. How many hours had passed since they locked her in this moldering cell, leaving her to rot in the endless dark beneath the streets of Salem?

It was persistently cold down here, the air infused with a raw and penetrating chill that seeped through her flesh and wormed itself into the marrow of her bones. She had no coat, no sweater. Only a pair of ripped maternity jeans and a thin black T-shirt.

It took considerable effort to concentrate on anything other than the cold. She sat on a bale of hay in the corner of her cell and hugged her knees to stay warm, trying her best to distract herself from the chill. But all it took was a single stray thought to break her concentration and set her teeth to chattering, and the bony echo of that never-ending vibration threatened to rob her of her sanity.

Maybe she deserved this. Maybe it was her penance for being such a shitty person. But Daniel, her unborn son, was innocent. Didn't he deserve to be born with a clean slate, not tainted by the sins of his parents?

She still held Daniel's plush blue rabbit in her hands, a spur-of-the-moment purchase that had likely betrayed her intentions to the Temple. She traced a finger along the edge of its nose, feeling the contours of the heart-shaped plastic.

Her stomach rumbled, and she pressed a hand against it, as if that might quell the hunger pangs. She couldn't remember when she'd last eaten, but she suspected the Temple brought her a meal once a day. The food was always the same—two hard biscuits, like a days-old dinner roll, and a tin cup filled with water. Depending on who brought it, the roll was either

281

dropped onto the floor between the bars or she was ordered to stand against the wall so Spider could pelt her with it. Sometimes the cup was filled with water, and sometimes it was filled with piss. On those latter occasions, Spider insisted on watching her drink it, holding his torch high so the light penetrated into her cell as she tipped the cup to her lips and gagged as the warm urine filled her throat.

He liked taunting the other prisoner too, but the girl's cell was far enough away that Naomi could barely hear what was happening. Sometimes, she heard Spider and his friend together, their voices echoing off the damp stone walls and rising into a crescendo of mean laughter. She knew now that the friend's nickname was Jackal, which couldn't be more fitting.

She'd heard Luther warn them more than once that the girl was special, that her blood would unleash a great power in the upcoming sacrifice, and that she was not to be defiled.

As much as she hated hearing Spider and Jackal's voices, she preferred it to the pitiful whimpering that often drifted to her from the other girl's cell. Naomi had called out to the girl once, but one of the guards—she thought Jackal—warned her that any communication between prisoners would result in skipped rations.

And maybe it was better that way, better the girl never had a name, never had a face, because the rest of their lives could be measured in hours... and the clock was ever ticking.

CHAPTER FORTY-EIGHT

After the trucks hauled out the last of the debris, Ray and Martinez inspected the site where the warehouse once stood. If there was ever a tunnel inside, it was gone now, the entire floorplan reduced to rubble, like a riverbed run dry.

Martinez let out her breath in a huff. "I don't understand how the Temple has the resources to do all this."

"I don't either, but somebody a lot smarter than Evan Brody is pulling the strings."

"They're running out the clock," Martinez said.

She was right. Between Brody, the van, and the DNA under Brittany's fingernails, the threads were beginning to unravel. But if they didn't piece it all together within the next two days, Cassie would be killed in a ritualistic sacrifice.

Martinez's cell phone buzzed, and she reached into her blazer to retrieve it.

"Who is it?" Ray asked.

She glanced at the number and shrugged, then answered it on speaker. "This is Martinez."

"Detective," a male voice said. "It's Alex Whitehall."

Her eyes widened. "Yes?"

"I've got information that might help with Cassie."

Ray and Martinez locked gazes, and he signaled for her to continue.

"What kind of information?" she asked.

"There's a guy that I defended a few years ago. I thought he was still in jail, but I just found out he was released six months ago."

"What's his connection to Cassie?"

"It's more about what he had against me. He blamed me when the judge handed down a harsh sentence. As the bailiff hauled him away, he cursed me out and vowed to get revenge when he got out of prison."

"And you think he kidnapped Cassie to get back at you?"

"A couple weeks ago, Cassie and I were on a date, and I could swear we were being followed."

"What was he driving?" Ray asked, finally jumping in.

"I'm not sure. It was big though, like a white SUV."

"Are you sure it wasn't a van?" Ray asked.

"It may have been, but I'm not positive. All I know is that he tailgated us for a while and was blinding me with his headlights. I felt threatened enough that I drove to the police station, but when I pulled into the lot, he kept on driving. Cassie was freaking out by that point, and I was trying to calm her down, so I didn't get a good look as he passed us."

"Are you sure it was a man?" Martinez asked.

"No. I'm just assuming," Alex said.

"This guy you defended," Ray said. "What was he on trial for and why did he blame you for his conviction?"

"It was a statutory rape charge, and I thought we had a good chance of getting probation since it was consensual and there was only a few years age difference between him and the victim."

Ray blinked at Martinez. Why did that sound so familiar?

"Unfortunately," Alex continued, "the prosecutor was friends with the girl's father, and I couldn't negotiate a reasonable plea. Long story short, it went to trial, and he was sentenced to three years at MCI Walpole."

"Wait a minute," Martinez said. "Was his name Eddie Fischer?"

Alex sucked in his breath. "How did you know?"

CHAPTER FORTY-NINE

"We do it quietly this time," Ray said. "Just the three of us." He eyed Garrison and Martinez across Mystical Brew's café table, a mug of coffee warming his hands.

"When did you last question Eddie Fischer?" Garrison asked.

"About a week ago," Martinez said. "At the Broad Street apartments. He's got a business called *Van-Go Painters*. He said they hired him to paint a bunch of empty units. It's possible he's not finished yet."

"You searched his van last time?" Garrison asked.

"Just a quick peek," Martinez said. "Nothing obvious jumped out, but that doesn't mean Cassie's DNA isn't in there somewhere."

"Now that we're looking at a cult," Ray said, "Eddie does fit the psychological profile—a loner who sees himself as a victim of society, someone who blames the world for his own problems."

Martinez frowned. "We shouldn't have been so quick to dismiss him."

"I don't know," Ray said. "He let us look inside the van and showed us the receipt for his vehicle wrap. If he did kidnap Cassie, then he's a damned good liar. And a ballsy one too."

"What's the deal with this vehicle wrap?" Garrison asked.

"It cost him two grand," Ray said, "and he installed it a few months ago. You can't take those things on and off without ruining them."

"Maybe he got two," Garrison said, "and only showed you one receipt. Or maybe the Temple bought him another one after the kidnapping."

"Either scenario is possible," Ray said. "Let's check to see if he bought more than one from that same vendor."

"I already asked the vendor to give me all of their transactions with Eddie the last time," Martinez said.

"Maybe they were lazy," Ray said. "And didn't run a full check. Or maybe they were hiding something. Either way, we'll threaten them with a warrant this time, make them cough it up."

Garrison finished his coffee and dabbed his lips with a napkin. "What about Alex's story? Did it check out?"

Martinez nodded. "The court stenographer's transcript corroborates everything he told us. Eddie made it clear he wanted revenge after prison."

Ray fished his phone from his pocket and checked the time. "We'd better get a move on if we want to catch Eddie before lunch."

***

As Ray steered the Explorer into the parking lot of the Broad Street apartments, Garrison halted his cruiser at the corner of Winthrop Street, where he was obscured by the stone wall and towering oaks bordering the Broad Street Cemetery.

Eddie Fischer's van sat in the parking lot of the apartment building, adorned by the same vehicle wrap as before, the words *Van-Go Commercial and Residential Painters* emblazoned on the sides and back, the block lettering filled with swirls of bluish-green impressionist brush strokes. The only other vehicle in the lot was a black Ford F-150 with a magnetic decal for *Sparkman's Electrical Service.*

Ray and Martinez climbed out of the Explorer and gazed up at the three-story brick apartment building. Ray noticed that none of the windows had any curtains or blinds. "Looks like the whole place is under renovation," he said. "Eddie could be in any one of those units."

THE BURYING POINT

They strode across the parking lot to a concrete stoop, ascending the stairs to a blue door that was propped open with a brick. Ray pulled it fully open, and they emerged into an empty hallway that smelled of fresh paint. Music emanated from one of the apartments, but it was too far away to decipher the lyrics.

They followed the sound up a flight of stairs, the hardwood glossy and newly resurfaced. The music grew louder as they reached the second floor, and somewhere down the hall Mick Jagger belted out the chorus to "Sympathy for the Devil."

Ray drew his gun and hugged the wall, creeping toward the open door of Apartment 203. Martinez was right behind him, so close he could feel the heat of her breath against his neck. He stopped at the edge of the doorway. Men were speaking inside, but their words were drowned out by the music.

Ray peered into the apartment and saw two middle-aged men positioning a ladder beneath a coil of yellow wire that dangled from the ceiling. He stepped inside and motioned for Martinez to follow.

"We're looking for Eddie Fischer," Ray said, holding up his badge.

The men were old enough to be Eddie's father, one of them tall and lean, the other stocky and balding. Neither said a word.

"Where's Eddie?" Ray asked again.

The stocky man pointed at the wall, indicating the apartment next door.

Ray and Martinez darted into the hall just in time to hear the click of Apartment 205's locks being engaged. Martinez pounded her fist against the door. "Open up, Eddie! Salem Police!"

It took Ray three kicks to break down the door, and another second to realize Eddie had escaped through the living room window.

"I see him." Martinez pointed to a figure running into the parking lot.

Ray holstered his gun and dialed Garrison. "He's headed for the van!"

Mick Jagger's voice drifted through the wall as Martinez climbed through the window.

Just call me Lucifer...

Ray hurried after Martinez, scaling down the fire escape and jumping the last few feet into the bushes. As he rounded the corner to the parking lot, Garrison's cruiser screeched to a halt in front of the van.

Eddie fumbled with the gearshift and was about to jam it into reverse when Martinez flung open the passenger door and jumped into the seat next to him.

She pointed her gun at his face. "Out of the car!"

Eddie lifted his hands slowly into the air.

Garrison was there a moment later. He hauled Eddie out of the driver's seat and forced him onto the ground. "Hands behind your back."

Eddie did as he was told, and Garrison cuffed him and dragged him to his feet. "Don't even think about running."

Ray jogged over to them. "What are you trying to hide, Eddie? You know it's a crime to run from the police, don't you?"

"I didn't know it was the cops," Eddie said. "I heard someone looking for me and I bolted. Like I said before, I owe people money, and I'm not exactly up to date with my payments."

"Spare us the song and dance," Ray said. "We may have bought it before, but this time's different."

"What do you mean?"

"You're wanted for the kidnapping of Cassie Barnes," Martinez said.

"I told you I had nothing to do with that."

"You can drop the act," Ray said.

"It's not an act."

Garrison walked the perimeter of the van, running a hand over the vehicle wrap.

"What's he looking for?" Eddie asked.

Garrison stepped onto the van's running board and peered at the roof. "Hey Ray, come take a look at this."

Ray walked over to the van and stepped onto the running board beside Garrison. The roof was coated in a layer of filth, the kind where you could run your finger through the grime and write your initials. It was even worse near the front, where the grime looked caked on and sticky, as if it'd built up around something that had later been removed, leaving a gleaming white outline surrounded by dirt. In this case, the thing that had been removed was a string of letters, likely formed by magnetic decals.

"Does that say what I think it does?" Ray asked.

Garrison nodded. "No flow, call Joe."

Ray hopped down from the running board. "Eddie Fischer, you're under arrest."

CHAPTER FIFTY

Following the customary booking procedures, Officer Jeffries escorted Eddie into an interrogation room and guided him to a steel table with matching chairs. Eddie's street clothes had been replaced by a bright orange jumpsuit and a pair of handcuffs.

After Jeffries left the room, Eddie slumped forward and propped his elbows on the table, running his hands through a thick mop of curly brown hair. Eventually, he sat up, his eyes darting around the room, registering the heavy steel door, the security camera, and finally, the two-way glass mirror. He studied the mirror for a long time, probably wondering who was behind it and if he was being watched. Then he dropped his gaze and fidgeted in his chair, one leg shaking against the concrete as he curled a hand into his mouth and gnawed at his fingernails.

"He looks like a caged animal," Martinez said, observing him through the two-way glass.

"I say we let him sweat it out awhile longer," Ray said. "Get him good and panicked." He turned to Captain Barnes, who was standing beside Chief Sanderson, his gaze fixed on Eddie. "You want the first crack at him, Captain?"

Barnes squeezed his hands into fists, his jaw clenched so tight it looked as though he might grind his teeth into dust. "If I go in there, there's no telling what I might do."

Sanderson stepped between Barnes and the door, even though the captain hadn't budged an inch. "I think it's best if Detectives Hanley and Martinez handle it."

They turned back to the two-way glass and watched Eddie for a few more minutes without speaking. When Ray finally made a move for the door, Barnes grabbed his arm.

"You find out what that sonofabitch has done with my niece."

***

Eddie jerked in his chair as Ray and Martinez entered the room and took seats opposite him. "You can't hold me here. I didn't do anything."

"Where's Cassie?" Ray asked.

"I don't know."

"Where is she?" Ray said again, his voice low and menacing.

"I told you this is all a mistake. I don't know anything about her."

"She was Alex Whitehall's girlfriend," Martinez said. "Your ex-lawyer. The one you threatened when he lost your case. Does any of that ring a bell?"

Eddie shifted in his chair. "I... I didn't mean any of that. I was pissed about going to jail. I mean, Donna was my girlfriend, and she was only two years younger than me. How could I go to jail for that?"

"Statutory rape is illegal," Martinez said.

"But we were in love."

"Who's the leader of the Temple?" Ray asked.

Eddie wrinkled his brow. "The what?"

"The Temple of Six," Ray said.

Eddie shook his head slowly. "I don't know what that means."

"We don't believe you," Ray said.

Eddie slunk down in his chair and rubbed his eyes. "I don't understand why I'm here."

"Your van matches the one used to kidnap Cassie," Martinez said.

"But I didn't do it. There's a lot of vans that look like mine. I mean—"

"It matches," Ray said. "Right down to the decals you had on the roof."

Eddie looked defiant. "I didn't have any decals on the roof."

"Cassie's DNA was found in your van," Martinez said.

"What do you mean, her DNA?"

"Strands of hair," Ray said. "Traces of blood."

"That... that can't be."

"We also found one of her earrings under your paint shelves," Martinez said. "A silver moon with a partial fingerprint that matches hers. The same earrings she was seen wearing on the morning she disappeared."

Eddie stared past them, his eyes glazing over with a look of hopelessness. "I want to talk to my lawyer."

Ray leaned forward. "Where's Cassie?"

"I don't know."

"Tell us where she is," Ray said again.

"I don't know!"

"Listen," Ray said, "if Cassie's still alive, we may be able to cut you a deal. But you need to tell us where she is."

"Who put you up to this?" Martinez asked.

"I want my lawyer."

"You sure about that?" Ray asked. "Didn't your last lawyer screw you over? Isn't that why you kidnapped Cassie?"

"Or was it the Temple's idea?" Martinez asked.

Eddie folded his arms. "I know my rights. I don't have to tell you anything."

"Come on, Eddie," Ray said. "What happened? Where is she?"

Eddie shook his head and made a gesture like he was zipping his lips.

After a few minutes, they gave up trying to make him talk. They left him sitting alone in the interrogation room and went next door to confer with Chief Sanderson and Captain Barnes.

"Judge Reynolds approved the search warrant for Eddie's house," Sanderson said. "State police are leading the search, but why don't you meet Garrison over there and give him a hand."

"In the meantime," Barnes said, "we'll meet with the prosecutor and the public defender and see if we can convince Eddie to make a deal. With any luck, maybe we'll find something at his house that'll lead us straight to Cassie."

***

Eddie lived in a dilapidated apartment building near the railroad tracks. His unit was halfway up a beige brick tower that formed part of a sprawling complex of Section 8 housing. The elevator was busted, so Ray and Martinez hoofed it up seven flights of stairs.

The hallway on either side of Eddie's apartment was roped off with yellow police tape. They flashed their badges to the trooper guarding the perimeter and ducked underneath the tape. Inside the apartment, the kitchen cabinets and drawers yawned open, couch cushions were upended, and the contents of Eddie's closet were strewn about the floor. The apartment was less than a thousand square feet, and it felt claustrophobic with a half dozen members of the Crime Scene Services unit sifting through Eddie's belongings, snapping pictures, dusting for prints, and scanning for traces of blood with a blacklight.

Garrison spotted them standing in the living room and strode over to them. "We're almost wrapped up." He led them into the hallway so they could have some breathing room.

"What's the verdict?" Ray asked.

"Well, unless the print analysis comes back positive, there's no evidence Eddie ever held Cassie here."

"He probably snatched her and delivered her straight into the tunnels," Martinez said.

"Any word on his search history?" Ray asked.

"He doesn't own a computer, but the warrant authorized us to unlock his phone. So far, we haven't found anything incriminating. His top interests appear to be porn, sports, and bass fishing. He also seems to have a fetish for Asian girl-on-girl action, which makes Cassie an odd choice if the motive was sexual."

"What about occult searches or paraphernalia?" Ray asked.

Garrison shook his head. "Nothing like that. And before you ask, his phone records show him at home the morning Cassie disappeared. Based on the cell tower pings, it looks like he rolled into work around noon."

"He could've left his phone at home while he kidnapped her," Martinez said.

"He told us he was in work by seven thirty that morning," Ray said, "so we've already caught him in a lie."

"Is there any record of him calling Brody or Danielle?" Martinez asked.

"Their numbers aren't in his history," Garrison said. "I even checked for that burner phone used by Brittany's killers, but no dice."

"Who else does he talk to on a regular basis?" Ray asked.

"Pretty much just his mom and an uncle who lives in Michigan. He's only been out of jail for six months. I guess he hasn't connected with many people."

"I find it hard to believe Eddie did this all on his own," Ray said. "Or that his only motive was revenge against Alex."

"He could still be part of the cult," Martinez said. "Maybe they avoid calling each other and only interact in person for their rituals."

Ray rubbed a hand across his cheek and grunted. Something about this didn't sit right with him.

Garrison pulled out his phone and angled it toward them. "I wanted to show you something else. Look at these pictures." The first one displayed Eddie standing in front of his van smiling proudly, one thumb cocked at the *Van-Go* logo. The next photo showed the van parked at the evidence impound yard.

"Notice anything different?" Garrison asked. He swiped back and forth between the pictures.

Ray stared at the photos and shrugged. "What are we supposed to see?"

Martinez reached for the phone and studied the photos, her eyes suddenly lighting up. "They're different!"

Ray leaned in for a closer look. "How?"

Martinez pointed to the lettering. "See the way the paint swirls are oriented inside the letters? It's counterclockwise in this photo, but clockwise in this one."

"Ding, ding," Garrison said. "The lady wins another prize."

CHAPTER FIFTY-ONE

The muscular bald guy tending bar at Kettle & Cauldron was named Kyle Jackman. He claimed to have no idea about the Temple of Six or Evan Brody's whereabouts, but he came across as defensive and tight-lipped, someone who Ray figured might be worth watching.

When Ray finished questioning him, he walked back to the table where Martinez, Garrison, and Frank were looking at their menus.

"Everything's either fried or frozen," Garrison said, glancing down in disgust. "And something on this table is sticky."

Frank eyed Garrison over his pint of Guiness. "Why are you always a pain in the ass when we go to restaurants?"

"Because he's a health nut," Ray said. "And a germaphobe."

"Just order a burger and add fifteen minutes onto your workout," Martinez said. "That's what I always do."

When the waitress came over, Garrison ordered a grilled chicken breast, which wasn't on the menu. The waitress responded with an exaggerated eyeroll, which was never a good sign. The rest of them ordered burgers—the only decent thing on the menu.

Ray sipped his Coke and gazed at Frank. "What is it you wanted to show us?"

"You remember that guy I told you about?" Frank asked. "The one who's an expert on rare books and the occult?"

"Did he find something on the demons?" Martinez asked. "The legion of Six?"

THE BURYING POINT

Frank pulled a pen and notepad from his jacket pocket and laid them on the table. "He says these demons aren't well known and aren't mentioned in the usual sources. But he came across a manuscript written by a seminary school student. Apparently, this student worked with a team that translated a collection of ancient scrolls discovered in some Middle Eastern cave about thirty years ago. The manuscript claims the scrolls are a lost chapter to the Book of Revelations and the demons play a pivotal role in bringing about the end of times."

"What is it they're supposed to do?" Ray asked.

"It says they break out of hell and pave the way for the Four Horsemen of the Apocalypse. Except that once the demons are in our world, they discover their combined power is greater than the Devil himself, and they conspire to stop Judgement Day."

"Why would they do that?" Martinez asked.

Frank glanced up from the notebook and frowned, the creases that lined his face deepening. "It says here they plan to conquer the earth, subjugate the human race, and give rise to an everlasting reign of darkness."

CHAPTER FIFTY-TWO

"My client says he didn't do it."

The public defender folded his hands on the conference table and leaned back, as if resting his case. He was young, barely out of law school, and his ill-fitting tan suit gave him the appearance of a kid playing dress-up on career day.

Ray turned to the prosecutor, Daley, who was wedged between Chief Sanderson and Captain Barnes. She bore a striking resemblance to a middle-aged Meryl Streep and spoke with an unquestionable air of authority.

"Mr. Peters, the evidence against your client is overwhelming. Insurmountable, really. We have a motive, surveillance footage, and the victim's DNA, which was discovered inside your client's van. Not only that, but the alibi your client provided is contradicted by his phone records. Thus, between the kidnapping, resisting arrest, and the strong possibility of sexual assault, your client is easily looking at twenty-five to thirty years in state prison. However, if he has Cassie locked up somewhere and she dies of neglect, your client's looking at a life sentence."

Mr. Peters fidgeted with his tie. "What are you offering?"

"If Cassie is recovered alive and in good health, the state's willing to agree to a term of not more than twelve and a half years."

Peters nodded, standing up eagerly. "Let me confer with my client and see if he's willing to deal."

When Peters returned to the conference room a few minutes later, the look on his face said it all. "Mr. Fischer appreciates the offer, but he's unable to accept it."

"Why the hell not?" Ray asked.

Peters frowned. "He insists he's innocent."

Captain Barnes pounded his fist against the table, hard enough to send coffee splashing out of his mug. "Bullshit, he's innocent!"

Ray fixed his gaze on Peters. "I want to have a talk with Eddie."

***

Ray and Martinez strode into the interrogation room and sat at the steel table opposite Eddie and Peters. Eddie's eyes were swollen and bloodshot, his bushy beard matted with what Ray could only guess were tears. The question was, were they tears of remorse or self-pity?

"Why aren't you taking the deal?" Ray asked.

"Because I didn't do it."

"If you didn't do it," Martinez said, "then how do you explain Cassie's DNA in your van?"

"I can't. That's the thing."

"You lied about where you were on the morning of Cassie's disappearance, didn't you?" Ray asked.

Peters held up a hand. "Don't answer that."

"He doesn't need to," Martinez said. "It's right there in the phone records."

"He could've forgotten his phone when he left for work," Peters said. "It doesn't prove anything."

"It's okay," Eddie said. "I'll tell them."

"Tell us what?" Ray asked.

"I think someone framed me."

"How?" Ray asked.

"I went out drinking the night before. I don't remember how I got home, but I know I slept most of the day."

"How much is most of the day?" Martinez asked.

"I climbed out of bed at three in the afternoon. I remember because I debated going into work late."

"Why'd you lie about where you were?" Ray asked.

"Don't answer that," Peters said.

"It's okay," Eddie said. "I know I shouldn't have lied—that was stupid—but I thought it might get you guys off my back. Not because I did it, but because I didn't want the hassle."

"Good luck convincing a jury of that," Ray said.

"Don't you think I'd tell you if I knew where she was? I mean, why wouldn't I want a reduced sentence?"

Ray exchanged glances with Martinez. Could he really be that dumb?

"If you killed her," Martinez said, "you can't exactly take the deal, can you?"

Eddie's mouth dropped open.

Christ, Ray thought, *he is that dumb*.

"I'm telling you the truth," Eddie said. "I'll take a lie detector test."

Peters sucked air through his teeth. "I wouldn't advise that, Eddie. Those tests aren't admissible in court, and you might get a false reading due to, um, nerves."

"Where'd you get the replacement vehicle wrap?" Martinez asked.

"Replacement? I've never taken that wrap off."

Martinez showed him the before and after photos on her phone.

Eddie rubbed his forehead in confusion. "That's messed up, man. I didn't do that. You know how much those things cost?"

"What time did you leave the bar the night before Cassie disappeared?" Ray asked.

"I don't know, I think it was early. I only had two drinks, but they knocked me on my ass."

"Who were you with?" Martinez asked.

"I went by myself."

"Did you meet anyone?" Martinez asked.

"I remember talking to this girl at the bar, but everything after that is like… missing, you know?"

"What if someone put something in his drink?" Peters said. "He could've been roofied."

"Will you submit to testing?" Ray asked. "Or do I need to get a court order?"

"I'll take the tests," Eddie said.

"Where did you have the drinks?" Martinez asked.

"Some dive bar near the waterfront. A place called Kettle & Cauldron."

CHAPTER FIFTY-THREE

"We've got the wrong guy," Ray said.

"You don't seriously believe him?" Chief Sanderson said.

They were gathered in the briefing room with Garrison, Martinez, Captain Barnes, and Prosecutor Daley.

"I don't think Eddie's smart enough to pull off an operation like this," Ray said.

"He spends a lot of time at Kettle & Cauldron," Martinez said. "Brody could've seen him as an easy mark."

"How long until we get the results of the drug test?" Barnes asked.

"We put a rush on it," Ray said. "But we probably won't see anything until tomorrow."

"I'm afraid it won't be definitive," Daley said.

"What do you mean?" Garrison asked.

"I've tried a number of cases involving Rohypnol," Daley said. "It only remains in the blood for twenty-four hours, and in urine for sixty. And while it lasts much longer in hair samples, it's not detectable in the follicles until two weeks after ingestion."

"Does that mean we need to retest him in a few days if we want to be certain of the results?" Garrison asked.

"That would be my recommendation," Daley said.

"We don't have that kind of time," Ray said. "Halloween is in two days."

"If he does test positive," Barnes said, "it still doesn't absolve him. He could've taken the drug deliberately to give himself plausible deniability."

"You're giving him too much credit," Martinez said. "There's no way Eddie's that smart."

"We've got to find a way to make him talk," Sanderson said. "If we can identify where the second vehicle wrap came from, it might give us the leverage we need."

"We didn't have any luck with the place Eddie bought the first one from," Garrison said. "None of the other local dealers manufactured it either. And since nothing came up in Eddie's browsing history, we've got no choice but to start cold-calling online vendors."

"That doesn't sound promising," Ray said.

"Was the lab able to analyze the adhesive side for prints?" Martinez asked.

"It came back negative," Garrison said.

"We've gotta be missing something," Barnes said.

"What we need," Ray said, "is a search warrant on Evan Brody."

"Then you'd better find something to justify it," Sanderson said. "Because the evidence you have right now isn't enough. And don't let me catch you going to Judge Reynolds again without my permission. Do you understand?"

CHAPTER FIFTY-FOUR

Naomi stared into the darkness and cast her thoughts into the endless void of the universe. The discomfort of the prison cell dissolved around her—the fatigue in her muscles, the swelling in her extremities, the raw and persistent chill—fading into oblivion as she centered her being and concentrated on whatever transcendental revelations the spirits had to offer.

Sometimes, when she reached the deepest level of meditation, she gleaned visions of the future, bits of knowledge or forewarning she could later use to guide her actions. The last time she meditated, she had a premonition of masked men dragging her into a black SUV. That vision had come to pass, but maybe this time it would be different.

She breathed in through her nose, expanding her diaphragm, before exhaling in a long, relaxing *aaaahhhhhhhh*. She imagined her body deflating like a balloon, and as she inhaled her next breath, a tingling sensation coursed through her body like a low-grade electric current, which grew stronger with each new breath.

She closed her eyes and observed a shift in the spectrum of darkness, a progression from obsidian black to a deep and flowering purple. A moment later, she was somewhere else, her mind transported to the subterranean chamber where the Temple held its most sacred rituals. A place where the screams of the damned echoed among the rocky walls but didn't penetrate the world beyond.

She hung suspended above a throng of masked congregants, her back pressed against something hard and unyielding. Gleaming torchlight flickered in the whites of so many upturned eyes, ravenous in their lust for blood. Their lips moved in the shadows, giving voice to a dark and guttural chant.

She felt a sudden lightness in her womb, and her gaze turned toward the hot caress of blood at her midsection, where the great mound of her belly was now sunken and flapped open, revealing a dark, bloody chasm robbed of its prize.

Blood seeped from the gaping wound and rained down onto the floor, where it collected in grooves etched into the stones and traced a gleaming ruby outline of a Baphomet.

A sound boomed like a thunderclap, and she watched the bloody Baphomet flare a brilliant orange, as if backlit by the fires of hell. Suddenly, the grooves were no longer grooves, but fissures... and, at last, she understood. The Baphomet was more than just a symbol—it was also a gate.

Now parted for the coming of the Six.

CHAPTER FIFTY-FIVE

It was Friday night, October 29th, and the streets of Salem teemed with costumed revelers in ghoulish apparel. Everywhere Martinez looked, there were witches, warlocks, devils, skeletons, grim reapers, wolfmen—and every slutty variation thereof—assimilating into a burgeoning crowd, which shuffled toward bars, parties, haunted houses, and countless other venues.

The last thing Martinez wanted to be doing after a frustrating day of work was weaving through a drunken group of killer clowns as she tried to enter the market on the corner of Derby Street. The Naked Fig Organic Market had the best selection of organic food in the city, and Martinez's ex-girlfriend, Stephanie, made a habit of stopping in most nights after locking up the bank.

After fighting her way inside, Martinez shrugged off the cold and wandered through the aisles. She eventually spotted Steph in the produce section, sifting through a bin of unripened bananas, her blonde hair done up in a clip. She was dressed in a knee-length black skirt paired with a royal-blue cardigan, an outfit that managed to be both elegant and sexy.

For a moment, Martinez considered turning around and melting back into the crowd outside, but something caused Steph to glance in her direction. "Elena? What are you doing here?" She looked surprised, but also a little annoyed.

"Um, I was just gonna grab something for dinner. How are you doing?"

"Okay," Steph said, placing a few loose bananas into her basket. "You?"

"Honestly, not so great."

"I'm sorry to hear that." Steph's voice held the cool neutrality of a doctor conveying a cancer diagnosis.

"I've been doing a lot of thinking about what you said. And you're right. I do have a problem expressing my feelings. I put up barriers because I'm afraid if I let people get too close, I'm gonna get hurt."

Steph's face softened a degree. "That's real progress, Elena. I'm proud of you."

"I've also been selfish with my time," Martinez said. "I realize I need to scale back and give priority to the people I love."

A smile touched Steph's lips, but quickly vanished— once Steph had made up her mind about something, there was no going back. But Martinez decided to go for it, anyway.

"I miss you, Steph… your laugh, your touch. The way you scrunch up your nose when you eat something you don't like. I was an idiot to take you for granted. I'm so sorry."

Martinez stepped toward her, closing the distance between them. Steph's lips twitched, and for a moment Martinez didn't know if she meant to laugh or cry. But Steph held eye contact, and that was the important thing. She reached for Steph's hand, and their fingers intertwined.

"I want to be with you, Steph. Always. Whether we're shopping in Paris, surfing in Costa Rica, or curling up under the blankets watching a scary movie. I love you. More than you could know."

A tear slid down Steph's cheek, and she wiped it away, laughing and sobbing at once. "Do you realize that's the first time you've said, *I love you.*"

"I know," Martinez said. "But it won't be the last." She drew Steph into her arms and kissed her.

Steph dropped the shopping basket and wrapped her arms around Martinez, kissing her back just as passionately. When the kiss was through, they clung to each other, foreheads still touching. "I missed you too," Steph whispered.

***

They went back to Martinez's apartment and kissed their way down the hall—jackets, blouses, and skirts dropping to the floor along the way. When they got to her room, they steamed up the bedside window in a marathon love-making session that left them both shuddering with exhaustion.

Afterward, Steph lay on her side and grinned at Martinez, her hair so perfectly tousled it looked almost deliberate. "That was amazing," Steph said. She pointed to her bare leg, which protruded from the blankets up to her thigh. "I literally have goosebumps."

Martinez ran her fingertips down Steph's cheek and kissed her softly on the lips. "*You're* amazing."

Something buzzed on the nightstand, and Martinez turned to see her phone lighting up with a call from Thalia, the owner of Raven's Wing.

"Do you need to get that?" Steph asked.

Martinez sent it to voicemail. "I'll listen to it later." She slipped her arm around Steph's shoulders and pulled her close. "After you're asleep."

"Mmm," Steph said. "Mind-blowing sex always makes me tired."

Martinez kissed her on the forehead. "We're gonna sleep extra hard this weekend."

Steph giggled, but her breathing was already getting deeper. "I love you, Elena."

"I love you, Steph."

And a few moments later, they were both asleep.

CHAPTER FIFTY-SIX

"Can I have another one, Daddy, *please*?"

Allie gazed up at Ray, her big blue eyes framed by the hood of her kitty cat Halloween costume, which featured bright pink ears, a long black tail, and whiskers drawn on her face with Michelle's eyeliner pencil. She had pink cotton candy crusted at the corners of her lips and was pointing at the stall where Ray had bought her the first one.

It was their school's fall festival, which they held every year on the Friday before Halloween. Michelle and a horde of other volunteers had spent all day transforming the soccer field into a spooky village, complete with a haunted maze, games, concessions, hayrides, and trick-or-treating stations.

Ray glanced over his shoulder to get Michelle's opinion on Allie's request, but she was busy chatting with Megan and a couple of women from the PTA, all of them holding plastic cups filled with wine. He turned back to Allie. "You're gonna get a ton of candy on Sunday, Allie-cat. Maybe you should wait a couple days to rot your teeth out."

Allie cupped a hand against her mouth and leaned forward, her eyes twinkling. "What if we don't tell Mommy?" she whispered.

"Will you share with your brothers?"

Allie nodded, clapping her hands excitedly.

As Ray dug out his wallet, he caught a glimpse of his brother shaking his head.

"You're gonna regret that," Jacob said.

"You're probably right." Ray handed five bucks to the man working the stall.

Allie accepted the bag of cotton candy from the man, favoring him with a toothy grin. Then she darted off into the crowd to find her friends, her cat's tail wagging in the breeze.

"What are the chances she gives any of that to her brothers?" Jacob asked.

"Literally zero."

"Where are the boys?" Jacob asked.

"Jason's hanging out in the maze with his buddies, scaring the younger kids."

Jacob pointed to Michelle and Megan. "There's the little guy."

Ray turned to see Petey zipping around in his bee costume, one finger held out at his nose as he pretended to sting people.

Ray chuckled. "That kid's gonna be trouble."

"Where'd they get that wine?" Jacob asked, motioning to their wives.

"A few of the ladies brought it. And I was already informed that it's for volunteers only."

"Then why does Megan have a glass?" Jacob asked.

"It's all about who you know, apparently. Go over there, I'm sure she'll give you a sip."

"I don't want to get sucked into small talk with the other moms."

"Better get used to it," Ray said. "Once you have kids, you've gotta pretend you like their friends' parents. Except if you're me; I don't do pretend."

Jacob laughed. "You never have."

"Life's too short to waste on people you don't like," Ray said, "which is why I need you to leave."

Jacob punched him on the shoulder. "Go ahead, you'll be all alone."

"At least I'll finally be in good company." Ray resisted the urge to massage his shoulder. Not because Jacob hit it hard, but because the old gunshot wound was still tender.

"You know you'd be lost without me," Jacob said.

"You're right. Thanks for sticking by me. These last few months have been rough."

"How's it going with Michelle?"

"Ever since that night with the undercover PI, it's been going great. I think Michelle just needed to prove to herself I wouldn't hurt her again."

"I'm really happy for you guys."

"Thanks, Jacob. I wouldn't have gotten through it without you."

"I'm just glad I could help."

"Actually," Ray said, "there's something else you could help me with, but it's work related."

"The missing girl?"

"Right. I need a hand with some company research. I figured that'd be right up your alley, being a bean counter and all."

"You know we don't actually count beans, right?"

"Don't ruin it for me," Ray said. "Now shut up and listen."

CHAPTER FIFTY-SEVEN

Martinez awakened to find Steph curled up beside her, one hand stretched over her head, the other draped across Martinez's chest. Bright arcs of morning sunlight sluiced through the blinds and painted the headboard in a pattern of gilded crescents. The clock on the nightstand read 7:13 a.m., which was two minutes before her alarm was set to go off.

Martinez rolled over and disabled the alarm, trying not to disturb Steph, who looked angelic lying on the downy white comforter, her wavy blonde hair fanned out over the pillow. Except for a single freckle high on her left cheekbone, Steph's complexion was flawless, and she had full lips that were irresistibly kissable.

Steph uttered a sleepy sigh of contentment and drew a deep breath. "Were you watching me sleep?" she asked, her eyes fluttering open.

Martinez ran a hand through Steph's hair and nodded. "I'm so glad you're here."

"Me too. I haven't slept that well in ages. What time do you have to be at work?"

"Forty-five minutes. Will I see you tonight?"

Steph kissed her on the lips. "I'll be here waiting."

***

Martinez didn't notice the voicemail until she was almost out the door. She'd completely forgotten about Thalia's missed call and had fallen asleep before she could check it. "Shit," she muttered, playing the message as she trudged downstairs.

"Hi, Detective Martinez. This is Thalia from Raven's Wing. I hope I'm not catching you at a bad time, but... well, you and your partner had asked about that cult, the Temple of Six. I was being honest when I said I'd never heard of it. But I overheard somebody mentioning it today and, um, I wanted to let you know. So, I guess call me back when you can. Thanks."

"Shit," Martinez muttered again. She hit redial, but it went straight to voicemail.

Instead of heading to the station, Martinez hopped into her Corolla and drove to Thalia's house since Raven's Wing didn't open for another couple of hours.

Thalia lived in a single-story cottage on English Street with chestnut-brown siding and stained-glass windows that were impossible to peer through. She'd decorated the stoop with a family of jack-o-lanterns arranged on mini bales of hay. Planted in the wilted grass beside it was a painted wooden cutout of a grinning witch stirring a cauldron.

Martinez knocked on the door. "Thalia? It's Detective Martinez. Open up." After the third round of knocking, Martinez tried the knob, which turned easily in her hand. "Thalia?" She stepped into the foyer. "Are you here?"

The stained-glass windows blocked out most of the light, and it took Martinez a few moments for her eyes to adjust to the darkness. The interior layout was a perfect square, with the door opening directly into the living room, which then merged into the kitchen. There were two doors on the wall to her left, which she guessed led to a bathroom and a bedroom, which meant the entire cottage couldn't measure more than 600 square feet. The ceilings were high, with rustic wooden rafters crisscrossing above the kitchen and living room.

That's where she spotted Thalia—dangling from a noose in the shadows of the ceiling, her feet tracing a slow, pendulous arc above the kitchen countertop.

CHAPTER FIFTY-EIGHT

"Christ," Ray said, gazing up at the rafters. "Did you touch anything?" He turned to Martinez, who appeared uncharacteristically rattled.

Martinez shook her head slowly.

"No suicide note?" he asked.

"Not that I could find. Everything looks in order, no signs of forced entry." She motioned to the overturned saucepan that lay on the hardwood floor in front of the countertop island. "It looks like she stood on the saucepan to reach the noose. Or maybe that's what someone wants us to think, anyway."

"Let me hear that voicemail," Ray said.

Martinez played it on speaker. "Do you think the person she overheard came into the store? It would make sense, right? It is an occult shop."

"Maybe Fiona overheard the same conversation," Ray said. "Let's head to Raven's Wing when it opens."

Martinez balled her hands into fists. "This is what I get for silencing my phone."

"Don't do that to yourself, Martinez. If she thought she was in any danger, she would've called 911, not an off-duty detective."

"But I saw the call and ignored it. I meant to listen to it last night, but I passed out. And because of that, some psycho strung her up while I was sleeping."

"If you'd taken the call," Ray said, "we might've gotten a lead, but it wouldn't have saved her. As soon as she hung up, the same damn thing would've happened."

"Not if I'd come over here."

"Come on, Martinez. That wouldn't have been necessary, and you know it. You can't be on duty 24/7, and no matter how hard you try, you can't save everybody."

She drew a deep breath and closed her eyes. "It's the day before Halloween, Ray. What was she trying to tell us?"

"We're gonna figure this out. Don't go losing hope now."

***

Crime Scene Services arrived at Thalia's house a half hour later, and Ray gave them strict instructions to treat it like a murder scene. While CSS snapped pictures and dusted for prints, Ray and Martinez searched through Thalia's bookshelves and personal belongings for any possible connections to the Temple.

Her phone and computer were both locked, and after a couple of wrong guesses at the passwords, Ray reluctantly let CSS bag them up as evidence. If they could convince Judge Reynolds to issue a warrant, their IT specialists would be able to access her devices.

"It could be too late by then," Martinez said, watching CSS haul the electronics away.

Ray didn't want to say it but he was thinking the same thing. "We need a breakthrough," he said, "and we need it now."

"We need one of Brody or Danielle's coworkers to come forward," Martinez said. "One of them must know something."

Ray agreed, but their coworkers had been under surveillance for days, and so far, nobody had done anything suspicious. "What do you think about the seminary student's manuscript?" Ray asked. "All that nonsense about the lost Book of Revelations and the six demons bringing about the apocalypse? You think the Temple really believes that?"

"If they're planning to go through with the sacrifice, they must believe it."

"For what it's worth," Ray said, "I think the prophecy is bullshit."

"So do I," Martinez said. "But I saw something in Abby's bedroom, and I think you did too. I don't know what the Temple is planning, but they're messing with forces that none of us understand."

Ray recalled the terrifying moments in Abby's bedroom when he sensed dark things zipping around his peripheral vision, their whispered voices taunting him, naming his sins, while Abby's mouth transformed into a spiral of fangs.

"Ray? You okay?"

"Yeah. But you're right; I did see something."

"What was it?"

"You know what I saw."

"I want to hear you say it."

"Fine," he said. "It was like Abby's face disappeared, and there was another one looming behind it. Something freaky and demonic with a mouthful of fangs."

"We need to talk to that seminary student," Martinez said, "and see what else he knows."

"That's not gonna happen," Ray said.

"Why not?"

"Because I asked Frank for more details on the author, and he told me the manuscript is in terrible condition. The title page is all smudged, and all that's legible are the words *Jason* and *Divinity School*. And before you ask, a lot of the bigger universities have divinity schools, so there's no way of knowing if we're talking about Harvard Divinity, Duke Divinity, or even the University of Chicago Divinity School."

"Was there a publisher?" Martinez asked.

"Frank's friend thinks this Jason guy printed and bound it himself, but he's only ever seen the one copy."

"Great. We've hit another dead end."

"For now," Ray said. "But like my old partner used to say, when you lose one thread, go tug on another. Eventually, the sonofabitch will unravel."

***

They found Fiona sitting behind the register at Raven's Wing, sipping a coffee and scrolling through social media on her phone. Sunlight filtered through the window behind her, illuminating her flaming red hair and endowing her with an angelic quality that was betrayed by her perpetual scowl.

Martinez cleared her throat. "Good morning, Fiona. Do you know where Thalia is?"

Fiona raised her eyes slowly. Reluctantly. "She doesn't usually get here until noon."

"When's the last time you heard from her?" Martinez asked.

"At closing yesterday." Fiona's eyes migrated back to her phone, as if she'd lost interest in the conversation.

Martinez cleared her throat again. "I'm afraid we have some bad news."

Fiona looked up, finally paying attention. Her emerald-green eyes reflected the steely defiance of someone who'd hardened herself to a lifetime of bad news. "What is it?"

"Thalia is dead. We found her this morning."

Fiona's face twisted into a mask of anguish. The phone slipped between her fingers and clattered to the floor. If she was faking it, it was the best damn performance Ray had ever seen. It took more than a minute for her to regain her composure.

"What happened?" Fiona asked, her voice cracking.

"We can't share those details right now," Ray said. "But if you could tell us her frame of mind these last few days, it would help our investigation."

A look of horror flashed across Fiona's face. "What do you mean by *investigation*? Was she murdered?"

"We're in the process of making that determination," Martinez said. "But we need your help to figure out what happened."

Fiona massaged her temples and stared into space, her eyes glistening. "I can't believe this. How can she be dead?"

"Did Thalia have any enemies?" Ray asked. "Anyone who might've wanted to cause her harm? Maybe someone from the coven?"

Fiona shook her head. "Everyone loved her. She was like a mother to me. Someone who really cared, you know?"

"What about the Temple of Six?" Martinez asked.

"I told you I don't know anything about the Temple."

"But you've heard of it," Ray said.

"Only from you guys."

"How was business going?" Ray asked. "Was she struggling to make ends meet?" He glanced around the store, which hadn't had a single customer since he and Martinez walked in.

Fiona shrugged. "The last couple years have been slow. A rival shop opened around the corner, and since then, it's been half as busy here. Thalia was hoping for a strong Halloween, but we haven't seen the traffic."

"She called me last night," Martinez said. "She said she overheard something about the Temple of Six. Did she mention anything to you about it?"

"No," Fiona said, shaking her head.

"Do you know who she might have heard it from?" Martinez asked.

"She didn't say anything to me. And I didn't overhear anyone talking about the Temple."

"Where were you last night?" Ray asked.

"I went to Kettle & Cauldron after work."

"Were you with anyone?" Martinez asked.

"Tracy."

Ray cocked a thumb in the direction of Mystical Brew. "That Tracy? Your roommate?"

Fiona nodded, wiping a tear from her eyes. "I need to tell her about Thalia."

Martinez laid a hand on Fiona's shoulder. "I'm sorry for your loss. But if you think of anything else, please give us a call."

318

CHAPTER FIFTY-NINE

"Where are you going?" Martinez asked.

She had turned the corner out of Raven's Wing and was headed toward Mystical Brew, but Ray was making a beeline for the Explorer, keys in hand.

"We're not interviewing Tracy right now," he said.

"Why not?"

"Because Eddie Fischer says he got roofied at Kettle & Cauldron. And Officer Jeffries followed Tracy and Fiona there last week when they were under surveillance. I'm starting to think they might be regulars."

Martinez followed him to the Explorer without a word, and they drove to Salem Police headquarters. They went straight to Eddie's holding cell, where they found him lying on his bunk staring up at the ceiling. He sat up quickly when they strode over to the bars.

"What is it?" he asked.

"I want you to look at a couple pictures," Ray said. He pulled up a photo of Fiona and held it so Eddie could see. "You know this girl?" he asked.

Eddie shook his head. "Doesn't look familiar."

"What about this one?" Ray said, swiping to a photo of Tracy.

Eddie's eyes lit up. "That's her, the girl from the bar! The one I was talking to when I got roofied."

CHAPTER SIXTY

Father Maroney stared into the darkened living room and wondered what he should do. He'd polished off the last of his liquor cabinet hours ago and had staggered to the couch before passing out. But now that he'd stirred awake, the effects of alcohol had receded, leaving behind nothing but guilt and self-loathing.

Kill yourself.

It's what he deserved, what his sins demanded. Satan had corrupted him with lust and bought his silence with vanity. Even if he threw himself at the feet of the bishop and confessed, the severity of his crimes against God and Church would surely result in his defrocking. And what would he do then? Travel the world as a disgrace, a man without a shred of dignity?

Father Maroney closed his eyes and wept. He'd committed the most horrific acts of blasphemy imaginable. Would God really forgive him if he did confess? Or was it better to end his life and fall on the sword of damnation? Was he damned if he did... or damned if he didn't?

He must've still been drunk, because the last thought made him giggle. The sound was high-pitched and maniacal, like a man gone mad. A moment later, something thumped at his front door, and he sat up with a start.

The lock turned and the door swung slowly open. The shadow of a man stepped inside and clicked on a flashlight, the brightness making Father Maroney shield his eyes and squint.

"Who are you? What do you want?"

He could see the man now, backlit by the glow of the flashlight beam. He appeared muscular, with curly dark hair and a Salem Police patch emblazoned on his left sleeve.

"Relax, Father Maroney. Just your friendly neighborhood officer stopping in for a welfare check." He paused to sniff the air. "Have you been drinking? It's not becoming of a man of the cloth."

Father Maroney's heart thudded in his chest. "What are you doing in my home?"

"I'm here to escort you to the Temple of Six." He threw a garment at Father Maroney. "Now put on that robe and walk quietly to the van. Act like we're taking a trip to the police station to pick perps out of a lineup."

"And if I say no?"

"Then I'll summon my associates, who will gladly break your bones and haul you out of here on a stretcher."

"What do you want with me?"

"The high priest requires your attendance at an important mass. It seems you're to be a guest of honor."

CHAPTER SIXTY-ONE

Ray called everyone into the briefing room to share the update on Tracy Lasher. "I think she's working with Brody and the other cult members," he said, turning to Captain Barnes, who had pretty much become a permanent fixture at Salem Police headquarters these last few days. "We can either haul her in for questioning or follow her and see where she goes. If we go with the first option, she might clam up. And if we go with the second option, there's no guarantee she'll lead us to Cassie. I think you should make the call, Captain."

Captain Barnes took a moment to consider the options. "Let's drag her in here and find out what she knows."

"Alright," Ray said. "Martinez and I—"

Garrison stormed into the briefing room. "I'm sorry to interrupt, but we got a match on the DNA results from under Brittany's nails. One of the ancestry databases identified a direct relative of her killer."

"Who's the match?" Barnes asked.

"A woman named Lily Whitehall," Garrison said. "Alex Whitehall's mother."

"Sonofabitch," Ray said. "If Alex killed Brittany, he for sure had something to do with Cassie's disappearance."

Chief Sanderson pointed at Garrison. "Get that report over to Judge Reynolds right away. We'll need a warrant to search Alex's house and car. In the meantime, find him and arrest him."

Ray stood up and gestured to Martinez and Garrison. "We'll go after Alex."

Sanderson nodded. "Officer Jeffries will bring Tracy Lasher in for questioning." He regarded them with a stern gaze.

"You've all worked damned hard to get us to this point, so be safe out there... and don't screw it up."

***

Ray stood in the Salem Police parking lot with Garrison and Martinez, strategizing their next move. Judge Reynolds had already signed off on the search warrant. Sanderson said the judge was understandably distraught and described Alex as a bright young attorney who worked diligently during the week and often did pro bono work on Saturdays. But like any good judge, she put her personal feelings aside and approved the search warrant.

Garrison glanced at his watch. "It's almost noon, and Alex could either be at home or at the office doing his pro bono work."

"We should split up," Martinez said.

Garrison nodded. "I can take Officer Frasier with me to Alex's house. If he's not there, we'll go inside and execute the search warrant."

"Martinez and I will go to his office," Ray said, "and take the same approach." He would've preferred swapping the assignments, but Brittany's murder was Garrison's case, so it was only fair.

"Let's stay off the radios and keep this operation tight," Garrison said. "I don't want the calvary spooking this guy." He held up his phone. "We'll use our chat group to stay in contact."

Ray squeezed Garrison's shoulder. "We'll see you on the other side."

CHAPTER SIXTY-TWO

Alex lived across the street from the Salem Common in a stately home with white siding and black shutters. Garrison drove past it and parked a half block away where he'd still have a view of the front porch. He turned to Officer Frasier, who was riding shotgun. "Pretty nice digs for a public defender."

"I hear he comes from money," Frasier said. "Trust fund or something like that."

"Yeah, well he's gonna need OJ money to dodge a conviction with the evidence we've got."

"I don't see his car," Frasier said. "He might not be home."

Garrison texted an update to the group chat, then turned back to Frasier. "Let's wait fifteen minutes to see if he shows."

As they watched the house in silence, Garrison found himself wondering about Holly, the girl who'd befriended Brittany and lured her to the pagan festival on the afternoon of her murder. Although the DNA evidence suggested Alex had struck the mortal blow, the statements from Brittany's roommate pointed to Holly as an accessory.

Garrison reached into the cruiser's center console for his notepad and thumbed through the pages for the description he'd recorded for Holly.

White girl, dark hair, gave off '80s metal vibe, presence of tattoos unknown.

A thought suddenly occurred to him, and he wrote a single question beneath the description.

Does Holly = Tracy Lasher?

CHAPTER SIXTY-THREE

Ray and Martinez arrived at the courthouse just as Alex exited the building and jogged down the steps, briefcase in hand. He wore dark jeans and a gray peacoat, and he kept glancing over his shoulder, as if he expected someone to follow.

Martinez shrugged off her seatbelt. "Do you think he knows?"

Ray opened the door and hopped out of the Explorer.

Alex's head swiveled in their direction.

Ray lifted a hand in greeting. "Hey, Alex. You got a second?"

Alex hesitated at the sight of them, then whirled around and ran in the direction of North Street.

Ray and Martinez exchanged a glance before taking off after him. "I hope you brought your running shoes," Ray said.

Martinez cupped a hand against the side of her mouth and shouted at Alex. "Stop, you're under arrest!"

Alex darted into oncoming traffic, eliciting a cacophony of honking horns and screeching brakes. He halted at the center line, standing ramrod straight and raising his briefcase into the air as cars zipped past him in both directions.

By the time Ray and Martinez reached the intersection, traffic had snarled enough to let Alex across. Ray waved his badge at the cars and signaled his intent to follow. Once they reached the other side, Ray and Martinez pursued Alex down North Street. He was leading them by a dozen paces, but they were slowly shrinking the gap.

Alex hooked a right onto Essex Street, rounding the bend at the Witch House Museum, which loomed over the corner like a colonial relic with its dark wood siding, gabled roof, and diamond-pattern windowpanes.

Ray yelled at Alex as he turned the corner, Martinez matching him stride for stride. "It's over, Alex!"

Alex glanced over his shoulder, anger contorting his features as he continued past a medieval stone church, his briefcase still clutched at his side.

They were close enough now to hear Alex's labored breathing, but he somehow managed to pick up speed as he approached the sign for Ropes Mansion. The palatial estate had a wrought iron fence and a pathway leading into a massive garden arranged in a pattern of concentric circles.

A couple dozen tourists milled about the garden, wandering through the mazelike circles, gawking at the hardy fall plants and greenery. Alex merged into the crowd and appeared to be headed for the open field beyond. Ray's view of him cut in and out like the flickering images of an old movie reel, stolen glimpses between the crush of bodies. In one frame, Ray saw Alex's briefcase flap open like a clamshell. In another, the briefcase was lying on the ground.

Ray fought his way through the crowd, attempting to go after Alex in a direct line. Meanwhile, Martinez hustled toward the outer ring of the circle, trying to outflank Alex before he reached the open field.

The next time Alex emerged into view, he was waving a gun in one hand and reaching for someone with the other. Ray had time only to think—*it was in his briefcase*—before Alex hoisted a small boy into the air and pressed a gun against his head.

"Stay back!" Alex yelled.

The crowd dispersed at the sight of the gun, people running and screaming in every direction.

The boy wore a black goose-down jacket and a Patriots knit hat, his legs flailing as Alex hugged him against his chest.

"Let him go!" a woman screamed. "Don't hurt my son!"

THE BURYING POINT

The boy reached his arms toward her, his face flushed, tears coursing down his cheeks. "Mommy!"

Alex pointed the gun at Ray. "Get your hands up and don't come any closer."

Ray lifted his hands into the air. "Put him down, Alex." Although his eyes were focused on the gun, Ray could see Martinez moving in his peripheral vision. She was a half dozen paces behind Alex and in danger of being spotted if he turned around.

"You're gonna let me walk out of here," Alex said. He shifted his gaze to the boy's mother. "And you, you're gonna reach under the detective's jacket, get his gun, and walk it over to me, keeping the muzzle pointed at yourself the whole time. You got that?"

As the woman nodded, Martinez crouched down behind a juniper bush ten feet from where Alex stood.

"Where's your partner?" Alex asked, glancing behind him.

Ray shook his head. "I don't know."

"Where is she?" he repeated, shouting now.

"Just calm down," Ray said, "and stick to the plan. The lady hands you my gun, and you let her kid go. That's the deal, right?"

The woman shuffled toward Ray and reached under his sports jacket, groping for his shoulder holster with trembling hands. "Easy," Ray said. "Watch the trigger."

A moment later, she had the gun and began walking it over to Alex.

"Put it in the briefcase," Alex said, motioning to the open case lying on the ground. "Then close it up and spin the dial on the combination."

The woman did as she was instructed. "Please," she said. "My son."

Alex shook his head. "Sorry, but I need the insurance." He whirled around and made a beeline for the open field, the kid

327

still clutched against his chest, the gun pointed toward the ground as he ran.

Martinez sprang out of the bushes and fired her Taser into Alex's back. He dropped to his knees and thrashed his arms as the metal leads bit into his flesh and pumped him full of electricity. The kid flew out of Alex's hands and tumbled into the grass. He popped up a moment later and raced into his mother's outstretched arms.

Martinez strode over to Alex, delivering another jolt from her Taser before she cuffed him and hauled him to his feet. "You're under arrest for the murder of Brittany Cooper." She rattled off his Miranda Rights.

Ray approached the mom and son, who were locked in an embrace, the boy's head buried in her chest. Ray nudged him in the arm. "You okay, buddy?"

The boy glanced up, tears running down his cheeks.

"If you weren't so brave, we wouldn't have caught the bad guy. We owe you a big thanks." He reached for the boy's hand and shook it, grinning as a smile broke through the boy's tears.

He slipped a business card into the boy's hand. "Once you've had a chance to catch your breath, I'll need you and your mom to come to the station to file a witness statement. We want to make sure attempted kidnapping gets added to his charges. And I'll have a special deputy's badge waiting there for you. We only give them out to real heroes."

The boy puffed out his chest, and Ray patted him on the back. "I'll see you later, buddy."

He turned around and jogged to catch up to Martinez, who was marching Alex down the pathway toward the street. "Just so we're clear," Ray said, glaring at Alex, "I always knew you were a piece of shit."

Alex stared ahead as if he hadn't heard, his face stoic.

"If you tell us where Cassie is," Ray said, "maybe you'll get a lighter sentence."

Alex smirked at him. "In thirty-six hours, when the legion of Six breaches the gate in fulfillment of the prophecy, I'll walk out of my jail cell and step over your rotting corpses."

"Go easy on that Kool-Aid, will you?" Ray said.

When they reached the wrought iron gate at the edge of the street, Ray pulled out his handcuffs and secured Alex's ankle to the gatepost. "You'd better behave while I pull the car around."

"Don't worry," Martinez said. "If he tries anything, I'll light him up like a Roman candle."

CHAPTER SIXTY-FOUR

Garrison's phone lit up with a text alert from Ray. He pumped his fist when he finished reading.

"What is it?" Frasier asked.

"They got Alex!"

"Where?"

"They ran him down outside the courthouse. They're headed back to the station now." Garrison unbuckled his seat belt and opened the door to the cruiser. "Let's go search his place."

Garrison retrieved the battering ram from his trunk. It was a single officer model—matte black, cylindrical, and weighing thirty-five pounds. He gripped it in one hand as he strode toward Alex's house with Frasier in tow. He would've preferred one of his own men, but he was in a rush when the warrant came through, and bringing Frasier was safer than going alone.

They ascended the stairs to Alex's porch, which was draped in a gauzy white lattice of cobwebs. A trio of motion-activated tarantulas hissed and vibrated at their approach. A life-sized statue of the Grim Reaper stood sentinel at the front door, its lurid red eyes staring at them from the shadowy recesses of its hood.

As Garrison approached the door, the Grim Reaper lunged forward with a menacing growl, its scythe coming down in an animatronic chopping motion. Garrison jerked backward and dropped the battering ram, punching a hole in the floorboards and nearly breaking his own foot.

Frasier burst out laughing, one hand clutching his stomach.

"Goddamnit!" Garrison yelled. "I hate this holiday." He picked up the battering ram and pointed at Frasier. "It's not funny."

"You should've seen your face."

Garrison drew back the battering ram and smashed it into the door beneath the knob, busting through on the first try. He lowered the ram and shoved the Grim Reaper with his other hand, toppling the statue onto its back, making its eyes light up as it growled at the ceiling.

He entered the foyer, which opened into an opulent living room, complete with large stone hearth, crystal chandelier, and gleaming hardwood throughout. The wall opposite the fireplace contained a built-in bookshelf, the wood a rich, dark mahogany that wrapped around a cushioned reading nook overlooking the side yard.

Definitely a trust fund baby, Garrison thought.

"You didn't call Crime Scene Services yet, did you?" Frasier asked.

Garrison shook his head. "I want to have a look around first."

Frasier shut the front door, using the battering ram to keep it from popping back open since the guts of the locking mechanism bulged out of the frame like a ruined eye hanging from its socket.

Garrison scanned the bookshelves. Most of the books were encyclopedic volumes with names like *Federal Reporter* or *American Law Reports*, but the shelves near the reading nook were old leatherbound texts with occult markings—pentagrams, stars, moons, upside down crosses.

"Looks like we found our cult member," Garrison said. He pulled one of the books off the shelf and turned around to show Frasier, but instead found himself staring into the muzzle of Frasier's gun.

"Put your hands up," Frasier said.

"What the hell are you doing?" Garrison asked. He raised his hands over his head, still gripping the book.

"I'm doing my part for the Six."

"You're one of them?" Garrison asked. "A cult member?"

Frasier laughed. "Who do you think opened a back door to the traffic camera footage? Your tech nerds still haven't figured it out, have they?"

Garrison swallowed, his throat suddenly bone-dry. He had to keep Frasier talking, had to buy time in hopes of Ray or Martinez showing up.

"Where'd you learn how to hack security cameras?"

"All I did was open the door," Frasier said. "One of our guys did the rest. As you know, we're a very resourceful group."

"You tipped off Alex, didn't you?"

"We look after our own," Frasier said.

"What about Brody?"

"Why don't you ask him yourself?"

A rough scraping emanated from the hearth, and Garrison watched as the fireplace grate slid back against the wall, revealing a dark chasm underneath. A pair of hands reached up through the hole, followed by a head, as if someone was ascending a ladder from below.

Frasier grinned. "Did you know that some of the town's wealthiest merchants connected the old smuggling tunnels right up to their fireplaces? Pretty wild, isn't it?"

Garrison thought about all the times they'd assigned someone to watch Alex's house. He'd been able to come and go as he pleased right under their noses. That's why the reports always said he never left.

"I believe you two know each other," Frasier said, motioning to Evan Brody, who was now standing in the living room holding a bo staff.

Frasier's attention strayed from Garrison for a split second, but it was long enough for Garrison to strike. He hurled the occult volume at Frasier, throwing it like a ninja star. The book spun end for end before striking Frasier dead in the face and sending him staggering.

Garrison reached to his hip and drew his gun, but a swipe from Brody's staff knocked it away almost immediately. Garrison raised his fists and squared against Brody.

Brody spun the staff so fast, it looked like it had six ends instead of two. Garrison rocked on his heels, ready for anything. Suddenly, Brody lunged at him with a cross strike that landed on the side of his ribs.

Garrison grunted, but cinched his arm down on the staff and yanked it with his other hand, making Brody stumble forward. Garrison pivoted, trying to wrestle the staff out of Brody's hands. Brody let go at the last moment, and Garrison lost his balance and fell backward into the bookshelves.

Brody charged at him, and there was no time to lift the staff, so Garrison let it clatter to the floor and kicked it out of reach before dodging a punch from Brody that landed against a row of legal texts, splintering the old leather spines.

Brody was one of the few criminals Garrison had faced who matched his six-foot-six, two-hundred-fifty-pound frame. The guy bulged with muscles, his bare arms roped with tattoos glorifying death and the Devil.

Brody threw another punch, and Garrison parried away, countering with a body blow to the ribs and a nasty uppercut that Brody somehow teetered away from. Garrison circled right and shoved Brody against the bookshelf, following it up with another body blow and a jab to the face.

There'd been a time when Garrison considered pro boxing as a career, back when he was training at the police academy and dominating in the ring. He ended up going 5–0 in professional matches across New England, winning them all by knockout in the first round. But the exhilaration and the glory were outweighed by the brutality of the sport and the emerging threat of CTE and cognitive decline.

You're too smart to risk all that, his Momma would've said. And she was right.

But now that he had Brody backed against the bookshelf, that old feeling of exhilaration returned. He could

333

almost hear the crowd cheering as he hammered his fists into the sonofabitch like he was a heavy bag, alternating between body blows and head punches so that Brody didn't know where to protect.

After landing a devastating jab-cross-uppercut combo, Brody went lights out, his eyes turned up as he fell against the bookshelf and slid down to the floor. Garrison loomed over him, his chest heaving. When he turned around, he saw Frasier standing with his Taser pointed at him, a gash under his eye from where the book had struck him.

Garrison spun out of the way, reaching for his own Taser, but Frasier pivoted and fired. The metallic leads hit Garrison in the throat, biting into his flesh, before delivering a debilitating shock that dropped him to his knees. His whole body seized up, jaw clenching, muscles straining, the smell of ozone filling the air.

When the feeling subsided, Frasier shocked him again, and the whole process started over. He slipped in and out of consciousness, unsure of the passage of time. When he finally looked up, Brody was standing over him, reaching for his feet.

Garrison felt himself being dragged across the hardwood floor while he stared up groggily at the crystal chandelier and the coffered ceiling. It felt like something was pinching his wrists, and it took him a moment to realize he was handcuffed.

"Hurry up," Frasier said, his voice sounding far away. "Get him into the tunnel. This ritual needs all the blood we can get."

CHAPTER SIXTY-FIVE

Ray tried getting Alex to talk on the drive back to headquarters, but Alex just stared out the window and pretended not to hear. Finally, Ray said, "You don't honestly believe in this prophecy, do you? In the coming of the Six?"

Alex met Ray's gaze in the rearview mirror. "People pray to God all their lives and never get results. But the Six have given me everything I've wanted, and their reign is only just begun."

"Unless we stop it," Martinez said.

Alex shook his head. "No one can stop the Six."

Ray looked at Martinez. "Remember those guys who were supposed to catch a ride on the Hale-Bopp comet?"

"You mean the Heaven's Gate cult?" Martinez asked. "Their ride wasn't on the comet. It was supposed to be on the UFO trailing behind it."

"The UFO never picked them up, did it?" Ray asked.

Martinez shook her head. "They died by ritual suicide."

"Exactly. Because they were a bunch of wack jobs. Does that remind you of anybody we know?"

"You'll see," Alex said. "After the ritual, everything in this world will be transformed."

"I'll take that bet," Ray said.

When Alex didn't respond, Martinez said, "What can you tell us about Jason, the seminary student who wrote about the Six? Is he a member of the Temple? Your high priest, maybe?"

Alex snickered. "I'll let you figure that out for yourselves."

Ray pulled the Explorer into the parking lot of Salem Police headquarters. "You ever been to prison, Alex? I have a feeling you're not gonna like it."

Ray shifted into park and killed the engine. He climbed out of the SUV, opened the rear door, and hauled Alex out of the back seat. Alex's hands were still cuffed behind his back, and Ray and Martinez each grabbed an arm and escorted Alex toward the station's front entrance.

When they were a half dozen paces from the door, Alex swayed on his feet and slumped against the brick wall, the left side of his face disintegrating into a bloody mist.

"Get down!" Ray yelled, dropping to the pavement and pulling Martinez with him.

He swept his gaze across the parking lot but didn't see the shooter, most of his view obstructed by a row of police cruisers. He fumbled for his radio and reported an active shooter, his voice drowned out by the sound of screeching tires in the street.

He jumped up and caught a glimpse of an SUV turning the corner at high speed. "Black SUV," he said, speaking into his radio. "I'm not sure of the make or model."

He gazed at Martinez, who had Alex's blood spattered across her face. "Are you okay?"

"Yeah, you?"

Ray nodded, observing Alex's blood and gray matter trickling down the wall. "He's dead," Ray said.

"But why?"

"Because somebody didn't want him to talk."

CHAPTER SIXTY-SIX

Within minutes, the parking lot had transformed into a bustling crime scene roped off by yellow police tape, the perimeter crawling with investigators snapping pictures and laying down evidence markers. The Crime Scene Services techs discovered two bullet casings on Margin Street, lying on the pavement opposite the parking lot.

When they rolled the tape on the security cameras, it showed a black Cadillac Escalade with darkly tinted windows and a phony paper tag halting outside the police station. The passenger side window cracked open to reveal the silenced muzzle of a rifle, which fired two shots before the car sped away.

They found the second bullet lodged into the brick wall at a height of about six feet, which meant it had probably been intended for Ray.

"You're lucky to be alive," Chief Sanderson said, peering down at the shell casings in a paper evidence bag. They were standing in the parking lot, just inside the taped-off perimeter.

"Let me have a look at that," Captain Barnes said. Sanderson passed him the evidence bag, and Barnes stared inside for a long moment. When he looked up, he said, "They're 7.62 x 51 mm rounds, which means they came from a sniper rifle similar to an M24."

"How common are those?" Ray asked.

"The M24 is a favored weapon of the US military and police SWAT teams, so it's not hard to come by."

"Ballistics will be able to tell us more," Sanderson said.

Barnes handed the evidence bag to Martinez. "Alex didn't say anything about Cassie? Not even a hint of her whereabouts?"

"We tried getting him to talk," Martinez said, "but he wouldn't say much beyond the Temple. I think he actually believed in the prophecy. But the Temple killed him anyway."

"Whoever's calling the shots wanted to prevent Alex from giving up the location of the ritual," Ray said, "These guys are highly organized, ruthless, and a hell of a lot smarter than we've given them credit for. They've had a contingency for everything."

"What do you mean?" Sanderson asked.

"Besides rigging the church and the warehouse with explosives, they set up Eddie from day one. But they only played that card when we got too close to Brody."

"But why wait?" Martinez asked. "Alex could've dropped a hint about Eddie from the beginning."

"That's true," Ray said, "but there was a risk it could backfire, especially if Eddie sounded credible enough. Or if he could ID Brody or Tracy as having drugged him."

"You're assuming Eddie's telling the truth," Sanderson said.

Ray folded his arms. "I'd bet my pension on it."

"Are you sure you want to do that?" Sanderson asked. "His blood and urine results came back negative for roofies."

"You heard Prosecutor Daley," Ray said. "It doesn't last long in the blood or urine, but it'll show up in his hair in a day or so when he's retested."

"What about Tracy?" Martinez asked. "Did Officer Jeffries arrest her?"

Sanderson frowned. "Tracy's coworkers spotted her leaving the coffee shop right before Jeffries got there."

"Christ!" Ray said. "Alex must've tipped her off. I swear he knew something was up when we spotted him leaving the courthouse."

"We've issued an APB on Tracy Lasher and the Cadillac Escalade," Sanderson said. "And we've got a team looking at the traffic footage."

"The Temple knows how to exploit the cameras," Martinez said. "They'll delete whatever they don't want us to see."

"And then they'll go into hiding," Ray said, "and lie low while they prepare for the ritual. All we can hope is that the search of Alex's house gives us clues to where they're holding it."

"I'd like to ride with you to Alex's house," Captain Barnes said. "Have you heard anything from Garrison?"

Ray shook his head. "Last time I called, his phone went straight to voicemail."

CHAPTER SIXTY-SEVEN

"What is that?" Martinez asked, leaning over Ray's shoulder from the back seat. "Is that smoke?"

Ray and Barnes stared out the windshield in the direction she pointed. At first Ray didn't see it—gray clouds had rolled in as the afternoon wore on, and he'd mistaken the plumes of smoke rising over Salem Common as fast-moving thunderheads.

He caught Martinez's eye in the rearview mirror. "Try Garrison again." He made a left, then a right, bringing them within a block of the Common, where the smoke was thicker. Closer.

Martinez lowered the phone and shook her head. "Voicemail again."

Ray turned onto Alex's street and rolled past Garrison's cruiser, peering into the empty front seat.

"Oh my God," Martinez muttered.

Ray turned and looked up the street, where flickering orange flames danced behind the windows of Alex's house, illuminating an interior engulfed by a roaring inferno. Dark smoke belched from the eaves and swirled into the air, adding to the clouds hovering over the Common.

At least twenty people were gathered in the street outside, staring at the burning house, their gazes transfixed. Ray shifted into park and jumped out of the Explorer.

"Police!" he yelled. "Everyone back!" He scanned the faces of the retreating crowd, searching for Garrison or Frasier, but he didn't see them anywhere.

Captain Barnes grabbed a roll of yellow police tape from the glovebox and worked with Martinez to rope off the perimeter as Ray forced the onlookers back. "Clear the street! Make room for the Fire Depart—"

An explosion rocked the foundation, shattering the windows and eliciting a chorus of shrieks from the crowd. The front porch collapsed a moment later, followed by the roof, which caved in with a resounding crash that sent a swarm of sparks spiraling up into the darkening sky.

Ray yelled for Garrison and tried to rush forward, but Barnes held him back. "It's too dangerous, Ray. There's nothing we can do."

As the warble of sirens rose into the air, Ray stood huddled in the street beside Martinez and Barnes, thinking about all the times that Garrison had saved his life... and wondering if he'd ever get the chance to repay him.

CHAPTER SIXTY-EIGHT

Officer Frasier staggered into the street, silhouetted against the glow of the roaring flames. He was bloodied and bruised, his face covered in soot.

Ray and Martinez rushed forward to meet him, and Frasier collapsed into their arms. They carried him across the street and laid him down on the curb.

"Are you okay?" Ray asked.

Frasier turned his head and coughed, the sound dry and raspy. "Need water."

Martinez found someone in the crowd with a bottle of water. She brought it over and guided the bottle to Frasier's lips.

He coughed and sputtered at first, but managed to keep the rest down. "Better," he said. "Thanks."

"Where's Garrison?" Ray asked. "Was he with you?"

"We were ambushed inside the house," Frasier said. "Two guys wearing ski masks. We fought them off, but one guy hit me with a bo staff and knocked me out cold. When I came to, the place was on fire."

"Did you see Garrison when you woke up?" Ray asked.

Frasier coughed again. "I couldn't see anything through the smoke. I crawled out the side window and was running toward the street when the place exploded."

"Before you got knocked out," Martinez said, "did you happen to notice if Garrison was hurt?"

"I don't know. It happened so fast."

The firetrucks finally arrived, along with an ambulance, their sirens wailing. "Over here!" Captain Barnes yelled, signaling to the paramedics.

THE BURYING POINT

The paramedics lifted Frasier onto a gurney and administered oxygen before loading him into the ambulance and speeding away.

Two hours later, the fire was out, but there was still no sign of Garrison. The Salem Fire department had prevented the blaze from spreading, but that was the only miracle of the night. Given the instability of the burned-out ruins, it would be at least a day before they could search for casualties and conduct an arson investigation.

"Maybe he's not in there," Martinez said. "Maybe they took him prisoner."

Ray leaned against the Explorer and stared at the smoldering ruins. "The Temple's goal was to destroy the evidence and get out without being seen. If they ran into Garrison, it would've been easier just to kill him."

Martinez frowned as she reached for the car door. "I'm just saying, we don't know anything until it's confirmed."

***

Ray barely slept that night. He arrived at the station the next morning bleary-eyed and filled with an impending sense of doom. He'd hoped for an overnight breakthrough in the case, but the morning briefing was a colossal disappointment.

There was still no sign of Evan Brody or Tracy Lasher, and the officer who was supposed to keep an eye on Tracy's roommate, Fiona, reported that she'd disappeared. A search of Thalia's phone and computer hadn't identified any evidence to suggest her death wasn't a suicide, and Eddie Fischer's apartment tested negative for Cassie's DNA.

The only promising development was the seizure of Alex's work computer, though so far the crime lab hadn't found anything incriminating. By all accounts, it seemed he'd lived a double life and had erected a solid wall between the two.

His parents refused to believe he'd been involved in anything so nefarious. His mom insisted the DNA result was either a computer glitch or a scientific blunder. His work colleagues were equally shocked and in denial.

Lacking any obvious leads, Chief Sanderson dispatched Ray and Martinez to interview a few of Alex's old college friends, but Ray had a feeling it was a waste of time.

"We're missing something," he said to Martinez. "I just wish I knew what the hell it was."

CHAPTER SIXTY-NINE

Ray strangled the steering wheel and fumed about their absolute waste of a day. The interviews with Alex's college friends had failed to produce a single shred of evidence. Now, it was a few minutes to sundown on Halloween, and they were fresh out of leads.

He hated to admit it, but the Temple had outmaneuvered them at every turn, hitting them with one distraction after another, leaving them chasing their tails. Finding Cassie now would take an eleventh-hour miracle, and the odds of that happening diminished with every grain of sand through the hourglass.

They were headed back to the station, but traffic was snarled, the roads leading into Salem choked with gridlock as throngs of Halloween revelers spilled into the streets, awaiting the coming of dusk.

A crackle of static emanated from the radio, and the dispatcher cut in to report a domestic disturbance—one person stabbed, another fleeing the scene.

Martinez snatched the radio and brought it to her lips. "This is unit twenty-eight. We're on it."

Ray scowled. "Do we really have time for that?"

"Didn't you hear the address? It's Abby's house."

Ray cut the wheel and made an abrupt U-turn, sending a Grim Reaper and his entourage of slutty nuns scampering onto the sidewalk. He activated the portable flashers on the dash and proceeded to weave through traffic.

When they arrived at Abby's house, they found Mrs. Garcia sitting on her stoop. She had both hands pressed over her stomach, dark rivulets of blood seeping through her fingers.

They climbed out of the Explorer and rushed over to her. "Are you okay?" Martinez asked.

Mrs. Garcia winced. "I'll be fine."

"What happened?" Ray asked.

"I don't know what got into her. All of a sudden, she climbed out of bed and ran to the front door like she had somewhere to be."

"You tried stopping her?" Martinez asked.

Mrs. Garcia nodded, her lips quivering. "Abby grabbed a knife from the butcher's block and waved it at me. I didn't think she'd hurt me, but when I stepped into her path, she stabbed me." She shook her head, tears rolling down her cheeks. "I'm so stupid... what am I even doing?"

Martinez crouched down beside her. "You're not stupid, Mrs. Garcia. You were trying to protect your daughter."

Ray stared through the open door and saw a knife lying on the ground, spatters of blood painting the blade crimson. Something small and metallic lay next to it.

He walked inside as the sirens of an approaching ambulance rang out in the distance. He strode across the foyer and bent down over the mystery object, which he recognized as a Baphomet ring with gleaming rubies for eyes. He picked it up and brought it outside, showing it to Mrs. Garcia.

"Was Abby wearing this?" he asked.

Mrs. Garcia nodded. "I threw that thing away months ago, but she must've dug it out of the trash and hid it somewhere. I don't know why she put it on tonight."

"Why was it on the floor?" Martinez asked.

"I grabbed her hand when she stabbed me, and the ring slipped off in all the blood."

The paramedics arrived a few minutes later and lifted Mrs. Garcia onto a gurney. As they wheeled her toward the ambulance and loaded her inside, she fingered the gold cross that dangled around her neck.

"Find Abby," she said. "Please!"

THE BURYING POINT

And then the doors closed behind her, leaving Ray staring at the bloody ring in his palm as the ambulance pulled away from the curb, its sirens carrying into the darkening night, howling at the rising moon.

CHAPTER SEVENTY

Ray wiped Mrs. Garcia's blood off the Baphomet ring with a crumpled-up napkin he'd saved from Mystical Brew. He slipped it into his breast pocket and watched the ambulance disappear around the corner.

"Where do you think Abby's headed?" Martinez asked.

Ray was about to answer when his cell phone rang. He debated sending it to voicemail, but picked up when he saw it was Jacob. "This isn't a good time. I'll call you later."

"Wait, don't hang up. It's about the companies you asked me to research."

Ray climbed into the Explorer and put the phone on speaker. "You found something?"

"The companies aren't related," Jacob said, "but there is a connection."

"What companies?" Martinez asked.

"I asked Jacob to see what he could dig up on the demolished warehouse and Rancic's haunted house."

"Let's hear it," Martinez said.

Jacob cleared his throat. "The warehouse is a foreclosed property owned by the Salem Fiduciary Bank & Trust, and the haunted house is part of a portfolio of properties inside a real estate investment trust, what's known in the business as a REIT."

"We already looked into that," Martinez said. "The bank and the REIT aren't related."

"That's true," Jacob said. "But the REIT is owned by a string of offshore companies, which in turn are owned by a joint venture and a nested loop of other entities. It was a bitch to unravel, but ultimately there's a hedge fund that sits on top of the chain leading down to the REIT. The majority partner of the hedge fund happens to be on the board of directors of the bank. He's also on the bank's credit committee, which means he'd have veto power over any plans to sell the warehouse."

"Skip to the punchline," Ray said. "Who the hell is this guy?"

Jacob lowered his voice. "Someone you should be very familiar with."

CHAPTER SEVENTY-ONE

Captain Barnes shook his head. "It's got to be a mistake."

Ray understood the captain's reservations, but there was no denying the facts. The captain's brother was the link between both companies. The captain had said himself at the beginning of the investigation that Paul had once studied to be a priest before switching majors.

"It can't be," Barnes said.

"Paul's middle name is Jason," Martinez said, "which matches the only legible part of the seminary student's manuscript."

"He didn't drop out of divinity school, did he?" Ray asked. "He was kicked out."

Barnes nodded slowly, his eyes dreamy and far away. "It could be a coincidence. I'm sure Paul controls thousands of properties. It doesn't mean he's responsible for everything that happens inside them."

Ray unbuckled his seat belt. "Let's go inside and find out."

Ray and Martinez ascended the stairs to the old Victorian, Barnes trailing a half step behind, as if his mind was struggling to catch up. Ray recalled his first trip to Cassie's house—standing on this porch, eyeing the historical plaque from 1711—and he wondered if the investigation really had come full circle.

Elizabeth Barnes answered the door, and it looked as if she'd aged five years in the past two weeks. Her features were gaunt, her blue eyes no longer so vibrant. "Jake, what are you doing here?"

"Where's Paul?" Barnes asked.

"He's on a business trip." She motioned for them to follow her into the living room. She sat down on the sofa and reached for a highball glass on the coffee table.

"When did he leave?" Barnes asked.

"This morning," Elizabeth said, pausing to take a sip.

"The detectives think Paul is involved in Cassie's disappearance."

Elizabeth barely reacted. She stared forward, shaking her head almost imperceptibly. "No, he wouldn't do that." She took another sip.

"He's not answering his phone," Barnes said. "How long is he gone for?"

"All week."

Ray leaned forward on the loveseat. "What is it you're not telling us, Mrs. Barnes?"

Elizabeth closed her eyes and drew a shuddering breath.

"This is very important," Martinez said. "Please... for your daughter."

Elizabeth nodded slowly, wiping a tear from her eye. "A few years ago, Cassie told me Paul had... *visited* her bedroom late one night. I didn't believe her. I told her to stop making up lies."

Elizabeth lowered her head and began to weep, her right hand held against her brow, as if shielding herself from judgement. "After Cassie went missing, I found her diary. She said the bedroom visits had become more frequent, that Paul insisted on calling it their special connection—a father daughter bond. She said he took pains to keep her pure... to honor her virginity."

"You told me she didn't have a diary," Ray said, clenching his teeth.

Barnes shot to his feet, a thick vein pulsing on his forehead. "My God, Elizabeth, how could you keep this from us?"

Elizabeth finished her drink and averted her eyes. "I didn't want to dredge up a terrible secret if it wasn't relevant."

"This is your daughter's life!" Martinez said. "Isn't that worth more than your family's good name?"

***

The hotel in Manhattan had a record of Paul checking in that morning, but when NYPD entered his room, the only thing they found was his cell phone sitting beside the bed. Hotel security had standing orders to call Captain Barnes the moment anyone spotted Paul, but Ray knew that would never happen.

"He's establishing an alibi," Ray said. "Flying to New York, checking into a hotel, using his phone to provide a false geolocation."

He and Martinez were in Paul's office, searching through the files in his desk drawers. So far, the documents were all work-related—business plans, spreadsheets, budgets, and blueprints. He'd taken his laptop with him, so they had no choice but to comb through an old-fashioned paper trail.

"We've been at this for two hours," Martinez said. "What if we don't find anything?"

They could hear the ticking of the grandfather clock in the living room, and with every passing second, it seemed as if the sound grew more mocking.

On any other weekend, they wouldn't have had a problem securing surveillance video of Paul leaving the hotel. The way midtown Manhattan was wired, they could've followed him just about anywhere, tracking one camera to the next until they saw what car he got into or what train he hopped.

But it was Halloween, and Paul had chosen a hotel that was hosting a horror convention. Nearly everyone was in costume. All he had to do was dress up, melt into the crowd, and stroll into the street in full disguise.

You almost had to admire his planning, right down to the call history on the phone he'd left behind, which included only work contacts and Elizabeth. No doubt he had a burner phone and a car waiting somewhere to take him back to Salem.

Ray frowned at Martinez and glanced at his phone. "It's almost eight o'clock." He dialed the captain, who was upstairs searching the bedrooms. "How are you making out?"

"Nothing yet," Barnes said.

Ray peeked his head out of the office and saw Elizabeth sitting on the sofa where they'd left her, the highball glass raised to her lips. "We're running out of time, Captain. Even if we do find something in here, I'm afraid it'll be too late."

"Do you have another suggestion?"

"As a matter of fact," Ray said, "I do."

CHAPTER SEVENTY-TWO

Garrison rolled over and groaned, fighting his way back to consciousness. When his eyes finally peeled open, he found himself lying on the floor, the room around him draped in shadows. He lifted his head and glanced around, tracing the room's dark contours. A gritty residue clung to his cheek, and dampness seeped through his uniform, chilling him to the bone.

He groped for his gun, but the holster was empty, every tool and weapon stripped from his utility belt. For a moment, he struggled to recall how he ended up here, but then the memories returned to him in a flood, and he sat bolt upright, realizing with dawning horror that his arms and legs were shackled together and connected to a stone wall by a three-foot length of chain.

He stood up and tugged at his restraints, but a wave of dizziness washed over him. He staggered against the wall and slid down to the floor, staring at the chains in confusion, wondering how he'd lost his balance.

A voice spoke up beside him. "They drugged you."

Garrison turned toward the voice and could barely discern the silhouette of a man sitting a few feet to his right. They were in a dungeon, confined to an eight-by-eight cell carved into the rock, the door fashioned out of iron bars. Torchlight flickered somewhere beyond the cell, the flames so weak the light barely penetrated.

"Where are we?" Garrison asked, trying to clear the cobwebs from his mind.

"Somewhere under the streets of Salem."

"How long have I been out?"

"An hour, maybe two."

"Who are you?" Garrison's eyes were beginning to adjust to the darkness, and he could see his cellmate was a white man in his early forties.

"I'm afraid I haven't been myself lately," the man said, "but my parishioners know me as Father Maroney."

Garrison blinked. "I know that name. Your church burned down, didn't it?"

"Yes."

"And you tried to expel Abby's demons."

"Tried, yes. Succeeded, no."

"I assume my colleagues told you about the Temple of Six and the ritual they've planned for tonight?"

Father Maroney nodded. "It'll be a fitting end to my story."

"Father, I'm—"

"Please. I'm not deserving of that title."

"Did the other detectives tell you about the prophecy?"

"I know no prophecy other than the word of God."

Garrison told him about the seminary student's manuscript and the demons' role in the apocalypse. "If any of it's true, maybe you can help stop it."

Father Maroney shook his head. "I couldn't even defeat the demon inside Abby Garcia."

"Is it possible you've lost your way?" Garrison asked, recalling Ray's use of the term *tainted priest*.

"I've done more than lose my way."

"Can't you pray for forgiveness?"

"I'm afraid my sins go well beyond that. Besides, the sacrament of confession requires a Catholic priest."

"Right now," Garrison said, "I'm all you've got. And if nothing else, at least you can make your peace."

Father Maroney nodded. "Perhaps you're right."

The echo of distant footsteps emanated from the hall, and Garrison pictured a company of guards marching through the tunnels.

Father Maroney kneeled down and made the sign of the cross. "Forgive me, Father, for I have sinned. It has been one year since my last confession."

The footfalls grew steadily louder, the sound interspersed with the deep voices of an approaching mob.

"Hurry!" Garrison whispered.

Father Maroney spoke quickly, a litany of sins pouring from his lips, each more shocking than the last. When he finished his confession, he said, "Oh Father, I ask that you cleanse me of my sins and grant me strength against thine enemies."

Garrison crossed himself and stood up just as the mob arrived.

A key rattled in the lock, and the cell door swung open with a reluctant groan of hinges. Evan Brody's hulking form appeared inside the door.

"The High Priest will see you now."

CHAPTER SEVENTY-THREE

Ray flew down Cassie's porch steps, taking them two at a time.

"Are you gonna tell me the plan?" Martinez asked, chasing after him.

Ray halted on the sidewalk and waited for her to catch up. "Let's assume Abby really is possessed," Ray said. "Where do you think she'd be going on this night, of all nights?"

Martinez's eyes lit up. "The ritual!"

"Exactly," Ray said.

"But we still don't know where it's being held."

"Remember that line in Abby's poem about sunlight yielding to life's long curse?" Ray asked. "Well, that got me thinking about Brittany Cooper buried in an open grave. And when I tried connecting that to Abby, I thought about where the cops found her after she first went missing."

Martinez locked eyes with him. "The cemetery... the Burying Point!"

"It would be a perfect place for a tunnel, wouldn't it?" Ray said.

Martinez shook her head in disbelief. "How did we not see that before? The poem even starts with *to the point*."

Ray eyed the crowd of trick-or-treaters swarming between traffic in the street. "How far of a walk is it?" he asked.

"About five minutes."

"Alright then. Let's hoof it."

"Hold on," Martinez said. "Let me get the *Book of Shadows* from the truck."

***

The crowd thinned as they moved away from Salem Common and followed Hawthorne Boulevard to Charter Street. By the time they arrived at the old colonial home that stood sentinel over the Witch Trials Memorial, a full moon was rising over its gabled roof, large and luminous against a violet sky.

Skeletal trees towered over a rectangular section of grass at the center of the memorial. A dirt path framed the edges of the rectangle, and a four-foot-high granite wall surrounded the site on three sides. Stone benches were set into the wall at even intervals, each one etched with the name of a witch trial victim, along with the date and manner of their execution. The inscription on the bench nearest to them read:

Giles Corey
Pressed to Death
September 19, 1692

Another one read:

John Proctor
Hanged
August 19, 1692

The Burying Point loomed beyond the wall of the memorial, the grassy field dotted with crooked rows of tombstones pitched at different angles. The thin stone markers were weathered by time, their inscriptions faded and crusted with lichen.

"Where was Abby found?" Ray asked.

"Frasier said she was lying next to one of the crypts." Martinez pointed to what looked like an oversized concrete sarcophagus with a heavy stone lid.

"You don't know which one?"

"Let me call Frasier." She dialed his number, leaving a message when it went to voicemail. "Hey, it's Martinez. We need to know exactly where you found Abby at the Burying Point. Call me as soon as you get this."

"What about the riddle?" Ray asked, after she'd hung up.

Martinez laid the *Book of Shadows* on the memorial wall and leafed through the pages until she found the poem.

> *To the point and past the nurse,*
> *Where sunlight yields to life's long curse,*
> *And through the halls of torchlit walls,*
> *Where conjured thoughts of decay and rot,*
> *Harken back to the rites of yore,*
> *With darkness, blood, and dripping gore,*
> *Where dancing flames paint the night,*
> *As the Temple prepares for sacrifice,*
> *With the offer of a virgin heart,*
> *The gates that hold the Six shall part.*

"We're at the point," Ray said, tapping his finger against the first line. "But what does she mean about the nurse?"

"It's gotta be Rebecca," Martinez said.

"Who's Rebecca?"

"Rebecca Nurse was one of the victims of the witch trials. A seventy-one-year-old grandmother. Come on, help me find her marker."

They hurried from one bench to the other. "Here it is!" Martinez said, sweeping aside a pink carnation that someone had left on the bench.

> *Rebecca Nurse*
> *Hanged*
> *July 19, 1692*

Ray leaned over Rebecca's marker and sighted an invisible line into the cemetery, which pointed directly at a mausoleum. "Come on," Ray said. "Let's check it out."

As Ray climbed over the wall, Martinez flashed her badge to a handful of tourists congregated near the benches, dissuading anyone from following. She joined Ray a few moments later, the *Book of Shadows* clutched against her chest.

With the cemetery closed for the night, they were the only two living souls in it, their shoes crunching over the frost-covered grass as they strode toward the mausoleum.

It was a ten-by-ten block of limestone with a gabled roof and a decorative frieze depicting ships navigating turbulent seas. The front door was solid steel, painted dark green, and bore the image of a winged angel. Above the door, carved into the limestone, were the words *Nathaniel Cartwright, 1722.*

"That's the name from Cassie's porch, isn't?" Martinez asked. "The one from the historical plaque."

"Elizabeth's ancestors were wealthy merchants," Ray said. "They might've had something to do with the old smuggling tunnels." He reached for the door and pushed, but it wouldn't budge.

"There's no hinges," Martinez said. "It's just ornamental."

"There's gotta be a way in," Ray said, sweeping his hands over the limestone, looking for a loose stone or a hollow compartment. When he gave up, he turned to Martinez, but she'd disappeared. "Martinez?"

"Over here."

Ray circled to the rear of the mausoleum, which concealed them from anyone who might be watching from the memorial benches.

"Look at this," Martinez said. She pointed to a nickel-sized hole drilled into the limestone near the edge of the wall. She clicked on her flashlight and shone it inside, revealing that the hole terminated at a metallic silver barrier about an inch deep.

"Maybe it used to be a doorknob," Ray said. He pushed against the wall to see if it had any give. When that didn't work, he poked his index finger into the hole and tried pulling the wall

360

up, down, left, and right. When that failed, he stepped back from the wall and shrugged. "Maybe this is the wrong tomb."

Martinez held up a hand. "Hold on a second. Do you still have that ring from Abby's house?"

Ray reached into his pocket and withdrew the grinning Baphomet ring. It was identical to the one Jeffries had found in the farmer's field where the cows had been slaughtered and blood let.

"What if it doesn't just signify rank or belonging?" Martinez said. "What if it's also a key?"

Ray's eyes shifted to the hole in the wall. Christ, could she be right? He slid the ring into the opening, horns pointed up, and pressed it against the interior piece of metal. It must've lined up perfectly, because the ring suddenly sank a half inch deeper, like a finger slipping into a glove.

A hidden locking mechanism clicked, and the rear wall sank slowly into the ground, as if they'd activated an old pulley and counterweight system. The door to the crypt yawned wide open, and a musky scent wafted toward them like the fetid breath of an ancient beast awakened from a centuries-long slumber.

CHAPTER SEVENTY-FOUR

Ray stared into the awaiting cloak of darkness, immobilized by a suffocating dread. He flashed back to the moment three months ago when he pursued the Artist into his lair without a plan, without any backup.

He turned to Martinez. "You'd better let Frasier know about the tunnel. Tell him to get the other Baphomet ring out of evidence."

As Martinez texted Frasier, Ray reached into his pocket and dialed the captain.

Come on, he thought. *Pick up.*

The captain was probably tied up with the crime scene techs, who were no doubt tearing apart the Barnes residence as Elizabeth drank herself into oblivion. He left a detailed message for the captain in case Frasier was MIA.

And because Ray had learned from his mistakes, he also called Officer Jeffries, who picked up on the first ring. "We found a tunnel," Ray said. "Frasier and the captain both have the details, but I need you to make sure they heard the messages. We're gonna need backup."

"I'm on it," Jeffries said.

Ray hung up and glanced at Martinez.

"We don't know what time this ritual is supposed to happen," Martinez said. "We can't afford to wait for backup."

Ray had been thinking the same thing. "We'll go inside and assess the situation, but if things go sideways, you get the hell out, understand? I don't want you becoming a martyr."

Martinez gave him the side-eye. "Do you plan on taking your own advice?"

"I guess we'll have to see." He motioned to the yawning maw of darkness. "You ready?"

"I've been waiting my whole career for this."

"That's what worries me."

He followed her inside, their flashlight beams lancing through the dark illuminating a screen of cobwebs peppered with dead insects. In the center of the mausoleum, a large marble sarcophagus sat on a pedestal. Nathaniel Cartright's likeness was carved into the lid, his face appearing serene but regal.

"Looks like someone had a high opinion of himself," Ray said. As he stepped toward the sarcophagus, a stone beneath his foot sank several inches into the floor, which triggered the rear wall of the mausoleum to close behind them, sealing them inside.

Martinez gasped, her flashlight aimed at the floor beside the sarcophagus, where a trap door had opened to reveal a stone stairway descending into darkness. "That wasn't there a minute ago."

"It must be connected to the wall," Ray said. "One goes up, the other goes down. Christ, Garrison would've hated this." He drew a shuddering breath. "I can't believe he's gone."

"Me neither. But he'd want us to finish this."

"You're right. He would." Ray pointed to the *Book of Shadows* cradled in Martinez's left arm. "Better leave that here. You're gonna need two hands."

Martinez opened the book and tore a page out before setting it down on a bench near the sarcophagus. The motion caused a cloud of dust to swirl up into their flashlight beams. Ray coughed into the crook of his arm. "Christ, Martinez, you're gonna kill us before we get down there."

Martinez had already started creeping down the stairs, her gun crossed over the hand holding her flashlight like they taught in the academy. "You might want to lay off the blasphemy," she said. "I have a feeling we're gonna need all the help we can get from the man upstairs."

"Who?" Ray asked. "Cartwright?"

Martinez rolled her eyes. "You're going straight to hell."

"If the Six get their way," Ray said, "the whole world's going to hell... assuming you believe in that bullshit."

The stairs descended ten feet underground, leading into a brick-lined tunnel that was barely wide enough for two people to walk side by side. It was old masonry, the red brick crusted with calcified lime, similar to the tunnel beneath Rancic's haunted house.

Ray paused at the bottom of the steps and pointed the flashlight at the floor of the tunnel. It was paved with cobblestones and coated in a scrim of dirt. He raised the beam, tracing a path away from the stairs. The light revealed dozens of footprints pointed in either direction, confirming his suspicion this was a well-travelled path.

The congregants could be anywhere—on their way in, on their way out. Maybe lurking in the dark, lying in wait.

"There's gonna be guards," Ray said. "We'll have to take them out quietly, before they can sound the alarm."

Martinez nodded, a wrinkle of concern creasing her brow. "I'm ready."

They started walking, their shoes rasping against the cobblestones, flashlights sweeping over the walls. The passageway ran straight back for more than a hundred yards, and Ray imagined crowds of trick-or-treaters roaming the streets above them, oblivious to the labyrinth below.

There were no torches on the walls, no visible means of underground lighting, so maybe they weren't the only ones using flashlights. If someone spotted them from a distance, maybe they'd look like a pair of stragglers running late for the ritual. Then again, maybe there was a station for torches that they'd missed, and he and Martinez were gonna stick out like clowns at a rodeo.

Christ, he thought. *Happy freaking Halloween.*

As they approached a bend in the tunnel, Martinez gave a start and clicked off her flashlight.

"What is it?" Ray asked, extinguishing his own light.

"I thought I heard something."

"Where?"

"Behind us."

Ray turned around, but all he could see was an endless void of darkness that made him think of the universe in the instant before its birth. A few moments later, far into the tunnel, he detected a flicker of light. Faint at first, then growing brighter, until it coalesced into an orange flame.

A torch.

First one, then another.

"Let's get around that corner." He reached out and groped for the wall, letting it guide him around the bend. He scanned the dark for Martinez but couldn't see a goddamn thing. "You in position?"

"I'm here," Martinez said. "Taser ready."

Ray drew his own Taser and crouched against the wall. "Hold your position until they turn the corner."

It was a full minute before they heard the approaching footfalls, the dim glow of the torches brightening the tunnel in gradual degrees. They were speaking in hushed tones, their voices low and raspy.

Shadows suddenly appeared on the wall, looming large and misshapen in the flickering light. Ray and Martinez held the line for another moment before springing from the wall and firing.

The men were dressed in scarlet cloaks, their faces shrouded in the darkness of their hoods. Martinez's Taser scored a direct hit, taking out the smaller of the two men. He dropped to the ground in a heap, both darts striking him in the chest, twin lines of copper wire delivering a debilitating shock.

One of Ray's darts penetrated the bigger man's stomach, but the other dart deflected off the torch and skittered to the floor. It was the equivalent of a misfire, since both darts were required to complete the circuit.

"Shit!" Ray said, ducking as the big man swung the torch like a club. It barely missed his head, smashing into the wall above him and creating a shower of sparks. The man yanked on the copper wire, pulling the dart out of his stomach and wrenching the Taser out of Ray's hands.

Ray lowered his shoulder and charged, hitting the man dead center and driving him against the wall. The man's head rocked back, and as his hood slipped off, Ray saw it was Kyle Jackman, one of the bartenders from Kettle & Cauldron.

Kyle still had the copper wire snagged around his hand, and as he lunged forward, he wrapped the wire around Ray's neck.

Ray felt the wire bite into his flesh and choke off his windpipe. He managed to slide two fingers underneath it to alleviate the pressure, but it was a losing battle. He caught sight of Martinez in his peripheral vision, stooped over the other cult member as she secured his wrists with handcuffs.

Ray tried calling out to her, but couldn't manage a sound. He quickly became lightheaded, a cluster of purple spots bursting like fireworks at the corners of his vision, a prelude to blacking out. Panicking, he drove his hips backward, knocking Kyle off balance. He maneuvered his foot between Kyle's legs and swept upward at an angle, striking the back of Kyle's knee and causing his leg to buckle.

As Kyle fell backward, the wire slackened. Ray pivoted and ducked beneath the wire. He jumped on top of Kyle, pinning him to the ground.

Martinez was there a moment later to slap the cuffs on him. "Are you okay?" she asked.

Ray staggered to his feet and winced, running a hand over his throat; his fingertips came away bloody. "I've been better. But at least we know we're on the right track."

"You're wasting your time," Kyle said, rolling onto his side. "You'll never defeat the Six."

The other man craned his neck and leered at Martinez, the fallen torch burning on the cobblestones near his head. "You should've come to Cabo with me. It would've saved you a whole lot of trouble."

"I'd rather be skinned alive," Martinez said.

Rancic chuckled. "Where you're headed, that can be arranged. There's plenty who'd do it just for the fun of it."

Both men had managed to sit up, and Ray realized there was nothing to prevent them from staggering to their feet and coming after them. "Let's reconfigure the cuffs," Ray said. He planted a foot on Rancic's chest and pushed him over, sprawling him onto his back.

He flipped Rancic onto his stomach and kneeled on the base of his spine. "Move the cuffs to his ankles and then link them up to the ones on Kyle's hands. That'll keep them from going anywhere."

As Martinez made the switch, Ray peeled off Rancic's robe, thankful the dirtbag was wearing a T-shirt and boxer shorts underneath. "Get his too," Ray said, motioning to Kyle. "We might be able to use them to sneak into the ritual."

Martinez had to cut Kyle's sleeves with her pocketknife to get the robe around the cuffs. When she was done, she cut two long strips of fabric and tossed one to Ray. "To gag them," she said.

Ray cinched the fabric tight around Kyle's lips and suppressed a grin as Martinez did the same to Rancic. "About time you two fools shut up," he said. He slipped Kyle's robe over his shoulders and stooped down to pick up the torch.

As Martinez followed suit, Ray noticed a beam of light lancing through the tunnel in the direction they'd come from. "We've got company," he whispered, reaching to his belt for the Taser's spare cartridge.

"It's a flashlight," Martinez said. "Not a torch."

A man's voice echoed through the tunnel. "Ray? Martinez? Is that you?"

Martinez pushed her hood back and waved to the figure in the distance. "It's Frasier."

Officer Frasier caught up to them a minute later, his face still scraped and bruised from his near-death experience the day before. "Looks like I missed out on the action," he said, staring down at Kyle and Rancic.

"Don't worry," Ray said, "there's gonna be plenty more opportunities."

"Where's the rest of the backup?" Martinez asked.

"On their way," Frasier said. "I had a head start."

Ray cocked his thumb at the prisoners. "Neither one of them is armed. We might be able to press forward with just the three of us. Even if the congregants have a knife or two, we've got guns, and the element of surprise."

"If we run into anyone in the tunnels," Frasier said, "you can pretend you've taken me prisoner."

Martinez nodded. "Let's do it."

They continued through the tunnel, Ray and Martinez leading with the torches, Frasier trailing a step behind. The path sloped gradually downward, leading them deeper into the earth. The ceiling seemed to grow taller too, transitioning from bricks to bedrock, as if merging into an underground cave.

Fifteen minutes later, the path ended at a wall of solid stone. Its surface was dark and rough, flecked with mica, but it looked slightly out of place next to the surrounding bedrock. Ray rapped his knuckles against it, but couldn't gauge its thickness.

Martinez pressed her ear to the wall, her eyes moving side to side as she listened. "I think I hear voices."

Ray scanned the wall. "Maybe there's another keyhole somewhere."

"There." Frasier pointed to a spot on the upper left, the impression well camouflaged by the stone's reflective properties.

Ray fished the Baphomet ring out of his pocket and handed the torch to Frasier. Martinez set her own torch on the ground and placed her hands against the wall, ready to push.

"Alright," Ray said, holding the ring near the impression. "On the count of three. One... two... thr—"

A paralyzing jolt of electricity shot through Ray's body, his muscles seizing up, his jaw clenching. The next thing he knew, he was on the ground, the twin leads of Frasier's Taser biting into his lower back beneath his Kevlar vest. A split second later, he saw Frasier strike Martinez with his baton. It connected with the base of her neck and dropped her to the ground.

Ray tried to roll over and lunge at Frasier, but another jolt of electricity coursed through him, and his mind went blank.

CHAPTER SEVENTY-FIVE

Garrison's eyes fluttered open, but the room around him appeared blurred and out of focus, as if he was viewing the world through a fishbowl. He didn't know where he was, but he remembered Brody entering the cell with three other men. They'd marched him and Father Maroney down a torchlit hall, their arms and legs shackled.

He'd pretended to pass out and collapsed against the wall. When one of the men came over to haul him back up, Garrison strangled him with his chains. The others tried to intervene, but the man was dead before he hit the floor.

He remembered thinking that if he had to kill them one by one, he would. After all, they were taking him to… to where? He'd slammed the second guy so hard against the wall that the man's head traced a bloody smear down to the ground. But then Brody hit him with the bo staff, distracting him long enough for the last guy to jab a needle into his leg.

And that's where his memories ended.

It was a struggle to keep his eyes open. He was tempted to ignore whatever was happening and drift back to sleep. He was exhausted—drained and delirious like he was home in bed, laid up with a fever.

Except it felt like he was sitting up, rather than lying down. And his arms were cramped. He wanted to rub the cobwebs from his eyes, but for some reason, he couldn't move his arms.

Panic washed over him, and the surge of adrenaline jolted him fully awake. He glanced around, seeing his surroundings for the first time. He was suspended above the ground in a torchlit cavern, strapped to a wooden cross, his arms

370

and legs secured with iron cuffs latched with carabiner clips. They'd stripped him of his uniform, leaving him naked, exposed, and on display.

A square of wood protruded a few inches from the vertical part of the cross below his waist, providing a meager bench to support his weight and take the pressure off his wrists and ankles. The wood was cold against his back, the damp air of the cavern prickling his skin with gooseflesh.

Father Maroney hung from a cross to his left, and a pregnant woman with shoulder-length blond hair hung from a cross to his right. Like him, they were naked and appeared to have been drugged, both still dozing in a hapless stupor. Someone had drawn a dashed line on the woman's pregnant belly with a black marker, tracing a rough circle, as if to indicate cut marks.

It took a moment for Garrison to realize that they weren't alone. A man in a scarlet cloak stood five feet below them, his features obscured by the shadows of his hood.

"Hello, Trooper. I trust you had a good nap."

Garrison stared down at him, but it was a struggle to hold his head steady. It felt like it weighed fifty pounds. "What... is this place?" he asked, finding it difficult to form the words.

"You'll find out soon enough. Are you comfortable?"

"Go to... hell."

The man in the cloak chuckled. "You should consider yourself lucky. We used to nail people onto those crosses... mostly drifters and homeless guys, the sort of people nobody misses when they disappear. And you really can't beat the symbolism of nailing someone to a fucking cross, can you? But, sadly, it's not very functional.

"At the end of our rituals, we turn our victims upside down and slit their throats, allowing their blood to flow onto a symbol carved in the floor. But whenever we tried that, the shifting weight of their bodies would tear them right off the nails. Sometimes, it'd leave behind long strips of flesh that dangled like bloody ribbons, and although that was a satisfying side effect, it interrupted the flow of the ritual."

"Who are you?"

"Your friends have figured that out already, but after tonight's ritual, none of that will matter."

"Who are you?" Garrison asked again, hoping the knowledge might provide some small satisfaction.

"Don't you know?" the man asked, a teasing lilt to his voice. "I'm your worst nightmare."

CHAPTER SEVENTY-SIX

"Pretty fucking cool, isn't it?" Frasier asked as the door rolled open to reveal an enormous underground cavern.

The ceiling stretched at least a hundred feet high and featured rows of jagged stalactites, like a lion's jaw frozen in a snarl. The cavern itself was circular, the approximate size and shape of Fenway Park. Except Ray was pretty sure the two-dozen red-cloaked figures illuminated by the flickering torchlight weren't on any official roster.

"Christ," he muttered, catching his first glimpse of the crosses rising up from the rock, his eyes settling on the naked forms strapped to them.

Under other circumstances, he would've been thrilled to discover Garrison had survived, but he wondered if burning to death would've been a mercy compared to what was in store for him.

Frasier slapped him on the back of the head, driving him forward at gunpoint. Martinez matched his stride, the two of them walking into the cavern, their hands secured behind their backs with heavy-duty zip ties. They restricted range of motion even more than handcuffs, which is probably why Frasier had brought them.

Martinez turned her head and glared at Frasier. "I should've known you were dirty. That night you followed me to the old mental hospital, you were planning to kill me, weren't you?"

Frasier smirked. "I was gonna rape you first."

Martinez lunged at him, but Frasier punched her in the nose, sending her sprawling. "You're gonna regret that," she said, climbing to her feet. She held her head high, a bright rivulet of blood leaking from one nostril.

"I doubt it," Frasier said.

The curt clearing of someone's throat drew their attention, and they gazed toward the center of the cavern, where a pair of hooded figures stood before a stone altar near the crosses. The other congregants had given them a wide berth, standing a respectful distance away and forming a loose ring around them.

A unified voice rang out from the congregation as they all bent a knee.

"All hail the high priest and priestess of the Temple of Six!"

"So good of you to come, detectives," the high priest said. "We were just getting started."

The pair made a show of removing their hoods and revealing their identities.

"I believe you already know Judge Reynolds," Paul Barnes said, motioning to the high priestess. "Isn't she beautiful?" He laid a hand on her shoulder and stroked her lustrous dark hair.

Reynolds extended her arms toward them, as if in benediction. "The Temple thanks you for this offering, Master Frasier. We need all the blood we can get on this sacred night."

"Where's Cassie?" Ray asked. "What have you done with her?"

"You're like a dog with a bone, aren't you, Detective?" Paul said, his voice assuming a mocking tone. *"Where's Cassie? What have you done with her?"*

"You'll see her in due time," Reynolds said.

"Why are you doing this?" Ray asked, trying to stall them. "You went to seminary school, Paul. You should know better."

"Ah, but I do know better," Paul said. "That's why we're all here, that's what this is all for."

"What are you talking about?" Ray asked.

"It's all about choices, Detective. And when we're born into this world, we're told there's only two—you either live a good life and go to heaven, or you live a bad one and go to hell. So, let me ask you, do you really want to live a boring, pious life in exchange for a harp and a pair of wings? Confined to a bland eternity of supplication and servitude? Sure, it's better than spending perpetuity getting fucked in the ass by the Devil's hot poker, but what if there was another choice?

"What if behind door number three, you could live forever as an immortal king, free to do whatever you please, eat whatever you want, fuck whoever you want, kill whoever you want... all without fear of consequences?"

"I'm not sure I believe in any of those options," Ray said, "the third one least of all. You're taking a big risk on something that's probably bullshit."

"Let's just say I'm a man of faith who also enjoys a good gamble."

"But you'd be killing your own daughter in the bargain," Martinez said, jumping in. "What kind of man does that?"

"What you need to understand," Paul said, "is there's power in sacrifice, especially when it's your own blood. And virgin blood, at that. If you want examples, you needn't look further than the Bible. After all, didn't God take Jesus's life? Allowing a mob to crucify his only son as he watched from his throne and did nothing. And didn't God command Abraham to sacrifice Isaac to prove his faith and obedience? How is this any different? How can you condemn me but exalt God with a straight face?"

"With this plan of yours," Ray said, "you'd be responsible for the deaths of millions of innocent people. You sure you can live with all that blood on your hands?"

"What about the innocent who lived among those at Sodom and Gomorrah?" Paul said. "Or all those who perished in the great flood? If I had a dime for every time God smited the world, I'd be a rich man. The truth is, Detective, when it serves His will, God is the most ruthless murderer of them all. Any true student of the scripture knows that. So forgive me for wanting to grab my slice of the pie, but I've got my own judge and jury, thank you very much."

"You're twisting the scripture to fit your own narrative," Father Maroney said, suddenly stirring from his place on the cross. "God is love. Jesus is love. And any biblical suffering was in service of the greater good."

"And yet you spat in God's face, didn't you, Father? Where was your piety when Naomi was sucking your cock in the nave?" Paul strode over to where the woman hung from the cross. He stroked the swell of her belly, then trailed his hand down her pelvis and slipped his fingers inside her, staring at Father Maroney as he rooted around. "You're baby's almost here, Father. And right on time. But is it a boy... a girl... or an unholy bastard?"

The congregants laughed like hyenas. "*Unholy bastard!*" they repeated, as if answering a responsorial psalm.

Paul's fingers emerged coated in blood-slicked amniotic fluid, which he traced along Naomi's belly, forming an upside down cross. Then he pointed to one of the congregants, who came forward and disrobed, revealing long, dark hair and a voluptuous, tattooed body.

Tracy Lasher.

She leaned forward eagerly, sucking the slime off his fingers. Then she turned around and made a show of licking her lips, before blowing a kiss to Ray.

A slant of silvery light materialized inside a carved circle near Paul's feet as a moonbeam lanced through a shaft in the rocky ceiling. He held out his arms and surveyed the crowd of congregants. "Are you ready to summon the Six? Are you ready to usher in the eternal reign of hell on earth and scatter the Four Horseman to the wind?"

The congregants responded with a raucous cheer, their celebration echoing throughout the cavern.

"You think you can put a leash on a demon?" Father Maroney asked. "Walk it around the park and make it play fetch?" He laughed dryly. "Only a fool bargains with the Devil."

"You're wrong," Paul said. "I've been planning this for over twenty years. You have no idea how rare and significant this night is, or how much power can be drawn from the convergence of celestial events and black magic, the combination of bloodlines, corruption, and sacrifice. And you'll all play a part in it, all bear witness to the collision of destiny and infamy."

Martinez fidgeted beside Ray as Paul droned on. "Where's Abby?" she whispered.

Ray scanned the crowd of congregants. The vast majority were dressed in red cloaks, some with their hoods on, some wearing goat's masks. He spotted Kyle and Rancic among them, but saw no sign of Abby. "I don't see her."

Frasier thumped him on the back of the head. "Didn't your mom ever tell you it's rude to talk in church?"

"You're not gonna get away with this," Ray said. "But if you let us go, maybe the DA will cut you a deal."

Frasier chuckled. "You actually think somebody's coming, don't you? Sorry to break it to you, but I told Jeffries and the captain that your voicemail was a false alarm. You're on your own."

Frasier's words sunk in as Paul and Reynolds donned the elaborate goat masks they'd worn in Father Maroney's church. With the transformation complete, they moved behind the altar and prepared to deliver their sermon.

In response, the congregation drew back their hoods and slipped their own masks into place. They stepped forward, tightening the ring around their high priest and priestess, the trio of crosses included in the circle.

The altar's legs were intricately carved, adorned with grinning demons and the tortured faces of the damned. A thick, stone slab rested on top and held a variety of objects: a ceremonial dagger; a golden chalice; black candles protruding from a cluster of human skulls; and a large leatherbound volume, which was folded open near the middle.

Paul lifted his arms toward the ceiling and began to preach. The words that rolled from his lips were guttural and profane, and in a language Ray didn't recognize.

Reynolds handed him the dagger, its blade gleaming wickedly in the torchlight. Paul intoned over it, then passed it back to Reynolds, who laid it down and exchanged it for the chalice. They took turns drinking from it, leaving dark red smears glistening on their upper lips.

Frasier nudged Ray in the arm. "That's the blood of Brittany Murphy... and I bet it's extra sweet."

Reynolds walked the chalice over to the congregants, who took turns receiving the unholy communion.

Frasier motioned to Brody, who'd been standing beside them with his bo staff since they first entered the cavern. The door was closed now, but there was another guard standing nearby—a man Frasier had called Luther—who was also carrying a bo staff. "Will you watch these two while I get a drink?" Frasier asked.

Brody stood in front of them and smirked, his lips glistening with Brittany's blood.

Before ushering Ray and Martinez through the door, Frasier had stripped them of their weapons and doled out their guns to Brody and Luther, who had them tucked into the pockets of their robes. Ray doubted any of the other congregants were armed, which meant if they could find a way out of these zip ties, the odds weren't terrible.

When Frasier returned, he tried to kiss Martinez with his blood-smeared lips, but Martinez headbutted him, connecting with the bridge of his nose. Frasier staggered back, covering his face, blood running between his fingers.

Paul stopped his sermon and glared at them. "Enough with the interruptions!"

Fraser spat onto the ground and wiped his bloody nose against his sleeve. "You'll pay for that."

A door creaked open further into the cavern, somewhere to the left of the altar, and a woman emerged wearing a bridal gown, a sheer white veil covering her face. She had blonde hair—Ray could see that much—and she was being hustled forward by a disheveled woman with wild, dark hair and a stained nightgown.

"Oh my God," Martinez muttered. "That's Abby and Cassie."

Ray felt his stomach twist into knots. They had to stop this, but how? It was almost too painful to watch, but he couldn't look away, couldn't turn a blind eye to Cassie's suffering. At the very least, he owed it to her to bear witness to her fate.

The congregation fell quiet as Abby brought Cassie over to Paul, her gut-wrenching sobs echoing throughout the cavern. He lifted Cassie's veil over her head, but her eyes remained downcast, her lips trembling as she refused to meet his gaze.

Paul lifted Cassie's chin, forcing her to stare at him as he removed his mask and revealed his identity. Cassie jerked backward, gasping audibly, her eyes progressing through a heartbreaking range of emotions—surprise, doubt, and fear.

"*Daddy?*" The tremor in her voice was so pronounced, the word was barely recognizable.

"Hello, Cassie." His tone was smug and condescending.

"What… what is this?"

Paul chuckled. "It's your destiny, Cassie. Atonement for your ancestor's sins."

Cassie stared at him, dumbfounded.

Paul continued. "John Proctor never repented for those he condemned to the hangman's noose. Perhaps this will make it right. And while it's largely symbolic, there's power in symbolism… power in bloodlines."

"Why?" It was only a single word, but it conveyed a lifetime of hurt.

"Because you've been a naughty girl, haven't you?"

"No."

"You told your mother about our special times in your bedroom, didn't you? And when she didn't listen, you told a police officer. *Didn't you?*" He almost spat the words. "Why don't you wave to the friendly officer over there?" He pointed at Frasier, who waved back enthusiastically.

"Please, Daddy." She shook her head. "Don't do this."

"I assigned Alex to watch over you, to be your pretend boyfriend who would keep you chaste until it was time. And that time is now. But first, I want to introduce you to your new stepmom." He gestured to Reynolds, who removed her mask.

"Don't worry, darling. You won't survive long enough to hate me." She snatched the dagger off the altar and showed it to Cassie, who shrank back in terror. Reynolds laughed. "Not yet, dear, but your time will come."

Cassie tried to run away, but Abby grabbed her by the shoulders and held her in place.

Reynolds strode over to the trio of crosses and waved the dagger at them, cutting tiny circles into the air. "Eeny, meeny, miny, moe," she sang. "Catch a traitor by the toe. If she hollers, stab that ho. Eeny, meeny, miny... *MOE!*"

Reynolds screamed the last word and plunged the knife into Naomi's stomach, cackling as she sawed along the dotted line.

The congregants erupted in a cheer, drowning out the sound of Naomi's blood-curdling screams.

Ray and Martinez both tried to rush forward, but Brody was lightning-quick with the bo staff, stunting their progress with body blows, which gave Frasier enough time to grab their arms and restrain them.

Martinez turned her head. "I can't look."

"Stop it!" Garrison yelled. "You sick sonsofbitches!"

Reynolds grinned at him, but kept on cutting.

Naomi's head lolled on her chest. She'd finally passed out from the pain. A dark river of blood ran down her legs and trickled onto the stone floor, gurgling as it drained into the grooves of a carved symbol, which Ray was only just now realizing was a giant Baphomet set against a six-pointed star, the entire symbol inscribed in a circle.

Reynolds reached inside the ragged hole she'd carved into Naomi's womb and extracted the baby, whose umbilical cord she cut with a triumphant yell. She held the baby up high, hoisting it into the air like a trophy, and the congregants went wild.

"Stop!" Martinez yelled. "You're all insane!"

"Be patient, Detective," Paul said. "Your part will come soon enough."

Ray wiggled his wrists behind his back, struggling to break free of the zip ties, but they showed no signs of loosening. "Come on, Paul," he said. "Think it through. You can't believe in the Six without believing in God, and how do you expect to beat Him? It's a losing gamble."

"Would someone please muzzle these two?" Paul asked.

One of the congregants raised her hand and removed her mask. "I know where there's duct tape."

It was Fiona from Raven's Wing.

"Go get it," Paul said.

Fiona ran in the direction Abby and Cassie had come from. Ray craned his neck and saw a door there. It was solid steel and cut into the rock.

As Reynolds laid the baby on the altar, Paul fiddled with a lever on Naomi's cross. Its vertical axis consisted of two beams, one laid directly over the other. When he released the lever, the vertical beam in the front spun one hundred eighty degrees, which turned the entire cross upside down.

Reynolds left the baby unattended on the altar, and Ray could see now that it was a boy. He lay on his back crying, his tiny limbs twitching, hands reaching up for a mother he'd never know.

Reynolds stalked over to the cross where Naomi hung upside down, her blonde hair hanging in tangles just inches from the floor, inches from the outer ring of the Baphomet symbol.

Reynolds brandished the dagger, showing it to the congregants before sweeping it across Naomi's throat.

Despite the barbaric delivery, Naomi's body still contained a surprising amount of blood. It poured from her throat in gushes, raining down onto the symbol and trickling into its grooves. For a few horrible seconds, Naomi's hands clenched and unclenched, her fingernails clawing at the wood below the iron cuffs.

Paul pulled the levers on the other crosses, flipping Garrison and Father Maroney upside down. Father Maroney's lips moved silently as he prayed, the pace of his prayers quickening after he'd flipped.

Paul loomed over him, shaking his head. "Why don't you pray on this, Father?" He parted his robe and urinated on Father Maroney's face, making him cough and sputter.

The congregation erupted in laughter.

Paul shook off the last drop and tucked it back inside the robe. "Your God has forsaken you, Father. And if you need any more evidence, I'll have one of our congregants squat over your face."

Paul glanced at Naomi on his way back to the altar. Her hands were no longer moving. All the tension had drained from her body, the flow of her blood slowed to a trickle. She resembled a deer that had been field dressed after a hunt—strung up and bled out, eyes glassy and bulging, ready to be skinned.

Paul loomed over the altar and chanted over the baby, which kicked and mewled in protest. Reynolds passed him the dagger, which he held over the baby while continuing to chant.

Abby escorted Cassie to the altar, gripping her by the shoulders.

"It's time to do your part," Paul said.

Cassie's voice quavered. "Wh... what part?"

"The part where you kill the baby."

"No..."

"Oh, but you must. Nothing draws power like one innocent killing another." He handed the dagger to Reynolds, who placed it in Cassie's hand. "Now, stab the baby."

Cassie shook her head vehemently.

"Stab the baby!"

"No." The dagger slipped from her hand and clattered to the floor.

Reynolds picked it up and forced it back into her hand. "Stab the fucking baby, Cassie!"

"That's enough!" Ray yelled, trying to break free of Frasier's grip. "Have you lost your goddamn minds?"

Fiona suddenly returned, weaving through the congregants and waving a roll of silver duct tape in the air. "I found it!"

"Make it quick!" Paul roared. "No more interruptions."

Reynolds glared at Abby. "Strap her down to the altar. If she won't stab the baby, then she'll hold him while I do it."

Brody and Frasier moved aside as Fiona approached with the roll of tape. She peeled off a strip, cut it with a Bowie knife, and slapped it over Martinez's lips. She repeated the process with Ray. As she did so, she held Ray's gaze, and what he saw in her eyes wasn't malice but something else.

Understanding? Sympathy?

Frasier and the two guards directed their attention to the altar, watching as Abby lifted Cassie onto the dark stone and restrained her with a series of leather cords. While they were distracted, Fiona inched closer to Ray and Martinez and cut the zip ties securing their wrists.

Before Ray had a chance to whisper his plan, Martinez grabbed the knife from Fiona's hand and spun around, plunging the blade into Frasier's heart.

As Frasier fell to his knees and pitched forward, Ray drew Frasier's gun from its holster and turned to face Luther, who was charging at him with the bo staff. He pulled the trigger and shot him through the heart. Luther collapsed to the ground, the bo staff rolling across the floor toward them.

Martinez dropped Fiona's knife and grabbed the staff, blocking an incoming blow from Brody, who had charged at them from the other direction. She used the staff to push him backward, then spun around, dodged a counterblow, and struck him on the side of his skull.

Brody wavered on his feet, taking a stutter step, but Martinez spun the staff in the opposite direction and clocked the other side of his face, bending his neck at an unnatural angle. He toppled like a giant redwood and lay motionless—unconscious, maybe even dead.

Martinez grabbed the gun from Brody's robe pocket. Ray did the same to Luther, then he and Martinez both stood up and faced the altar, where Cassie was strapped down with the baby lying on her chest.

Ray ripped the tape off his lips. "It's over!" he yelled, inching forward with a gun in each hand. "Drop the dagger and back the hell away from them!"

Martinez moved with him, pointing her gun at the congregants. "Everyone over to one side! Do it now!"

"You too," Ray said, motioning to Paul and Reynolds. "Get away from the altar and join the others."

He eyed them closely as Paul set the dagger on the altar and put his hands in the air. Reynolds followed suit. A moment later, they were shuffling into the back corner of the cavern with the others.

Fiona crept up beside Ray and whispered in his ear. "I know another way out. We can take Cassie and the baby."

"How do I know we can trust you?" Ray asked.

"Because I just saved your asses, and this has gone way too far. They killed Thalia... and they were going to kill the baby."

Ray considered their options, then nodded slowly. "Get Cassie and the baby out as fast as you can. We'll follow with the others."

Fiona was in motion before he even finished speaking. She dashed to the altar and used the dagger to cut the leather cords securing Cassie. Cassie swung her legs onto the floor and hugged the baby to her chest. Together, they raced toward the steel door set into the rock.

Paul whispered something to the congregants surrounding him. A moment later, Steve Rancic broke ranks and charged after Fiona and Cassie.

Ray didn't hesitate. He adjusted his aim and shot Rancic through the back. Momentum carried him for a few steps before he crumpled face-first to the ground and lay still.

Ray eyed the congregants, trying to read their body language. "You'd better think twice before making a move."

With the congregation corralled in one spot, Martinez was able to maintain cover while Ray walked over to the crosses. He unhooked the carabiner clips securing the iron cuffs around Garrison's hands and feet, and Garrison tumbled off the cross, landing on the stones with a meaty thud.

Ray reached down and hauled the big man to his feet. "Good to have you back."

"Took you long enough."

He handed Garrison one of his guns. "Help Father Maroney down. And for Christ's sake, put on a robe, will you?"

Ray kept his gun aimed at the crowd as Garrison helped Father Maroney to his feet. The Father cupped his hands over his crotch to hide his nakedness, his arms ridged with goosebumps.

"Give me a second," Garrison said. He hurried over to the bodies of Brody and Luther and stripped off their cloaks. He put one on and handed the other to Father Maroney. A few moments later, they joined Martinez and began creeping toward the steel door.

Abby stepped into their path, her mouth drawn into a snarl. Red light glowed in the depths of her eyes. She gestured to the ceiling and uttered a monstrous roar as she lowered her arm in a chopping motion.

A thunderous crack emanated from the ceiling as an enormous cluster of stalactites broke away from the rock and plummeted to the ground. It landed in a heap near the door, shaking the ground and creating a pile of rubble that sealed off their exit.

Paul doubled over in hysterics. "You have no idea what you're up against. It seems you'll be sticking around for the rest of the ritual after all. I guarantee it will blow your pants off. Hell, it might even shatter your reality... or break your fucking minds."

Ray aimed his gun at Paul, while Martinez and Garrison aimed at the congregation and Reynolds.

Undeterred, Barnes strode over to the altar. "Are you planning to shoot us for practicing our religion? Need I remind you that it's protected under the First Amendment? Or would you prefer I turn around so you can put a bullet in my back?" He gestured to Rancic, who lay buried beneath the boulders with only his sneakers protruding from the rubble. "I'm pretty sure what you did violates police procedure."

"Then give yourselves up," Ray said, "and file a complaint at the station."

Abby extended her arms again, horizontally this time, and Ray felt a cold wind creep past him. He glanced over his shoulder and saw that Frasier's body had begun to stir, his limbs twitching.

Garrison backed away, his eyes huge. "Huh-uh... nope."

As Abby drew her hand toward her chest, Frasier's body slid across the floor and came to a stop near the altar, tracing a bloody smear against the stones. The bodies of Brody and Luther soon followed, and Ray had to blink several times to convince himself that he wasn't seeing things. Had Frasier cooked his brain with that Taser?

He glanced at the stone wall behind them, at the secret door they'd entered through. There was no opening it without a ring, without a key. Frasier had taken their ring and now had two of them around his fingers. Ray had seen a few of the congregants wearing similar rings, but not everyone, so maybe it had to do with rank.

Reynolds stalked over to the bodies with her dagger. She stooped down and slit their throats one by one, like a rancher in a slaughterhouse. Paul helped her position the bodies at the edge of the Baphomet symbol, directing their blood so it gurgled into the crevices, mixed together, and began to fill every nook and cranny.

Martinez crept over to Ray, her gun still pointed at the congregants. "What do we do?"

"We can't let them complete the ritual," Father Maroney said. "It has to be stopped."

"Are you suggesting that we shoot them?" Ray asked.

"I'm not saying that, but…" He shrugged, trailing off.

"There's too many of them," Garrison said. "If we try to engage them, it'll be a bloodbath."

"We should retreat into the tunnel," Martinez said, "go back the way we came."

Garrison nodded. "That might be our best option. We can keep them penned up here while one of us runs for reinforcements."

"You're assuming we can get our hands on a key," Ray said. He kept his eye on Reynolds as she stepped away from the bodies and stared up at the ceiling.

Her gaze followed the path of the moonbeam down to the Baphomet symbol. In the last several minutes, the silvery light had moved from the lower quadrant of the six-pointed star to the edge of the Baphomet's jawline.

Reynolds lifted her arms to the sky. "Almost time," she said, her voice filled with reverence. She gazed into the crowd of congregants. "Tracy, come forth!"

Tracy Lasher emerged from the crowd and walked over, her dark hair flowing over her bare shoulders. A spiderweb tattoo stretched upward from her naval and connected to the piercings on her nipples, creating the illusion of a lace bustier.

Reynolds motioned to the moonbeam. "You were instrumental in bringing about this moment, Tracy. As repayment for your services, the Temple bestows this honor upon you."

She leaned forward and kissed Tracy on the lips. Passionately. Lovingly. One hand trailed down Tracy's back... while the other drove the dagger into her heart.

Tracy's eyes snapped open. A ribbon of blood spurted from her mouth and dribbled down her chin. Reynolds smiled kindly, lowering her gently to the floor. "There's power in sacrifice, Tracy, especially when it's someone we love."

In the next breath, Reynolds yanked the dagger out of her chest and swept the blade across Tracy's throat.

As the congregation voiced its approval, Paul read from the leatherbound volume at the altar, leading them in a guttural incantation.

Reynolds joined the chant and gazed down at the Baphomet symbol. Tracy's blood seeped into it, mingling with the others, until every groove was filled—an unbroken symbol awash in sacrificial blood.

Ray couldn't believe what he was seeing. Reynolds had murdered Tracy... right in front of their eyes. They'd stood there and watched. Stood there and done nothing. It'd happened so fast, but at the same time, it seemed inevitable.

Christ!

Ray suddenly broke free of his paralysis and sprang into action, charging toward the Baphomet symbol, intending to retrieve the ring from Frasier's hand no matter the consequences. But an invisible force stopped him in his tracks and hurled him backward, his arms and legs flailing in the air.

Garrison broke his fall, and they tumbled to the ground. Ray struggled to his feet just as the moonbeam shifted, illuminating the eyes of the Baphomet and reflecting back toward the ceiling like laser beams. The pool of blood tracing the outline of the symbol glowed bright red and began to boil.

"Does anyone else see that?" Martinez asked.

Garrison made the sign of the cross. "I wish I wasn't."

The chanting grew louder, and Paul hands gesticulated wildly as he read from the leatherbound volume.

Ray made another run at Frasier's body, but was met with the same result. He winced as he staggered to his feet, his mind reeling. How the hell was this happening? How was it even possible? He'd written off the strange occurrence in Abby's bedroom as a stress-induced hallucination... but this?

The blood in the symbol grew brighter. Pinpricks of orange light appeared within the grooves and radiated upward, multiplying. It took Ray a moment to realize that the rock inside the grooves was disintegrating, dropping into some unknown abyss, until the outline of the symbol was drawn entirely with the flaming orange of hellfire.

Father Maroney sank to his knees and prayed, clutching the gold crucifix that dangled around his neck, his head bowed.

Something flew out of the glowing fissures in the symbol and swooped over the congregation. It was sinewy and batlike, the size of a bulldog, with leathery wings, black talons, and a beaklike snout bristling with fangs.

It was joined by another... and then another.

They flew in circles throughout the cavern, swooping and gliding, their eyes bright red and luminescent.

The congregation continued chanting, uninterrupted, the cadence ebbing and flowing like a dark symphony of madness.

Suddenly, the winged demons executed a synchronized dive and landed on one of the congregants, tearing flesh from bone like piranhas skeletonizing their prey.

"What the hell is happening?"

Ray had no idea he'd even spoken the thought aloud until Father Maroney answered. "The demons demand more blood for their sacrifice. You can presume we'll be next."

"Not if I can help it." Ray lifted his gun and sighted the demons as they flew through the cavern. He pulled the trigger—again and again—but the damn things were too fast. They streaked toward the ceiling, and he lost them among the stalactites.

"There's only three," Martinez said. "I thought there were supposed to be six."

Father Maroney frowned. "I'm afraid that's just the opening act."

"What do you mean?" Martinez asked.

"Those things you see flying around... they're nothing but mindless lesser demons. Believe me, when one of the Six arrives, you'll know it."

Garrison swore. "Have I mentioned how much I hate this holiday?"

"You and I have that in common," Father Maroney said.

Ray shifted his attention to the altar. Reynolds was pointing to a congregant, beckoning him to join her.

"Spider," she said. "Come forth."

The man called Spider came willingly, dropping his cloak, his goat mask still in place.

Reynolds shrugged off her cloak and bent over the altar. She spread her legs, her dark hair fanning out over the leatherbound volume as Paul continued his sermon. Spider mounted her from behind, thrusting until completion. When the deed was done, she gestured for him to stand at the center of the Baphomet symbol.

He stepped onto the symbol reluctantly, eyeing the latticework of fissures glowing beneath his feet. Moments later, a high-pitched chittering emanated throughout the cavern, seeming to come from everywhere at once. The skin on Spider's face began to quiver as if something was tugging his cheeks in different directions. At first, it was almost comical, but then a wet, ripping sound rang out, and the flesh was torn from his body like a glove peeled from a hand. His skin dropped to the ground next to him—all in one piece, like a wet raincoat.

He stood frozen before them, eyes blinking, for a moment completely unaware that he resembled a glistening cadaver—all blood, guts, and bone. Then he gazed down at the raw meat of his arms and touched a finger to the exposed tendons of his jaw. The horror in his eyes blossomed into madness, and he tipped his head back and cackled. A moment later, the symbol crumbled beneath his feet, and he vanished into the fiery abyss.

Ray turned to his companions, wondering if they'd witnessed the same thing he had. Their shocked expressions confirmed it. "You were right," Ray said, looking at Father Maroney. "We need to stop the ritual."

Father Maroney nodded. "What I need is the names of those demons."

But Ray barely heard him. He had Paul in his sights. He squeezed the trigger, firing off two shots in rapid succession, the sound pealing like thunder.

They should've been kill shots, but somehow Abby got in the way. One moment she was standing among the congregants, the next she'd materialized in front of Paul. The bullets struck her in the chest, but bounced off, as if her filthy nightgown was made of Kevlar.

Ray lowered his gun, not wanting to kill Abby, but damned if he knew what to do next. They didn't teach this in the academy.

Abby stepped toward him, and a grin spread across her face, her lips parting like the petals of a decaying flower. Her gaze was penetrating, those horrible red eyes boring into his soul. He heard a loud crack, like the snapping of bones, and watched Abby's jaw unhinge. Her face blurred and elongated as her mouth filled in with an unending spiral of fangs.

Ray inched backward, unable to look away, drawn to the light that had appeared in her eyes like a mesmerizing whirl of galaxies. He could see Father Maroney in his peripheral vision—a crucifix in one hand, the torn-out page of Abby's *Book of Shadows* in the other.

Abby pounced on Ray like a lioness taking down its prey. The jolt of the landing shook the gun from his hand, and he turned to see Abby's nightmarish face pressed near his, tendrils of drool dangling from her jaws.

"By the power of Christ," Father Maroney shouted, "I command you—release this child!"

The demon within Abby wailed in pain, and Ray looked up in time to see Father Maroney plant the crucifix against Abby's forehead, where it sizzled like a branding iron.

"May the holy cross be my light!"

Ray scrambled backward on his butt, retrieving his gun and huddling beside Garrison and Martinez.

The Abby-thing staggered to its feet and faced off against Father Maroney. They moved in a slow circle, both opponents hesitant to make the next move.

"God has deserted you, tainted priest. Your soul belongs to me."

"I've confessed my sins to a God who is merciful."

The Abby-thing let out a guttural laugh. "I am your god now."

Further into the cavern, Paul and Reynolds were still leading the congregation in a chant, while nearly a dozen winged demons wheeled through the air. One of the demons snatched a congregant in its talons and hurled him into the fiery abyss.

Father Maroney brandished the crucifix and recited a prayer in Latin.

CRUX SACRA SIT MIHI LUX,
NUNQUAM DRACO SIT MIHI DUX.
VADE RETRO SATANA!
NUNQUAM SUADE MIHI VANA!
SUNT MALA QUAE LIBAS.
IPSE VENENA BIBAS!

The Abby-thing's jaws opened wider, its voice emanating from somewhere deep inside. "Your words are powerless, your cross nothing but a golden bauble. You cannot prevent the coming of the Six."

"What is your name, demon?"

"My name is death."

Father Maroney glanced down at the crumpled page from the *Book of Shadows*. "All things in heaven and earth shall bend the knee in the name of Christ our Lord. Tell me thy name!"

"No!" the Abby-thing shouted.

"Are you Exilenus?"

"No!"

"Malsedar?"

"No!"

"Septival?"

No answer.

Father Maroney grinned, then shouted. "May the Lord God lay hold of the beast Septival and cast it into the abyss!"

The Abby-thing jerked backward and collapsed to the ground.

"Quick!" Father Maroney shouted. "Hold her down!"

Garrison and Martinez each grabbed an arm, while Ray sat on her legs and kept one eye on the winged demons, which soared through the cavern like hawks searching for prey.

Father Maroney laid the cross on Abby's forehead. She tried to fight him, thrashing from side to side, but the prayers had weakened it. The spiral of fangs had vanished, and it was Abby's face once again... save for the eyes.

"Say a prayer," Father Maroney said, turning toward them. "Anything you can recall from memory."

As Garrison and Martinez began reciting the Hail Mary, Father Maroney leaned over Abby. "By the power of Christ, I command thee, Septival, release this child!" And then to Abby, he said, "You must fight this evil, Abby. Reject Satan and his minions. Ask forgiveness for your sins and let the love of God into your heart."

Abby's lips moved without sound, her head turning, like she was lost in a dream.

One of the winged demons flew toward them, and Ray jumped to his feet, following the arc of its flight, squeezing off a volley of gunshots. His last shot clipped a wing and sent the demon shrieking away, climbing into the stalactites for cover.

Something gargantuan flew out of the abyss, jet-black and wraithlike, a nightmare fusion of talons, scales, and fangs.

"Malsedar!" Paul shouted triumphantly from the altar.

Abby was still lying on the floor, fighting an unknowable battle as the others prayed over her. Father Maroney motioned to Ray. "Pray with us."

But Ray's attention was drawn to the altar as Paul announced the arrival of another demon, which rose from the abyss like the essence of some evil genie.

"Tortomal!"

"Quickly," Father Maroney said. "Kneel and pray."

But Ray shook his head. "You do your thing, Father, and I'll do mine." He raised his gun and leveled it at Paul, who was still chanting and gesticulating, reading from the blasphemous book.

Ray had lost count of his shots, but his Glock held seventeen rounds. With any luck, that would be enough.

He pulled the trigger, and the gun responded with a roar... and this time, there was no intervention. The bullet tore a hole in the center of Paul's forehead and blew out the back of his skull. He collapsed to the stone floor, his body seemingly lost in the folds of his cloak, as if drowning in a sea of rags.

As soon as he released the trigger, Ray charged forward and snatched the book off the altar. It weighed more than he expected. The rawhide cover felt warm, waxen, and surprisingly soft.

It's not leather, he realized. *It's human flesh.*

He fought a wave of revulsion and hoisted the book over his head as he ran toward the abyss. Reynolds tried to head him off, but he had her beat by three paces. As he prepared to heave the book into hell where it belonged, one of the winged demons divebombed him.

He spun to his left and lost his balance, the demon raking a talon across his shoulder as it flew by. The book slipped out of his hand, tumbling end for end. It landed near the edge of the abyss, but Reynolds was there.

She threw her body in front of it like a goalie making a sliding save. As she staggered to her feet and lifted the book in celebration, Ray saw Malsedar and Tortomal fly into the ceiling and disappear like phantoms through the rock.

A moment later, the winged demon returned to finish Ray off, and as he scrabbled across the floor to retrieve his gun, he caught a blur of movement out of the corner of his eye.

Reynolds stood at the edge of the abyss, the book in her hands. She flipped through its pages, searching for where Paul had left off. She didn't see Father Maroney until it was too late.

The priest charged her like a defensive lineman and wrapped her into a crushing bear hug, sending them both careening into the abyss, along with the Temple's unholy bible.

As they vanished from view, a concussive blast rang out from within the abyss, and the winged demons dropped from the sky. They landed on the stones below, thrashing and wailing as the earth began to shake.

Martinez rushed over to Frasier's body and pulled the ring off his finger. "Come on!" she yelled. "Hurry!"

Ray peeled himself off the ground and ran to catch up. Garrison lifted Abby into his arms and joined them. She still looked like she was dreaming, but her face was serene now.

As Martinez pressed the ring into the secret lock, triggering the door to roll open, Ray ventured a final glance into the cavern.

The congregants were eyeing each other nervously, mourning the loss of their high priest and priestess, and wondering if the shaking earth was a welcoming sign... or a foreboding of things to come.

Ray and the others didn't stick around to find out.

CHAPTER SEVENTY-SEVEN

It turned out to be the right move. The earthquake triggered a cave-in, which collapsed the entire cavern and made it impossible to ever recover the bodies.

They encountered Captain Barnes and Officer Jeffries in the tunnel just beyond the secret door. The captain hadn't trusted Frasier's story, and he and Jeffries had made their way through the mausoleum, arriving just in time for the earthquake.

Fiona had guided Cassie through the tunnels and back to the street before melting into a crowd of trick-or-treaters and vanishing into the night. Cassie eventually found her way to the police station with the baby, where she later had a tearful reunion with her mother and Captain Barnes. Although the family unit was broken beyond repair, at least there was the Cartwright family fortune to spend on therapy.

Prosecutor Daley dismissed the charges against Eddie Fischer after Cassie failed to identify him in a lineup and the latest lab results showed he tested positive for roofies.

Abby didn't remember a damn thing, which was the biggest blessing of all, and the update from the hospital was that Mrs. Garcia was expected to make a full recovery from the stabbing at her daughter's hands.

Ray, Martinez, and Garrison spent the rest of Halloween night typing up their report.

When Chief Sanderson read it, he was skeptical. "Let me get this straight," he said. "After you observed the Temple preparing for sacrifice, you rescued Cassie and Garrison and then somehow caught wind that the place was rigged to explode?"

They all nodded in agreement.

"Why would the Temple go through all that trouble only to blow themselves up in the end?" Sanderson asked.

"Ritual suicide," Martinez said. "Like the Heaven's Gate cult."

They'd told Sanderson as much as they could without revealing the supernatural parts, but to his credit, the chief sensed that something was missing.

Sanderson folded his hands on his desk and leaned forward. "That's it, then? That's your story?"

"What's the matter, Chief?" Ray said. "You want the Halloween version? If you want us to say that a couple of demons escaped into town, we could always make that edit."

Sanderson chuckled. "That won't be necessary, Detective. This town's already got more demons than it can handle."

Author's Note

One of my goals when writing this book was to describe the setting in enough detail to make the readers feel like they were experiencing the story through the eyes of the characters. To that end, I endeavored to describe the city of Salem and the history of the witch trials as accurately as possible. Almost everywhere the characters go in this novel are real places, and if you're so inclined, you can retrace their footsteps—street by street and landmark by landmark.

I have, however, taken certain liberties with the Boston and Salem police precincts, as well as the location of the Salem public defender and judicial offices. And although the Salem Witch Museum, Boston College, and Hub City Bookshop are real places, the employees in this story are entirely fictional. The following places are also fictional: Steve Rancic's haunted house, Mystical Brew, Kettle & Cauldron, and Raven's Wing Books & Magick.

The Burying Point Cemetery, on the other hand, is not fictional. Founded in 1637, it's the oldest cemetery in Salem and is also known as the Charter Street Cemetery. It's the final resting place of several notable historical figures, including John Hathorne, one of the judges who presided over the Salem witch trials.

Although the Burying Point Cemetery is a great place to visit, I want to be clear that it does not contain a mausoleum for Nathaniel Cartwright, who is a fictional character. This probably goes without saying, but please don't attempt to open any crypts or disturb any graves in search of a secret tunnel. That part of the story is entirely fictional. Likewise, the tunnels under the Danvers Lunatic Asylum no longer exist, and the ruins of the old power plant are boarded up and are not safe to enter.

If you're wondering about the smuggling tunnels under the streets of Salem, it's true their construction was funded by wealthy merchants and politicians in the early 1800s to avoid paying import taxes at the customs house. Some of those tunnels did, in fact, connect to the basements and fireplaces of their mansions.

Apart from the history of Salem, this book also delves into the history and beliefs of Wiccans. As I mention in the book, Wicca is widely misunderstood and is often confused with satanism. I'd like to reiterate that Wiccans don't worship the devil, they don't sacrifice animals, and they don't practice black magick. It's a peaceful religion that teaches 'Do no harm, lest it return to you threefold.'

Much of the material I wrote about Wicca comes from online sources and articles written by practicing Wiccans. I put their knowledge and experiences into my own words, drawing on their unique perspectives to provide what I hope is an accurate depiction of Wicca. Wiccan spells and chants, on the other hand, have been passed down for generations. They're often taught at festivals and public rituals. Like nursery rhymes or traditional folksongs, they generally lack attribution and are old enough to be considered in the public domain. Accordingly, they are not subject to copyright. I've used bits and pieces of these spells and chants in this book, although I've taken certain liberties to bend the words to suit the story.

Writing about satanic cults is a tricky business. As I started on that leg of my research, I made a few queries to online horror forums and consulted with other members of the HWA. I was surprised (and a bit spooked) by the number of warnings I received advising me to stay away from certain occult texts. These individuals strongly recommended that I read the adjacent material rather than the original source... and even those materials proved to be a bit of a mindfuck.

The Temple of Six is a fictional cult, and the names of the demons in this book are also fictional. Why, you ask? Because there is power in names, and I didn't want to give voice to any demons cited in religious or demonology texts. You can decide for yourself if that was superstition, or perhaps a reasonable precaution against accidentally summoning a demon.

Shockingly, I didn't need to exaggerate many of the deeds performed by the Temple of Six. If you believe the research, much of what the Temple did is documented in various non-fiction books on the study of cults and occult crime. Some of the texts I consulted when researching this book included:

- *Cults that Kill* by Larry Kahaner
- *The Occult Criminal Investigation: Reference Material* by the Michigan State Police Child Abuse Unit and Criminal Investigation Division (November 1988)
- *An Exorcist Tells His Story* by Father Gabriele Amorth

If you enjoyed **The Burying Point**, please consider rating it on Amazon or Goodreads. And if you're interested in another thrilling read, turn the page for a preview of **Colony of the Lost**, a horror novel about an ancient evil that returns to the site of a lost colony.

COLONY OF THE LOST

The tall man stared into the dark and wondered about the voices. It seemed that lately, he could think of little else. They haunted him at home. They haunted him at work. All hours of the day. Whispered promises of death's dark purpose.

Shadows draped his living room. Darkness stretched its tentacles into every corner, every crevice. The blinds were drawn tight, shutting out the pale light of dusk and the fluorescent glow of the street lamps.

He hadn't cleaned in weeks. Dishes loomed over the sink in teetering stacks, rising from a cesspool of stagnant water. A bag of trash overflowed beside the refrigerator; its rotting contents buzzed with flies.

He barely noticed the stench. He was far too used to it by now, far too absorbed in his problems to even care.

He was losing his mind.
Bit by bit.
It happened in a span of weeks. The seed of madness had taken root and blossomed, sprouting spidery vines that wormed into his brain. It seemed hard to believe that his sanity could slip away so suddenly. More likely, he'd always been crazy and just never knew it.

But who could he ask? Ever since Mary died, he had all but broken off from the rest of the world. He had no children, no immediate family to speak of... at least not since his brother died in that car wreck on I-95. He had no friends at work. Just acquaintances. And he'd stopped joining them months ago for the occasional beer after his shift.

He lowered his face into his hands. *Please, God, let me be insane. Let this all be part of some crazed delusion.*

But it wasn't a delusion. A small part of him knew that. He had imprisoned the truth in the darkest corner of his mind, had bound it in chains and locked it away from the rest of his consciousness.

But sometimes it escaped.

Images appeared when he least expected them, grisly scenes too horrifying to watch. Flashes of light, bursts of sound... phantom memories of events that he wasn't conscious of at the time.

Fact or fantasy? Reality or madness?

Only the prisoner in his mind knew for sure.

Eventually, he'd have to confront the prisoner and discover the truth, but would he be ready to hear what the prisoner might say? Or would it be the last words he heard before the thread of his sanity snapped, and he plunged headlong into the abyss?

His eyes slipped shut, and suddenly, the images appeared. He tried in vain to force them away, to resist the horrors he knew would be revealed, but his efforts proved futile.

***

Leaves and twigs crunched beneath his feet as he picked his way through the midnight forest. Starlight filtered through a canopy of skeletal limbs, the trail ahead steeped in shadows. Ragged clouds of breath plumed before him, lingering for a moment before vanishing into the dark.

His respiration was heavy, his lips salty and slick. His arms struggled to restrain their writhing burden. The boy jerked and squirmed and tried to scream, but the duct tape pressed over his lips muffled the sound.

Laughter echoed through the forest. Voices circled his mind in a maddening frenzy.

THE BURYING POINT

He staggered toward a moonlit glen, drawn toward the mouth of the gaping earth, strung along by the whisper of death's dark purpose, the promise of life begun anew. His shoes rasped against a rocky floor as he wound through a drafty passageway and spiraled down, ever down, toward the restless voices and the beating of an ancient heart.

He emerged into a cavern adorned by seeping stalactites. A phosphorescent glow emanated from the walls and floor, illuminating a subterranean pool in the center of the chamber, its onyx water as smooth as glass.

The whispering voices became a chant, and all at once he could hear them everywhere, an urgent susurration that compelled him nearer to the pool. He shuffled toward the water's edge, drew a knife from the sheath at his ankle.

The chanting built into a guttural swell, into a dark symphony of madness. The blade reflected the ghostly light. Steel plunged into flesh, spattering hot ribbons of blood across his face.

The boy's screams became a choked garble. The chanting ceased. The cave fell quiet. All that could be heard was blood dripping into the pool, swirling and rippling its black waters.

When the boy's lifeblood was fully drained, he released the body and watched the once-still water begin to bubble and roil.

For more information about the author, visit:

www.amazon.com/author/cavignano

www.derikcavignano.com

dcavignano@hotmail.com

Instagram: @dcavignano

X @DerikCavignano

Facebook: www.facebook.com/DerikCavignanoAuthor/

Made in the USA
Middletown, DE
29 February 2024